RHAPSODY

Other Novels by Judith Gould

Sins
Love-Makers
Dazzle
Never Too Rich
Texas Born
Forever
Too Damn Rich
Second Love
Till the End of Time

Judith Gould

RHAPSODY

A Love Story

A DUTTON BOOK

DUTTON
Published by the Penguin Group
Penguin Putnam Inc., 375 Hudson Street, New York, New York 10014, U.S.A.
Penguin Books Ltd, 27 Wrights Lane, London W8 5TZ, England
Penguin Books Australia Ltd, Ringwood, Victoria, Australia
Penguin Books Canada Ltd, 10 Alcorn Avenue, Toronto, Ontario, Canada M4V 3B2
Penguin Books (N.Z.) Ltd, 182–190 Wairau Road, Auckland 10, New Zealand

Penguin Books Ltd, Registered Offices:
Harmondsworth, Middlesex, England

First published by Dutton, a member of Penguin Putnam Inc.

First Printing, November, 1999
10 9 8 7 6 5 4 3 2 1

Copyright © Judith Gould, 1999
All rights reserved

 REGISTERED TRADEMARK—MARCA REGISTRADA

LIBRARY OF CONGRESS CATALOGING-IN-PUBLICATION DATA:

Gould, Judith.
   Rhapsody / Judith Gould.
      p.   cm.
   ISBN 0-525-94516-4
   I. Title.
PS3557.0867N64   1999
813'.54—dc21   99-20067
                                                        CIP

Printed in the United States of America
Set in Goudy
Designed by Leonard Telesca

PUBLISHER'S NOTE
This is a work of fiction. Names, characters, places, and incidents either are the products of the author's imagination or are used fictitiously, and any resemblance to actual persons, living or dead, events, or locales is entirely coincidental.

Without limiting the rights under copyright reserved above, no part of this publication may be reproduced, stored in or introduced into a retrieval system, or transmitted, in any form, or by any means (electronic, mechanical, photocopying, recording, or otherwise), without the prior written permission of both the copyright owner and the above publisher of this book.

This book is printed on acid-free paper. ∞

The novel is dedicated to
the memories of
T. Ray Rucker, Renaissance man and friend,
and
Happy "Hap" Gould,
the most golden of retrievers,
whose unconditional love was a
blessing in weather both foul and fair.
R.I.P. my friends.

And to the living whose unflagging support and friendship
will never be forgotten:
Nancy Austin, assertive woman extraordinaire;
Bill Cawley, prince among men;
and
Peter Bevacqua and Stephen King,
the Penny and Igor who were put here
to brighten lives.

Of splendour in the grass, of glory in the flower;
We will grieve not, rather find
Strength in what remains behind.

—Wordsworth, "Ode:
Intimations of Immortality"

RHAPSODY

Prologue

⏤⏤

Brighton Beach, Brooklyn

Steam rose in dense clouds. They were as thick as fog, and it was difficult for the young man to see more than two or three feet ahead. Bodies passing beyond that distance appeared to be ghostly apparitions, barely discernible as human forms through the hot, gauzy vapor. The heat was intense, almost unbearable, as it was supposed to be, inducing copious amounts of sweat from the bodies, which lay prone or sat up on the white ceramic tile seats that rose in tiers like bleachers nearly to the ceiling.

An occasional hiss of water, malevolent and unsettling, hit the heated rocks, producing more steam. Voices muted and unintelligible rose and fell in the near distance. The remote swishing of the doorway announced unseen newcomers or never seen departures.

This must be what hell is like, *the man thought.*

He hated the sheen of sweat on his body and breathing the humidity-laden air into his lungs. The feel of the soggy, thin white towel against his flesh repulsed him, and the loathsome cracked white tile—so filthy with germs, he thought—made his skin crawl.

A shadowy figure, huge in the smothering haze, appeared at his side almost before he realized it, sitting next to him on the third tier. Tall, broad, and muscular under layers of fat, the man adjusted his towel, then, without preamble, began speaking in a whisper. They both stared ahead into the fog, as if unwilling to acknowledge each other.

"You have the job?" the huge older man asked.

The younger man nodded. "Yes," he replied.

The older man grunted, then adjusted the towel around his waist.

The younger man waited for him to continue, but the older man stared off into the haze, as if he didn't exist. Suddenly there was a loud hiss of water hitting rocks, and the young man jerked involuntarily.

"Not nervous, are you?" the older man asked.

"No, no," the younger man replied. "Of course not."

Using both hands, the older man swept his sweat-soaked hair back away from his face. His hands looked like gnarled bear's paws to the younger man, huge and battered and ugly. Lethal, too, he thought.

"Nothing to be nervous about," the older man said. "Just do your job. Call the number I gave you last time. Once a week. Saturday nights after nine."

"What if I can't?" the young man asked, his voice rising slightly. "What if—?"

"No excuses," came the gruff reply.

The older man got to his feet. He loomed over the younger man like a Neanderthal, hairy, barbaric, and evil. He turned his powerful body and looked down.

Wolf's eyes, the younger man thought. He has eyes like a wolf on the steppes.

"No excuses," the older man repeated. Then he turned and disappeared into the steam.

The younger man's lips drew into an ugly sneer. Stupid barbarian, he thought contemptuously. He felt like spitting on the dingy ceramic tile. He hated these older Russians with their gangland mentality. But he also knew that in this case at least, beneath the barbaric and hideous exterior, there was a mind that was anything but stupid.

I mustn't let appearances fool me, he thought. The ugly wolf's mind is keen, with well-honed instincts. Whether for business or . . . killing.

He sat, waiting patiently, giving the older man time to shower, dress, and leave the baths. He hated the place and the older Russian men it catered to.

They're so different from me, he thought. And my new associate. Yes. Misha Levin and I represent a new breed of Russian emigré.

Part One

❧

TODAY

Chapter One

Vienna, November 1998

Under a *Mittel Europa* wintry sky, a chill wind swept through the grand parks and streets of central Vienna. It was as if the jealous ghosts of Mozart, Schubert, and the Strausses were carried on the wind, protecting their city against interlopers from the more modern world.

It occurred to Misha Levin that New York was gearing up for the Macy's Thanksgiving Day Parade. But this was Vienna, *Alt Wien*, the crown jewel of the Hapsburgs, where the palaces and monuments of the Austro-Hungarian empire in all their operatic pomp and circumstance made the very idea of such a parade seem hopelessly gauche and unsophisticated.

Misha pulled up the collar of his perfectly tailored black cashmere overcoat and adjusted the silk and cashmere scarf around his neck. His leonine mane of slightly curly, rich jet-black hair, which he always wore a little too long, was picked up by the breeze and fluttered about his head. He was tall, six feet, four inches, with perfect proportions and the defined musculature of one who ate properly and exercised relentlessly. His large, luminous dark brown eyes were almost black in their intense depths. Liquid, bedroom eyes they were frequently called, with their long, thick lashes, and they glittered in the pale light as he pulled on black leather gloves to protect his long, artistic fingers.

To the casual observer on the streets of Vienna, he might have appeared to be overreacting to the chill. But Misha Levin's fingers were his fortune. He was one of the world's most sought-after classical concert pianists, with a career that, at thirty-one years of age, held the promise of a Horowitz or Rubinstein. He also had movie-star looks, and for this reason he appealed to a far larger audience than that which normally listened to classical music.

He was a darling of the recording industry because of his crossover commercial appeal, and he was sometimes touted as the "rock and roll" star of the classical world, a soubriquet he did nothing to discourage.

As he strode down Bösendorfer Strasse, he garnered stares of appreciation. His forehead was high and broad, and his nose was straight but prominent. His high cheekbones and strong, deeply cleft chin were complemented by wide, sensuous lips. He had about him a virile masculinity and a commanding—some would say arrogant—air, and to those who didn't know him, he could seem both dashing and intimidating at once. But there was no denying that he cut a decidedly romantic figure, with an edge of mystery and danger that only enhanced it.

Misha made his way through the throng of shoppers and tourists on the city's streets, enjoying the crisp air and the beauty of Vienna's architecture. After hours of intense early morning rehearsal at Schönbrunn Palace, he had dismissed his chauffeur and limousine, deciding to walk to a late lunch with his wife and agent at Zu den Drei Husaren on Weihburggasse.

His gaze had shifted from the neo-Renaissance facade of the Wiener Staatsoper to the neoclassical Hotel Sacher when he suddenly saw the familiar figure just ahead of him on Kärntner Strasse. She was idly window-shopping. Her height and long, shiny black hair—as raven black as his own—flying in the wind behind were surely hers. The tomboyish stride was unmistakable, and the toss of the head was like no one else's.

It has to be! he thought.

Misha stopped in his tracks, still studying the figure ahead of him. His heart began to pound and his pulse began to race, thudding in his ears.

Yes, it has to be! he thought, certain now that he was right.

He hastened his pace, quickly closing the space between them. A shiver—most definitely not caused by the cold—ran through him. He slowed as he came up behind the figure, stopping before a shop window. The chalk-striped black suit she wore was tailored like a man's, but the stilleto-heeled black leather Gucci boots were pure female. Over her shoulder was slung a huge black leather bag.

With a camera in it, he thought. *She never went anywhere without a camera.*

He stood there, practically breathless, and watched her for a moment longer, in profile, not yet speaking her name. He quickly discerned that she had hardly changed at all since he had last seen her. If anything, the slight maturity made her even more ravishing than before.

She was at least six feet tall in her heels, slender, and lightly tanned as always, from her various athletic outdoor pursuits. Her high forehead, prominent cheekbones, and long, straight nose and full, bee-stung lips were precisely as he remembered them. And that swan's neck, so elegant and fragile-looking. He'd always told her that she should be on the other side of the camera's lenses—modeling instead of taking pictures.

Misha took a deep breath. "Serena?" he said tentatively, in his rich, deep baritone.

She jerked slightly, then stood stone still for a moment before turning on a heel to face him. She wore huge, dark sunglasses, but there was no mistaking that it was she.

She stared at him through the dark lenses, momentarily stunned—he could see that, even through the glasses. Then a smile—conditional and nervous at first—formed on her painted lips, and her beautiful features gradually blossomed to life.

"Misha?" she said in her smoky voice.

"Yes," he almost whispered, "it's Misha."

"Oh, my God! I don't believe it!" Serena tried to control her fluttering heartbeat, but her voice was testimony to the genuine delight and excitement she felt at seeing him.

"I don't, either!" he said. There was a note of wonder in his voice. "How long has it been?"

"Five years," she answered without hesitation. *Five long, lonely years,* she thought.

"Five years," he repeated. Then he stepped closer and held his arms out to embrace her.

Serena hesitated momentarily, thinking that she should perhaps not be so demonstrative, that she should conceal the utter joy—*and* vexation—that seeing him had caused. Usually in command of almost any given situation, she found that her mind was a whirlwind of indecision, of contradictory thoughts and feelings.

Oh, what the hell, she finally resolved.

She impetuously moved into his arms, throwing her long arms around him and hugging tightly. He kissed both her cheeks in the Continental fashion, and she kissed his. Serena immediately felt comfortable in his arms, as if she belonged there, despite her initial shock at seeing him.

We must look like two old friends meeting for the first time in a long while, she thought as shoppers made a path around them on the sidewalk. *But we were much more than that. So much more.*

Misha hugged her to him, thrilled at the feel and smell of her, that familiar, exotic scent. It was a mingling of musk and citrus, of the Orient, of mystery and allure.

They drew apart, but still he held her, a hand on each arm. He was reluctant to release her. "You look beautiful," he said, eyeing her up and down. "More beautiful than ever, if that's possible. Fame suits you, I think."

Serena laughed and smiled. "Thank you, Misha," she said. "And you look more handsome than ever." She took off her sunglasses and gestured with them toward the wall behind her. "Better than your picture even."

Misha looked at the wall, to the spot she'd indicated, and saw his face, blown up in black and white, staring back at him. It was one of the posters advertising the United Nations land mine benefit concert for which he was playing tonight. He had been so preoccupied with her, he hadn't noticed it before.

"Do you think so?" he asked. "Those photographs are always so dramatic, aren't they?" Then he laughed. "But you know that better than anyone, I guess."

"It's a good photo," Serena said. "He did a good job, I think."

"That's certainly a compliment, coming from you," Misha said.

"Yes," Serena said, "it is. It's a good thing he did, too, because they're plastered all over Vienna."

"So, of course, you knew I was here." It was a statement, not a question.

She looked at him levelly, her hazel eyes glittering with the same remarkable energy and passion for life that had always attracted him. "Yes, Misha," she said. "I knew you were here."

He wanted to ask her if she had planned on getting in touch with him, but wasn't sure he was ready to hear her answer. "What brings you to Vienna?" he asked instead.

"I'm doing a shoot with some of the newly elected political leaders in Middle and Eastern Europe," she said. "They're here for a conference, so I'm getting them all together. Czechs, Serbs, and so on. For *Vanity Fair*."

"It sounds exciting," he said.

Serena smiled mischievously. "It might be a lot more exciting if a good old-fashioned fight broke out among them. Then I might get some really interesting pictures."

"I see you haven't changed too much," Misha said with a smile. He looked into her eyes. "You've really come a long way, Serena."

She shrugged. "Yes and no," she said in a self-deprecating manner.

"What do you mean?" he asked.

"Oh . . . I don't know," she said evasively. "Never mind."

Misha glanced quickly at the Rolex Oyster on his wrist, the one he'd been given for doing a print ad for them. "Have you got time for a quick cup of coffee?" he asked.

Serena shook her head. "Sorry, no. I have to get going, Misha. I'm on my way to meet Coral for lunch. We have to go over some business."

"How is Coral?" he asked, an amused expression on his face.

"You know Coral. She's the same as always." Serena laughed. "Mother. Father. Sister. Brother. Jailer. And agent, of course. Still smothering me with too much attention." She paused, then asked: "How's your family?"

"Very well," he replied matter-of-factly.

Serena thought she detected a storm cloud momentarily scud across his handsome countenance. What is it? she wondered. Regret, sorrow, doubt? Unhappiness?

He looked at her intently. "Are you . . . are you going to be here for a while?" he ventured.

"Yes, but just another couple of days," she said. "Then it's back to New York."

"Do you mind if I call you?" His dark brown eyes were pleading with her to say yes. He didn't want to push her, but he couldn't let her go without at least trying to see her again. Not if there was any possibility, however remote, that she might be willing.

Serena gazed at him for a long moment with those large hazel eyes of hers. They were golden brown, with scintillating shards of green and blue glittering in the light, and they mesmerized him now as they always had. "I'd like that, Misha," she finally said. "Very much."

He felt a sudden excitement churning in the pit of his stomach and knew that he would be living in a state of unbearable anticipation until the next time he got to see her. "I would, too, Serena," he uttered.

She put her sunglasses back on. "I'm at the König von Ungarn. On Schulerstrasse," she said, more casually than she felt. "I'll be free late tonight and tomorrow afternoon." What am I doing? she asked herself. I must have lost my mind. That's the only explanation for agreeing to see this man again.

"I'll call you tonight, then. Okay?" he said.

"Yes," she said, turning on her heel to go. "I'll be there. Bye, Misha." She tossed her long hair and walked away, thinking: I'm crazy. Completely crazy. But I don't care. I want to see him again. I must see him again.

"Good-bye, Serena," he whispered to her swiftly departing back.

He stood then, watching her go, and expelled a sigh. I already miss her, he thought. After all these years, seeing her for mere minutes had left him with a great empty feeling, like a profound physical hunger, that was frightening—and inescapable.

Chapter Two

〜

"It's all sugar coating," Emanuel Cygelman said. "The Ringstrasse was only built in the last century. Neo-Renaissance, neo-Baroque, neo-Gothic, neo-You-Name-It. It's all poured concrete. Just all mock-ups of the real thing."

"You're joking, Manny," Vera Levin said, brushing a strand of pale blond hair away from her face with perfectly manicured fingernails. Her blue eyes, a cool pale delft, gazed at him as she forked up a small bite of pike soufflé.

"It's true, Vera." Manny leaned across the table. "The Parliament Building, City Hall, the Imperial Museum, the Court Opera, the Bourse— you name it. They're all like a theatrical backdrop for some monstrous operetta," he continued. "I mean, sure, Vienna is an ancient city. But the Ringstrasse? It's pure nineteenth century, all done in one fell swoop."

Vera took a sip of her wine and looked at Misha, but her husband, seated on her left and staring off toward one of the restaurant's magnificent Gobelin tapestries, was apparently in another world.

"Well, Manny," Vera said, "I, for one, am glad they built the Ringstrasse. Concrete or not, it's part of Vienna's wonderful magic."

Manny took a bite of his rich *Kalbsbrüken* Metternich, a justly famous veal dish, and frowned thoughtfully as he chewed. "Still it's part of the sugar coating," he finally went on with relentless determination. "Vienna has its dark side, too, Vera. Don't forget, it was home to the melancholy Dr. Freud. Not to mention its popularity with that most infamous of all Austrians, Herr Hitler, who, I might add, had a huge following here."

He took off his tortoiseshell glasses and made a production of polishing them with a crisp linen handkerchief. "And what about Herr Kurt Waldheim? Hmm?" He eyed her quizzically. "He ruled the roost not so long ago. So you see? Vienna's not only great musicians and marvelous pastry chefs—"

"Oh, Manny!" Vera snapped irritably. "Do give it a rest. Aren't you supposed to be busy at Knize being fitted for new suits? Dietrich swore by them, you know. Clotheshorses the world over think they're better than Savile Row."

Manny, who never donned anything but the finest custom-made clothing and shoes, adjusted his silk tie a fraction. "I," he pronounced, "shall never set foot anywhere but Huntsmann, no matter what they say."

"You," Vera sighed, "are a hopeless Anglophile—and snob." She smiled then. He really *was* a terrible snob, she thought, but there was so much more about Manny that remained a mystery to her. Even after knowing him for years, he and Sasha, his associate who had remained behind in New York, both were an enigma.

Once again she glanced at Misha, but he was still staring off into space. He hadn't heard a word of their discussion.

"Misha?" prodded Vera gently. "Are you nervous about tonight, darling?"

He drew in his gaze and turned to her. "No, no," he said with a smile. "I was just thinking about . . . oh, nothing really." He shrugged.

Nothing, indeed! he thought. Talk about a U.S.D.A. prime lie. In truth—and he didn't dare divulge it—he hadn't been able to think of anything except Serena Gibbons since the moment he'd laid eyes on her. It was as if they had never parted, as if they were still the impassioned lovers they had been five long years ago.

"You've hardly touched your food," Vera admonished. "You ignored the hors d'oeuvre trolley, and I think you had two spoons of that delicious lobster soup. Your guinea fowl looks delicious. I hope—"

"You know very well I seldom eat anything much before a performance, Vera," he said mildly. "I'll have something after the concert tonight."

"Okay," Vera said resignedly. She smiled at her husband and dropped the subject.

Vera Levin was possessed of an elegant, rare—some said decidedly icy—beauty, and one might easily be forgiven for forgetting that she was also possessed of a daunting intelligence, which had served her well in her marriage to Misha.

Vera glanced surreptitiously at him. His gaze was already once again diverted from the luncheon table, his eyes apparently sweeping around the restaurant. Was it the extravagant flower arrangements that had attracted his attention? The fine antique furnishings and carpets? Or those delightful plaster mannequins of the Hungarian officers who'd founded the restaurant at the end of World War I?

No, she didn't think so. He was lost in thought again. *Very curious,* she thought.

She could sense that he was much more preoccupied than usual before a concert, and she wasn't satisfied with his response to her about not eating. *Misha is dissimulating,* she surmised. But she knew when to leave well enough alone, and was wise enough not to question him any further. She knew when she married him that music was Misha's mistress, and a more demanding, time-consuming mistress she couldn't imagine. She had reconciled herself to this fact, and thought that if he took up a mistress of flesh and bone . . . well, she would cross that bridge when she came to it.

Besides, she told herself, the benefits of marriage to a world-renowned pianist were incalculable, both socially and financially, and Vera thrived in the monied, cosmopolitan artistic circles in which they moved.

Manny, who had been studying his most important client with interest, took a sip of his wine, then set the glass down and touched Misha's hand with one of his own. "Misha," he asked, "what did you think of the posters?"

"What?" Misha said. Then Manny's question registered in his preoccupied mind. "Oh, they're all right," he said, turning his attention back to the table. "Although, quite frankly, I don't see the point of them. They're unnecessary. The concert was sold out the day the tickets went on sale. And that was two days *before* the posters went up."

"They did the posters as a courtesy to you," Manny said. "And a well-deserved one, too, if you ask me. You're performing this concert at your own expense."

"Well, it's for a worthy cause," Misha replied matter-of-factly.

"And it's making *tons* of money for them," Manny said.

"The tickets were thousands of dollars apiece," Vera added.

"You couldn't ask for better advertising," Manny continued. "You couldn't *buy* this kind of advertising!"

"No," Misha said, "I don't suppose you could. Anyway, I just hope they get their money's worth."

"I don't think there's any doubt about that," Vera said, with both certainty and loyalty in her voice. "I've never known you to disappoint your audience."

"Aha!" Manny exclaimed. "I do believe I spy the waiter approaching to take our dessert orders!" He rubbed his plump pink hands together in gleeful anticipation.

"Manny," Vera said, "your enthusiasm is sometimes de trop."

"I've heard great things about their desserts," Manny said.

The waiter graciously asked how their meals were, and they voiced their appreciation. Then he noticed Misha's plate, and his expression became one of utter consternation, as if he had somehow offended.

"Monsieur Levin," he asked anxiously, "was the guinea fowl not to your satisfaction?"

"I'm sure it was sublime," Misha replied. "Please assure the chef that everything was to our satisfaction. It's just that I don't usually eat anything at all before performing."

The waiter looked relieved. "Perhaps you can honor us by returning, then," he said. "We hope you can try our cuisine another time."

"Yes," Misha said, "I certainly plan to." He turned to Vera. "Are you having dessert, darling?"

"Hmm. Maybe just a taste," Vera said. She looked up at the waiter. "The cheese crepe, I think. With the chocolate sauce."

"Manny?" Misha asked. "Need I ask?"

Manny laughed. "No," he said. "I'll have the same as Mrs. Levin," he said to the waiter.

"And coffee all around," Misha said.

"No dessert, then, Monsieur?" the waiter asked.

"No, thank you," Misha said. And he thought: *I just want to get out of here.*

After their coffee and desserts came, the discussion moved to the Austrian minister of culture's recent efforts to begin returning the vast quantities of art seized from Jews by the Nazis during World War II. Austrian museums—including the Kunsthistorische and the Belvedere, both venerable institutions—were filled with treasures that had belonged to Jewish families prior to the war.

"It's outrageous," Vera said, finishing the last bite of her cheese crepe, "one of the French Rothschilds who I met at a couture show in Paris told me that the Austrian branch of the family had many priceless paintings seized." She lifted a brow significantly. "And *loads* of valuable furniture and other things. If Baroness der Rothschild wants to see her things, she has to go visit them at Viennese museums because they're on display."

"It's disgusting," Manny said. "It's high time something's done. The government has waited half a century to begin to make any kind of restitution. I know that the Rothschilds and a lot of other families have repeatedly tried to get satisfaction of some sort, but the Austrian government has always turned a deaf ear."

Misha put a hand over his mouth and stifled a yawn. "Excuse me," he said. "It's not the company or the conversation."

Vera looked at him with an indulgent smile. "Would you like to get back to the hotel to have your nap before tonight's concert?"

"Yes," Misha said, returning her smile. "I think that's a very good idea." And he thought: *I want to be alone. Alone to think about Serena.*

"Just what you need, old sport," Manny said, neatly folding his big linen napkin and placing it beside his plate. "A good snooze before you dazzle them tonight."

Within minutes, the trio had left Zu den Drei Husaren and was ensconced in the luxurious black leather rear seat of the black Mercedes limousine that awaited them, serenely rolling toward their suites at the Palais Schwarzenberg, the grand country house–hotel owned by Prince Schwarzenberg. Vera was wrapped in an Oscar de la Renta suit and honey-colored sable, Manny in his fine English tailoring and handmade Lobb shoes, and Misha in his obsessive thoughts of the hauntingly beautiful Serena Gibbons.

Chapter Three

❦

Coral Randolph—normally the essence of urbane sophistication and the epitome of control—dropped her fork, unaware of its clatter on the beautiful porcelain plate in front of her. She was too self-assured to notice or care that several sets of eyes had snapped in her direction from nearby tables at Steirereck, reputed to be Austria's finest restaurant. Coral's eyes, the color of Colombian emeralds, narrowed to slits, and her pencil-thin, drawn-on eyebrows arched.

"I *trust,*" she enunciated sweetly and clearly in her best boarding school lockjaw, "that you kicked the son of a bitch in his precious family jewels, leaving him rolling in the gutter in agony?"

Serena shrugged nonchalantly. She took another bite of her delicious, calorie-rich *Wildschwein*—succulent wild boar—before answering her formidable agent, whose cheeks burned with adrenaline-induced war paint that no cosmetics manufacturer had yet invented.

Serena had suspected that Coral might react like a lioness trying to protect her cub, but the news of seeing Misha had been altogether too exciting to hold back.

"As a matter of fact," Serena said at long last, "I was the essence of cordiality. I mean, Jesus! It's been ages, Coral, and I decided to let bygones be bygones. You should know from all those years of your own therapy how stoking resentments can eat you alive. All that negative energy bouncing around inside you like lethal atoms is self-defeating, and I just thought—"

"You didn't *think* anything," Coral interrupted with biting precision. "If you had, you would have either socked him or walked off. And don't try to feed me any of your New Age psychobabble, either! I refuse to listen to it!"

She sat fuming for a moment, ignoring the salad she invariably ordered for lunch, no matter what the restaurant. In this case, she was particularly disdainful of the salad's beet root and potatoes, typical of

Austrian cuisine. Those all-knowing emerald eyes of hers glared malevo-lently across the table at her star photographer.

Serena took a sip of her wine, admitting to herself that she was deriv-ing a little sadistic pleasure from Coral's outrage about Misha. As much as she loved her, Serena relished torturing Coral from time to time. After all, she thought, time about's fair play.

Her eyes swept over Coral briefly. *What an unlikely mother-figure-warrior-agent the woman was,* Serena thought, as she had a thousand times in the past.

This ruthless warrior was chicly thin and forty-fiveish. It was difficult to discern Coral's age beneath her elaborate maquillage and her meticu-lous grooming—and some would vow numerous nips and tucks here and there by famous but discreet plastic surgeons—and it was a secret she guarded as if it were the Crown Jewels of England. She was all angles with hardly an ounce of fat on her. Her obviously dyed hair was always se-verely cut into a shoe-polish black page boy helmet. It was one of Coral's trademarks, this hairstyle, and had not varied an iota since her days as a debutante. Serena knew that maintaining its perfection required two vis-its every single week to the hairdresser, one for a trim and the other for dyeing. It contrasted dramatically—"spookily" was the description prof-fered by many of international society's wags—with the palest ivory rice powder she brushed on her face and neck. Her nose was a prominent beak, and her rather thin mouth was a vivid slash of a mulberry-shaded lipstick, which resembled nothing so much as dried blood. Her clothes were always exquisite and severely cut, as was today's black wool Jil Sander suit. Though not extensive, her collection of jewelry was not only real but of the very finest quality. She favored vintage pieces designed by the late, great Count Fulco di Verdura, and was a fixture at the jewelry sales at Sotheby's and Christie's auction rooms.

Thus, Coral was one of Manhattan's much ballyhooed social X rays, a clothes hanger par excellence, only in her case with a major difference: behind that urbane, refined facade, was a woman with a street-fighter's guts and instincts, coupled with an acute mind for business. She may have attended the most exclusive boarding and finishing schools in both the United States and Europe, but there was nothing in the least bit de-mure, spoiled, or flighty about her. No, for Coral Randolph relished a bat-tle and without exception went straight for the jugular.

When she was deciding on a career, she came to the conclusion that because of her great love for photography, coupled with her unerring nose for spotting talent, she could become a successful—even great—photographer's representative. Over the years she had put together an extraordinary stable of photographers. If they remained with her, Coral got them top dollar and the best assignments. Nobody liked to negotiate with Coral Randolph—be it a testosterone-driven male or a female much like herself.

She was also a lesbian, known in the chicest realms of that demi-monde as Randi—from her surname, of course—and had lived for years with a well-known casting director, Brandace Sargeant, known as Brandi. They were not militant or political lesbians, and their sexual orientation would never be questioned by the casual observer, so elegant were they both. And at the highest levels of international society they were not only accepted but also held with great respect.

Randi and Brandi. Hell on wheels, Serena thought. *And God, am I lucky to have them on my side.*

"Serena," Coral continued, after she had calmed herself down considerably, "you know I'm thinking of your own welfare, when I say do *not*, I repeat, do *not* see Misha Levin again."

Serena looked at Coral but didn't respond. Her gaze traveled to the restaurant's lovely wall murals and rustic beams and archways.

"You're not paying attention to me, as usual," Coral said. "And this is a very serious matter, Serena." She took a sip of her mineral water, her ring clicking against the crystal, then set the glass down and cleared her throat.

"Sometimes I think what we need is a good, old-fashioned war," she said. "For you to photograph. It's too bad you weren't around for Vietnam. The way you go looking for trouble, young lady, it would've been right up your alley."

Serena put down her wineglass and dabbed her lips with a corner of the napkin. "Coral, I don't want to have a battle over this. How many times do I have to tell you that Misha Levin is a thing of the past? My God, it's been five years! It's over. *Finito. Kaput!*" she exclaimed. "There's nothing—*nada! zilch!*—for you to worry about."

Coral scrutinized the beautiful, obstinate young woman. *Serena is so ravishing, so talented, and in many ways, so strong*, she thought. *But her character is also, in some ways, extremely weak, extremely needy, extremely vulnerable, and far too trusting—especially where men are concerned.*

Coral cleared her throat again. "Serena, I won't say anything else about this, I promise." She reached across the table and patted one of Serena's hands with her own. "But please, please, *please*," she begged. "Don't allow this man to toy with you like he did the last time. I honestly believe that he is capable of doing you great harm. I think he is *evil*, Serena."

She raised her eyebrows significantly, looking into Serena's eyes. "You know that I don't use the word lightly. I've heard all sorts of stories about the things he's done to other women, and some of them were very . . . unsavory. I think he's very dangerous. Just remember, Misha Levin is looking out for one thing and one thing only: that weapon he's got between his legs."

Serena had listened intently, but now she burst out into laughter. "Coral!" she protested with a sputter. "Not all men are like that, you know?"

"This is no laughing matter, Serena," Coral said with irritation. "Misha Levin *is* like that," she said emphatically. "And besides, you have to remember that he's a married man now. There's Vera Levin to consider, and from what I hear, she is a formidable woman. Oh, she may *look* cool as a cucumber and be oh so very social and on a lot of benefit committees and all that sort of thing, but she's also a wife and mother—and an aggressive social climber. I don't think you'd want to cross swords with her."

Serena slammed her wineglass down on the table. "Coral," she said with exasperation, her hazel eyes flashing, "I am *not* planning on having an affair with Misha Levin. I simply *saw* the man in the street, okay? So drop it, will you? *Jesus!*"

Coral held up one long, slender hand, a finger of which was adorned with a large, perfect pearl set in gold. One of her treasured Verdura pieces. "I'm finished," she said. "I won't say another word."

"Promise?" Serena said.

"Scout's honor," Coral replied. "Now then, have you got everything lined up for the shoots?"

"Yes," Serena said. "It's all taken care of. Jason and Bennett are taking care of a lot of the details."

"Oh, and how are the boys?" Coral asked.

"They're great," Serena replied. "Like sponges, the two of them. Soaking up everything I know."

"Good," Coral said. "That's hard to find in assistants these days."

"Anyway," Serena continued, "everybody's been a lot more cooperative than I expected, so barring unforeseen difficulties, it ought to be a piece of cake."

"You've worked your usual charm on these great Middle European politicians, I assume," Coral said knowingly.

"You might say that." Serena smiled. "It doesn't hurt to stroke their egos a little to get them to cooperate."

"Good," Coral said. "Sometimes, I don't know how you do it. This group seems so . . . *gray*. So dull. All bad suits and bad haircuts."

"Well . . . ," Serena said mirthfully, "they *are* easy to resist."

"Well, thank God for that," Coral said, sitting back in her chair.

Serena looked at Coral, then at her plate. "You're not eating. Don't you like the salad?" she asked.

Coral made a moue of distaste. "No," she said. "It's not to my taste."

"But this food is scrumptious," Serena enthused. "The goose-liver Steirereck—sublime!" She rubbed her tummy with a hand and rolled her eyes heavenward. "The caviar-semolina dumplings—yummy! Everything—"

Serena noticed the pained look on Coral's face. "What?" she said. "What is it?"

"I don't know how you can do this to your body," Coral said. "Putting all this rich, unhealthy food into yourself. It almost makes me sick. I know you work out all the time, but it just seems so . . . *excessive.*"

Serena fixed her with a stare. "I don't eat like this all the time, Coral," she said defensively. "In fact, you know very well that most of the time I'm on a very strict fruit and veggie diet. This is a treat."

"If you say so," Coral said, "but I wish you could treat yourself to something healthier."

"Drop it, Coral," Serena said.

"Thy will be done," Coral intoned. "Now, do you want to do some sightseeing this afternoon? Or maybe some shopping? There's a lot to see and do."

"I've got to do some more lighting tests," Serena said. "I trust Bennett and Jason, but I want to make sure there're no hitches when we shoot."

"What about tonight, then?" Coral went on. "You want to have dinner? Maybe go to a club or something?"

"I don't want to have a late night," Serena said, stretching. "I'm a bit jet-lagged, and I think I'll turn in early."

I've got to be there for Misha's call, she thought. *I can't miss him. No way.*

"Okay," Coral said. "Maybe lunch tomorrow, then. I'm off to Paris tomorrow evening for some meetings there." She opened a gold compact and began whisking her face with more ghostly rice powder. When she finished, she snapped the compact shut with a loud clack and stared at Serena. "I just hope you're not going to be waiting around for that *evil* piano-playing *putz* to call you."

Serena rolled her eyes but chose to ignore the pointed barb.

Coral picked up a tube of lipstick and gave her lips a fresh coat of dried-blood mulberry. When she was finished, she tossed the compact and lipstick back into her black alligator Hèrmes Kelly bag, closed it, and looked at Serena. "You having dessert?" she asked.

"You bet I am," Serena replied, smiling. "I'll have to see what they've got. Why don't you have some? Live a little, Coral. This is Vienna, home of the Sacher torte and a zillion other gorgeous, yummy pastries."

"Nooooo," Coral said. "Thank you very much, but my body couldn't take the abuse."

"Don't you want some coffee?"

"Yes," Coral said. "I think I'll have some decaf."

"On the way back to the hotel," Serena said, "let's stop by Demel's. I want to pick up some of their famous pastries to munch on tonight."

"God!" Coral said in exasperation. "You're going to be purging for days, if I know you."

"What can I say?" Serena said. "I'm just an excessive sort of person, Coral. I like extremes, I guess."

"I guess you do," Coral said somewhat haughtily. "It always seems to be feast or famine with you."

"I guess you're right," Serena agreed. And she thought: *My life has been like a famine for far too long, and it's time for a feast. Yes . . . some sort of feast. . . .*

"Are you ready to order dessert?" Coral asked.

"Yes, I'm ready," Serena said. And she wondered: *For what?*

Chapter Four

❦

Schönbrunn Palace was ablaze with light, all of its 1,441 rooms lit for tonight's performance, an unnecessary but magnificent extravagance. The Baroque and Rococo palace, named "beautiful spring" for the stream that meandered through the woodland in which it had been built, was far and away the Hapsburgs' favorite. It was situated away from the formality, intrigue, and rigid protocol of the court at the Hofburg Palace, in central Vienna. Here, the family could live in relative "simplicity," pursuing their hobbies and interests without the watchful eyes of courtiers, comfortable in a setting they considered *intime*, but built to rival Versailles, as were so many extravagant European palaces.

Many of the guests tonight were accustomed to such grandeur, being descendants of families such as the Hapsburgs, and some still lived in the remnants of properties that such vast largesse could provide. For the concert they entered through the main courtyard. At the doorway two enormous obelisks, crowned with Napoleonic eagles, stood guard. Napoleon had them placed there during visits early in the nineteenth century.

Tonight's visitors had been assembled for nearly two hours now, seated in gilt bamboo-turned ballroom chairs, intently listening to Misha play, or pretending to. The air was heady with expensive perfume, the intoxicating scent from thousands of flowers, and, of course, the beauty of the music itself.

With a flourish Misha Levin's hands descended, striking the final notes of Mozart's Rondo in A Minor, K.511. A more exciting finale to this performance could hardly have been imagined. After a moment of suspenseful silence, the audience burst into enthusiastic applause. Bravos resounded in the glittering hall, echoing off the gilt-and-mirrored walls and dazzling crystal chandeliers. Then, as if on cue, the audience rose to its feet, to pay the ultimate homage to one of the world's preeminent virtuoso classical pianists.

Misha sat for a moment, seemingly oblivious to the audience's response, his mind still in the music's thrall. Then as if abruptly relinquishing its hold with a snap of his head, he stood and turned to face his adoring fans. He placed a hand on his Steinway concert grand piano. It had been shipped from New York along with its tuner, expressly for tonight's performance. Graciously bowing his raven-haired head several times, he smiled, acknowledging the audience's appreciation, both gratified and relieved that he had been in top form.

Perfectionist that he was, he always strove for his best, no matter the venue, but this evening was special in several ways. European political, industrial, business, and social leaders from the highest stratum of society had paid thousands of dollars for the privilege of hearing him. Sprinkled among them were several royal and serene highnesses from Europe's oldest and most noble families. They were for the most part a discerning group, both accustomed to and appreciative of the very best, and that is what he had wanted to give them.

The beneficiary, the United Nations' land mine fund, was a cause that was close to his heart. In his travels he had witnessed the human devastation that these buried monsters could cause, and he had committed himself to raising money for the fund at every opportunity. Tonight's concert would add considerably to the fund's coffers and, at the same time, focus attention on the cause.

There was a unique consideration at play tonight, however, at least to the musician in Misha: the almost overwhelming emotional experience of playing in this room, steeped in history as it was. For it was here, in Schönbrunn Palace's Hall of Mirrors, that six-year-old Mozart and his ten-year-old sister, Nannerl, had performed for the Empress Maria Theresa. It was on that long-ago night that Mozart had declared that he wanted to marry the seven-year-old Marie Antoinette, who had sat with her mother, the empress. After his performance Mozart had kissed the empress, then made himself comfortable on her lap.

As the applause slowly died down, the corporeal reality of the distinguished audience intruded upon the sublime realm of the spirit, and Misha quickly found himself enveloped in a crowd of well-wishers. Their good intentions, while appreciated, only served to increase the growing impatience he felt, now that his performance had come to an end.

As was expected, he mingled among the extravagant flower arrangements, accepting lavish praise and making conversation with the perfumed ladies and fastidiously groomed gentlemen, all sipping champagne from crystal flutes and delicately eating Beluga Malossol caviar, which passing waiters proffered from silver trays. There were a few familiar faces—those ardent music lovers who traveled the world over, willing to pay any price to hear him or other great favorites—but there were also many introductions to industrial and political leaders who, while they may not truly appreciate music, could be important to his career and the event's cause.

For an hour or so he was at his most charming and courteous, but as time wore on, his efforts at socializing became more halfhearted. Wrapped up in his thoughts, he retreated to a distant corner of the hall.

"Darling?"

Misha started at the familiar voice, so deeply absorbed had he become. "Yes?" he said, forcing himself out of his reverie.

"Where *are* you tonight, darling?" It was Vera, and there was a note of concern in her voice.

"I'm here," he said, smiling indulgently at his wife. "I was just think- ing about . . . the performance." The lie—for that is what it was, he told himself—flowed glibly off his tongue.

"Well, you were practically rude to the countess," Vera went on, a hint of admonishment in her tone. "You know how influential she is, Misha. She's on the board at Salzburg, and has a great deal of say in the music festival."

"Sorry, Vera," he said. "I guess I'm a little weary. Jet lag or something." *What is she prattling on about anyway?* he asked himself. *Some ancient Countess von und zu Something-or-other.* He found that he was irrationally irritated, with Vera and this glittering party. It was his own preoccupa- tion, however, that disturbed him the most, for he couldn't seem to shake its hold over him.

"Do you feel ill?" she asked.

"No, no," he answered, trying to reassure her. "Just tired."

"You worry me, Misha," she persisted. "You're not yourself. You haven't been since lunch."

Why doesn't she leave me alone? he wondered. *God! How I would give anything to get out of this stifling atmosphere with all these relics of a by- gone age and get back to the hotel where I can—what?* But he knew what. Speak with Serena on the telephone. Arrange a meeting for tomorrow afternoon.

"I'll be fine," he said to his wife, a tired smile crossing his lips.

He saw the consternation etched into her elegant features. A sudden wave of guilt, like a fever, washed over him, and he realized that betray- ing her in his thoughts, as he surely was, was virtually tantamount to the actual deed. *But what choice do I have?* he asked himself.

"You look beautiful tonight," he said to her, hoping that his voice had the ring of sincerity, for it was true. "Ravishing."

"Thank you, Misha," she said, smiling. "I didn't think you'd noticed, and I made a very special effort for you tonight."

And indeed she had, he noticed. She was wearing an opulent Christian Lacroix couture ball gown. Its bodice, all creamy lace that ended in handkerchief sleeves, was gem encrusted, and its skirt was the same lace underlaid with a rose-colored satin petticoat. The gown had required three fittings in Paris and was a masterpiece of the couturier's art.

Her pale blond hair was pulled back into an elegant twist, with slightly curled tendrils framing her porcelain-skinned face. She wore diamonds, white and pink, on her ears, at her throat, and on her wrists. Normally a more conservative dresser, she had about her the air of a Marie Antoinette fantasy tonight.

Misha looked at her admiringly, asking himself how he could even think of betraying this lovely creature. But try as he might, he could not wrench his mind away from thoughts of Serena Gibbons. It was as if she had cast a spell on him, a spell he didn't have the power to break.

"Vera, *liebes Kind!*" An elegant lady of an ancient age tottered up to them and exchanged air kisses in the Continental fashion with Vera. She was dressed in a rather dowdy manner, Misha observed, old lace and satin hanging limply on her skeletal frame, but she wore what appeared to be the entire wealth of the Holy Roman Empire in precious stones.

"I must meet this divine man," the woman said to Vera, her English embroidered with the merest trace of a German accent. She nodded toward Misha, her wispy white hair riotously escaping the confines of the tiara she wore, its immense stones looking far too weighty for her head.

"Katharina," Vera obliged, "this is my husband, Misha. And this, Misha," she said, turning to her husband, "is Princess Katharina von Wallenburg."

Misha took the princess's bony, liver-spotted hand in his own and bent over to kiss it, careful of the enormous stones in her many rings. "I am very pleased to make your acquaintance," he said, making an effort to turn on his charm once again.

"Likewise," the princess replied, her smile exposing yellowing teeth. Her shrewd, hooded old eyes twinkled cornflower blue. "The concert was magnificent, as I'm certain everyone has told you, so I won't bore you about it any further. But it was so beautiful that Rudolph and I will be making an extra little gift to the fund. In your name."

"I am honored," Misha said humbly, "and I thank you very much." He noticed that Vera was smiling broadly, and knew that he had her to thank for this honor. It was her tireless socializing on his behalf that had brought the princess here.

"I won't keep you," the elderly princess said. "I know everyone wants to meet you. You must be exhausted with the chitchat." Then she turned to Vera. "We look forward to seeing you at dinner tomorrow evening, *liebes Kind*," she said.

Vera smiled. "We do, too, Katharina," she said. "We're staying over just for you."

"Only a few of us," the princess said. "Twenty-five or thirty *devoted* music lovers." She winked coquettishly at Misha. "With *very* deep pockets and *lots* of influence." She tottered off without another word, her old-fashioned lavender scent trailing behind her.

"Well, old chap, outdid yourself tonight." Manny Cygelman, resplendent in custom-made Savile Row white tie and tails, sidled up to Misha and Vera.

Misha smiled. "Yes. It did go very well, didn't it, Manny?" he said.

"Extremely pleased," Manny said in his most affected voice. "Everybody. Dazzling performance. Certainly won't hurt your career to have played this concert."

"No," Misha said, "I guess not."

"See you've met the queen of the European music festivals, Princess von Wallenburg."

"Yes," Misha said. "Vera knows her. She seems very nice."

"Pays to know her," Manny said. "Good woman to have on your side. Wouldn't want her for an enemy." He scrutinized his prize client closely. "Feeling all right, old boy? You seem a bit . . . bothered."

"Just tired," Misha said again. "I think I'll go on back to the hotel, Manny." He turned to his wife. "You don't mind, Vera, do you? Manny loves to squire you around. I'll send the limousine back to fetch you."

Vera put a hand on his arm. "If you want to leave, darling, I'll go with you."

"No, no," Misha said. "You two stay and enjoy yourselves. Work your very special magic on the crowd." He squeezed her hand. "Have a good time. I feel like being alone awhile to come down from the performance. Maybe I'll turn in early."

"Are you sure?" Vera asked, a worried expression on her face.

"Yes," Misha said definitely. "Don't worry. I'll be fine. I just need to rest." He turned to Manny. "You'll take care of this beautiful lady?"

"With pleasure, old boy," Manny said, taking Vera's arm.

Misha leaned down and gave Vera a peck on the cheek. "I'll see you in the morning, darling."

"You rest," Vera said in an even tone that she hoped didn't belie her concern and curiosity.

Misha turned and swiftly made his way through the crowd, not stopping until he was outside in Schönbrunn Palace's five-hundred-acre park, where the Mercedes limousine's chauffeur awaited him. In moments he was speeding off in the darkness toward his suite at the Palais Schwarzenberg, and the telephone.

Serena flung the door shut behind her, then slumped against it. "Oh, God!" she gasped, her chest heaving mightily. After a moment she half staggered into her hotel suite, still breathless from her nightly jog. Despite the chill Viennese winds outside, her body was sheathed in a sheen of perspiration.

She pulled off her red fleece gloves, briskly rubbing her hands together for warmth, then shrugged herself out of her silver nylon warm-up jacket, the one with the orange reflective stripes, and pulled the fleecy hot pink watch cap off her head, dropping everything onto the opulent suite's carpeting in a heap of mismatched color.

Without bothering to untie them, she nudged her long, slender feet out of her gray Nikes, one at a time, kicking the running shoes off and across the sitting room, where they thunked to a stop against an antique table. Then she leaned over and peeled off her sweat socks and tossed them in the direction of the heap on the floor.

"Basket!" she cried to the empty suite. Some of her hostility vented, she padded into the bathroom on bare feet, still more than a little angry with herself because of tonight's jog.

Running lukewarm water, she rinsed her hands off and splashed her face several times, then dried off vigorously, a little winded yet from her run. She ran the towel around the back of her neck, patting the sweat there.

No more Wildschwein for this girl! she thought. *No more yummy pastries, either!* All those beautiful little confections for which Vienna was so justly famous had undeniably affected her jogging tonight, weighing her down, tiring her faster.

She hadn't cut her run short, though. Oh, no. That was not Serena. She had run all the faster, covering more distance, telling herself that she could work off all that enormously caloric, body-abusive, and richly satisfying food she had so voraciously partaken of today.

Coral was right, she thought, with a grimace. *But then, she always is. I shouldn't be doing this to my body.*

She eyed the big bathtub and thought that she would run a tubful of water, hot as she could stand it. *I'll have a long, languid soak in aromatic, foamy bath salts.* Let all the tension and strain of the day and her nightly jog slowly ease their way out of her muscles.

First things first, she thought. She retraced her steps to the suite's sitting room, where she poured herself a glass of mineral water at the wet bar. She took long, thirsty swallows, finishing off the tall glass, and poured herself another. She sashayed into the bedroom, her long raven hair swinging behind her, and gradually peeled off the rest of her clothes, tossing them onto a chair. Then she grabbed a thick white terry cloth bathrobe, slipped it on, and tied it around her waist. Finally, she plopped down on the immaculate bed.

Her gaze shifted around the room, eventually coming to rest on the telephone, sitting on the nightstand next to the bed. *Maybe*, she thought, *maybe I should wait to bathe.* She shut her eyes, blotting out her view of the telephone. *Yes. Maybe I should wait. What if Misha calls while I'm in the bathtub? Or . . . maybe . . . maybe I should take a quick shower instead? That way I won't be too long.* She had already checked downstairs at the desk, and there'd been no messages, so she knew he hadn't tried her yet.

The she reminded herself that he was performing tonight. *He'll probably be at Schönbrunn Palace until midnight or later*, she thought. *Hobnobbing with all those charity-circuit bigwigs.* She quickly glanced at the little travel clock at her bedside: ten-thirty.

Should I wait? she wondered. *Or shouldn't I? What the hell should I do?* Then she abruptly sat up, slamming a fist into the bed.

"Shit!" she exclaimed aloud. "Shit, shit, *shit!*"

She leapt out of bed and marched purposefully to the bathroom. *I will not let this happen*, she told herself. *I will not fall into that deadly trap again. Not like I did the last time. Waiting for Misha Levin to call. Ha! What a joke! I'm a changed person now. Oh, yes, I am. Yes, indeed! I don't need this. I don't need* him! *I am* invulnerable *to him and his charm.*

She twirled on the taps with a vengeful forcefulness, poured scented bath salts in—a potent and erotic combination of musk, vetiver, and citrus—then tromped back into the bedroom. She snatched up the latest copy of *L'Uomo Vogue* to look once again at the fashion shoot she had done for it some months ago.

Back in the steamy bathroom, she turned off the taps and eased herself down into the tub, now filled with foamy, exotically perfumed water. *Ah, yes!* she thought, delighting in the heat of the steamy water on her weary flesh. *This is more like it.*

She began leafing through the magazine, studying its layouts, nodding to herself with satisfaction at the photos from her shoot and the way they had been used. The art director had done an excellent job, she decided, piecing together the story line in the photos in an artistic way. She never had to worry that her work would look cheap or be poorly displayed in the Italian fashion magazines.

Leafing back and forth, back and forth, she abruptly sighed and tossed the magazine over the side of the tub. It landed on the floor with a bang. She lay back, staring at the wall. All those male bodies in the latest fashions only served as a reminder of her own unattached and chaste state. At least for now.

But what will tomorrow bring? she wondered. And then it started again.

Thinking of him. Of Misha. And how extraordinary it was that she had run into him today—in Vienna of all places.

God, he looked so wonderful, she thought. *Better even than he did five years ago, if that were possible.* She could envision the wind in his longish blue-black hair, that prominent nose and those sensuous lips. His strong cleft chin and high cheekbones. And those piercing, liquid, dark, dark eyes. All of it embellishing a tall, strong Adonis of a body that she remembered only too well.

She felt that old sweet, maddening, almost uncontrollable physical urge—an urge that she had never felt with anyone else—suffuse her body with longing. She'd had a lot of men in her thirty years. *Too many men,* she thought. Some of them had been rich, some famous, some of them no more than feral brutes. Many of them had a foggy indistinctness in her memory. But in that pantheon of lust, none of them had compared with Misha Levin.

No, she thought, *none of them had held a candle to Misha Levin.*

Her hands traveled over her voluptuously charged body—neck, shoulders, breasts, torso, thighs, mound—remembering his hands on all those places, relishing the imprint they had left there, never to be forgotten.

Oh, my God, she wondered. *Why did he have to come back?*

Then: *Thank God he has.*

At the three-hundred-year-old Palais Schwarzenberg, Misha hurried through the striated-marble lobby, for once ignoring the breathtaking beauty of its noble antiques and Baroque gilt and crystal. He went straight up to his suite. Once inside the antique-filled duplex, he closed the door and poured himself a scotch neat, and drank it down in one swallow. Loosening his tie, he poured another one to nurse, this time adding ice cubes and a splash of water. Then, taking his drink and the bottle of scotch, he climbed the stairs to his bedroom. There, he slowly began to undress, neatly hanging his clothes in the closet, although they would be taken to the cleaners when he was back in New York.

Once naked, he spread out on the luxurious bed and sipped his scotch, mentally preparing himself to telephone Serena. *You want to do this*, he told himself. *Yes, you may regret it for the rest of your life if you don't.* Then, before he could lose his nerve or change his mind, he set down his drink and dialed Serena's number at the König von Ungarn.

"Hello?" She picked up on the first ring, her voice breathy.

"It's Misha," he said.

"I know," she said, a hint of amusement in her voice.

"What have you been up to?" he asked. "You sound like you're out of breath."

"Nothing really," Serena replied. "I was just finishing up in the bathroom. I had a nice, long soak after my jog tonight."

"So you're still running," he said. He could see that long, lithe body of hers, speeding through the streets.

"Yes," Serena answered. "And I bet you're still torturing yourself with racquetball and swimming and the weight-lifting thing." His body, in all its masculine definition and hardness, flashed before her mind's eye.

"You know me too well," Misha said with a little laugh. He paused a moment, then said: "I . . . I still can't quite believe we ran into each other today."

"It is a coincidence, isn't it?" Serena said. "All those years with both of us living in New York, and we've never once crossed paths."

"Maybe it's fate," Misha said uncertainly.

"I don't know that I believe in fate," Serena said warily.

"Whatever it is," he said, "I'm glad, Serena."

"I am, too, Misha," she replied.

She sounds as if she really means it, he thought. *Maybe . . . just maybe . . . something will . . .* He quickly tried to put his hopes and desires on hold.

"Do you think we can get together tomorrow?" He was making an effort not to sound too pushy or too anxious. *I mustn't scare her off*, he thought.

"Yes . . . I think so," Serena said. "But I . . . I don't want to mislead you, Misha. I mean, I don't want you to think that we can just pick up where we left off."

"No, no, *no*, Serena," Misha rushed to assure her. "I don't have any expectations. I just . . . I just want to see you."

"I'd like that," she said. "Very much." *Do I sound too excited?* she wondered. *Will he think I'm desperate to see him?*

"Is sometime around four okay?" he asked.

"Make it four-thirty," Serena said. "Is that okay?"

"That's perfect," he replied. "Shall we meet at your hotel . . . in the bar downstairs?"

"Come on up to the room," she said. "I have several appointments, so it would be easier for me."

"Great," Misha said. "I'll see you then."

"Bye," Serena said. She hung up the telephone and took a deep breath. *If he only knew!* she thought. *How I can hardly wait to see him!*

"Good night, Serena," he said, then realized that she'd already hung up the telephone.

Misha took a sip of his scotch and closed his eyes. He could see her, that lush raven black hair, her long swan's neck, those huge hazel eyes and sensual, even lascivious, lips. Then: her perfect, small, but ample breasts with their strawberry nipples, her long trim torso and narrow waist, and the beautiful mound of black lusciousness between her creamy thighs.

He felt a stirring in his loins that he hadn't felt in—*How long has it been?* he wondered. He couldn't remember, but he knew that it had been too long. Far too long. And now, the sensation was both intoxicating and irresistible.

Later, after a long, hot shower, he lay in bed thinking about the past, all those years ago when he and Serena had spent time together. It had been a torrid affair of operatically dramatic highs and equally dramatic lows. They'd always seemed to be devouring each other with an all-consuming, lusty sexual passion—a passion he hadn't known could exist.

Serena, Misha knew, had been all wrong for him. In fact, he thought, had he tried to conjure up the worst of all possible choices in a lover, she would have surely been that woman.

He was of Russian descent and Jewish, though nonpracticing. Serena was American, southern—a Florida cracker, really—and a Protestant, though she had long since abandoned faith in anything or anybody but herself. He was obsessed with his career and needed a woman who would devote herself to him and his music. Serena was equally as obsessed with her own career and wasn't about to sacrifice herself to him and his ambitions.

Misha picked up his scotch and took another sip, savoring its smooth, heated descent down his throat to his stomach, where its fiery warmth spread out like a blanket.

Yes, two such different people, he thought.

Yet . . . Yet, I still don't think I've ever loved anybody like I loved her. I've certainly never had that same profound physical craving for anyone else.

He sipped the last of his scotch, then set down the empty glass again.

He leaned over and clicked off the lamp on the night table, then closed his eyes to sleep. But sleep eluded him, and he tossed and turned, obsessed with his thoughts of Serena, of their past together, and, finally, of their date tomorrow.

What will tomorrow bring? he wondered. He didn't know, but in his heightened state of physical longing, of arousal, he prayed for release.

Chapter Five

The day dawned bleak and gray, a chill wind sweeping in from the east, a harbinger of the winter to come. Misha opened his eyes. In the diffuse light coming through the elaborate draperies at the windows, the first thing in his line of vision was Vera's pale blond hair fanned out over the pillow. Never had her porcelain profile looked more beautiful, her neck and shoulders more beckoning. Her breathing was deep and regular. She was still sound asleep.

Perhaps, he thought, perhaps . . . I should slide my arms around her, and wake her as I . . .

He furrowed his brow.

No, let her sleep. For suddenly, Serena's Madonna-like face, framed by its raven black hair, and her resplendent body, in all its tantalizing eroticism, flashed before his mind's eye. A wave of sensuous pleasure engulfed him. He was aroused—doubly so by the mere thought that he would be seeing her today.

He felt deep down inside that their running into each other had been fate, that somehow or other it was meant to be. That his urges—*their* urges, surely—were meant to be assuaged. There was an inevitability about it, Misha decided, a powerlessness to control it that was not characteristic of him at all.

Slowly he sat up and looked around the grand second-floor bedroom of the suite. The exquisite ball gown that Vera had worn last evening was carefully laid over a chair, its gemstones twinkling in the dim light. What a magnificent piece of work it is, Misha thought. And Vera looked beautiful in it, more beautiful than ever. She really had made a supreme effort. He smiled ruefully. But then, Vera always did, didn't she?

Guilt, as it had last night, began to worm its way into his consciousness. This woman had done everything in her power to be the perfect wife and mother, to try to satisfy him. Running a hand through his long, black hair, he slammed a mental door shut on this line of thought.

He quietly pulled off the covers, swung his legs out of bed, and stood up, stretching his long limbs. He padded into the bathroom, where he lathered up and stood under a hot steamy shower for long minutes, all the while thinking about last night's performance.

After weeks of practice and rehearsal, and finally the performance itself, he was usually left physically and emotionally drained, and last evening had taken its toll. Oddly enough, however, he felt energized today, still a little high, more so than usual after performing.

Generally, adrenaline relentlessly drove him during the final weeks of preparing for a performance, then enveloped him in a fever-pitch high during and after the performance itself, the rush heightened all the more in intensity if the concert was a success, such as last night's. The glow of success and the accompanying festivities dissipated quickly, however, and his spirits inevitably sank, sometimes plunging into a near-crippling depression.

Gradually, however, he had learned to cope with this aftermath. He came to realize that he was simply tired and sad. Sad that it was over. Slowly life would interest him again. Music, its siren call beckoning, would entice him anew, and he would answer that call, mercilessly throwing himself into practice for the next performance, for the next recording session.

Misha turned off the shower and began to dry himself with a towel. Today he still felt the remnants of the high he'd experienced for the previous weeks. Curious that it hasn't dissipated yet, he thought, but perhaps it was because he hadn't really celebrated. He'd been too preoccupied at the party afterward to enjoy himself. Yes, he decided, carefully shaving now, that was it. He hadn't celebrated.

So today would be just that. A little celebration. He deserved it, and Vera, too. She had worked almost as hard as he had to see that last night was a success. When he'd left her there with Manny, she'd been charming the powers that be. So typical of Vera, he thought. She left little to chance where his career was concerned, and often explored avenues that even Manny overlooked or was too busy to pursue.

Today, Misha decided, he would arrange something special for Vera and himself, perhaps a tour of the Hofburg, a celebratory lunch afterward, and then . . . well, then he would make his excuses.

Trying not to disturb his still slumbering wife, he quickly dressed. Black cashmere turtleneck sweater, black wool trousers and sports jacket, black Gucci loafers. Ready for a hearty breakfast downstairs, where he could read the papers and enjoy a little time alone.

*   *   *

The moment he stepped into the elegant dining room, Manny waved to him. Well, Misha thought, forget a quiet perusal of the papers. But what the hell. He was feeling particularly expansive this morning, generous with his time and himself.

He strode over to the table, the maître d' scurrying along behind him, and took a seat, then the proffered menu.

"How're you feeling this morning, old chap?" Manny asked, looking up from his newspaper. He was dressed to the nines as usual, today in his pinstripe international banker-diplomat mode. "Better, I trust."

"Much," Misha said. "All I needed was a good night's sleep. I guess this trip and the concert took more out of me than I thought."

Manny pointed at the newspaper. "Well, it was worth it, my boy," he said, "well worth it. There'll be more reviews in *Der Standard* and *Die Presse*, but this one is superb. Superb!"

The waiter materialized, and Misha ordered breakfast. Ham, sausages, three fried eggs, fried potatoes, and toast. Orange juice and coffee. He was ravenous, as he always was the day after a concert.

"Who wrote it, Manny?" Misha asked.

"Gertler. Here, have a look?" Manny extended the newspaper across the table to Misha.

"No," he said, waving the paper away. "Just give me the gist. I don't want to read it."

"What?" Manny said, eyeing him through his tortoiseshell glasses. "I told you the review's superb, and it is."

Misha stirred cream and sugar into his coffee. "Look, Manny," he replied. "I don't mean to be arrogant, but I was at my very best last night. You know it, and I know it." He looked Manny in the eye. "So fuck the critics."

Manny grunted noncommittally. "You're right," he said, "but you never know when they'll send in a hatchet man to chop you into little pieces because somebody happens to be pissed off at you."

Misha sipped his coffee and didn't reply.

"Anyway," Manny continued, "Herr Gertler's review is all 'dazzling transcriptions.' 'Old-fashioned virtuoso.' " He thumped the newspaper. " 'Bold' and 'lushly moody.' You get the picture."

"Yes," Misha said. "I get the picture." His food arrived, and he began eating voraciously.

"So," Manny asked, "what would you like to do today? There's nothing on the agenda until that party at Prince and Princess von Wallenburg's tonight."

"I thought maybe Vera would like to see the Hofburg," Misha said between bites of sausage. "You know the Hapsburg jewels. All that." He took a sip of coffee before continuing. "Then, this afternoon, I want to do some shopping. Alone."

"You?" Manny exclaimed. *"Shop?"*

"Yes. Why not?" Misha said, his eyebrows raised questioningly. "I want to pick up some things for Nicky. Maybe a surprise for Vera."

Manny looked at him with a quizzical expression. This was not like Misha. Misha never shopped unless he had to. "What's up?" he finally asked.

"Up?" Misha replied. "Nothing's up. I just want to be alone, do some shopping and . . . soak up some of the atmosphere."

"Gimme a break," Manny said. He abruptly dropped his Anglophile pose, his voice and manner reverting to the streets of Brooklyn from which he hailed. "I know you well enough to know you've got something on your mind, Misha. You've been acting weird ever since lunch yesterday. Now, what's cooking? What is it?"

Misha's eyes strayed out the windows to the Palais Schwarzenburg's lushly planted fifteen-acre gardens. He could see that the sun was beginning to break through the clouds, with the promise of a crystal clear, if chilly, day. His gaze returned to Manny across the table. There was a secretive smile on Misha's lips, but he didn't utter a word.

"Uh-oh," Manny said, looking at him. "I smell trouble. *T-r-o-u-b-l-e,* trouble."

Misha took a sip of coffee, then put down his cup. "Just take care of Vera this afternoon after lunch. Would you?" he said.

"Jesus!" Manny exclaimed. "It's a fucking woman, isn't it?"

Misha ignored him, concentrating on his food again.

"Give!" Manny said in exasperation. *"Talk* to me, Misha! This is Manny, remember?"

When Misha remained silent, chewing on a piece of toast, Manny emitted a loud sigh. "Shit," he said. "I'll do it. I'll take care of Vera, but I hope I don't live to regret this."

Misha continued eating contentedly, knowing that Manny would do exactly what he'd asked him to do.

"A little more to your left," Serena called out. "Please!" She waved her arm, indicating the direction in which she wanted the men to move.

There was hesitation, stumbling, laughter, and general chaos, as there had been all morning.

"Left!" she cried, waving furiously. "Left, gentlemen, *left!*"

Jason, one of her assistants, jumped to his feet and bounded over to help the men align themselves properly.

She stifled a growl of exasperation but smiled politely. *Heads of state,* she thought with frustration. *Assholes of state is more like it.* Most of them understood and spoke English well, so the language barrier wasn't the problem. No, the problem with this shoot, she decided, was that these political big shots weren't taking her or the shoot very seriously.

Locker room clowns, she thought with rising disgust. If she could shoot them individually, she didn't think she'd be having this problem. But she couldn't do that—she was stuck with The Group—whether she liked it or not. And like a lot of men in a group, they had to pump up their testosterone levels for one another—and her.

Arms akimbo, she studied the men, lined up as they were in the *Zeremoniensaal,* one of the Hofburg palace's throne rooms. She liked the juxtaposition of their contemporary, if somewhat dull, appearance with the overwrought Baroque gilt and marble splendor of this, the Hapsburgs' former seat of power.

"Okay!" she enthused. "That's good. Great! Hold it." She put her eye back down to the Hasselblad's viewer for a moment. "Don't move!" she cried.

With a flick of a button the camera's motor drive started whirring away. She shot frame after frame of these, the new faces of *Mittel* and Eastern Europe. Faces she would like to shove her fist in right now. She'd been shooting for over two hours, with limited help. She'd only brought Jason and Bennett, her favorite and most knowledgeable assistants with her from New York. She knew that she had plenty of acceptable shots for the magazine. But she still wasn't satisfied. Despite the setting, she just didn't feel that she'd captured anything beyond the ordinary, the mundane.

Face it, she told herself. There's simply no magic happening here today. Part of the problem, she realized, was her subjects. They were reacting to her as a woman first and a photographer second. For some reason her usual tactics, including her "disguise," weren't working today.

Long ago, Serena had developed this disguise, born of ingenuity and necessity. She'd quickly learned the importance of dressing *down* for photo shoots. There were the practical considerations, or course. Most shoots encompassed long hours of physically grueling labor, and it was sometimes very dirty work—even here in a palace like the Hofburg, where all that marble wasn't necessarily as pristine as it looked.

Practicality aside, the single most important lesson she'd learned was that whether a shoot was with men or women, or both, she could accomplish a lot more if she minimalized her own, undeniably exotic, presence on the set, drawing as little attention to herself as possible. For her appearance, she'd soon discovered, was distracting to clients and hindered their cooperation. She was a threat to many of the women, and an object to be conquered by most of the men.

That explained the disguise and her look today: the complete lack of makeup, the loose ponytail low on her neck, and the ratty old baseball cap worn on her head. Plus, the wrinkled work shirt and paint-splotched, torn Levi's. All worn with down-at-the-heel, high-top sneakers. But the clincher, she thought, were the nerdy, black-framed eyeglasses perched on her nose. The ones with the dirty masking tape wrapped around the temples. She didn't need them, of course—they had clear lenses so they didn't distort her vision—but they were essential to her disguise.

Why was today different? she wondered. Don't I look like somebody's plain-Jane cousin? Perhaps, she thought, they were merely excited by being photographed here in the splendor of the former court of the Holy Roman Empire. Or perhaps it was coming together like this for the first time.

She didn't know, but she wanted to get this shoot over with. Pronto. Get out of here and get back to the hotel.

And that, she knew, was the key to the larger part of the problem. *Me,* she thought. Her usual patience had deserted her today. She was not trying her hardest, not giving it her usual best shot. The reason for this she knew unequivocally: she was nervous, and had been ever since yesterday, after running into *him.* Misha Levin.

Before she had spoken to him last evening, she'd promised herself that she would set certain ground rules over the telephone. That she would tell him yes, that she would like to see him, but that they must meet on "neutral" ground—neither's hotel room—and that under no circumstances should he expect anything more than a friendly chat, a catching up with each other.

The sound of his voice had changed all that. *A total meltdown of defenses,* she thought. *That's what it was.* The deep, resonant baritone, with the merest hint of an accent, had immediately weakened her resolve, made any rules or restrictions seem unimportant—silly even—in the light of the possibilities that were held within its promising timbre.

Misha had been as excited as she by their encounter, of that she was certain. And it was most definitely not the excitement of two old friends running into each other. No. It was much more than that. It was as if two electrically charged elements had crossed paths, creating a heretofore unknown form of power and magic, that in its potency was an all-consuming force of such depth and dimension that it could not be denied. Their encounter had been one of two former *lovers* meeting.

Serena shook her head, as if to clear it of these obsessive thoughts. *I've got to get busy,* she thought. *Forget this shit.* She turned her attention back to the task at hand.

"Bennett," she said, "move that umbrella on the right about a foot toward me."

"You got it." He jumped up to do as she'd asked.

Serena watched him, then nodded when the reflector was repositioned exactly like she wanted. Then she turned to the men before her. "Just a couple more shots, gentlemen," she said, smiling. "Then I'll let you go."

Thirty minutes later, she had thanked her subjects profusely and was busy helping Jason and Bennett pack up. There was a lot of equipment, but Serena didn't mind helping out. She hated traveling with an entourage of assistants, so she'd trained Jason and Bennett to do nearly everything. What the three of them couldn't do together, or was simply too time-consuming, she usually hired local freelancers for. Like the hair stylists and makeup artists she'd used today.

They had left now, and she and "the boys," as everyone referred to them, were just about ready to start taking equipment down to the rented van outside, when the staccato click of Coral's Manolo Blahnik heels on the marble announced her arrival. "How did it go?" she asked.

"It was not a picnic," Serena said simply, turning to look at Coral. She looks like a modern-day empress, Serena thought. Dressed to guide paying tourists through her throne room.

"What happened?" Coral asked, a look of alarm on her magnolia white face.

"Nothing, Coral. Nothing important, anyway," Serena replied. "It's just that they acted like a bunch of guys that just found out what they've got in their pants, if you know what I mean."

Coral's right eyebrow lifted in an arch, and she nodded. "I see," she said. "But you got all the shots you needed?"

Serena shot her agent a scornful look. "Of course I got what I needed, Coral," she said. "I always get what I need."

Coral flinched. "I was just asking, Serena," she said defensively. She brushed at imaginary lint on the sleeve of her black wool, sable-trimmed coat, an Yves Saint Laurent. "I see that you're a little testy. Shall we go back to the hotel so you can change? Then go to lunch?"

"I'm taking Jason and Bennett to lunch," Serena said, winking at the two of them. "But you're welcome to join us, Coral." She hadn't planned on this, but decided it would be just the diversion she needed to take her mind off Misha Levin. She pulled off her baseball cap and eyeglasses and loosened her long, black hair, shaking it out.

The boys shot each other amused glances, knowing that Serena was deliberately baiting Coral.

"Why, yes," Coral said, surprising them all. "I would like that very much, I think." She turned to Jason and Bennett. "It's time we talked, boys," she said. "I've looked at some of your proofs, and I think that you have great promise as photographers in your own right."

Jason and Bennett exchanged glances again, more a mixture of surprise and awe than amusement this time. This news—and it was fantastic for them—came from straight out of the blue.

"That'd be great, Coral," Jason said.

"Yeah," Bennett seconded.

"Good," Coral said, her brows knitted as her eyes ran up and down the two of them, scrutinizing them closely. *My God!* she thought. She had a feeling that they might as well forget a restaurant with any stars to its name. For that matter, was there *any* restaurant in Vienna that would even admit them? "I hope you have some clothes at the hotel," she said, smiling sweetly. "Something a little more . . . suitable, perhaps?"

Jason shrugged, and Bennett just stared at her. They were both dressed as always, as if headed for an East Village club. Jason, his nearly waist-length dark brown hair with bold, blond skunk stripes, wore shiny black PVC pants with logger boots and an artfully slashed, asymmetrical Helmut Lang T-shirt, which exposed his numerous tattoos. Black leather pants with futuristic sneakers and a leopard print shirt adorned Bennett's skinny frame. His wildly chopped—that was the only word to describe it, Coral thought—hair was dyed platinum and had black roots, an effect he worked hard to achieve.

"Their clothes aren't a problem," Serena piped up, ruffling Bennett's hair with her fingers. "In fact, I'm not going to bother to change. We're going to a really hip bar I heard about." She threw her agent a lofty glance. "*You're* the one who'd better change, Coral," she said. "Unless you want to chance getting that sable spray-painted."

As they stepped into the sunlit courtyard, Vera's head was still aswirl with the glories of the *Schatzkammer*, the Hofburg's Imperial Treasury. "It's like going to a really fabulous art exhibition," Vera said, turning to Misha. "My mind will be flashing a kaleidoscope of colors for days. All those beautiful things." She sighed somewhat wistfully. "And to think that the Hapsburgs took nearly all the imperial jewels with them into exile."

"What was your favorite?" Misha asked her, putting an arm around her waist. "Oh, wait. I think I can guess."

Vera laughed. "You know me too well, Misha," she said.

"Emeralds and rubies and sapphires and diamonds," Manny sang. "These are a few of my favorite things." He turned to Vera and grinned. "Am I right?"

"You know me almost as well," Vera said.

"If I were a betting man," Misha said, "I would guess that your very favorite *objet* was perhaps green? As in emerald?"

"Certainly not the 1,680-carat Colombian Emerald," Manny joked.

"I don't think I've ever seen a precious stone that big," Vera said. "And the old imperial crown! It's enormous, with all those diamonds and rubies and sapphires!"

"Hitler liked it so much he took it to Nürnberg in '38," Manny said.

"All the gold and precious stones were dazzling," Vera said seriously, "but you know what?"

"What?" Misha asked, looking at her.

"My very favorite things," Vera said thoughtfully, "were actually the christening robes that Maria Theresa embroidered for her grandchildren."

"They were magnificent," Misha said.

"Yes," Vera nodded, "but they were also sweet. I mean, the work that went into them, the thought. It's not something that an empress has to do for the grand . . ."

Vera suddenly slowed her pace and peered off to her left.

Wasn't that . . . ?

She was certain that she recognized the tall, thin raven-haired beauty loaded down with photographic equipment who was striding across the *In der Burg* courtyard, two wildly clothed young men alongside her, and . . .

My God! It has to be! she thought.

. . . Coral Randolph, jet black helmet of hair and white-white face, in a sable-trimmed coat, leading the way.

Unmistakably. Unmistakably Coral, therefore almost certainly . . .

Vera quickly resumed her pace.

. . . *Serena Gibbons.*

"What is it, darling?" Misha asked. "You look as if you've seen a ghost."

"Nothing," Vera said lightly. "Nothing at all. I thought I had something in my shoe for a minute, but I don't." She smiled up at him, searching for any indication that he had seen what she had. *If he had seen her,* she thought, *I would be able to tell it from his face.* But apparently he hadn't, for she saw nothing in his expression or manner that was a tip-off.

"You two still game for the crypt?" Manny said quickly. *Oh, God!* he thought. *I've got to get them out of here. And fast!* He couldn't believe what he'd just seen, but knew his eyes hadn't fooled him—especially considering Misha's peculiar behavior since lunch yesterday.

Serena Gibbons. She explained everything.

Chapter Six

~~~~

Serena eyed herself critically in the bathroom mirror, then made hollows of her cheeks by sucking them in. She picked up her sable-tipped makeup brush, dipped it in the tinted powder, and whisked another touch of Mata Hari blusher onto her cheekbones. She looked again. "Purrr-fect," she told her reflection. Then on second thought, she puckered her Cabaret-coated lips just so. "No more," she decided. "Enough's enough." She bent over double and began brushing her hair furiously, from the base of her neck over her head, back to front, back to front, then stood back up, swung her head from side to side, shaking her hair, and gave it a few strokes from under the ears down. "There," she said. "All done."

With that, she twirled out of the bathroom and into the suite's bedroom, where she quickly slipped on a black wool boat-neck sweater and quilted black leather micro-miniskirt. Both by Iceberg, but anything but cold. She eyed herself in the bedroom mirror for a moment, then heaved a sigh. "Shit!" she said. She turned and slumped down onto the bed, arms on her knees, chin in her hands.

Another promise broken, she thought. *And to the most important person around: me.*

She sighed again, then got up and poured herself a glass of mineral water and brought it over to the bed. She put the glass on the nightstand and spread out. She'd promised herself that she wouldn't make any special efforts for her meeting with Misha today, that she would take their seeing each other in stride. She would *not* let nervousness and excitement rule the day.

Famous last words.

During lunch with Coral and the boys, she had been anything but helpful in the discussion of the boys' careers. She simply couldn't concentrate and had gotten increasingly anxious, finally becoming so overwrought that she'd jumped up from the table, told them she didn't feel well, and deserted them there in the restaurant. Same reason, of course. She'd fallen prey to her thoughts of Misha.

She took a sip of the mineral water and sat up in bed. I'd better finish getting ready myself, she thought. Now, what have I forgotten? I know I've forgotten something, but what? Then it dawned on her: perfume. She jumped to her feet and dashed into the bathroom, where she'd left a bottle of exotic scent that had been specially concocted for her in Paris. She dabbed the stopper on her neck, behind her ears, between her breasts, at her wrists, and reaching up under her skirt, she swiped drops down her thighs.

At that moment she heard a knock at the door.

Shit! she thought. *Countdown's over! It's ground zero!*

She dashed back to the bedroom but didn't see her shoes. *Screw it!* She forced herself to stand still for a minute, taking deep breaths of air. Then, forcing herself to take slow, measured steps, she padded on bare feet through the sitting room to the door. When she reached it, she squared her shoulders and took another deep breath, then opened it wide.

Misha stood in the hallway, his hands crossed in front of him, a shopping bag dangling from them. He stood there a moment, mute, his dark, liquid eyes feasting on her.

His lips spread into a disarming smile. "Hello," he said simply. Ah, the beauty of her! he thought. The long raven hair. The perfect skin on those exquisite features. The hint of ample breasts that he knew were concealed beneath the sweater. The endlessly long, slender legs beneath the minuscule leather skirt.

Serena returned his smile. "Come in, Misha," she said in her smoky contralto. *Oh, my God,* she thought. She'd already forgotten how handsome he was, how he exuded a kind of power. How his very presence was so commanding.

He stepped into the suite, and Serena closed the door and followed him in. "Here," she said, "let me take your coat."

He set his shopping bag down and shrugged out of his long cashmere overcoat. When she started to take it from him, he said: "I can hang it up, Serena." He smiled. "As I remember, you weren't all that keen on hanging up clothes."

"You would remember that," Serena said with laughter in her voice. "Let me have it anyway." She took the coat from him and hung it in a closet. "I've gotten a wee bit better about housekeeping," she said, turning to him. "Not much"—she held her thumb and forefinger up—"but a little better anyway."

They stood, looking at each other in the suite's sitting room.

"Oh, here," Misha said, reaching down into the shopping bag. "I had to do some shopping on the way over, and I picked these up." He extracted a small bouquet of roses, blushed with the palest pink and almost completely open. They were wrapped in an elegant sleeve and tied with satin ribbon. He held them out to her. "For you," he said.

Serena looked at the bouquet and smiled. "They're beautiful, Misha." Her voice was soft and wistful. "My favorite color. And almost fullblown. Just like I like them." She looked up at him. "You didn't forget."

"No," he said. "How could I?" At this moment he wanted nothing more desperately than to take her in his arms and tell her that he had forgotten nothing about her.

Serena felt a rush of embarrassment and wondered if he noticed as a tingling flush rose from her chest, up her neck, and into her face, suffusing it with heat.

She quickly turned away. "Come in and sit down," she said. "Make yourself comfortable. I'll get something to put the flowers in."

She went into the bathroom and got a glass that she half-filled with tepid tap water. She carefully untied the bouquet, unwrapped it, and put it in the glass. She returned to the sitting room and ceremoniously placed the roses on the coffee table.

"There," she said. "Perfect."

"Yes, perfect," Misha echoed, his dark eyes ignoring the flowers and coming to rest on her.

Serena sat down on the couch and drew her long legs up underneath her.

Misha looked over at her. "You look more beautiful than ever," he said, "if that's possible."

Serena laughed nervously. "Thanks," she said. "I try. Sometimes." She focused on the flowers, trying to avoid his eyes, then decided to quickly change the subject. "How was your performance last night?" she asked.

"It went very well," Misha said, not adding that he had been totally preoccupied with thoughts of her the entire evening. "How did your shoot go?"

"Don't ask," she replied, tossing long strands of hair away from her face.

"That bad?" he said.

"Oh, not really, but it wasn't exactly inspiring," Serena said. She reached for her mineral water, but it wasn't there.

Suddenly she jumped up. "Oh, God, Misha, I'm such a terrible hostess," she cried. "Would you like something to drink? There're all kinds of goodies in the minibar."

"What're you having?" Misha asked. "Are you on one of your crazy diets?"

"Noooo . . . ," Serena said. "Well, I *am* trying to sort of do a purge starting right now. Just mineral water for a couple of days. Nothing else. All this Viennese food, you know. Everything drenched in whipped cream."

Misha laughed. "I see that money and fame haven't changed you all that much," he said.

"I guess not," Serena said as she looked at the contents of the mini-bar's refrigerator. "Oh, look," she said. "There're two splits of champagne. Why don't we have them?" She turned to Misha with a questioning look on her face.

"Definitely," he said. "Here, let me open them."

"No," Serena said, "I can do it."

But Misha got up and walked over to the minibar. He held out his hand for the bottle of Taittinger. "Let me," he said. "I insist."

Serena was suddenly disconcerted by his nearness. She could feel his warm breath on her, could smell his masculine smell, could swear that she sensed about him a heightened arousal that was charging the very atmosphere between and around them.

Wordlessly, she handed him the bottle, and as she did, Misha took her hand and held it in his for a moment. Serena felt a surge of desire rush through her, like an electrical charge, suffusing her not with embarrassment but with a heated lust, galvanizing her entire body, melting her resolve, weakening her knees. Her pulse pounded in her ears, and she suddenly felt breathless. She desperately wanted nothing more than for him to take her in his powerful arms and wrap himself around her. To take her here and now, on this very spot, and devour her passionately,

Oh, God, she thought. *I want him! And . . . and I want him to want me!*

With a barely perceptible, but sharp, intake of breath, she forced herself to remove her hand from his. She was certain that she was visibly shaken, that she must look like a fool. Without a word she turned and went back over to the couch, where she sat down and pulled her legs up underneath her again.

Misha, who was anything but oblivious to Serena's disconcertedness, quickly popped the cork on one of the splits and poured the pale, golden liquid into two glasses at the minibar. He walked back over to the couch and handed one to Serena, then sat down at the other end of the couch, turning to face her. He extended his arm with the glass and smiled.

"To . . . old friends," he said, looking into her hazel eyes.

Serena clinked her glass against his. "To old friends," she repeated. She took a sip of the champagne. It tasted delicious and bubbly against her tongue.

Misha sipped, then set down his glass and looked over at her. "Now tell me," he said. "About your day. You didn't finish."

"Oh, it's such a bore," Serena said. "You don't want to hear about it, Misha."

"Yes, I do," he said definitely. "Tell me."

"Well, the men were a little rowdy. You know, I was photographing some of the new leaders of Eastern and Middle Europe. And"—she looked at him—"I guess I'm just getting a little tired of some of the assignments I get." She took another sip of her champagne.

"What?" Misha looked surprised. "But you're doing so well, Serena. I'd have thought you were very happy. I read about the huge contract Coral negotiated for you."

"Everybody did, didn't they?" Serena said in a somewhat embittered tone of voice.

"That goes with the territory," Misha said. "But I don't understand why you're not happy. All that money! And you get exposure in the best magazines. You get to travel all over the world. Meet all those famous people. You're even a celebrity yourself now."

"I know. I know." Serena groaned. "I must sound like an ungrateful child. "It's just . . . well, the money's great, and I love the travel. I guess I'm just tired of the shoots. Doing fashion shoots and taking pictures of celebrities year after year can get to be a bore, you know?"

"I'd have thought it would be very exciting," Misha said.

"It can be," she said. "It *was* in the beginning, but it's gotten to be old hat. It seems like I'm always surrounded by a thousand assistants. Hair stylists, makeup artists, shoot stylists, the clothing people, publicity people, a huge technical crew. You know, the last time I did a shoot in L.A.—a big movie star—there were *twenty-two* of us there to get the pictures." She sighed and looked at him. "Is that ridiculous? Sometimes I wonder what happened to me and the camera. *Just* me and the camera. Do you know what I mean?"

"I think so," he said. "It's like the music business. Recording and performing. It seems like sometimes the least important things are me and the piano or me and the music. All the business of recording and performing, all the hoopla surrounding it, take precedence. It's like last night's performance was important because the big European connections to Salzburg and Bayreuth were there. The business going on there was probably more important than the performance."

"Exactly," Serena said. "Sometimes I think I'd like to start over, or go in a new direction. I know I'm lucky. I make tons of money and all that. But I think I'd like to start concentrating more on *what* I photo-graph. Take off somewhere with nothing but me and the camera."

"Sounds to me like you want to do some experimenting," Misha said. "Maybe you're getting more interested in art photography."

Serena nodded. "Yes," she said, "I guess that's it. People are talking more about the money I make and the celebrities I shoot than about the *pictures* themselves." She laughed. "I guess I want some respect."

"From critics?" he asked.

"Yes," she said, "that, too. I want to be taken seriously, and do some work that's more meaningful to me. Even if I'm not sure what that is."

"You'll find out, Serena," he said confidently. "I'm certain of it."

She took another sip of champagne and tossed her head. "Oh, well, enough about me and my luxury problems," she said. "Come on, tell me all about yourself. It *has* been five years."

Misha looked into his champagne glass, then looked over at her. He shrugged. "What do you want to know?"

Serena lasered him with those brilliant hazel eyes of hers. They gleamed golden brown in the light, punctuated by shards of blue and green. "Come on, Misha," she said. "You can do better than that."

"I don't know what to say," he demurred.

"I know your career is going great guns," she said. "I mean, I do read the *New York Times*, so I'm always seeing that you're performing some-where. And you can't miss the ads for your new CDs when they come out. Not many classical artists get full-page ads in the *Times* and do per-sonal appearances at record stores." She paused a moment, tilting her head as she looked at him. "Next thing you know, you'll be like the three tenors."

He laughed lightly. "Yes," he said, "I do get a lot of publicity." He took another sip of his champagne.

"What about the rest of your life?" she cajoled. "Why are you being so mysterious?"

"I'm not being mysterious," he protested. He looked at her seriously now. "You mean my family life."

Serena returned his look. "Yes." She nodded. "Your family life."

"You know about my marriage . . . ," he began.

". . . To Vera," Serena finished. "Yes. I've seen her picture in the *Times*, too. She's very beautiful."

"Yes," Misha said.

Serena got up to retrieve the second split of champagne. "Are you happy, Misha?"

He looked lost in thought for long moments, staring off into space,

before he finally turned back to her. "I . . . I'm feeling a little . . . neglected, I guess," he finally said. "Vera's always so busy with social obligations. You know, she's on the boards of God knows how many music
organizations. And all her auction clients. It seems like there's always
another party or some kind of function that I'm supposed to lend my
presence to."

Serena listened while she popped the cork on the second split of Taittinger. She brought the bottle over to the couch and poured a refill into
his glass.

"Thanks," Misha said.

She refilled her own and sat back down again.

"Sounds like she's very good for your career," Serena said.

"Yes." He nodded. "She is that."

Serena looked at him. "What about the rest of it?" she asked.

"The rest of it?" Misha said.

"I think I read somewhere that you have a kid now," she said. "Ring a
bell?"

Misha laughed. "My God, of course. It has been a long time, hasn't it?
Nicholai. He's three years old now. And he's wonderful."

Serena smiled. "I think I detect just a little pride on your part,"
she said.

"Oh, yes," he said, a sheepish grin spreading across his lips. "He's
adorable and brilliant. I don't get to spend as much time with him as I
should. Traveling so much and all. We have a great time when we're together, but it's not very often."

There was a moment of silence as Serena sat, seemingly somewhere in
another world, rubbing a finger around the rim of her glass, starting to
make it chime.

"What about you, Serena?" he asked.

"What about me?" she said, looking over at him.

"Has there been a man?" he asked. "Anything . . . serious?"

"Ah, you know me. Everywhere I go, I leave a trail of broken hearts
behind." She laughed shortly. "Actually," she said with a rueful smile,
"there *have* been men, but . . . oh, you know. Nothing really serious.
Just . . . *men*. Just a few little flings."

"Your career must make it very difficult," Misha said.

"Yes," she said, nodding. "I'm on the road a lot, like you, and I've just
never met . . . you know. The right man." She shrugged and looked at
him. "I haven't really been *involved* with anyone. Well, not like I was . . .
with you."

As he heard her words, Misha felt a flood of emotions wash over him—guilt, remorse, self-conscious embarrassment—but overriding all his other feelings was the distinct frisson of pleasure he derived from knowing that she hadn't found anyone in the last five years to replace him in her affections. It was a guilty pleasure to be sure, but he couldn't deny it.

She's still in love with me, he thought. *As I am with her.* His heart leapt with joy, and the fear and self-consciousness he had felt—because he did still love her—dissipated with this realization.

After a moment he cleared his throat and then spoke. "I don't know whether you can believe me, Serena," he said, looking into her eyes, "but I . . . I haven't felt what I felt for you with anyone else, either. I've thought about you every single day since the last time I saw you. I've *wanted* you ever since the day we parted."

Suddenly a thrill rushed through Serena, because she knew now that he felt the same way she did. At the same time new fears and anxieties formed a knot in her stomach, giving rise to more questions and more puzzlement. Gone now was any effort at appearing casual about his visit.

Tears, unbidden, began to fill her eyes. *Oh, God,* she thought, *he really does mean it, doesn't he?* His pride, she knew, was a significant aspect of his character. Misha always seemed in control. Yet, underlying his pride was a fragility that few ever glimpsed. And it was because of this essentially delicate nature that she didn't believe Misha could possibly admit such vulnerability unless it were true, unless it was something that he really felt.

He still feels the same way, she thought. *He still loves me after all these years.*

Serena looked up at him, into those dark eyes, a solemn expression on her face. He reached over and brushed the tears from her eyes with a finger, gently, reverently, silently.

She reveled in his nearness to her, the touch of his finger, his arm around her shoulder, his tender ministrations. She could feel his breath upon her, could smell his uniquely masculine and erotic aroma. And she sensed his urgent desire for her.

"I love you," he whispered, lightly tracing a finger upon her exquisite features. "I've never stopped loving you, Serena."

She almost gasped aloud at the words, and she felt anew the overwhelming power that these particular words from this particular man held over her. She felt a swoon of desire—that was the only way to describe it—rise from deep down within her. It overshadowed any resistance to him she might have had, rendered any considerations but for this moment, in this place, inconsequential.

"I . . . I've always loved you, too, Misha," she whispered. "I've never loved anyone like I love you."

He pulled her closer, encircling her in his powerful arms, as his lips sought out hers. When they closed over hers, her body trembled in a kind of ecstasy, and she wanted the moment to last forever in its tender sublimity. Then his tongue, so warm, so sweet, so langorous, parted her lips, and he began to explore her mouth, slowly at first, delving, probing, licking. Gradually, the flames of his desire began to build, and he began to plunge more hungrily, lustily, devouring her with his passion, his urgency driving him deeper, faster. She gave herself up to him, her own desire consuming her, devouring him as he did her, her body afire now with an urgency and ardor she had virtually forgotten was possible but that she now remembered with a shock that was powerful but welcome in all it entailed.

He abruptly stopped and pulled back, and she almost whimpered at the sudden need for him. "Oh, my God, Serena," he rasped, "I've missed you so much. So much."

"Oh, yes," she whispered. "And I've missed you, Misha. So much."

His arms hugged her even closer to him, and his hands began to run up and down her back, up her neck, into her luxuriant black hair. He gently pulled her head back, and his mouth plunged to her long, swanlike neck, and he licked at her feverishly, then kissed and sucked at her as if he could never taste enough of her deliciousness.

Serena moaned with pleasure, holding his head in her hands, running her fingers through his hair, up and down his strong, muscular back, over his hard, round buttocks. She gloried in his body and the return of this hunger that she hadn't known for so long. She realized that she had been starved for the touch of *this* man, for the banquet that was *his* magnificent body in its love for her. Nobody in all those years had come close to arousing her as he did now, as he always had.

He rolled onto his side and pulled her with him, so that they lay face-to-face on the couch, one of his arms under her, the other free to explore. His mouth sought out hers again as his hand ran up her leg, under her skirt, and over her silken buttocks, pulling her to him, pelvis to pelvis.

She could feel his hard tumescence riding against her and was enthralled with this potent physical manifestation of the sheer power that together they generated.

"Oh, Misha," she gasped, "I want you. I want you in me!"

"Yes," he whispered, peppering her face with kisses. "Yes, my darling." He drew back slightly, looking into her eyes. "Let's go into the bedroom."

"Yes," she said, "let's go. Now."

Misha rose to his feet and extended a hand to her. She took it, and he pulled her up to him, taking her into his arms, kissing her passionately once more. Then he put an arm around her waist, and together, they walked into the bedroom, where he began to undress her.

Slowly and reverently, he gently slid her sweater over her head, dropping it to the floor. Then he unhooked her bra and let it slide from his fingers to join the sweater. He took her breasts in his hands, stroking them softly and gently as his mouth covered hers and he kissed her more ravenously than ever.

Serena moaned, relishing the touch of his hands on her nakedness, and returned his kisses, anxious for the feel of his hard, muscular bare flesh against her own.

His hands, moving more forcefully now, began to thrum her small, strawberry nipples between fingertips, exciting them to hardness. He kissed her neck, nibbling and licking, his tongue darting across her flesh, slowly moving down, down, inexorably down, to her breasts, where he kissed and licked with rapacious desire.

Serena felt the sudden wetness between her thighs and moaned again in exquisite pleasure as her body readied itself for him.

His hands found the zipper on her leather skirt and pulled it down. With his mouth still at her breasts, he slid her skirt down, over her slim hips, and let it slide to the floor. He went down on one knee, his hands moving to Serena's buttocks, his mouth to her waist, kissing and licking her.

Serena trembled with almost uncontrollable desire, her hands in his hair, drawing his head to her, but he drew back slightly as his hands slowly slid her panty hose down to her feet. She stepped out of them and her skirt, kicking them away in a single motion.

Misha looked up at her momentarily, an expression of awe on his face. Then his mouth went to her thighs, kissing and licking in long strokes, slowly moving ever more closely to her raven black mound, until at last he delicately began to kiss and lick there.

Yet another tremor ran through Serena as she felt his heat on her there, his tongue delicately exploring until it found that glorious treasure between her legs. She gasped aloud, savoring the feel of him, tempted to push his head into her harder, to beg him to go faster, deeper, but letting him take his time, teasing her as he was to excruciating heights of bliss. She almost cried out as his tongue suddenly dove into her, his hands pushing her buttocks hard against his face as he began to devour her in a frenzy.

"Oh, Misha," she whispered. "I want you in me, Misha. Oh, my God. Now. Please."

Misha abruptly jerked back, his breath coming in rasps. "Oh, my God," he breathed. "Oh, Serena." He stood up and took her in his arms again, kissing her hard, his tongue plunging into her mouth. Then just as suddenly he drew back and led her to the bed. She sat down, and he stood before her and began taking his clothes off. First, his black turtleneck sweater and undershirt, exposing his strong chest and powerfully muscular arms. Then, after reaching down and pulling off his shoes and socks, he unbuckled his belt and unzipped his trousers, which he quickly pulled off.

Serena watched, enthralled at the sight of his body, remembering her initial surprise all those years ago that a classical musician would have such a powerfully muscular build, and mesmerized anew by his hard masculinity.

Misha pulled down his Jockey shorts now, and his tumescence sprang before her in all its glory. He stood there, naked, without a trace of embarrassment, taking pride in his powerful manhood just as he reveled in the sight of her exquisite body in its nakedness. After a few moments, he joined her on the bed, where he guided her with a hand, spreading her out on her back. He bent over her, his knees between her legs, staring into her eyes, his expression feverish with desire. His hands slowly moved to her breasts, and he stroked them softly, gently, teasing her before moving down her slender torso to her thighs and her mound, which he stroked ever so delicately.

Serena, tantalized to almost unbearable heights of passion, began to writhe with her own desire and reached out with a hand and encircled his cock, stroking its length, then brushed along his balls lightly before returning to his cock. Misha gasped involuntarily, his eyes closing in ecstasy, and he slid his fingers into her, feeling her wetness.

In a frenzy now, he was unable to wait any longer. He took her hand off his cock and put it back over her head, then brought her other hand there to join it. He held them both with one of his, then spread her thighs with his other hand, before finally lowering himself to her mound, poised to take her, hesitating a brief moment, then entering her, slowly, but deliberately, shoving himself all the way in.

Serena jerked from side to side at first, almost overwhelmed by his hugeness within her, but wanting it, needing it, loving it, opening herself up to him with all of her might.

Misha withdrew very slowly, and she whimpered, before he plunged in again, impaling her as she surely never had been before. He could wait no longer, his passion overcoming his restraint, and he began to ride her faster, harder, plunging in and out like a man possessed. He released her hands and placed both of his under her buttocks, lifting them, pushing them hard against him, then relentlessly riding her, intent now on release.

Serena moved with him, gasping, moaning, crying out as wave after wave of carnal pleasure engulfed her in an ecstasy of timelessness, then thrashed madly as the floodgates of orgasm rolled over her, her cries joining his as he finally plunged in to the hilt and spasmed, jerking wildly as he let out a bellow of release.

After a moment, he collapsed on top of her, hugging her hard to him, noisily peppering her face and neck and breasts with kisses, his breath coming in loud gasps. "I love you, I love you, I love you," he rasped repeatedly, his body trembling in the aftermath of release. "Oh, Serena, I love you."

Serena wrapped her arms around him, gasping for air, the flood tide of their pleasure warming her to the very core of her being. She felt as one with this extraordinary man, completely satisfied and content as with no one else, wishing the feeling could go on forever, knowing of course that it could not be sustained, that she could only hope to reexperience it. She grasped him to her harder, squeezing, her breath still coming in deep, noisy rasps, her heart still hammering in her chest. "I love you, too, Misha," she finally managed, returning his kisses. "I love you, too."

After a few more moments, he lay with his head on her shoulder, both of them still, letting their breathing return to normal, content to hold each other, to plant solemn kisses, he on her shoulder, she on his head.

Misha finally raised himself on an elbow and stared into her eyes. "That was wonderful," he said. "Unforgettable." He hugged her to him and kissed her on the mouth.

Serena returned his affection, then said: "I'd forgotten how wonderful it can be. How extraordinary." She squeezed his buttocks. "Misha, there's nobody else like you."

He began running his hands up and down her body, slowly, savoring its lustrous afterglow, beginning to explore it anew, all the time looking into her hazel eyes, a look of adoration on his features. Then his mouth went back to her breasts, where he began to lick and suck, the heat of his passion flaming up again, not quite spent by their first coupling.

He had remained inside her, inert but large, and now Serena could feel him growing, his tumescence engorging once more, his hands and mouth exploring with renewed vigor, his pace gradually increasing. She moaned aloud when he mounted her again, her passion rekindled, and fell into the rhythm of their lovemaking with a natural ease.

They were slower this time but once again came together in a frenzy of release, after which they lay side by side on the bed, arms entwined, unable to part.

"I don't know what I've done without you all these years," Misha said, looking at her. "I really don't."

Serena smiled. "I feel the same way," she said, returning his look. "Exactly the same way."

"Nothing else has compared with this," he went on, "and now I wonder how I can live without it. Without you."

Serena remained silent, a wisp of a smile on her face. A smile of satiation, of contentment. She didn't want to point out the obvious to him: he didn't have to live without it. Without her. That she was there for him.

Misha kissed her lips again, chastely, then her eyes, her nose, her cheekbones, her forehead and chin. Heaving a sigh, he hugged her to him. "I can't let you go again, Serena," he said. "I can't lose you again."

She wanted to believe him, and as far as she was concerned, she certainly didn't want to give him up. She was not a fool, however. She knew that their situation was a very difficult one at best. "I don't want to lose you, either, Misha," she finally said. "I want to be with you." She looked into those black eyes of his. "But what do you want to do? What *can* we do?"

He was thoughtful for a few moments, gently running a hand up and down her spine, her arm, over her buttocks. "We can go on seeing each other," he said. "That's all I know to do. Just go on seeing each other as much as we can manage." He looked at her.

"I want to," Serena said quietly. "But what about Vera and your family?"

"Vera," he repeated. He sighed. "I don't know, Serena," he said. "I just don't know what will happen." He squeezed her hand and stared into her eyes again. "I can't promise you anything. Right now I just know that I want to see you more than anything else in the world. I can't lose you again."

Serena ran a hand through his tousled hair. "I know," she said. "I know you can't make any promises, and I don't expect you to right now." She paused a moment before continuing. "As much as I detest all the furtiveness, all the lying and cheating"—she looked at him with a serious expression—"and that's what seeing you would entail. Make no mistake about that. But I don't want to give you up either, Misha. And, if we can work it out, somehow or other . . ."

He pulled her to him, covering her mouth with his, kissing her passionately again. When he pulled back, he said: "We *will* work it out, Serena. Somehow. I know we will. I just *know* it." His hands were all over her again, his mouth devouring hers, and once again they feasted on each other, as if starved for the drug that they were to each other, until they finally lay spent once again, reveling in the rediscovery of their great passion, delighting in its pleasures.

Misha finally began disentangling himself from Serena. "Oh, God," he said with a sigh. "I wish I could stay here like this forever."

"But you can't," Serena said.

He rose from the bed to dress with the greatest reluctance.

"Do you want to shower?" Serena asked from the bed, where she watched him pick up his clothes.

He sat back down on the bed next to her. "No," he said in a whisper, looking into her eyes, then kissing her. "I want to smell you on me tonight."

Then he got to his feet again and began to dress. He would have to hurry now because he was expected back at the Palais Schwarzenberg in time to change into black tie for a formal dinner at eight. He quickly donned his clothes, and Serena stood up to walk him to the suite's door.

He turned to her at the door and took her into his arms again. "Oh, God," he said, "I've never hated to leave a place so much in my life. I really don't want to go."

"You've got to," she said, slipping him a note. "You've got all my telephone numbers now, and my schedule, so call as soon as you can."

"It won't be long," Misha said. "We'll see each other again soon."

"I hope so," Serena said. "Now go, before you're late."

Misha kissed her once more, then turned and left.

Serena returned to the bedroom and spread out, happier than she had been in years. Her happiness was tempered, however, with the trepidation she felt over this clandestine affair. She hoped against hope that it would evolve into something that was positive and life-enhancing for them both. Then it suddenly occurred to her that she might be counting her chickens before they hatched.

What if Misha didn't call her? What if he didn't really want to see her again? What if this was just a one-night stand for him, despite what he said?

She shivered and began rubbing herself with her arms. Then she remembered the things he'd said and the way he'd said them. She remembered his extraordinary passion in bed.

I don't think he was faking it, she told herself. *No. I think Misha truly loves me, as I truly love him.*

Misha hailed a taxi and gave the driver instructions. "Palais Schwarzenberg," he said. He leaned back into the seat, his mind spinning with their encounter. He no longer felt the self-conscious embarrassment he had experienced when he realized that he still loved Serena. He didn't think, in fact, that he'd ever felt this satisfied, this contented in his life. Their meeting had been destined, he believed, a gift that the Fates had for some reason given both of them.

Yes, he decided, that was it. And it was a gift of such powerful love that it could not be denied. God, he thought, I wish I could shout it from the rooftops!

But of course that was out of the question, the very last thing he could do. No. He would have to keep this love bottled up inside him, sharing it only with Serena.

He turned and gazed out the taxi's window at the splendid procession of Vienna's pastiche of architectural wonders. *It's the perfect setting for the rekindling of our love*, he thought. *And love it is. True love.*

Oh, yes. An undeniably great love.

Unfortunately, he reminded himself, there were many other considerations to ponder. Vera, of course. Nicholai. His family. Protecting all of them from the painful truth of reality. A reality of deceit, subterfuge, unfaithfulness.

I still love Vera, he thought. *Undeniably, odd as that might seem to her.* He sighed. *It would be so much easier if I didn't.*

It was a different kind of love from what he felt for Serena. Was it perhaps a more mature form of love? He wasn't really certain. What he did know without any doubts was that he also loved Serena, a love that was almost overwhelming in its intensity of feeling.

I may be asking for trouble, he thought. His relationship with Serena all those years ago had been an explosive one and had failed miserably. But that, he felt, was partly because they had been too young and had come from such totally different worlds. That was not as true now as it had once been, and they were both a little older.

Her image, in all its exquisite beauty, flashed before his mind's eye, and he smiled. She had matured so much in the last five years, and he had meant what he'd said: her fame and fortune suited her. She had be-

come more self-assured, more sophisticated and worldly wise, more toler-
ant and less explosive.

Still, that inevitable poisonous snake, guilt, had wormed its way into
his consciousness. He had everything in the world. A beautiful and devoted wife. A healthy, brilliant, and adoring son. A career that few pianists in history could lay claim to. Fame. Money.

Last night I played before royalty in Schönbrunn Palace, he thought. *No
mean feat. And now I'm on my way to the Palais Schwarzenberg to dress for a
dinner with Prince and Princess von Wallenburg.*

Why endanger all of it? he asked himself. *I've been so damned lucky,* he
thought. *So fortunate.*

Life had not always offered so much, had not always been so abundant
with its gifts. Life, in fact, could be a lot worse . . . *had* been a lot
worse. . . .

Part Two

YESTERDAY: 1968–1998

Brighton Beach, Brooklyn

The club was one of the tackiest and most depressing places the young man had ever seen. But then, what else should I have expected? he asked himself with smug superiority. At night it looked glitzy, all silver and gold, gleaming black and red, polished steel and brass. At night, too, it was always packed, banquette to banquette, dance floor to orchestra stage, with well-dressed men in custom-made suits or tuxedos, their hair slicked back, and their elaborately coiffed and heavily made-up wives or girlfriends, in jewels, gowns, and, in any but the warmest weather, fur coats.

Now in daylight, with the lights turned up to their full wattage, he discovered it was but a tawdry, dirty, and gimcrack stage set that could ill afford close inspection. Soiled, sticky carpeting—he almost recoiled at even having to walk on it in his expensive shoes—went with the frayed and befouled upholstering. At night, matte black paint effectively concealed an ugly maze of overhead electrical conduits, water pipes, ductwork, and the cheap light fixtures mounted helter-skelter that were aimed at various areas of the club. In the light, it all looked makeshift and filthy with accumulated grime.

Two goons, stony-faced behemoths in black mock turtleneck sweaters that matched their black suits, led him down a long hallway to what he knew must be the club's offices. The goons, muscles seemingly about to split the seams of their suits, lumbered along in black lizard skin cowboy boots.

Leningrad cowboys! the young man thought. Ridiculous! His eagle eye didn't fail to see that the black paint on the walls was lumpy and peeling, and the carpeting beneath his feet—the color the British referred to, appropriately enough, as mouseback—was like the rest, soiled and worn.

They came to a stop at a door all the way at the end of the hallway. A video-camera mounted above the door focused its lens on them. One of the goons rapped on the steel door with a huge, muscular fist. The young man couldn't help but observe that there were at least three cheap-looking gold rings set with gaudy stones on his massive fingers.

There's no accounting for bad taste, *the young man thought snidely.* But they go awfully well with the big gold watch and chain-link bracelets on his thick wrist.

He heard the sound of a buzzer, and then the door clicked open. Straight ahead was a large, messy office, with cheap utilitarian furniture, all of it worn and derelict. The air was tainted with a miasma of blue-gray smoke that stank of cigars and cigarettes.

Jesus! *he thought.* Don't they ever air the cesspool out?

The goons propelled him into the office, one on each of his arms, then stood at either side of him. The mammoth behind the desk, which was a scarred, paper-strewn clutter, looked up, his ugly face expressionless. There was a tiny cell phone at his ear.

The young man waited, despising every minute of it, bored with the theatrics employed by these barbarians. He guessed that he was supposed to be intimidated by their strong-arm, gangland tactics, but he found them merely repellent. Their ridiculous sense of drama was off-putting in the extreme. He'd thought these kinds of Russians had surely gone the way of Stalin and Khrushchev and the rest of the old-time hardliners. These hooligans may not be Communists, he thought—they were hard-core capitalists of the first order, as a matter of fact—but they certainly were enamored of the worst of the old-fashioned Communist tactics.

The Neanderthal behind the desk finally finished his call and put the phone down on the desk. When he looked up, his wolf's eyes locked on the young man's.

"You've missed calling in a couple of Saturday nights." *His voice was a deep baritone growl with a Russian accent.*

"We were out of the country," *the young man answered.*

"I don't give a shit where you were," *the Neanderthal spat.* "You call me every Saturday night no matter where the fuck you are. You understand me?"

"Yes, I understand you," *the young man answered calmly.* "But you've got to understand that sometimes we're at functions, parties and stuff, and it's practically impossible for me to get away without arousing suspicions."

The wolf's eyes remained locked to his, never once wavering. "You've got a cell phone. You can use it in the fucking john or someplace. If that doesn't work, you'll think of something. You're getting paid to think, right?"

"Right," *the young man answered, a hint of anger in his voice.*

The older man leaned back in the black leather desk chair and put his thick legs up on the desk, his arms akimbo back behind his head, which rested in his hands. "We've got some more instructions for you," *he said casually. He eyed the younger man through deceptively sleepy-looking eyes now.*

The young man didn't respond but stood waiting silently. He knew the old Neanderthal liked to take his time, tease him with his assignments, keep him guessing. He also knew that he irritated the shit out of the older man when he didn't act like an anxious puppy, dying to know what was next.

Suddenly, the older man swung his feet on the desk and sprang forward in his chair, slamming his fists on the desk. All in one swift movement. "You're going to get Misha Levin to do a tour of Russia," he snarled. "No matter what it takes. You're going to talk him into it. Right?"

"I'll try," the younger man said, "but I've already told you how he feels about that."

"I don't give a shit how he feels about it," the man growled. "You're going to present him with an offer he can't refuse." He pointed a meaty finger at the young man. "You're going to change his mind."

"I said I'd try," the younger man repeated.

"You don't have any choice," the older man said. "There's a ton of money in this for us. Concert hall deals, CD deals. Distribution deals. All over Russia. All over the former Soviet Union."

The mammoth put a paw on a toothpick, which lay among several scattered about the paperwork on the desk. He began cleaning his teeth.

The younger man cringed inside. He loathed being witness to such uncouth behavior, but he didn't show it.

"This is going to take a lot of time," he said in a firm voice to the older man. "You've got to understand that."

The Neanderthal jerked the toothpick out of his mouth. "Just do it," he spat. "You don't want to end up on a garbage barge, somebody else doing your work, do you? Am I right? You got that through your smart-assed head?"

"I got it," the younger man said, apparently unruffled by the threat. "If anybody can do this, I can," he added with confidence.

"Good," the man growled. "Now get out of here. And don't miss any more calls. There'll be more specific instructions."

"Right." The younger man turned and started out of the office but halted when he heard the older man's voice behind him.

"And you can lose the smart-assed superior attitude," the man said.

The younger man stood still for a moment, silent, then continued on out of the office. One of the goons sidled up to him, taking one of his arms.

"I'll show you out," the goon said with a thick Russian accent.

"I don't need your help," the young man said with irritation.

"You're going to get it, though," the goon said, propelling him down the dingy hallway, into the club's entrance hall, and out the door.

Filthy barbarians, the young man thought for the millionth time. Why did

I ever get mixed up with them? *But he knew the answer to that question was very simple. He was after the same thing they were: dollars. And lots of them.*

Besides, *he thought,* nothing would give me greater pleasure than screwing over the imperious and talented Misha Levin, his perfect and beautiful wife, and his entire family.

Chapter Seven

❧

Moscow

A bitter Arctic wind swept through the deserted snow- and ice-laden streets of Moscow on that January night in 1968, when Sonia Levin gave birth to her first and only child, Mikail, called Misha.

For two months the city had been under a deep blanket of snow, and today the steel gray skies held the portent of yet another blizzard. It was a grim and desolate world, and Sonia's labor was long and arduous.

She was a tall and long-boned woman, with olive skin, raven hair, and large, Gypsy-dark eyes. She was often described as regal, not beautiful, but imposing and handsome. It was her strength—an inner strength of daunting proportions—and boundless energy, however, that friends and acquaintances would unfailingly speak of when describing Sonia Levin.

Today, however, Sonia felt anything but regal, and her normal vigor and optimism seemed to have deserted her entirely.

Not an auspicious beginning, she couldn't help thinking as she lay, racked with pain and fearing for the life of the child within her, in the ill-equipped, outmoded, and far from sanitary maternity ward in one of Moscow's state-run hospitals. *No, indeed,* she thought tearfully. *This excruciating pain and sapping struggle in this cheerless, wintry place do not bode well.*

But when she was finally delivered of a perfectly healthy seven-pound, eleven-ounce baby boy with a downy fuzz of jet black on his head, her exhaustion and pain were swept away. As her spirits lifted, she became absorbed in this miraculous bundle of joy.

His birth *was* miraculous. She knew that better than anyone. Hadn't she and her husband, Dmitri, tried for years to conceive? At thirty-nine years of age, she had begun to give up hope of ever getting pregnant.

Now, as she held little Mikhail, endearingly known as Misha, in her arms, that despair was replaced with an awe such as she had never known. Sonia had thought that she was prepared for this moment, but nothing she had ever imagined had readied her for the immense emotions stirred up within her by the arrival of this child.

She was overwhelmed by the powerful and sublime sense of wonder she felt, and the accompanying sense of responsibility ignited every maternal instinct within her, instincts whose existence she hadn't been aware of before. Oh, yes, she had heard other mothers and fathers chattering on ad infinitum, and she had read everything that dealt with the subject.

Still, brilliantly intellectual as she was, she hadn't had a clue that her feelings would be *this* powerful, that her desire to protect and nurture this child would become the all-consuming purpose in her life.

So it was with thanks to a beneficent God and a determination to give Misha everything humanly possible that she and Dmitri Levin took their child home. It was on January 12, three days after giving birth, that she and Dmitri slowly but excitedly trudged up the four flights of dark and rickety stairs to their apartment with Misha. Dmitri unlocked the door to their Prussian blue parlor and immediately helped comfortably settle Sonia, babe in arms, on a Karelian birch daybed, which was swathed in old throws of wild boar and Moldavian kilims. Here she received their friends and acquaintances to show off their infant, Misha.

In later years Sonia delighted in telling anyone who would listen that it was on the Becker concert grand piano in that very room that little Misha had first focused his dark, bright eyes. On her very first glimpse of the newborn infant, in fact, she had noticed his long, slim fingers—so suitable for playing that same grand piano. As she greeted the endless procession of friends who came to visit, Sonia felt like a czarina, surrounded as she was by the faded grandeur and beautiful objects of their parlor, the baby in her arms.

The Levins, Sonia knew only too well, were very fortunate to be able to bring their baby home to such rooms in Moscow. It was an attic apartment in one of the few remaining old mansion blocks within walking distance of the Kremlin, in one of Moscow's oldest districts. Like many apartments in that precinct, it had been purposely kept empty during Stalin's reign of terror, for fear that it could be used as a sniper's lair. After the dictator's death, artists were gradually permitted to move into the attics, and the Levins had lived there ever since, thanks to their prodigious talent as musicians and painters—and the ever-watchful eye of the Ministry of Culture.

Sonia's and Dmitri's immediate forebears had managed to survive the waves of terror, from the revolution of 1917 on through the world war, plus the deeply entrenched anti-Semitism that had always pervaded daily life in both czarist and now Soviet Russia. But survive they had, even though any vestige of their religious faith and Jewish culture had been driven underground.

Sonia and Dmitri, like their deceased parents before them, were brilliant and hardworking musicians—pianists in their case—performers and teachers, who belonged to the union. Membership in the powerful unions was a rare privilege for Jews, and as a result they lived luxuriously by Soviet standards, even though they had to share an antiquated kitchen and a single, somewhat primitive, bathroom with seven other families in the old mansion attic.

It was a crumbling, once grand, house, with high ceilings, glittering chandeliers, beautiful plaster molding, and fireplaces with ornately carved marble mantels. Their two private rooms were chockablock with antique furnishings and artwork rescued from rubbish dumps and demolition squads over the years. Some of the grander pieces had been scavenged by their parents after the revolution. Magnificent icons, salvaged from churches closed during Khrushchev's era—many traded for no more than a bottle of vodka—hung on the walls alongside nineteenth-century paintings. Porcelains from former imperial factories graced the Karelian birch and mahogany consoles and tables.

The only evidence of their faith was a small gilt menorah, which rested, almost hidden among family photographs and bibelots, on an ormolu-encrusted neoclassical sideboard.

It was into these splendid if time-worn rooms that their friends and neighbors came to get their first glimpse of the newborn, bringing gifts and glad tidings. Naturally enough, they were all in agreement with the doting parents: Mikhail Levin was destined for great things.

Just how great a destiny at that moment neither Sonia nor Dmitri— nor any of their visitors—had a clue.

Four years passed before they had their first inkling. At that tender age Misha gave them proof positive that he had a truly miraculous gift: he was a musical prodigy.

During those first four years, life for them had gone on much as usual, though it was infinitely more abundant since the birth of their son. Those years for Misha were radically unlike what most Russian youngsters experienced. He was never placed in one of the multitude of state-run day-care facilities, but was coddled in the much grander and more cultivated atmosphere of home. If both Dmitri and Sonia were working or performing at the same time, one of the other musicians or painters who lived in the house would watch over the boy.

In that fourth year, on the day in question, Dmitri was at home, reading a musical score while watching over his son. Sonia was shopping, waiting in the inevitable and often horrendously long lines for the meager selection of groceries at various shops. At first Dmitri thought he had heard music on the radio; but he knew that the radio wasn't turned on. Then he rationalized that the music was coming from a neighboring apartment, even though he knew that theirs was the only piano in the building that he could hear with this degree of intimate proximity.

Finally, he put down his score and looked over his half-glasses across the room. There, perched on the stool at the grand piano, his chubby little legs dangling over its edge, sat Misha, playing a Bach piece, its rendering technically correct, though slow and strained, because of the size of the child's hands.

Dmitri was so astonished that for long moments he couldn't speak. When he eventually found his tongue, he could only whisper: "Misha?"

The boy didn't hear him and continued playing, strenuously making the effort to reach the correct keys.

"Misha?" Dmitri uttered again.

When the child still didn't hear him, Dmitri rose to his feet and strode over to the piano. He gently placed a hand on Misha's shoulder and cleared his throat. "Misha," he repeated.

Misha looked up at his father, his large, dark eyes shining. "Yes, Papa?" He was grinning happily, perhaps a little mischievously.

"Misha," Dmitri said, "when did you learn to do this? How—?"

"I don't know, Papa," the child answered. "I've just been watching and listening."

Tears sprang into Dmitri's eyes, and his body trembled all over as the realization of what he was witnessing dawned on him. It was frightening in all its implications, this scene he had just beheld. The profound responsibility he had felt with Misha's birth was now compounded a hundredfold, for the child had a God-given talent that was so rare and so precious, that Dmitri knew that he and Sonia must sacrifice all else to it.

When Sonia came home, her string bag bulging with purchases, she dropped the bag onto the floor, looking from her son to her husband and back again. Then she quietly sat down in shocked stupefaction, listening to her son as he switched from Bach to Mozart. When at last her initial shock had worn off, she and Dmitri quietly discussed the spectacle before them, then sat at the piano with Misha, testing him, trying to determine what he knew and what he was capable of.

After they had worked with him at the piano for an hour or more, she kissed Misha, and he tottered off to his building blocks. She and Dmitri debated the best way to deal with the prodigy in their midst, although any discussion was an unnecessary formality for Sonia, because she knew deep down inside exactly what they must do. She wiped her eyes with a finger and cleared her throat, then turned to her husband. "Dmitri?"

He looked at her. "Yes, Sonia?" He could tell from the bright intensity of her eyes that a plan was feverishly developing in her mind and that she could hardly contain her excitement.

Sonia took one of his hands in her own and looked into his eyes. "Dmitri, you know and I know that Misha is very special."

"Yes, Sonia," Dmitri answered, his voice almost quavering. He sighed. "You are right, as always, Sonia. You are right. But we'll simply have to do the best we can. What else can we do?"

Sonia's eyes gleamed with fiery determination as she gripped his hand hard and said in a low, intense voice, "We will emigrate, Dmitri! We will leave Russia so that Misha can get the training he has to have. We both know that the only place he can get what he needs is New York."

Dmitri jerked at her words and remained speechless for a long while. Finally he said: "You are tempting fate, Sonia. It's very difficult to emigrate."

"But—" Sonia interjected heatedly.

"But," Dmitri said quickly, squeezing her hand with his, "I think you are right, as usual."

Sonia felt relief flood through her, and tears of joy came into her eyes. She was reminded now of why she first fell in love with Dmitri Levin. He had never been afraid of taking chances, not with her. When they went into something together, no matter how hare-brained the scheme might seem, she felt indomitable and fearless, for Dmitri was at her side. And now, once again, Dmitri would back up her—and Misha—all the way.

She wrapped her arms around her husband, and Dmitri hugged her to him tightly.

She drew back at last and said to him: "Then it is settled. We will start the proceedings to get exit visas at once. Perhaps in a year to two, maybe even sooner, we will be able to leave."

"Yes, Sonia. Yes, yes," Dmitri said, hugging her again.

Sonia leaned back. "We may have to go to Israel first," she said. "But no matter. He can get very good training there, to start. Then who knows? It's only a short hop from there to New York City."

She threw her arms about her husband's neck again and kissed him on the lips. "It will work, Dmitri. I know it will. It will work out perfectly."

Dmitri nodded enthusiastically, but thought: *Maybe in another world it would work out perfectly.* But he said: "You are right, Sonia. Yes, as usual, my Sonia is right."

Chapter Eight

It was on March 16, 1972, when the world of Sonia and Dmitri Levin and their son fell apart. The snow and ice had just started to thaw in Moscow after nearly five months. It had begun as a perfect day, the first hint of spring in the air exciting them with the prospect of being able to take Misha to one of the nearby parks, or perhaps for an all-day outing in Leninskiye Gory—the Lenin Hills.

It was not to be.

Early that morning, before they had finished their breakfast, they heard the sounds of thundering boots on the stairs leading up to their attic. Then there was a pounding on the parlor door.

Sonia looked with wide, wary eyes at Dmitri. "What . . . ?"

Dmitri shrugged, as if to say, Who knows?

But he did know. Oh, yes, he knew without any doubts whatsoever. He quietly set down his cup of black coffee, dabbed his lips with a napkin, then rose to his feet. His stomach was already twisted into a knot of fear, but he gave Sonia a reassuring squeeze on the shoulder as he passed her on his way to answer the door. A tight smile was fixed on his lips.

"What is it, Mama?" Misha asked.

"Nothing, Misha," Sonia answered. "Nothing at all. Eat your breakfast." She scooted her chair closer to his protectively, and tried to interest him in his food. His large, dark eyes, however, followed his father inquisitively.

Dmitri unlocked and swung the door open. There stood two official-looking bureaucrats in almost identical, cheaply tailored, dark gray suits under brown leather trench coats. They carried battered leather briefcases, and on their faces were the expressions of unrelentingly grim Soviet bureaucracy. They were, Dmitri thought, the sort of petty officials who enjoyed exercising their modicum of power. Behind the two men he saw four armed militiamen—boys, really—in ill-fitting uniforms. They stood waiting, their collective demeanor blank.

"May I—?" Dmitri began.

"Dmitri Levin?" barked one of the suits harshly. He flashed a red identity booklet, but Dmitri couldn't make out what it said before the man snapped it shut and replaced it in his jacket.

"Yes, I am Dmitri Levin," he responded, trying to keep the nervousness out of his voice. He was loath to let these minor functionaries hear the fear that he felt, but he was unable to control the cold sweat that suddenly broke out on his face or the slight tremor that made his hands appear to have a life of their own.

The men in suits, not waiting for an invitation, shoved their way past Dmitri into the room. The militiamen tromped in on their heels.

Dmitri slowly closed the door behind them, then turned to them, mustering up as much dignity as he could under the circumstances. "What do you want here?" he asked, knowing deep down inside what their answer would be.

"I am comrade Vladimir Sergeyovich Kazakov," the larger of the two men announced. His face was beet red and vodka-bloated. "This is comrade Ivan Mikhailovich Kuznetzov." He nodded toward the other suit, whose eyes were flicking from wall to wall, ceiling to floor, from paintings to consoles, chairs to porcelain, rugs to chandeliers, taking in the room's ornate furnishings. Kuznetzov didn't bother acknowledging Dmitri.

Sonia watched them intently from the table. She noticed that the young militiamen with their badly shorn fair hair and pale eyes, so typical of the north, were ogling the room, wide-eyed and open-mouthed.

Such stupid expressions on their faces, she thought unkindly. They were nearly all farm boys, these militiamen. Suspicious and ignorant provincials. And that, she knew, was all the more reason to give them a wide berth. *I must try to control my anger*, she thought.

Then the one called Kazakov unceremoniously placed his briefcase on the grand piano with a loud thud. Sonia recoiled with distaste, and glaring, she practically jumped to her feet, her back to Misha, as if to hide him from their sight.

"What do you want here?" she asked in an imperious tone of voice.

"You are the wife? Sonia?" Comrade Kazakov asked, flipping through thin sheets of official-looking documents he had produced from his leather briefcase. He didn't look over at her.

"Yes," she replied. "Who wants to know?" She watched him as he continued to riffle through the documents. "What do you *want* here?" she repeated, more irritably this time.

Dmitri quietly crossed the Bessarabian rug to his wife's side and took one of her hands in his, but she didn't seem to be aware of him, staring at Kazakov as she was.

Comrade Kazakov locked eyes with her, a smug expression on his face.

Piggy eyes, Sonia was thinking. *He's got little piggy eyes. Like so many of his sort. Little piggy eyes squinting out from between those ugly red folds of vodka fat.*

"It is my duty to inform you," Kazakov said, "that the housing authority will be taking over your apartment. I have your papers here. You will be moving to new, more appropriate accommodations."

"What—?" Dmitri gasped. He felt Sonia's hand squeeze his, as if trying to draw strength from him. He knew she was making a great effort to control her temper.

"These militiamen here," Comrade Kazakov continued, indicating the young men behind him, "will remain here to make certain that you finish packing today."

"Today!" Sonia burst out, unable to remain silent any longer. "That's . . . that's impossible!"

Despite the anger in her voice, Dmitri recognized the sound of defeat underlying it. He glanced at her and saw the sudden look of fear, of dread and loss, that appeared on her face as the realization of what was happening dawned in all its horror. He could see that she, too, finally knew what this was all about. Her words, he knew, were mere posturing.

Dmitri pressed her hand reassuringly, then put an arm around her shoulders.

"Papa, what—?" Misha began. He looked as if he might burst into tears at any moment. The boy didn't understand what was happening, but he knew that something was very wrong.

"Shhh," Dmitri whispered. He took his son's plump little hand in his free one. "Quiet now," he said, forcing a smile to his lips. "We have to hear what our visitors have to say."

He turned and directed his gaze at Comrade Kazakov. "We haven't been informed of any of this," Dmitri protested. "We—"

"You are being informed now," Comrade Kazakov snapped. "You are to begin packing immediately, and you are to finish by this evening. This apartment will be sealed off tonight. New tenants will be moving in tomorrow."

"This is criminal," Sonia spat. "*Criminal!* You don't know what you're doing! I'll go to the union with this!"

"It is your union which has taken this apartment," Comrade Kazakov said evenly. "For someone else." A smile revealed tobacco-stained teeth. He obviously relished his role. "So you can discuss it with whomever you choose, but it will do you no good."

With these words Sonia and Dmitri saw the futility of any further protests. Circumstances doubtless were even more serious than they had at first imagined. They had always been protected by their union membership and high-level teaching and performing careers. It appeared that now all of that was for nought. Their security had vanished in one fell swoop.

"You are to pack your clothing and other personal possessions," Comrade Kazakov went on. "You are to leave all furnishings as they are."

"You must be crazy!" Sonia shouted. "You can't *do* this! All of these things belong to us!" As she said them, she realized her words would have no effect, but she couldn't stop herself.

"You can see for yourself," Comrade Kazakov said, dramatically slapping one of his documents down on their breakfast table.

Sonia and Dmitri both glanced at the official-looking document, but there was no point in reading it. They knew what it said.

"The piano!" Dmitri suddenly protested. "It is our livelihood! We—?"

"You are to pack whatever you can in suitcases and boxes and *get out*," Kazakov interrupted. "There is a truck downstairs, and the militiamen will help you load it. They will take you to your new home." He nodded at his partner, who was examining a small porphyry urn decorated with ormolu, an avaricious gleam in his eye. "Comrade Kuznetzov will accompany you."

Sonia thought for a moment that she wouldn't be able to stop the tears that threatened to spill from her eyes, but she could not let these brutes see her cry. She simply stared at Comrade Kazakov, her eyes filled with pure, unadulterated hatred.

"But where are we to go?" Dmitri asked. "What will we do?" He despised the emasculated, helpless sound of his own voice in his ears.

"Your new address is listed on page three. There." Kazakov pointed at the document he had placed on the breakfast table, then turned his attention to Comrade Kuznetzov. "Ivan Mikhailovich."

His partner looked up at him and set down the porphyry urn, a guilty expression on his face. "Yes?"

"See that this move is completed tonight," Comrade Kazakov said. Without another word he turned and strode toward the door.

Dmitri had taken Misha in his arms. The boy watched over his father's shoulder as the stranger opened the door and let himself out, leaving the door ajar. Misha had never before been confronted with evil, and he didn't understand it. His eyes filled with tears, however, because he knew instinctively that their lives had been changed.

Sonia slumped down onto a chair, her head in her hands. *It's all my fault*, she thought, engulfed in self-hatred, its poison washing over her in bilious waves, threatening to make her sick. *All my fault. I should have been content to let Misha study here. I should have been content with what we've got. But, no. I had to apply for exit visas, didn't I?* She choked back tears. *The exit visas. That's why they're doing this. Now they'll never leave us alone. We'll never have any peace.*

She looked up and saw Misha, still in his father's arms, his large, dark eyes observing her worriedly. For an instant she wanted to scream, to tear her hair out, but instead she put all of her considerable resources into smiling up at her son. Then, she quickly got to her feet and kissed his cheek.

"Dmitri," she said, "we must hurry. We must take everything we can."

Chapter Nine

⌒⌒⌒

"Mama? What is it?" Misha looked at his mother, an anxious expression in his large, dark eyes. "Are you sad, Mama?"

Sonia was all choked up. For a moment she could not speak. Then she turned away, surreptitiously wiped a tear from her eye and squared her narrow shoulders, and turned back around. She smiled bravely.

The child has endured more than any child ever should, she thought.

"No, of course I'm not sad, Misha," she lied, distressed that she should cause her son worry.

He can read me like a book, she thought. It was perplexing to her, this ability of his to sense her every mood.

"I was simply thinking. Wondering when your father would be back, that's all."

"You shouldn't worry, Mama," he said in an effort to cheer her. "Probably the shop lines are long today."

Sonia and Dmitri took turns doing the shopping, and today it was Dmitri's turn to wait in the interminable lines for groceries.

"You're right." Sonia forced a smile onto her lips. "Now then, let me listen to your Chopin. Start with the nocturnes."

Misha sat down at the piano and adjusted the seat. He put his head down and closed his eyes, as if in prayer. It was a moment of mental preparation Sonia knew very well. She had seen it countless times in the last two years. He was clearing his mind for the music and the music alone.

She watched him as he began to practice, but after a few minutes she turned her head and gazed out through the rain-streaked window. She listened to the beautiful but melancholy music of Chopin wafting from behind her. What a contrast it was, this beautiful music, to the bleak landscape that greeted her eyes.

Cement and asphalt, she thought. *Nothing but desolate expanses of concrete and asphalt, nearly as far as the eye can see.* There was hardly a tree in sight, and the precious few there were had been mutilated by vandals, stripped of their lower branches, defaced by graffiti.

It was a numbing sight, this postapocalyptic landscape. Virtually barren, even now in spring, it was of a drab, uniform grayness, punctuated here and there by high-rises of dirty, weathered cement, parking lots with pathetically maintained cars—no fancy Zils or Chaikas here—and cheerless playgrounds. Stolen or abandoned cars, many of them stripped down to mere shells, sat on the streets, as if they were caught in some dreadful limbo.

Like us, she thought grimly. *Two years in limbo.*

She drew her gaze in, glancing at the buckets and basins she'd placed under leaks in the ceiling. The spring rains, which she'd always welcomed in the past, nourishing the city's plants and flowers as they did, were now no more than a dreaded nuisance. There were no plants or flowers in this district, none to speak of anyway, and the rain simply meant more work for her.

She sighed aloud. *That's certainly the least of it.* What was a leaking roof compared with the rest of the endless stream of problems that had confronted them in the two years since being forced to leave their beloved attic apartment in central Moscow?

It was like a palace in the sky, she thought wistfully.

There, she had never minded climbing the old, rickety stairs to their grand, but homey, rooms. Here, she begrudged every single step she had to take to reach the small, seventh-floor room the three of them shared. There was an elevator, but it rarely functioned. It had been broken down nearly every day since the week they had moved in. When it did work, it invariably stank of urine, and its walls were smeared with the vilest obscenities, sometimes in excrement.

Even the mailboxes downstairs didn't escape desecration. They were blackened from the fires that vandals regularly set to them. And the security! *It's a joke,* she thought. In a project such as this, where security was vital, the door locks to the lobby were nearly always broken. If not, no matter: the security code was scratched neatly on the door for all to see.

Sonia shivered and clasped her arms around herself, as if to give herself warmth and comfort. *It is disgusting,* she thought. *Utterly disgusting, this place. But what else could you expect?* she asked herself. *The people here—the very dregs of humanity, most of them—are cooped up in such an execrable, soulless place that it only reinforces their basest, most animalistic instincts.*

Their neighbors were no exception. There were three other families on their floor, and they shared a communal kitchen. The kitchen always reeked with the stench of boiled cabbage, an odor that permeated the entire building, seeping into their clothes, as did the strong, foul-smelling tobacco of the *papirosy*, the tube cigarettes that everybody in the building, young and old alike, seemed to chain-smoke. Sonia had quickly determined that she would have to get a minuscule refrigerator to keep in their room, but it wasn't only the unpleasant odors of the kitchen that had driven her to it. Their food in the communal refrigerator vanished as quickly as she put it there—more than once—with denials all around, of course. She could put a container of her borscht—the simplest, cheapest concoction!—in it to cool, and it would disappear before it even had a chance to lose its warmth. She had finally resorted to cooking on a hot plate in their room, inconvenient as it was, so as to avoid the kitchen and their neighbors as much as possible.

Pavel and Nyushka, their neighbors on one side, fought like wild animals, often arguing long into the night. Pavel frequently beat up his wife in drunken rages. Sonia didn't think she'd ever seen Nyushka without bruises, but when she tried to come to her aid, she was rebuffed, met with furious hostility, in fact. Old Ivan, on the other side, was a *zakhleba*, a guzzler. He reeked of cheap vodka day in and day out, sweating it from his very pores. He was often slumped downstairs, sometimes outside in deadly, freezing weather, incoherent, if not passed out, unable to climb to his room. Like so many of the men around these projects—even some of the women—he would swallow anything he could get his hands on to render himself unconscious. Paint thinner, she had discovered, was a popular alternative to vodka, and airplane glue and other inhalants—she didn't know what most of them were—were a staple as well.

The youngsters in these dreary environs had already learned all too well how to cope with such violent, unloving families and their gloomy prospects for the future. They emulated their elders, drinking, sniffing, snorting, smoking—anything they managed to find. Their youthful energies, when not focused on sex and fights, were used to defile every conceivable surface in their midst, rendering an already hideous world even more so. Nothing was spared, not even their own bodies, which they desecrated with abandon. Many of them proudly wore the scars of gang warfare and various initiation rites and ugly homemade tattoos.

Sometimes Sonia felt that she understood their utter hopelessness, their desire to simply abandon this awful world, slowly but surely killing themselves, leaving their problems behind them.

She had heard of this other Moscow when they had lived in the cushioned opulence of their attic, bu she had never actually encountered it firsthand. She had often visited friends in the monstrous, sterile projects

that housed most of Moscow, but they had been well kept, constantly pa-
trolled, and more modern.

We have been relegated to a gulag right here in the city, she told herself.
Thank God I've been able to protect Misha from the worst of it.

She turned, her dark eyes alighting on his long, slender, six-year-old
body. *So much like mine and his father's,* she mused with pride. He was going to be a strapping, handsome man one day.

He sat erect now, a look of control on his still childlike face. It was
certainly not a look that was always there, especially when he was having
difficulty with a piece of music, struggling to make it his own. But he was
still playing Chopin—music that seemed to be second nature to him—
and was having no such difficulty. As she listened, he switched from the
melancholy and relatively easy nocturnes to the Piano Concerto no. 1,
op. 11, in E Minor, a more challenging piece.

He was unaware of the smile that suddenly lit up Sonia's olive-
complexioned features, the warmth that suffused her heart with so much
love that sometimes she thought it would surely break, that it simply
couldn't contain the love she felt for this brilliant prodigy she and Dmitri had brought into the world. The struggle, the hardships, the daily
unpleasantness—all of it came to nothing when she looked upon her son.

We have been blessed with him, she thought. *And if truth be told, we've
had our share of luck since that dreadful day two years ago when we lost our
home. We've got a lot to be thankful for. Why, I could make a whole list of
mercies!*

She nodded to herself with satisfaction, and her thoughts turned
to Arkady and Mariya Yakovlevna, for they would surely be placed at
the very top of that list. The elderly couple—they were in their early
eighties—who lived downstairs had been like a gift from the angels in
this most unlikely, godless of places. They were retired teachers and, like
the Levins, had been relegated to this project, only years earlier. They
had been lucky not to be sent to one of the gulags. Their offense: conspir-
ing against the state. In their case, writing religious tracts in Yiddish that
were not "Communist-directed." Yet even amid the cultural wasteland
that surrounded them here, they had tried to create a little garden of
civilization.

Cautiously at first, then gradually becoming more expansive as they
let down their guard, they had opened up their lives to Sonia, Dmitri,
and Misha. It was a tiny, one-room world, but it was a jewellike micro-
cosm of a cultured world, much like that world that Sonia and Dmitri
had once known. It was their little spinet studio piano that was now in

the Levins' room, and that piano had made teaching Misha possible for the last two years.

Ah, yes, Sonia thought. *That's more like it. I feel better now. Much better.* Just seeing Misha at practice and thinking of Arkady and Mariya Yakovlevna had that effect.

It was Arkady and Mariya Yakovlevna who cared for Misha when neither Sonia nor Dmitri could be home. They were loathe to place him in one of the state-controlled day-care centers, and he became the child Arkady and Mariya had never been able to have, although he was more like their grandchild. They smothered him with affection, giving him welcome respite from the grueling hours at the piano that Sonia and Dmitri outlined for him. For it was their firm belief that Misha should be allowed to be a child as well as a prodigy.

Storytelling, card games, reading, and chess were part of their regimen. Injected into many of their discussions with the youngster were stories about the Jewish people and the Jewish faith. Arkady and Mariya Yakovlevna knew that Sonia and Dmitri were agnostic and had little appreciation for their cultural heritage or faith. They had descended from artists and considered themselves artists, first and foremost, with little or no interest in politics or religion.

Arkady and Mariya hoped that Misha would retain some of the stories they told him and that they could instill in him an awareness of his heritage and a degree of pride in it.

Sonia and Dmitri, for their part, knew what Arkady and Mariya Yakovlevna were up to, but they held the couple in such great respect and affection that they let them contribute whatever they might to Misha's education. Besides, Misha loved the old couple dearly, and they were doing no harm, the Levins felt.

In the meantime, she and Dmitri had worked out a program that would prepare him for a career in music. They took turns working with him, and he had blossomed during the last two years. The future, indeed, held the possibility of great promise. They had turned the losses of their home and their incomes into an opportunity. Their teaching and performing duties had been cut back significantly two years ago—and of course their pay with it—but as a result, one or the other could be at home to work with Misha nearly all of the time.

Increasingly, however, she fretted about his future. She and Dmitri had already taught him nearly everything they possibly could, and there was only one recourse open to them—at least here in Moscow. At the age of six, he should enter the famous Moscow Gnessin School of Music for Gifted Children. It would normally be a simple matter. Misha, after all, was extraordinarily gifted. She and Dmitri, of course, knew some of the faculty well, but intervening considerations had complicated the issue: the matter of their having applied for exit visas.

They had been told by the administrators that "perhaps" in the coming fall, Misha "might possibly" be admitted to a place in the school. As he had turned six on January the ninth, he hadn't been old enough the previous autumn, though exceptions were always being made. Despite the "perhaps" and "mights" of the administrators, Sonia felt heartened by the possibility. The Gnessin was a rigorous school, a great school, which turned out the best musicians in all of the USSR. If the Levins must be in Moscow, she surmised, then they could do no better. If indeed the school finally accepted him.

Sonia looked over at her son now, head bent in concentration. *If only we could provide the best for him!* she thought for the thousandth time. *If only we knew what to expect in the coming months from the authorities.*

They did know certain things. Through her various contacts in the music world, she had discovered that, if Misha were indeed admitted, under no circumstances would he be allowed to study under Anna Pavlovna Kantor. This, for Sonia and Dmitri, was a crushing blow. Kantor was without exception the greatest teacher in all of Russia, and orders—they had been told in the greatest confidence—had already been given that she would not be permitted to teach their son.

If only we would be permitted to emigrate! If only they would give us our exit visas! In the last two years many Jews had been permitted to leave. There had, in fact, been a veritable exodus of the Jewish intelligentsia to the West and to Israel. *Why,* she asked herself, *are we being held back here? Why are we being made to suffer?*

At that moment the thud of fists pounding heavily reverberated from the door. Sonia was jerked out of her reverie, and Misha missed a key on the piano, then abruptly stopped playing. He turned and looked questioningly at his mother.

When she nodded wearily, he hopped off the piano stool and cautiously approached the door. Sonia put down her knitting, which had lain unworked on her lap all this time, and reluctantly got to her feet and followed him.

Through the locked door she could hear old Arkady shouting . . . and it sounded as if he was raging incomprehensibly against heaven.

Misha undid the lock and opened the door. "Arkady!" he whispered.

The old man was slumped against the door frame, gasping for breath, his snow white hair in Einsteinian disarray.

"Arkady?" Sonia asked tremulously, barely able to subdue her panic as she reached the door.

She put an arm around him and helped him into the apartment. In her strong arms, he was tiny and felt practically weightless, like a wounded bird, and he was nearly limp with fatigue or fright or . . .

Sonia didn't yet know.

"What is it? Arkady! What has happened?" she asked.

Misha closed the door behind them and threw the bolt.

"I . . . I . . . oh . . . oh . . . *oh*," the old man muttered, weeping now as if he were a child, tears running down his creased cheeks in rivulets.

"Tell me, Arkady," Sonia persisted. "What is it?"

"Mariya . . . Mariya Yakovlevna," he cried.

"What *is* it?" she repeated. Sonia shook the old man by the shoulders. "What, Arkady? Tell me. What has happened to Mariya Yakovlevna?"

With a great effort the old man tried to compose himself. He took a perfectly pressed white linen handkerchief from a pocket in his trousers and wiped his face, then blew his nose. When he was done, he carefully refolded the handkerchief and replaced it in his trouser pocket.

Sonia took his shaky hands in hers while he caught his breath and began to speak.

"Mariya Yakovlevna was coming home from the shops." He looked up into Sonia's eyes. "You know . . . you know how I . . . I can't bear to see her go alone, but my hips were so bad today, my arthritis, I could hardly walk."

"Yes, yes," Sonia said. "Go on, Arcady. Go on." She felt her heart beating wildly in her chest as a mounting sense of horror gripped her.

"A gang of boys . . . hooligans . . . attacked her. Somewhere . . . somewhere near the project," Arkady gasped. "They . . . they stole her groceries and what . . . what little money she had." Suddenly his voice broke, and he began weeping like a child again. He couldn't continue.

Sonia held him in her arms, stroking his back with her hands. "Please, Arkady, You must finish. We must know, so we can do something."

After a few moments the old man recovered himself enough to resume his story. "They kicked her . . . and . . . beat her . . . and . . . and left her there to die," he cried.

"What is she, Ardady?" Sonia asked, her eyes huge with terror. "Where?"

"The hospital . . . the one over . . ." He was pointing to the east with one of his hands.

"The one near the ring road?" Sonia asked.

He nodded his head. "Yes, that one."

Sonia let go of the old man and grabbed her coat off its wall hook. "Misha," she said, "you stay here with Arkady. Make him some tea. Okay?"

"Sure, Mama," Misha said.

"No, no," Arkady said. "I must go, too." His voice was a pathetic plea.

"No, Arkady," she said. "You stay here and wait for Dmitri. He's out shopping and should be back any minute. The next hour or so at the most. When he gets back, he'll bring you to the hospital."

"But—" The old man had an imploring look on his wrinkled, distraught face.

"No," Sonia said with certainty. "You must stay here with Misha and rest. Have some tea. I will see to Mariya Yakovlevna." She quickly patted Arkady on the cheek, then leaned down and kissed Misha.

"You will take good care of Arkady for me?" she asked.

"Yes, Mama," Misha said. "Don't worry. I'll make him tea." He hoped that his mother didn't see the worry and fear that he felt, but if she did, she didn't acknowledge it.

Sonia shrugged into her coat and unlocked the door. "Lock it behind me," she said. Then she was gone, almost running to their friend.

Sonia rushed breathlessly into the vast white and yellow expanse of the hospital's lobby. Pausing to catch her breath, she looked about her. The lobby was soiled and ill-kept, its once white walls now gray, its yellow tiles beige with grime.

Oh, God, no, she thought. *One of the pigsties.*

In Moscow the hospitals and clinics could be pristine, like the Kremlin Clinic, but they could also be shabby and ill-equipped. Here, if the lobby was any indication, she could see that Mariya Yakovlevna would be lucky to get decent treatment. The trouble with many of the hospitals, even though they had adequate facilities and reputable physicians, was that patients would develop complications from infections because of the filth. The lack of adequate sterilization in many facilities was notorious.

She approached the information desk, where she nervously awaited her turn in the short line. When it finally came, she asked for Mariya Yakovlevna.

The attendant at the desk, twirling a strand of her dirty, garishly dyed hair around a finger, consulted a large registry. She seemed to take forever.

"Seven," she finally told Sonia. "The elevator's down that corridor." She pointed with a chubby hand, a finger with chipped orange nail polish extended.

"Thank you," Sonia said. She turned and strode purposefully down the corridor to the elevator bank and pushed the up button, grateful that here, at least, they appeared to work. She tapped her foot impatiently on the tile floor, willing the elevator to come. Within moments it arrived, and she entered the crowded car. After stops on every floor, Sonia finally got out on the seventh floor.

She spotted the nearest nurses station, just down the hallway, and made a beeline for it. "Mariya Yakovlevna," she said without preamble.

The nurse sitting behind the desk didn't look up or acknowledge her. Finally, Sonia repeated her request, a little louder this time. "Mariya Yakolevna? It's an emergency."

The nurse continued to fill in blanks on the sheet of paper set down in front of her. After a few more moments she lifted her head and glared at Sonia.

"What do you want?" she asked in an angry tone of voice.

"Mariya Yakovlevna," Sonia repeated. "What is her room number, please?"

Why are so many of them so angry? she wondered. *And so rude?* But she thought she knew the answer to that question. In many of the hospitals and clinics, you had to bribe the nurses and especially the *saniturki*, the nurses' aides, with gifts or money in order to get decent treatment for your loved ones.

The nurse looked down at her registry for a moment, then back up at Sonia. "Room seven-twenty-two," she said, sighing with exasperation. "But I think the doctors are in there now."

Without thanking her, Sonia hurried down the corridor, hoping she was headed in the right direction. She didn't want to wait and take the chance that the nurse would tell her she couldn't visit Mariya now.

As it was, she almost stumbled into room 722, trying to avoid a gurney, farther down the corridor. When she saw the numbers, she approached the door, which was ajar, with trepidation.

Pushing the door open wide, she leaned in. She could see that there were several patients in the small room, probably six, far too many for such a small space. She didn't see Mariya Yakovlevna, but over in the corner a group of four or five doctors and nurses surrounded one of the beds, hiding its patient from view.

Mariya Yakovlevna, she thought. *It must be.*

She started toward the group, but they were already turning in her direction, apparently preparing to leave the room. Behind them, she saw one of the *saniturki* pull a sheet up over a body, which lay prone on the bed. The sheet was gray with age and use.

Sonia cringed, then gasped. *It can't be!* she thought. *No, no, no! Oh, dear God, it can't be!*

She grasped one of the doctors by a sleeve. A woman, as nearly all of them were. "Mariya Yakovlevna?" she whispered.

The doctor didn't speak, but her thick, black-framed glasses nodded in the direction of the bed that they had just left. The doctor moved on past, toward the door.

Sonia stood there immobile, the doctors and nurses filing quietly out of the room around her. She felt rooted to the floor. *There's been a mistake,* she told herself. *Yes, a mistake. It happens all the time in these big Moscow hospitals.*

She squared her shoulders and walked over to the bed. The *saniturki*, bent over at the bedside, was lackadaisically throwing bloody bandages into a garbage can. She looked up at Sonia, an utterly blank expression on her face.

Sonia gingerly picked up a corner of the gray sheet and pulled it back, peering at the face that lay beneath it.

She had to stifle the urge to scream.

It was Mariya Yakovlevna, but it wasn't. Her little face with its parchmentlike skin was swollen purple and red with cuts and bruises, her lips split and bloody, her eyes shut from swelling before death. Her beautiful white hair was encrusted with blood and grime.

Sonia let the sheet drop.

For a moment she thought that she was going to be sick. She felt bile rise in her throat, and its nauseous taste almost overwhelmed her. Cold beads of sweat broke out on her face and her neck.

Oh, my God, she thought. *I'm going to faint. I'm going to faint right here on this filthy floor.*

But she didn't faint. She steadied herself on the bed's foot rail, taking deep breaths of air, trying to get her thoughts in order. Then, reaching into her coat pocket, she took out her little Moroccan leather change purse. She opened it and extracted a few rubles. Turning to the *saniturki*, she extended the rubles to her, and the woman took them, pocketing them quickly. "Please," Sonia said. "A clean sheet for Mariya Yakovlevna."

She turned and left the room without looking back, thinking: *It can never get worse than this,* she thought. *Can it?*

She wasn't so sure anymore.

Rain, light but steady, plastered her hair to her head. In her rush to the hospital, she'd forgotten to take her umbrella, but it didn't really matter. Nothing much did anymore.

Sonia thought: *If only this rain could wash away the ugliness that caused this senseless death. . . .*

She walked slowly, almost in a trance. A mixture of bitter rage and anguish churned crazily inside her. In all of her forty-five years, she didn't think she'd ever been as angry, or as full of sorrow.

Sonia knew that the sight of Mariya's body lying there, so still, so bruised, so heartbreaking, was burned into her mind forever.

On she walked through the rainy streets, the tears that periodically came to her eyes mixing with the spring rain that spattered her cheeks.

How do I tell Arkady? she wondered over and over. *How on earth will he live through this?*

She caught sight of their building rising up ahead, more cheerless and unwelcoming than ever. It seemed to have acquired a potent kind of malignancy in her absence.

I am a messenger of death.

I must be brave, she told herself. *I must be brave for Arkady. For Dmitri and Misha. No matter what anguish I feel, no matter my own rage. I must be their rock.*

Reaching the building, she pressed the security code into the lobby door's lock. She climbed the stairs, and when she reached their floor, she stopped to catch her breath. At the apartment door she stopped again, filling her lungs with more deep breaths, this time to prepare herself to tell Arkady about Mariya. She took her keys from her coat pocket and inserted the appropriate one, but the door pushed open before she could turn the key.

What—?

Two men—strangers—stood just inside the doorway, blocking her way into the apartment. Before she could ask them to move, Dmitri called to her from over their shoulders.

"Sonia! Sonia!" he cried. "Hurry! Come in. Come in!"

What is it? she wondered. Then she realized that these men must have come to give Arkady the news. But so soon?

Becoming aware of her behind them, the two men moved aside to permit her entry. Her cursory glance at them told her all she needed to know. She immediately recognized them for the minor state bureaucrats that they were. Cut from the identical mold as those who had come to force them out of their home. The same badly made, drab, gray suits, the same leather trench coats, the same battered leather briefcases. The same vodka-bloated faces.

Why are they here? she asked herself again. *Their sort wouldn't be coming to see Arkady.* Then she noticed them shuffling official-looking documents, paying no attention to her.

Sonia wanted to spit with disgust. *At a time like this, to have these idiots visited upon us!* she thought. *I need peace and quiet to deliver my message, to take care of Arkady and Dmitri and Misha.*

Looking around their room, she saw that neither Misha nor Arkady was here. She turned to Dmitri. "Where—?" She suddenly stopped when she saw the look on her husband's face.

My God, she thought. *Dmitri's face is lit up with a huge grin. It's as if nothing had happened. What's going on?*

"Dmitri," she said, a note of alarm in her voice, "where are Arkady and Misha?"

Dmitri stepped around a chair to her side. He put an arm around her shoulders, pressing her to him reassuringly. "They're downstairs at Arkady's, playing chess, I guess."

"But—?" Sonia began.

"Calm down," her husband said. "Listen to me, Sonia. These men are OVIR officers. The came just a little while ago."

Sonia looked at him questioningly. She hadn't really been listening, so absorbed was she in the task she had to perform.

"Sonia," Dmitri said, shaking her lightly, "listen. Don't you see? The OVIR police. The division that deals with exit visas." Dmitri looked into her dark eyes. "Sonia, we've been given permission to emigrate."

Realization dawned, and the full impact of his words nearly swept her off her feet. "Dmitri?" she asked, a quaver in her voice. "Are you certain?"

"Yes," he said. "But we don't have much time. We'll be leaving right away, so we must start getting ready."

"Oh, my God," she said, covering her face with her hands. She was afraid that she was going to cry. "I can hardly believe it." Then she abruptly lowered her hands, and questions came tumbling out of her. "Why is Misha not here. And Arkady? Why are they downstairs? Do they know?"

"Yes, yes," Dmitri said. "They know. Arkady took him downstairs the minute we found out. He said he wanted to play a last game of chess with Misha, but my guess is that Arkady is down there having a nice long chat with him about—who knows what?"

"But what about Mariya?" Sonia blurted. "My God, Dmitri—"

One of the men from OVIR interrupted. He flourished a pen on one of the many documents he was handling, then snapped a folder shut.

"You have all of your papers now, Levin," he said. "We will be going. Remember, your date and time of departure are on the forms. Don't miss it."

"No," Dmitri said, "we won't."

The men gathered up their briefcases and turned to the door.

"There may not be a second chance," one of them snapped. With that, they let themselves out, slamming the door behind them.

Dmitri grabbed Sonia and threw his arms around her, giving her a long, joyous kiss. She laughed and drew back after a moment.

"Dmitri," she said, "this is the greatest news in our lives. But I have to tell you something." Then she quickly told him what had happened to Mariya Yakovlevna.

Dmitri sat down, his head in his hands, not speaking, unmoving. When he finally looked up at Sonia, there were tears in his eyes, tears that subdued the joy that had been there only moments before.

"Arkady thought that she must be all right since he hadn't heard anything. He thought . . ." Dmitri suddenly choked.

Tears came to Sonia's eyes as well, and she put a hand on Dmitri's head, patting it tenderly.

"Sonia," he rasped throatily, "I'll tell Arkady. Let's give him a little more time with Misha, then I'll go down and talk to him."

"No," Sonia said, "we'll both talk to him, but it must be right away. We must see him before the authorities get here to tell him."

"Yes. You're right, of course," Dmitri said. He got to his feet and took one of her hands in his. "Shall we go?"

Misha, holding the cylindrical gold object in his hand, turned it around and around, studying it with intense curiosity. It was about five inches long and roughly the circumference of a pencil, and its filigree had been worn smooth by generations of people touching it. It was exquisite and beautifully ornate, like an exotic piece of jewelry. Only, he didn't quite know what to make of it. Arkady had retrieved it from an old, locked wooden box under the bed, and was explaining to Misha what it was.

"It's a mezuzah," he said. "Inside it is a tiny, rolled-up piece of parchment. Printed on one side is Deuteronomy 6:4 to 9 and 11:13 to 21, from the Bible. Deuteronomy is the fifth book of the Pentateuch, and it contains the second statement of the Mosaic law."

He paused, watching the boy handle the mezuzah.

"All this you will understand better someday," Arkady said.

"You said one side is printed with Deuteronomy," Misha said. "What about the other side?"

Arkady smiled. "On that side is printed the word *Shaddai*. That is a Jewish word for God."

He took the mezuzah from Misha for a moment. Holding it up to the light, he pointed. "See? Look through the aperture. *Shaddai*."

"*Shaddai*," Misha repeated in an awed whisper.

"Yes," Arkady nodded. "*Shaddai*. There, where you can always see it." The old man sat back and took a deep breath. "Many of our people put them up at their doorways. One day you can, too, if you choose to do so."

He patted Misha on the head. "It's been in my family for generations, Misha," Akady said. "And I want you to have it as a going-away present. For good luck in your new home. It will be a secret between us. Okay?"

"Okay," Misha said. "Thank you very much, Arkady." He looked over at the old man. "I will always think of you when I look at it."

"And I will think of you, Misha, every time I hear beautiful music," Arkady said.

There was a soft knock at the door, and they both looked over at it.

"That will be your folks," Arkady said. "Quick, put it in your pocket so no one else will know our secret." He winked conspiratorially at Misha.

Misha grinned and wrapped the mezuzah in its wrinkled old piece of tissue paper and shoved it in a trouser pocket.

"Now, Mikhail Levin," Arkady pronounced, "you are ready for a brilliant future."

Nearly a week had passed, and Mariya Yakovlevna had been laid to rest. Sonia and Dmitri had just about finished packing what few belongings they would take with them, not much more than musical scores and some clothing. Misha had gone downstairs with Arkady for his final good-bye.

"I still wonder about Arkady's reaction to Mariya's death," Sonia said. "He took the news so quietly, so . . . serenely."

"I suppose it makes sense, Sonia," Dmitri said thoughtfully. He buckled one of the straps on the old-fashioned leather suitcase that had belonged to his father, securing it tightly. Like all their luggage, it was bulging at the seams.

"He told me that he knew," Dmitri continued. "He said that when you didn't call from the hospital, he somehow knew that she was gone. He said that he felt it." He looked over at his wife and shrugged. "I guess after all those years with Mariya Yakovlevna, he has a sixth sense or something."

"I thought he would go all to pieces," Sonia said. "I thought he would be inconsolable. He was mad with grief when he came to tell us what had happened."

Sonia looked at the old brass menorah and rolled it up in a woolen scarf, then placed it in the last piece of open luggage. It had never been used, at least not in her memory, but she didn't want to leave it behind. Aside from some photographs, it was one of the few reminders of their families, of their lives in Moscow, of that magnificent old attic apartment that had once been their home.

"Make no mistake," Dmitri replied grimly, "Arkady is grieving and probably still in shock. Part of the 'serenity' you see is so we'll think he's okay. So we won't worry about him."

Dmitri buckled the last strap on his suitcase and, grunting with effort, cinched it as tightly as possible. He sat down on the closed suitcase and looked over at Sonia. "As terrible as Mariya Yakovlevna's death was—and believe me, Arkady will certainly never forget her or the horrible way she died—Arkady's embracing life, trying to go on."

Sonia nodded her head emphatically. "Yes," she said. "I think he's finding consolation in Misha."

Despite the sadness of the situation, Dmitri couldn't help but smile. "How like Arkady to turn to the future—Misha—to find solace, to try to heal the wounds of the past."

She sat down on the suitcase she had finished packing. "Dmitri, try to close it, will you?"

Her husband got to his feet and crossed the small room. "Put all your weight on it," he said. He got down on his knees, and after a struggle with the latches he got the old suitcase closed.

He stood up and extended a hand to Sonia, helping her to her feet, and into his arms. His dark eyes looked into hers, and he planted a solemn kiss on her lips.

"We have to do like Arkady, Sonia," he said. "Look to the future—our future, and Misha's future. We're finally getting what we asked for over two years ago."

"Yes," Sonia said, hugging him to her. "And I'm thrilled, Dmitri, but I'm a little scared, too."

Dmitri put a finger under her chin and raised her face to look at her again. "There's nothing to be afraid of, Sonia. You've got me and Misha, and we'll be in the Promised Land." He kissed her again and hugged her tightly, then let her go.

"We'd better go downstairs and get Misha and get on our way," Sonia said.

"Yes," Dmitri replied. "On our way. To a new life."

* * *

At Sheremetyevo Airport, the Levins relaxed in the lounge, waiting to board their plane. Their excitement was tempered by their sad leave-taking from Arkady, who, despite his best efforts to conceal his sorrow, was obviously grieved to see them leave.

The first leg of their journey would take them to Vienna. From there they would fly on to Tel Aviv. They were somewhat surprised to see that there was an international mixture of passengers awaiting the flight. They hadn't known what to expect but thought they might be on a flight filled only with Russian Jews like themselves who had been given exit visas.

There were only twenty more minutes to go before boarding when OVIR policemen, accompanied by airport emigration police, appeared in front of the seated Levins.

"Come with us," one of the policemen said.

"Why?" Sonia piped up angrily. "We have our visas. The plane will be boarding in minutes."

Dmitri put a hand on her arm. "What's this about?" he asked mildly.

"We have to inspect your luggage," the policeman answered. "Follow us. You'll still make your plane, unless . . ."

They got to their feet, Dmitri in the middle, a bag slung over one shoulder. Sonia had a lighter one, and Misha carried a small shoulder bag also. They dutifully followed the police to an enclosed secure area close by, where their carry-on luggage was placed on tables and opened. The police riffled through the contents of the bags, making a chaotic mess of their orderly packing.

"Is this really necessary?" Sonia asked angrily. "What in the world would we be taking out of the country that would matter?"

Her words were wasted on the police, who ignored her and continued to dig through their belongings as if they were searching for state secrets.

Misha became anxious as they began to go through his small shoulder bag. The policeman tossed his clothes, shaking them, letting them fall where they may. Misha cringed when he saw the familiar piece of old tissue paper surface from between the folds of a sweater. He bit his lower lip to keep from crying out when he saw the man feel the tissue, then proceed to unwrap it.

When the gold mezuzah rolled out of the tissue, the policeman grabbed it and studied it for a moment.

"What's this?" he murmured to himself. Then with a look of disgust, he said, "Garbage." And making a spitting noise, he threw the tissue paper to the floor and slid the mezuzah into the pocket of his trousers.

Misha bit his lip harder and harder, until a drop of blood beaded on his lip. Tears of pain welled up in his eyes, and a hatred such as he had never known consumed him. The mezuzah had been a special secret between him and Arkady. It was meant to bring luck to his future, and it was a special bond to this most loving part of his past. Now that, too, was gone.

Misha stood alone, turning his face away and choking back his tears.

No one will ever be able to treat me like this again. No one! And if I ever return to this place, it will be as a conqueror, in triumph!

Chapter Ten

Tel Aviv, 1979

"Misha!" Sonia called. "Hurry! Ben and Avi are waiting downstairs. You're going to be late!"

"I'm coming, Mama," he called back.

With a burst of youthful energy, his American sneakers pounding on the floors, Misha loped down the hallway from his bedroom, then slid to a squeaking stop in front of his mother.

"Do you see a baseball diamond in my living room?" she asked with good humor, a smile on her face.

Misha returned her smile. "Sorry, Mama, I'm just in a hurry." He dashed to the piano and began shuffling through the pile of scores that were neatly stacked on it.

His long, jet black hair—too long, Sonia thought—was still wet from the shower, and hung on his shoulders, dripping water onto the shirt she had just pressed for him.

Oh, well, Sonia thought, *what's the difference? He looks like a Greek god no matter what he wears, and his hair will be dry before the concert.*

"Misha," she said, "hurry up. I told you Ben and Avi are waiting."

"I can't find the right scores," he muttered, scowling as he continued to shuffle through the piles.

Sonia raised her arm and shook it. "See these, young man?" she said.

Misha turned his head and looked at her. She was waving the scores he was looking for. *She's always one step ahead of me,* Misha thought. He smiled brightly, his teeth gleaming white against his darkly tanned skin.

"Thanks, Mama," he said. He took the proffered scores from her hand, gave her a quick kiss on the cheek, and rushed to the door. "See you there, Mama," he called. " 'Bye!" The door slammed behind him.

In the building's hallway, Misha quickly reached up and, with one finger, rubbed the cheap silvery metal mezuzah that he'd bought and mounted on the door frame.

"Wish me luck, Arkady," he whispered, then he was off.

Inside, Sonia walked to the sliding glass doors, which led to the balcony. Opening them to the inferno of July, she stepped out and crossed to the metal balustrade, careful not to touch it, as it was fiery with the sun's heat. She looked down, her dark eyes searching the sidewalk five stories below for Misha. After a few moments her gaze was rewarded.

There he is, she thought, her heart swelling with pride. *Jumping into Ben's car. Eleven years old, and already so grown up. It seems impossible.*

Even five stories up, she thought she could hear rock and roll blasting from the car's radio. She watched the car pull away from the curb, heading toward Hayarkon Park. When it was finally out of sight, she raised her gaze to the Mediterranean beyond. There was a haze today from the heat, and even the sea looked boiling hot.

She stepped back inside to the cool of the apartment and went to her bedroom, where she began undressing, carefully hanging her clothes in the closet. She looked at the clock on the bedside table. Four o'clock. She would relax a few minutes, then take a shower before Dmitri got home from the university. They didn't have to be at the amphitheater in Hayarkon Park until eight o'clock.

Tying a lightweight cotton bathrobe around her waist, she went to the kitchen and poured herself a glass of iced tea, then returned to the bedroom with it. Passing the dresser, she caught sight of herself in the mirror over it and stopped, scrutinizing the image she saw reflected there.

So much white hair, she thought. *And so much more visible because of the way it contrasts with my black hair.* She drew closer to the mirror, flicking strands of it with one hand. *Oh, well, I'm fifty years old, and I've earned it. I have a right to it if anybody does. And I'll never do a thing to change it.*

She looked at herself closely once more. *Well, not unless . . . not unless Dmitri wants me to.*

She turned away from the mirror and spread out on the bed, sipping the cold tea. She was terribly excited and not just because of tonight's concert. Misha would be performing with the Philharmonic Orchestra, playing two Chopin concertos, two mazurkas, and a waltz. The concert, she was certain, would go well, because Misha was well rehearsed. This was music that was second nature to him, after all.

No, her nervous excitement stemmed more from the letter she and Dmitri had received last week. Then the telephone call that had followed it a couple of days later.

Are our fortunes going to change for the better? she wondered. She took a long sip of her tea. *We've been so extraordinarily fortunate,* she told herself. *So fortunate after the troubles we had in Russia. For us Israel has indeed been the Promised Land. Is it fair to expect even more good fortune?*

When they'd arrived in Tel Aviv in the spring of 1972, five years ago, they hadn't really been certain what to expect in this rough, young country. They had only their luggage with their few belongings with them, and a name and letter that Arkady had given them. The name was Haim Weill, and the letter was one of introduction to him.

They had dutifully contacted Haim Weill upon arrival—for Arkady's sake, actually—given him the letter, and presto! the magic had begun to happen. After only a few days the family had been settled into a two-bedroom apartment in Tel Aviv—the very apartment in which she now reminisced. It was in one of the International Style buildings that had been erected in the 1930s in the center of the city. Misha had always called it their "ship," because of its streamlined resemblance to an ocean liner. Only a few weeks later both she and Dmitri had prestigious jobs teaching music at the University of Tel Aviv. Then, as if their cups weren't already running over, a baby grand piano had arrived and was installed in the apartment's living room. Misha had begun intensive studies with the best instructors available.

Sonia had often thought that it was as if a genie had appeared from a magic bottle. In the beginning she and Dmitri assumed that they had Haim Weill to thank for such generous help. After all, he was a highly respected and very wealthy dealer in Tel Aviv's thriving diamond industry. But as kind and helpful as he had been, they'd soon discovered—from Haim Weill himself—that their true benefactors were a very wealthy family in New York City.

A family of Russian Jewish extraction, the Bunims had made a fortune in investment banking, a fortune they spent liberally to patronize the arts, in particular music. Haim Weill acted as one of their scouts in Israel, always on the lookout for talent.

Haim Weill had notified the Bunims at once of the Levin family's arrival in Tel Aviv, and thus Sonia, Dmitri, and Misha had seen their fortunes change overnight. They had been spared the struggles of most recently arrived Russian immigrants in communities like Nazerat Illit and Arad, and those working on the many kibbutzim and moshavim.

They had immersed themselves in the study of Hebrew, although their English, French, and Russian served their immediate needs in the small, multicultural state. There had been times in the beginning—despite the wondrous turn in fortune—when the three of them felt like aliens on a far-distant planet. Russia had, after all, been the only home they'd ever known, and harsh as it could be, Sonia sometimes reflected that it was in their blood, in their very souls. At times she'd longed for the birches and lindens, the onion domes, and the snow—a longing made all the more poignant by the predominantly dry, rocky, lunar landscape that was Israel.

The ways of its people were also unfamiliar. Ultra-Orthodox, Orthodox, and Reform Jews with all their various sects within sects, and Arabs and Christians with theirs, were perplexing to the Levins. Coming from a tradition of nonpracticing Jews, they cared little for the religion or culture of their antecedents, and in Russia the practice of the Jewish faith had been driven underground. As a consequence, they were faced with a people to which they were, in theory at least, supposed to belong, but with which they felt little or no identity.

The one thing that had kept loneliness at bay—aside from their abiding love for each other—was their unwavering belief in Misha's talent and their relentless ambition for his success as a pianist. Thus far he had done nothing to disappoint them. On the contrary, at eleven years old he had already played in Mann Auditorium, the preeminent performance hall in Israel, with the Philharmonic Orchestra. He had performed in the Jerusalem Convention Center and toured with the orchestra. The Israeli critics—and they were a severe, discerning lot—had hailed him as the next Rubinstein, the next Horowitz, the next—*well, you name it*, thought Sonia.

Yet there remained a niggling dissatisfaction, for she knew that Misha could never realize his full potential here in this Promised Land, wonderful as it had been to them.

She picked up her glass of tea from the bedside table and took another sip, holding a piece of ice to melt on her tongue, reflecting on tonight's concert. *He should be playing in Carnegie Hall tonight*, she thought. *Or Lincoln Center. And he should be continuing his studies with the best teachers in the world, in New York City.*

Misha deserved better. She also knew that her belief in him was not simply a matter of a mother's pride. She was herself a musician and a teacher and was certain that she was objective enough to assess Misha's abilities for what they really were. Dmitri had always supported her in this deeply felt belief and agreed with her, and now she knew that there were others who shared her convictions as well.

The letter. The telephone call.

Sonia expelled a loud breath, her wonderment over the recent turn of events still giving her moments of breathlessness. The clock caught her eye, and she decided she'd better take a shower now.

Quickly disrobing, she went to the bathroom and turned the taps, testing the water until it was barely warm, perfect for a sweltering day. She stepped in and lathered up quickly, then let the water run over her for a time, relaxing her tense muscles. *If only it would rinse away my nervous excitement*, she thought, knowing that it would not.

She stepped out of the shower and began to towel off vigorously. Suddenly the hair on the back of her neck stood up, and she had the distinct feeling that she was being watched. Slowly, she turned, and—

"Boo!"

It was Dmitri.

"You . . . you *devil*," she cried. "You scared me half out of my skin, Dmitri."

He took her into his arms and hugged her tightly. "I'm sorry," he said. "I just couldn't resist." He began peppering her wet face with kisses. "Will you forgive me?"

"Maybe," she said. "If you're good."

Dmitri leaned back from her. "I think I can be good," he said. "In fact, I think I can be very, very good." He grinned mischievously, eyeing her naked body.

Sonia smiled knowingly.

"Are we alone?" he asked.

"Yes," she said. "Misha's already left for the amphitheater."

"How about it, then?" he asked.

Sonia arched an eyebrow. "How about what?" she asked with feigned innocence.

He hugged her, pushing his groin at her playfully.

Sonia could feel his tumescence against her stomach. "Oh," she said. "That." She smiled up into his dark eyes. "I think we could do something about that."

Dmitri kissed her on the lips. "I'll see you in the bedroom."

He patted her playfully on the behind, then turned and walked out. Sonia finished drying off and dabbed herself with cologne. She looked at her reflection in the bathroom mirror and smiled. *I think I'll keep the gray,* she thought, then walked into the bedroom.

Dmitri lay on the bed, naked, his long, lean body still handsome, more rugged-looking now with its deep tan than it had ever been in Russia. He beckoned to her with a hand. She walked to the bedside, and Dmitri reached out and ran his hands gently over her taut flesh, up to her breasts, down to her thighs.

Sonia shivered at his touch, delight and desire beginning to create a fiery heat in her loins. She sat down beside him, and Dmitri pulled her down to him with his long, strong arms, kissing her deeply, his tongue thrusting into her mouth, exploring. She spread her length out on the bed, face to face with him, and their kisses became more passionate, more urgent.

Dmitri stroked her back, her buttocks, and her thighs, then took a breast in his hand. He lowered his mouth to it and began to kiss and lick it gently.

Sonia moaned with pleasure and need, one of her hands moving down to his tumescence, stroking it tenderly.

Dmitri gasped aloud, and he moved a hand to the mound between her legs, a finger entering her, feeling the wetness that was already there.

Sonia moaned again, anxious now for him to enter her. "Oh, Dmitri . . . Dmitri . . . please—"

The telephone at the bedside rang shrilly in their ears.

"Jesus!" Dmitri groaned. He looked at the offending instrument, then at his wife. "Let's turn it off," he said.

Sonia nodded with a smile, reaching over with a hand to it, but suddenly stopped. "The concert!" she said, looking at Dmitri. "Misha may have forgotten something. I'd better get it, Dmitri."

He emitted a low growl. "Shit."

Sonia picked up the receiver. "Hello?"

Dmitri, stroking one of her breasts, watched her as she listened to the voice at the other end. Slowly he sat up, his hand leaving her breast, as he saw the look of curiosity, then the growing horror that crept over her features.

"Where?" Sonia asked, her voice quavering, the telephone receiver trembling in her hand.

"Yes, yes," she said. "We're on our way." She abruptly slammed the receiver down in its cradle, and a pitiful mewling sound escaped her lips.

"What is it, Sonia?" Dmitri asked. "What is it?"

She shook her head back and forth, moaning, tears coming into her eyes.

Dmitri shook her arm. "Sonia!" he cried. "For God's sake, what is it?"

"Misha," she gasped. "Misha . . . he . . . he's been in a car accident." She burst into tears, but even as the tears flowed she leapt out of bed.

"We must hurry, Dmitri." She dashed to the closet. "Hurry. To the hospital."

Oh, my God! Dmitri thought, quickly jumping to his feet. Misha . . . the concert . . . his hands!

Chapter Eleven

Dmitri slammed on the brakes, and the car jerked to a stop. They could see the signs indicating the emergency room entrance. Even before he could kill the engine, Sonia had her door open and was getting out of the car, prepared to run ahead of him.

"Wait, Sonia!" he called to her. "Wait for me."

"Hurry, Dmitri. Hurry!" Her face was a mask of anguish, flushed from the heat and her fears.

Dmitri got out of the car, quickly locked it, and looked around. *No parking. What the hell.* He didn't care right now. He hurried over to where Sonia anxiously waited for him and put an arm around her shoulders. They rushed to the emergency room door together.

Once inside the cool of the hospital, they hurried to the information desk and asked for Misha. They were quickly led through swinging double doors toward a curtained-off cubicle in the emergency room. They heard groans and cries of pain from every direction, and Sonia grabbed Dmitri's arm tightly.

As they drew near the cubicle in a far corner where the nurse was leading them, Sonia was certain that she heard laughter. *It sounds like Misha!* she thought. She tightened her grip on Dmitri's arm and glanced at him, but he was staring grimly ahead.

The nurse pushed aside a curtain, and they saw their son, prone on a gurney, a doctor bent over him.

"Misha!" Sonia and Dmitri cried in unison.

He looked up at them with a wide smile. He had never looked so handsome, so well, so *alive* to his parents. Then they saw the bandage on his chin.

Sonia felt tears begin to form in her eyes yet again, but this time they were tears of relief. Her heart swelled with gratitude. She wanted to cradle Misha in her arms, but she didn't want to get in the doctor's way.

"What—?" Dmitri began.

"It's nothing," Misha said. "I'm all right, Dad."

The doctor looked up at them, shaking her head. "Your son is a very lucky young man," she said. Her hair was a mass of frizzy black ringlets, and she wore glasses with Coca-Cola bottle lenses. "A few stitches in his chin, a few in his knee, and he'll be as good as new."

"Oh, thank God," Sonia said. "You're sure? Everything else is okay?"

Misha grinned. "If you're worried about my hands, they're fine."

The doctor nodded and smiled, revealing widely spaced yellow teeth. Sonia noticed that her name tag read WEITZMANN. "He'll be able to play tonight if he wants to." She looked back down at Misha's knee, where she was dressing his wound.

"No," Dmitri said. "I think we'd better take you home to rest."

"No, Dad," Misha cried in a determined voice. "I'm perfectly all right. There's no reason for me not to play."

"How are Ben and Avi?" Sonia asked, suddenly remembering his friends.

"They're okay," Misha said. "Avi didn't have a scratch on him. He was sitting in the backseat. But Ben probably has a broken nose."

"Where is he?" she asked.

"In one of the other cubicles," Misha said.

"Can we see him?" Sonia asked Dr. Weitzmann.

The doctor looked back up. "If you'll wait a few minutes, I'll go see," she said.

"Thank you," Sonia said. She stepped closer to the gurney and leaned over, tenderly kissing Misha on the forehead. "We're so relieved," she said. "When they called, they couldn't tell us anything except that you'd been in an accident."

Misha grimaced. "You know how people drive in Tel Aviv," he said. "Some jerk—a real old man—ran a light and front-ended Ben. It was the other guy's fault."

"Well, never mind," Sonia said. "What's important is that you're all okay. Was the man who hit you injured?"

"No," Misha said. "He was just a little shook up. He wouldn't even go to the hospital." He looked over at his father. "You didn't mean what you said, did you, Dad? About going home?"

Dmitri nodded. "You've had a shock, Misha," his father said. "I really think it would be best if you came back home with us and had a good, long rest."

"Aw," Misha groaned in exasperation. "That is so stupid! I'm fine. You can see for yourself."

"You could have been killed!" Sonia interjected.

"Mama," Misha said, "do I look dead?"

Sonia couldn't help but laugh. "No," she said, "that you don't. But it's like your father said. You've had a shock to your system. Perhaps tonight you should—"

"No!" Misha said. "This may be the last time I get to perform in Israel for a long time, Mama. You know that. You, too, Dad." He looked at his father, an earnest expression on his face.

His parents knew the truth of his words, and remained silent.

"You know how much this means to me," Misha continued. "Besides, I owe it to my audience to show up, don't you agree?"

"Misha, people will understand if you have to cancel," Dmitri said.

"Maybe," Misha said, "but they'll be disappointed." He turned the full wattage of those large, bright eyes on his parents. "This country has been very good to us, and I don't want to let these people down. Surely you can understand that."

Dmitri looked at his son's imploring face. *He's so willful*, he thought. *But he knows what he wants, and he knows what he can do . . . at least I hope he does.*

Dmitri turned to Sonia. "What do you think?" he asked.

Sonia looked at Misha worriedly, then turned her gaze on Dmitri, her mind made up. "If he thinks he can do it, then I think . . . I think he should, Dmitri."

"Right on!" Misha almost shouted, shoving a fist in the air. "That's the spirit."

The humid air was still heat charged, the atmosphere stifling in the park, with no breeze tonight to alleviate the discomfort. Nevertheless, the audience seemed to find relief in Chopin's beautiful music as Misha's playing transported them—and that's what it does, Sonia thought, *transports*—to another, more gracious time.

She didn't believe it was her imagination, but she would swear that Misha had never played this professionally before, with such virtuosity.

He's putting his all into it tonight, she told herself. *He's glad to be alive, and he's grateful to these people who have given him this opportunity to play, who have come out to hear him.*

She squeezed Dmitri's hand, and he turned and looked at her, a smile on his lips. He put an arm around her waist and hugged her to him, then turned his attention back to the stage.

Even though they had good reason to be concerned, Sonia decided that they shouldn't have been worried about Misha performing tonight. He always pushed himself to the limit, but young as he was, he always seemed to know what he was capable of, just how far to go before pulling back.

He's like an athlete in training for the Olympics, she thought, *with hardly a break in the grueling routine.*

She often worried that his genius for music would leave him impoverished in other areas of his life, and she remembered Arkady's admonishments about allowing Misha to be a boy. A normal life was not an easy task for a prodigy who practiced for hours a day, every single day of the week, but she felt that they'd encouraged him in other pursuits, although they needn't have worried. Misha did well in school and had developed other interests, interests typical of the average young man, she supposed.

Without fail, he exercised every day, lifting weights, jogging, or playing racquetball. He sometimes fenced with friends. He loved loud, brash American and English rock music, volleyball at the beach, and—to her horror—skateboarding. She and Dmitri frequently had to remind themselves of Arkady's advice—he was a young man now—and let Misha pursue these interests.

She smiled to herself, watching him toss that mane of raven hair as he struck a chord onstage. *How handsome he is!* she thought for the millionth time. *And how dangerous that combination of looks, talent, and his willfulness could be! He's got the potential to be a real heartbreaker . . . a lady-killer.* She often hoped that his willful nature and the self-centered attention to his talent and ambition—attention that was a necessity if he was to succeed—would not make him a selfish partner.

She had known far too many artists, be they musicians, painters, writers, or sculptors, who had devoured those around them to serve their own needs. Whether unknowingly or deliberately, they left a path of emotional ruin behind them, destroying their families, their loved ones, in relationships that were essentially parasitic and utterly self-centered. All for their art, or so the excuse usually went. Deep down inside, she knew that Misha was like many of these artists, but she told herself that this would change with time . . . and the right woman.

Her mind drifted back to the letter they'd received. She remembered that day with extraordinary clarity. She had waited for Dmitri in her office, where she attended to administrative duties, while he finished his classes. In the late afternoon they had gone home from the university together, as they often did.

On the drive to the apartment, he had been unusually withdrawn, and Sonia had sensed that he was in a bad humor.

"What is it, Dmitri?" she'd finally asked. "You're so . . . distant."

He shrugged. "Nothing," he replied, staring ahead at the bumper-to-bumper traffic as they crept along.

"Dmitri, I know something's bothering you," she said. "Maybe you'd feel better if you talked about it."

He glanced at her, then turned back, staring out the windshield. "Oh, I guess I'm just frustrated, Sonia. With teaching. With students."

Sonia laughed lightly. "That sounds too familiar," she said. "Did anything in particular happen today?"

"No," Dmitri said, easing the car into the traffic circling around Magen David Square. "Nothing out of the ordinary. It's just the usual, I guess."

"What?" Sonia persisted. "The routine?"

"Maybe that's part of it," he answered. "But it's mostly the students. One after the other all day long, and half of them don't really want to be there. They don't have their hearts in it, you know?"

"Do I ever," Sonia replied dryly, gazing out the window at the palm trees.

"Another thirty or forty percent of them show some interest, and do what they have to to get by." He paused as he stopped for a traffic light, then continued when the traffic began to move again. "A lot of them don't have much ability. I guess about ten percent of my students actually want to be there, doing what they're doing and really working at it."

"But only one or two of those will ever go anyplace with it," Sonia said. "Right?"

"Exactly," Dmitri said. He glanced at her again. "I guess it just gets to me sometimes. I feel like I'm not accomplishing very much. I look at these kids, and I can't help but think about the way that Misha works, his drive and passion."

"Dmitri," Sonia interjected, "you've got to remember that Misha is one in a million. He's a prodigy. You can't expect that from your students."

"I know," Dmitri said. "I don't know why it bothers me today. Most of the time I don't think too much about it."

They reached their apartment building, and Dmitri pulled over and parked. Gathering up their briefcases, they walked together to the lobby, where Dmitri retrieved the mail. Then they waited a moment for the pristine and reliable elevator. Sonia never failed to be reminded of the squalid, graffiti-scrawled elevator in Moscow, and today, as on so many others, she said a silent prayer of thanks.

When they reached the cool of the apartment, Sonia went to the kitchen, and Dmitri put down his briefcase and started going through the mail. Bills and fliers, mostly. *So much junk,* he thought, separating the mail into two piles. He picked up the stack of fliers and promotional letters and started to throw it in the wastebasket. Then suddenly he noticed what appeared to be a letter. He pulled it out of the stack and looked at it.

From New York City. What could it be? he wondered, turning the expensive-looking envelope over in his hand. It was ecru paper of a very heavy stock. He took it to the living room couch, sat down, and tore the letter open.

Sonia came out of the kitchen with two tall glasses of iced tea, and put them down on cork coasters atop the coffee table. She sat down on a chair across from Dmitri and kicked off her sandals, wiggling her toes.

"Oh, it's so good to be home and out of the heat," she said, putting her bare feet up on an ottoman. She took a long sip of her tea.

Dmitri didn't respond, and she looked over at him. He was so absorbed in whatever he was reading—was it a letter?—that he apparently hadn't even heard her. As she watched him, she saw the expression on his face change, gradually altering from one of studious attention to one of complete—*what?*

"Dmitri?" she ventured in a quiet voice.

He read on, still ignoring her.

"Dmitri?" she repeated with growing apprehension and puzzlement. "What is it, Dmitri?"

He held up a hand to silence her and continued to read.

Sonia reluctantly held her tongue. Not only was she becoming increasingly anxious but she was also a little angry now. *Why is he ignoring me?* she asked herself. *What the hell could be so important he would react like this?*

A minute later, Dmitri looked over at her, then held the letter out. "I'll let you read this for yourself, Sonia."

"What is it?" she asked again.

"Just read it, Sonia," he replied.

She took the letter from his outstretched hand and began to read. Her irritation and alarm quickly turned to astonishment and wonderment. A strange sensation ran through her, as if the moment wasn't quite real, as if she were in a movie and this weren't actually happening to her. When she was finished, she quickly read through the letter again. Satisfied that her eyes were indeed not deceiving her, she put the letter down. She went to the couch and sat next to Dmitri.

He saw the tears that had already formed in her eyes, threatening to spill at any moment, and tears came into his eyes. He took her in his arms tenderly, and they wept, holding each other on the couch, trembling, crying for joy, for their lives would surely never be the same again.

After a time Sonia pulled back from her husband, though they still clung to each other. "What do you think, Dmitri?" she asked.

"What do I think?" he echoed. *"What do I think?"* He looked at her intensely, then almost shouted with sheer, unadulterated joy, "I think I believe in *miracles*, Sonia! That's what I think!"

He hugged her to him again, and they both laughed without restraint, with the glee of children. Dmitri drew back, and they smiled at each other.

"We've got to tell Misha," Sonia said excitedly, her laugher quieting.

"I'll call him now," Dmitri said. Then he turned to her. "Or do you think I should wait until his class is over?"

Sonia looked at her watch. "His class is almost over," she said thoughtfully. "Why don't we wait for him to get home? What do you say?"

"Yes," Dmitri said, "then he can read the letter himself."

Misha closed the door behind him. "Mama!" he called out. "Dad!"

"We're in here," Dmitri answered from the living room.

Misha walked in, his scuffed sneakers squeaking on the floor, his backpack, full to bursting, swinging from one hand. He stopped when he saw them, and looked at them curiously.

"What's going on?" he asked, smiling. "Why the wine? You celebrating something?" He dropped his backpack to the floor and went over to the couch, where he kissed his mother on the cheek, then his father.

"Sit down," Sonia said.

"What is it?" Misha asked again, sitting down sideways in a chair, his legs dangling over the arms.

Sonia handed him the letter. "Here, read this," she said.

Misha took the letter from her and quickly scanned it. When he was finished, he jumped to his feet, almost dancing around the living room. "All right!" he yelled jubilantly. *"All right!"* He kissed and hugged Sonia again, then his father. "We're going to New York! Finally!"

Sonia and Dmitri watched him, taking pleasure in his reaction. They had always dreamed of this moment for him. When he eventually sat down again, he looked over at his parents.

"When do we leave?" he asked.

"We have a lot of loose ends to tie up here," Dmitri said, "but I don't think it will take us too long."

"But Mr. Bunim says in the letter that we can come anytime," Misha said.

"I know," Sonia said, "but your father and I have discussed it and think that we should make sure the university has replacements for us before we go. Then, we have to look for an apartment in New York, and . . ."

Misha laughed. "There must be dozens of people lined up for your jobs," he said. "That'll take about a day."

"You're right," Dmitri said, "but the university will want to do a search for the best people for the jobs."

"And there're other things to do, too," Sonia said. "We'll have to sell the car and the furniture and pack, but it won't take too long."

"But the Bunims said they'd finance everything," Misha said. "We could just let somebody else—"

"It's a loan," Dmitri said. "A *loan*, Misha. You read the letter. He's *loaning* us the money to come to New York and get established. It's not a gift. So we don't want to just up and leave. We'll still have to be careful, son."

Misha was suddenly quiet, then looked at them thoughtfully. "I won-der why he didn't do this before?" he asked. "Why did he wait all this time. Why now?"

"Misha," Sonia said, "you're excited. You didn't read the letter very closely. He says in plain English that he wanted to be certain that you would benefit by the training in New York. You know, that you're quali-fied, that you're mature enough."

"Seems to me," Misha said, "he should've known that for a long time."

"Listen, son," Dmitri said. "The Bunims have been very generous, helping us through Haim to get established here in Tel Aviv. You know that."

"Yes," Misha said, "I know."

"And through Haim," Dmitri went on, "we've managed to pay them back for helping us get this apartment and everything else. But I guess they're like most rich people, they want value for their money. So Mr. Bunim's been waiting to make sure that we're worth it."

"In other words," Misha said, "he wanted to make sure that I have the talent to make it in New York? That I'm worth it?"

"That's it, exactly," Sonia said, nodding.

Misha looked at his father, then his mother, an intense look in his dark, fiery eyes. Sonia looked away. She didn't think she'd ever seen such naked determination in anyone's eyes before. It was a little frightening, this look, and made her uncomfortable. She told herself that it was only the harsh Israeli sunlight pouring in through the windows, striking his eyes at a certain angle. Yes, she decided, it must be a trick of the light. She looked back over at Misha.

"I'll show him," Misha said in a low voice that was almost a growl. "You just wait and see. I'll show him."

Chapter Twelve

⚛

New York City, 1986

"Afternoon, Misha," the doorman said, nodding his head as he held open the door. "Beautiful day, isn't it?"

"Hey, Sam," Misha said. "It sure is." He strolled on into the apartment building's darkly lit lobby, a big black leather gym bag in hand, his Walkman dangling loose around his neck, emitting a loud, tinny buzz.

"And Misha?" Sam called after him.

He turned around and looked questioningly at the doorman. "Yeah, Sam?"

"Good luck tonight," he said with a salute.

"Thanks, Sam," Misha replied, smiling at the doorman's gesture.

He walked on toward the elevator bank, his sneakers squishing on the floor, looking around the lobby's vast, tastefully restrained expanse of marble. As always, there were three massive bouquets of fresh flowers, one on an elegant French-looking commode against a wall, one on a low coffee table surrounded by couches, and another on a table between the elevators. The smell of huge pink and white lilies engulfed him.

Nice change after the street outside, he thought, punching the elevator call button.

Central Park South was one of the most prestigious addresses in New York City, but ironically, it nearly always smelled of horse manure. Like today, in the warm spring weather. Misha felt sorry for the pathetic old horses, most of which should have been put out to pasture long ago, pulling their tackily decorated buggies. They lined up along the length of the street here, day in, day out, waiting for the tourists who took rides in the park.

Like everything else in this city, you had to take the good with the bad. *Like horseshit on Central Park South*, Misha thought. *Every pleasure has its price.* It was a city of extremes, existing side by side, and no matter how insulated you thought you were, there was no escaping the realities that New York inflicted on you.

The elevator arrived, and he stepped back, allowing an elegantly dressed woman to step out. Her hair was all dyed blond flips and waves and twirls, firmly cemented into place, and her almost totally unlined face—a plastic surgeon's playground—was a palette of colors from the various concoctions skillfully applied to it.

"Good afternoon," Misha said, flashing a wide smile.

Her sharp blue eyes surveyed his sweat-soaked gym clothes and his long, still damp hair. She lifted her chin perceptibly, then grandly stared straight through him and hobbled out.

He idly wondered why she hadn't spoken, why she never did speak to him, for he ran into her occasionally, and she had yet to acknowledge him. Was it the way he was dressed? Probably not. She'd seen him in everything from white tie and tails to torn-up blue jeans. Did she know who he was—and he was almost certain she did—and want to pretend that she didn't?

He didn't really know, but his curiosity was piqued. The more well known he had become, he'd discovered, the more bizarrely the people around him reacted to him. He didn't really believe that celebrity had changed *him* all that much, but he knew that it had definitely changed the behavior of those *around* him.

He stepped into the car and punched the button for the penthouse, relishing the very word. *Penthouse*. On the very top of the building, with a view of the entirety of Central Park, the East Side across the East River to Long Island, and the West Side over the Hudson River to New Jersey. It seemed to be on the top of the very world.

Like me, he thought with a smile of satisfaction. *On top of the world*.

The elevator car bobbed to a halt, and Misha got off, fishing in his gym pants for the keys to the apartment. Before he unlocked the door, he rubbed the silver metal mezuzah on the door frame with a fingertip, then brushed it lightly with a reverent kiss. It was the mezuzah he'd bought to replace the one Arkady had given him all those years ago in Moscow.

Twelve years, Misha thought. *Arkady is long dead and buried, and I'm eighteen years old and living in New York City*.

Russia often seemed like a dream to him now—he'd only been six years old when they'd left—but Arkady was firmly imprinted in his mind forever, in every detail of physique and dress, every nuance of speech and manner, every loving little piece of advice, every little lecture. Misha would always remember him, and with a deep and abiding love, of that he was certain. Arkady was his only loving memory of Russia.

He stepped into the enormous mauve entry foyer to the grand old apartment he shared with his parents. He tossed his keys into a heavily carved Russian silver bowl set on a console—also Russian—in the entryway, then went through the tall double doors into the vast, double-height living room, its ceiling soaring to over twenty feet.

No one was about, and he skirted around the twin Steinway concert grand pianos set back to back in their ebony magnificence, and stepped over to the wall of windows, which faced north, over Central Park, straight ahead. The view through the floor-to-ceiling windows was breathtakingly beautiful and never failed to impress him with its majesty. He sometimes imagined that this view—*his* view—encompassed *his* park and *his* city, spread out at his feet, paying homage to the great artist that he was becoming. This was a thought, however, that he kept to himself. He knew that his family and friends would surely accuse him of a dangerous hubris.

"Misha!" It was his mother.

He jerked involuntarily, so rapt had he been in the view that he hadn't heard her approach.

"Where have you been?" Sonia asked. "I've been worried to death. My God, the concert tonight! And the party afterward!"

Misha turned from the window. His mother was already dressed for the evening, wearing a simple long black gown with a tailored silk-satin bodice and chiffon skirt and sleeves, a dress she'd had made several years ago for his concerts. She wore tiny diamond studs in her ears, a gift from Dmitri, and a small pearl and diamond brooch, a gift from Misha, on her bodice.

"You look beautiful, Mama," Misha said.

"Thank you, Misha," she replied, her anger somewhat mollified by the compliment. Sonia Levin at fifty-seven was almost totally white-haired, but she was a tall and regal woman, erect as a girl, who wore her age well. Those dark eyes set in her lightly lined but clear skin still flashed with youthful vitality, and her attitude toward life was unwaveringly optimistic.

"What took you so long?" she asked.

"I met somebody at the gym, Mama," Misha said, "and we got to talking and before I knew it . . ." He shrugged.

"Look at you!" she cried. "You're filthy from that place!"

"I didn't take the time to shower at the gym," Misha said. "I hurried on home to get cleaned up here because of the time."

"And who did you meet that made you forget the time?" she asked. "Who is so important?"

"A guy who's a musicians' agent," Misha replied. "He handles classical musicians. Manny Cygelman."

Sonia, arms akimbo, regarded him thoughtfully. "An agent," she said.

"Yes, Mama, an agent," Misha answered. "That's what I said."

"You can have any agent in the world," Sonia said. "You have agents beating down the doors to handle you. So why are you wasting your time with this Manny . . . this Manny Whoever that I never even heard of?"

"I like him, Mama," Misha said. "I like him a lot." Misha sank down onto a couch and started unlacing his sneakers.

"Good, so you like him," Sonia said. "But I wouldn't think about him representing you. Not if I were you. I don't remember his name on the list we made of the top agents." She strode over toward the couch, then sat down in a chair facing it.

Misha grimaced. "I didn't say he was going to represent me, Mama. But I like him. He's young and he's hungry. You know what I mean."

He held a sneaker up in his hand, gesturing with it. "He's got to earn his living, make his way in the world, you know? He's not like a lot of those people. Old and tired and bored. Just going through the motions."

Sonia was becoming irritated. "Misha, Misha," she said. "Who have you been talking to? This Manny person?"

"Nobody!" he said defensively. "Everybody in the music business knows this."

"Listen to me," she said. "Please. Don't do anything rash with this . . . this Manny . . . this Manny Whatever. He might be somebody out to rob you. This city is full of unscrupulous people. You know that. You're getting to be a famous pianist. This guy smells money. He comes on to you—"

"Mama," Misha said with exasperation, "it's not like that, okay? Just cool it. I like Manny as a person. And his name is Manny Cygelman. *Emmanuel Cygelman*. I didn't say he was going to be my agent, did I?"

"No. Not in so many words," Sonia conceded. "But I know you, Misha Levin. I know how you like to be different. I know how you like underdogs. And I also know you're headstrong and in too much of a hurry sometimes. I say—"

"*Mama*," Misha cried. "Cool it! For God's sake, Manny and I just met, okay?"

"Okay," Sonia said, "okay. If you say so." She squirmed slightly in her chair, not really wanting to drop the subject yet, but realizing that to pursue it now was not wise. Misha might storm out of the room and remain incommunicado for a while. She couldn't have that. Not now. Tonight was too important.

"Listen," she finally said. "You'd better start getting ready. And don't forget, we have to go to the Bunims after the concert tonight."

"I know," Misha said.

"Your clothes are all laid out up in your bedroom, ready for you," Sonia said. "Your father is getting dressed now. All you have to do is shave and shower. Okay?"

"Okay, Mama," Misha said. He stood up, grabbing his sneakers and gym bag, and headed for the stairs up to his bedroom. "They won't mind if I bring a friend or two, will they?"

"A friend? Or two?" Sonia's eyes widened with alarm, and she stared after her son as if he was mad.

"Yes," Misha said easily. "I asked Manny to come along after the concert. And I told him he could bring his friend Sasha."

"You . . . you asked this . . . this *stranger* to come along to a party at the *Bunims*'?" Sonia sputtered. "And to bring his friend? What's with you, Misha? Have you lost your mind? To the *Bunims*', of all people." She threw her arms into the air dramatically. "I don't believe you."

Misha started up the stairs. "It'll be okay, Mama," he said, turning to face her. "They won't mind at all. It's not like it's a sit-down dinner or anything."

"Misha, we have to do everything *perfectly* for them!" she cried. "These people expect nothing but the very best from all of us! After all they've done for us. Don't you understand that?"

"You bet I do, Mama," he said in a cynical tone of voice, turning his back to her. Then he disappeared down the second-floor hallway. "You bet I do," Sonia heard him repeat.

She sat mute, gritting her teeth in frustration. Misha was beginning to show signs of . . . of rebellion, she thought. He hadn't been himself for the past few months now. Oh, sure, he was basically still the same sweet and dutiful Misha who practiced relentlessly, pleased his teachers, and played as if he'd been kissed by an angel, but his behavior of late was definitely beginning to take on a kind of edge, a kind of cockiness, sometimes a sullenness, that she found disturbing.

Though she hated to admit it, this attitude change she'd witnessed lately, this growing arrogance, was a character trait she truly found unlikable. In some ways, she thought, Misha was becoming a stranger to her—and to his father. This she knew because she and Dmitri had discussed it at length, and she had discovered that he was as perplexed as she. When Dmitri had tried to discuss his son's behavior with him, Misha had simply clammed up, shutting his father out, really wounding Dmitri, who'd thought the two of them could discuss anything.

We've been wonderful parents to him, Dmitri and I, doing everything in our power to see to it that he realizes his ambitions. Could it be that we've been too smothering? she wondered. *Too demanding? Were our expectations for him too high?*

She didn't think so. He had always asked for more, begging for challenges, never being satisfied.

When they had first arrived in New York seven years ago, Misha had begun lessons with one of the world's greatest teachers, Joachim Hess, and he had worked indefatigably, startling Hess with his talent and hard work. Word quickly spread among the close-knit international classical music community that there was a new wunderkind in town. After his first public recital at Julliard, he had become the toast of the New York music world, extolled as the most exciting pianist to come along in years. The praise only drove him to work harder.

At that point Sonia, Dmitri, and Misha put their heads together to decide on the best strategy to use in handling his career, and a very clever one it turned out to be. Without the advice of agents, producers, instructors, or other luminaries in the music world, Misha himself had come up with a master plan, one that they now saw in retrospect as a stroke of genius.

"I'm not going to go to any of the competitions," he'd told them in no uncertain terms. "Not the Van Cliburn, not the Tchaikovsky, not *any* of them."

"But why?" Dmitri had asked, amazed at this piece of news. "This is unheard of, Misha. Every up-and-coming young pianist like yourself uses the competitions to get his name out there, to build an audience and a reputation."

"*No* competitions," Misha reiterated. "For the same reason that I'm not going to allow any recordings to be sold yet," he added.

"No recordings! But this is suicide!" Sonia had cried at the time. "What are you thinking of? They could be your biggest source of income! And make your fame!"

"*No* recordings sold," Misha repeated. "Not yet. And," he continued dramatically, seemingly paying no attention to their dumbfounded expressions, "for the same reason I'm only going to play in public on very rare occasions for very small audiences, at least for the next three or four years."

When he was finished speaking, he sat looking at them with a feverish gleam in his eyes.

Dmitri and Sonia were temporarily stunned, unable to grasp what he could possibly be thinking.

Misha abruptly jumped to his feet and began to pace the room excitedly. "Don't you see?" he said, stopping and turning to them. "This is the best way in the world to generate international interest in me. To have a hungry audience in the wings, just *waiting* for my concerts, *begging* to hear me play, *begging* for my CDs. They'll have heard all the rumors about me, and they'll want to find out for themselves."

"But—" Sonia began.

"I'll record my concerts," Misha said, pacing the room again, "but I won't allow the release of the CDs for the next few years. Can you imagine the storm of interest—of publicity—this will generate?"

"What—?" Dmitri started to speak.

Misha silenced his father by lifting his hand. "With your teaching positions at Julliard, plus my performance fees, even if there're only a few," he continued, "we won't have to worry about money, will we?" He looked at them.

"Nooo," Dmitri said, "we can manage. It's just that—"

"Good," Misha said. "It's settled, then." He leaned with a hand on one of the Steinway concert grand pianos, looking up at the ceiling dreamily. "I won't perform in Carnegie Recital Hall until I'm eighteen. Until then I'll tease the music world mercilessly, doing maybe one performance a year at Julliard. After I do Carnegie Recital Hall, I'll have them beating down my door."

"Misha," Dmitri said, "what you are proposing is the very opposite of what most young musicians would do."

"And that's the point," Misha had said.

That had been four years ago, Sonia remembered. He had been fourteen years old and already so wise in some ways. At first she and Dmitri had had misgivings, worrying that this strategy would backfire, that interest in Misha would die out and that any potential audience would gradually lose interest after waiting so long. They had played along, however, encouraging him, always being there for him, and had been relieved to see that the curiosity about him had finally evolved into what had virtually become an international clamor among the cognoscenti.

Now, she surmised, with a resignation that made her a little sad, she and Dmitri would finally be taking a backseat to agents, to producers, to recording companies, to conductors, to marketing experts, and to a host of others who would each have a part in carrying out their son's future in music.

Sonia anxiously rubbed her arms with her hands, then hugged herself. She hoped against hope that Misha had been right and that she and Dmitri had done the right thing in letting him carry out such an unusual approach to handling his career.

Well, she thought at last, with her usual practicality, *the proof is in the pudding. So we'll see—tonight.*

Tonight: Carnegie Recital Hall.

The glittering audience, usually so sedate at these affairs, was stamping its feet, to Sonia's and Dmitri's astonishment, demanding more and more, as if Maria Callas had finally left the stage after performing her last encore, leaving the audience begging for one more. Only in this case the thunderous noise of stamping feet, clapping hands, shrill whistles, and loud shouts of Bravo! was all for Misha.

Sonia turned to her husband with a wide smile on her face. "Do you suppose they're ever going to leave?" she asked.

"It's crazy!" Dmitri said. "Wild!" He hugged her. "And I love it!"

Gradually, the audience did finally begin to disperse. Sonia and Dmitri became surrounded by well-wishers on their way out, many who knew them and some who only knew who they were. They shook countless hands, accepted an untold number of compliments, and kissed numberless cheeks, and when they were finally left to themselves, they stood nearly exhausted, yet still exhilarated after the performance.

"I guess we'd better get back to the dressing room," Dmitri said.

"Yes," Sonia said. "It's time we got started to the Bunims'." She paused and looked at Dmitri curiously. "Did you see them, by the way?"

"Oh, yes," Dmitri said. "They were two or three rows behind us."

"Funny," Sonia said thoughtfully. "I would have thought they would say hello."

"I think they were just being very nice," Dmitri said, "and deliberately sparing us more handshakes and more compliments."

"You're probably right," Sonia said, nodding her head. "Besides, they must get home for their guests."

They made their way backstage, but couldn't get close to the dressing rooms. A noisy crowd was gathered outside Misha's door, many of them young women but with a sprinkling of men as well, all with programs in hand, waiting for autographs, jostling one another for space and proximity to Misha's door.

"Oh, my God," Sonia said. "He'll never get out of here at this rate. What're we going to do?"

"Step back, please," shouted a baritone, British-sounding voice with the ring of authority, firm yet polite. "Please, step back. Kindly clear a path."

A young man grasped Sonia by the arm and began to lead her forward, turning to Dmitri and indicating by a nod of his head that he should follow with another young man, who had sidled up to Dmitri. It was as if the Red Sea parted before them, with the short, overweight man in his resplendent tuxedo and tortoiseshell glasses continuing to cajole the crowd in his very posh-sounding voice. "Please, step back. Kindly clear a path, please."

They arrived at Misha's dressing room door none the worse for wear, and the stranger gave it five rapid, distinct knocks. The door opened a crack, and then was swung open just enough for them to slide in, first Sonia, then Dmitri, and finally the strangers.

Misha sat back down in a chair in the little dressing room, a towel draped around his shoulders. He was using the ends of it to rub his face over and over, wiping off the sweat from the combination of stage lights and nerves.

He looked up and smiled widely. "It was okay, huh?"

"Misha, it was fantastic!" Sonia enthused.

"The best you've ever played!" Dmitri said simultaneously.

Misha kissed his mother and father, then grabbed the towel from around his neck and used it to vigorously dry his sweat-soaked mane of hair. "I think they liked it, don't you?" he said, with laughter in his voice.

"Liked it?" Sonia cried. "My God, I've never seen an audience respond like that. The enthusiasm! The—"

Suddenly Misha stopped drying his hair and dropped the towel. "Mama," he said. "These are my friends Manny Cygelman and Sasha Soloviev."

Sonia turned first to the rotund young man with the balding pate and tortoiseshell spectacles, dressed elegantly in what appeared to be custommade clothes. Manny almost blushed under her assessing scrutiny. The other young man, Sasha, stood silently watching her. He was taller and thinner than Manny, but equally well dressed.

"So," she finally said, shaking his proffered hand, "you're the famous Manny Cygelman."

"Well, I'm not famous, Mrs. Levin," Manny replied, "but I am undeniably Manny Cygelman."

"Well, if you're as good at being an agent as you are at crowd control," Sonia said, "then I'm betting you're going to be top-notch." She gave him the benefit of her best smile.

"I will accept that as a compliment coming from you, Mrs. Levin," Manny said.

"And please, Manny," she said, "you're a friend of Misha's. So call me Sonia. Okay?"

"Okay," Manny said.

"And you're Sasha?" Sonia said to the taller and thinner man.

"Yes," he said, shaking her hand. He seemed slightly uncomfortable, she noticed.

"A friend of Manny's?" she asked.

"That, too," the young man said with a slight blush.

"Welcome," Sonia said. Then she turned to Misha and began fretting over his mass of hair.

"You're going to have to have a blow-dryer backstage, Misha," she said. "Or you're going to have to get all that . . . that mess cut off. A rock star you're not."

"No way," Misha said. "My fans love it."

"The fans," Sonia repeated. "The fans."

Misha gave his hair a final toss and rose to his feet. "Is everybody ready to party?"

"All right!" Manny said.

Sasha smiled tightly.

"Just remember, young man," Sonia said, "tonight was a great success, but don't forget where we're going. Best behavior. Understand?"

Misha laughed. "Manny, they're worried because the Bunims are so grand, you know? One generation off the boat from Russia, and they think they're the Romanovs."

Manny smiled, but a serious look came into his eyes. "From what I hear, they practically are the Romanovs."

"You," Sonia said, "have the right attitude, Manny Cygelman. Now, we'd better get moving, but oh, my God, what do we do about the crowd outside?"

"I'll take care of it," Manny said. "I'll get you two out, while Sasha maneuvers Misha through. He can give a few autographs on the way. It won't take too long, so we can wait out front. Okay?"

"I think that's a good idea," Dmitri said.

"I think he's brilliant," Sonia said, patting Manny's nearly bald pate. He took her arm, and away they went, Manny putting on his best British accent for the crowd.

Chapter Thirteen

The entry gallery, as it was referred to, left little doubt as to the character of the inhabitants of the vast apartment, set high above Fifth Avenue in the east Seventies. The floors were of gleaming black-and-white checkerboard marble with cabochon insets of malachite and lapis lazuli. Overhead, four matched crystal chandeliers, antique Russian ones of the waterfall shape, brilliantly lit the gallery.

Its walls were lined with neoclassical carved marble pilasters between which priceless paintings—Picassos, Mirós, Matisses, Legers, and Braques, among them—were hung against the gold silk damask fabric. Ornately carved gold-leafed French consoles with marble tops held large marble busts of antiquity and Meissen pots of enormous hothouse orchids, their brilliant blooms cascading to the tabletops. Heavily carved and gilded hall chairs, which once graced the entry halls of stately British homes, lined both of the long walls.

The entry gallery set the tone for the remainder of the Bunim family's thirty-six-room palace of treasures, dazzling those chosen few ever permitted beyond its gilded portals.

Manny tugged at Misha's sleeve. "Have you been here before, old chap?" he asked, wide-eyed despite his efforts at appearing to be a blasé sophisticate.

"Yeah," Misha replied. "A few times. You know, they sponsored us in Israel and helped us get to New York."

"The Bunims?" Manny gasped in genuine awe. "You hear that, Sasha?" he said, turning to his friend.

Sasha merely nodded and continued looking about the entry gallery.

"Yeah," Misha said, looking at Manny. "And believe me, nobody will ever forget it."

Manny looked surprised for a moment. "I think I catch your drift," he finally said. "But it is spectacularly beautiful, isn't it?"

Vaslav, the majordomo, ushered Sonia and Dmitri to the drawing room entry first.

"Mr. and Mrs. Dmitri Levin," he intoned in a firm, loud voice.

Misha, Manny, and Sasha heard the noise level of conversation drop considerably, followed by a polite scattering of applause. The applause was an unusual gesture, and the guests, of course, were demonstrating their appreciation of Misha's parents, knowing that the great pianist himself would most likely be waiting in the wings.

Vaslav, who was huge—tall and broad-shouldered—immediately returned and ushered Misha to the entry.

"Mr. Mikail Levin," he announced.

A loud round of applause ensued and continued for some time. In response Misha bowed his head several times to the assembled guests. As the applause died, the noise level of conversation grew much higher and more animated than before.

When Vaslav announced Emmanuel Cygelman, then Sasha Soloviev, hardly a head turned to look at them, but the Bunims, perfect hosts that they were, immediately took note of them both. They soon made their way over, introducing themselves, making pleasant conversation, knowing as they now did, that Manny and Sasha were friends of the evening's star.

Misha easily mingled with the guests, accepting their lavish praise for his performance with poise and self-confidence. It was not in his nature to be self-deprecating, but he didn't give the impression of being an accomplished egomaniac, either.

When the crowd of well-wishers had finally subsided, Misha retired to a corner of the drawing room, where he could quietly enjoy the vintage champagne and caviar lavishly lumped on toast points. Surveying the glittering crowd, he could see that Dmitri was engrossed in conversation with Ivan Bunim, the two of them talking as if they were the best of friends. Manny and Sasha, standing near one of the baronial marble fireplaces, appeared to be attentively listening to Tatiana Bunim.

Where was his mother? he idly wondered, surprised that he didn't see her in the thick of the action. Then he caught sight of her out of the corner of his eye, heading toward him—with one of the most stunning women he'd ever laid eyes on firmly in tow.

As they approached, he stopped eating and gazed at the beauty. She was very tall, at least five feet, nine inches, with long, pale blond hair pulled back into a chignon. She looked ethereal, he thought, angelic even, in her paleness. Her skin appeared to be flawless in its perfection, and her eyes were an intelligent but icy blue.

How perfect she looks in that white gown, he thought. *So pure, so innocent, so . . . virginal.*

"Misha," Sonia said as they drew near. "I knew I would find you hiding in plain view."

"Just taking a little break from the party, Mama," Misha said, returning her smile.

"I have someone very special for you to meet," Sonia went on. She patted the young woman's arm. "This is Vera Bunim, Ivan and Tatiana's daughter. My son, Misha Levin."

For a moment Misha was surprised. He had always heard about the Bunims' daughter but had never met her, had never, in fact, given her a thought. Nor had he ever paid any attention to the photographs in their Fabergé frames he'd seen scattered about the library the few times he'd been here.

He put out his hand, and Vera took it in hers. "It's a pleasure," Misha said, flashing his most winning smile. "I've heard so much about you."

Vera nodded, a smile on her perfect lips. "And I've heard a great deal about you, Misha."

Her voice, he thought, was also perfect. Not too little girl, but soft, cultured, with the slightest drawl. He supposed it was a boarding school voice.

"I hope you've only heard glowing reports," he said with a wink.

"In fact, that's all they've been," Vera said. "Glowing." There was a hint of amusement in her voice. "But now that I've finally seen you, I don't know that I trust my sources."

Misha laughed. "And why's that?"

"You're surely a little too good-looking not to've been up to a little mischief making," she replied.

Sonia laughed lightly. "I think I'll leave you two alone, if that's okay," she said. "I have to see about Dmitri."

"That's fine, Mrs. Levin," Vera said.

"Yes, Mama," Misha said. "You'd better go see what Dad's up to."

"I'll see you again before leaving, Vera," Sonia said, and then she turned and was gone.

Vera looked at Misha. "I hope I didn't offend your mother," she said without conviction. "I mean about the mischief making."

"I don't think so," Misha said. "She's not a woman who is easily offended."

"I wouldn't think so," Vera said. "I mean, with all you've been through over the years."

"I guess it does tend to . . . to harden one," Misha said.

"Ummm . . ." Vera looked up at him with what Misha thought was surely a challenging expression.

"So are you in town from school?" he asked, trying to make conversation. For the first time in his life he felt uncomfortable in a woman's presence. He sensed that Vera Bunim was not only beautiful but also extremely intelligent, insightful, and worldly-wise. She was not, he was certain, a woman to toy with.

"Yes," she said. "I just finished studying at the Courthault."

"So you're in town for a while?" Misha asked.

"I'm going to be here all summer," Vera replied. "Well, here and out in the Hamptons." She looked at him again, riveting him with those icy blue eyes. "What about you?"

"Yes," Misha said. "I'll be here for the summer at least. Then I'll probably start going on tour in the fall. Winter at the latest."

"Oh," she said playfully. "So you're finally going to let the world hear you?"

"Yes," Misha said. "It's time."

"I enjoyed your concert, by the way," Vera said. "Immensely. It really was a brilliant performance."

"Thanks," Misha said. "I appreciate that coming from you."

"Oh?" she said. "Why? I mean, coming from me?"

"Because I'm sure that you have very discriminating taste, for one thing," Misha said. "And since your family has helped us so much—"

"Please," Vera interjected, "let's don't bring that up. They were able to do it, and you deserved it. Case closed. Okay?"

"Okay," Misha said. He was somewhat surprised that she would want to sweep her family's patronage under the rug, but he also was relieved. "Case closed."

"Oh, God," Vera said. "Here comes that old dragon, Annabelle Lawrence. Let's make a run for it, shall we?"

"Sure," Misha said, laughing.

"Follow me," Vera said, and she turned on her heel, rushing toward a door that led into a hallway. Misha followed in her wake, enchanted and a little mystified by this angelic-looking creature, who he was somehow certain was anything but an angel.

In the hallway Vera turned to him. "Why don't we go upstairs and talk? Is that okay?"

"Sure," he said, intrigued more than ever, and beginning to feel a slight stirring in his loins.

She led him to a small elevator, exquisitely paneled in mahogany, and they ascended in it to the apartment's third floor. He followed her down a hallway to a door, which Vera opened, and he went in after her.

The room was obviously her private domain, with pale gray French boiserie-paneled walls, a huge, draped canopy bed, an Aubusson rug with pale creams, pinks, greens, and raspberry in it, a massive carved marble fireplace mantel, and French doors leading out to a terrace.

"Let's go outside," she said, leading the way.

Misha stepped out onto a lushly planted terrace. Set under its enormous trees, surrounded by flowers and shrubbery, were a table with a large umbrella, chairs, and chaise lounges, and under a canvas awning extending from the building were sofas, more chairs, and a drinks cart.

Misha walked to the parapet and looked out over the park. The city's lights twinkled magically in the distance, like diamonds in the dark. He could see Central Park South, his street, to the southwest, and straight ahead, the majestic towers of Central Park West.

She came up beside him. "It's beautiful from here, isn't it?" she said.

"Yes," Misha said, looking at her, standing there so closely beside him. The wind, which seemed much more powerful up here than down on the street, was whipping loose strands of her hair about her face, only enhancing her breathtaking beauty.

"Would you like a drink?" she asked. "A glass of wine? Some more champagne?"

"You have some here?" he asked.

"Oh, yes," she said. "I sometimes have a glass while I dress for evenings out." She went to the drinks cart and expertly pulled a silver-topped cork—in the shape of a tricorn hat, he noticed—from a bottle of already opened champagne. Filling two flutes with the golden liquid, she brought them over to the parapet and handed him one.

"Cheers," she said, touching his glass with hers. "I'm glad I've finally met the great Misha Levin."

"Cheers," Misha echoed, returning her gaze. "And I'm glad to have finally met the beautiful Vera Bunim."

She smiled, and they took sips of their champagne.

"It's odd," she said, "that our families have such a history, but we've never even met before. Isn't it?"

"Yes," Misha said. "I didn't know what to expect. I had no idea you were so . . . well, so beautiful."

"Thank you," she said, meaning it. "I knew you were enormously talented, and I'd heard you were very good-looking."

She paused, looking out over the city, and took another sip of her champagne. Then she gazed up into his eyes again. "But I didn't know that you would be quite as handsome and . . . *virile*-looking as you are."

Misha felt that powerful and unmistakable stirring in his loins once again. *Somehow or other,* he thought, *Vera Bunim knows exactly what buttons to push.*

"What did you expect?" he asked, cocking an eyebrow questioningly. "A pale, skinny nerd who never sees the out-of-doors? Somebody gay?"

"No," Vera said, "although there are some nerdy pianists like you say and some gay ones, too. Quite virile-looking gay ones at that. It's just that you're so obviously, so definitely . . . well . . ."

"Hetero?" he supplied.

"Yes," she said. "At least I think so."

"What if I weren't?" he asked.

"I would still be extremely attracted to you," Vera said with surprising bluntness. "But I wouldn't bother pursuing you, knowing that it would be a waste of time."

"You're a practical lady, I see," Misha said.

"Yes," Vera said softly, "actually I am. A very practical woman. When I see something I want, I usually don't hesitate to go after it."

"A woman as beautiful as you are, with all your money," Misha said, "could have anything in the world she wants."

"Not necessarily," Vera said, looking back out over the park. "I'm not going to play the poor little rich girl, because I'm lucky as hell and I know it. But sometimes girls who have my looks and my money don't get what they want."

"I have a feeling that you will," Misha said.

She turned her intense gaze back on him. "Do you mean that?" she asked.

"Yes," he said, shifting closer to her at the parapet, brushing against the softness of her chiffon gown. He was so close to her that her heavenly scent—flowery and sweet, but not cloying—was intoxicating. He set down his flute of champagne and slid an arm around her pale creamy shoulders, drawing her to him.

Vera shivered at his touch, a thrill rushing through her that she had never experienced before. It was a sensation that she had somehow felt certain—had known in her very being—that this man would arouse in her. She put down her champagne and looked up at his dark face.

Misha looked down at her longingly, her response to him stirring the heat within him. He took her in his arms and began to kiss her tenderly, inhaling the sweetness of her femininity, savoring her delicate lips, then exploring her receptive mouth.

Vera gave herself up to him, lost in his embrace, anxious to know this man. She felt his swollen manhood pressing against her, and shivered again, almost gasping aloud.

Misha lingered at her lips for a moment longer; then his mouth trailed to her ears and down to her neck, devouring the taste of her, the beautiful creaminess of her. His hands began to explore her breasts, slowly, gently, stroking them through the almost sheer white chiffon of her bodice. They moved down to her buttocks, pressing her against him as they both became more feverish in their desire.

Vera drew back a moment. "Let's go over there," she said, indicating one of the large white sofas under the awning.

He took her hand in his and led her to the sofa, where he took her in his arms again, then began to unzip the back of her dress. When it slipped to the terrace, she stood before him almost naked.

He drew in a quick breath. "You're so very beautiful," he said. "So very beautiful and desirable." He took her in his arms again, kissing her harder, ravenous for her body and its secrets. He unhooked her bra and let it slip to the terrace, then held her firm breasts in his hands, leaning down to kiss first one, then the other.

Vera shivered anew, enthralled in the passion that was driving them both relentlessly. She relished his tongue on her nipples, kissing and licking, before he went down on a knee and began to kiss her thighs, all the while sliding her panty hose down with a hand.

When they were all the way down, Misha could barely wait for Vera to step out of her shoes and slip the hose off her feet. He gazed at her pale golden mound, then his mouth inexorably found it, his tongue licking there, tasting her, adoring her, and finally entering her most private place, exploring it in a rapture of desire to have this woman, to know her as no other.

A quiver shot through Vera's entire body, and she didn't think she could wait another moment to have this man inside her. "Please," she rasped. "Oh, Misha, please . . ."

He quickly got to his feet and tore off his jacket, then practically ripped off his tie, suspenders, and shirt. He bent over, removing his shoes and socks, and then stood up and undid his trousers. His tumescence sprang out as his trousers slid to the floor. He was wearing no underwear.

Vera gasped aloud and reached out with a hand to touch his awesome manhood, encircling it, then stroking it. Misha jerked at her touch.

"Oh, my God," he groaned, "I've never been so excited in my life." He eased her down onto the couch, where she spread out ready to receive him, and he mounted her, both of them in a frenzy of desire such as they had never before known.

He rode her mercilessly, and she responded as she had never responded to anyone before, almost screaming as wave after wave of ecstatic spasms rent through her, carrying her, lifting her, to carnal heights she had only dreamed of before this night.

Misha suddenly stopped and groaned, then plunged in her to the hilt, unable to hold back any longer, almost bellowing as he released himself in her, in torrent after torrent, until his passion was spent. He collapsed atop her, hugging her to him almost violently, never wanting to let her go now that he had found her, already dreaming anxiously of the next time, and the next time after that.

Vera relished the weight of his body atop hers, the feel of him still inside her. She felt like a new and entirely different woman, fulfilled and complete, as if some vital missing part of the puzzle that was her being, her soul, had at last been found and made her whole. And she was certain that this was only the beginning, not the end.

Chapter Fourteen

"The Levin residence," Katya Petrovna said into the telephone receiver in her thickly accented Russian. She listened for a moment, then repeated the same litany she had been using day after day.

"I'm sorry, but no one is available at the moment. I will have to take your name and number and have someone get back to you as soon as possible." She then began scribbling furiously on a notepad in front of her on the desk.

"Yes, yes," she said. "*Ciao.*"

She replaced the receiver and looked up from the desk at Misha. Her beautiful face was tired, and her large brown eyes were beginning to lose some of their sparkle.

"Call number twenty-nine this morning," she said, brushing a tress of chestnut hair out of her eyes with a long, red-lacquered fingernail. She puckered her full, sensuous lips slightly. "It's unbelievable, this telephone. I don't have time to take a break."

"Who was it?" Misha asked, staring at the hint of cleavage exposed by the blouse she had unbuttoned as the morning wore on.

"A conductor," she said. "From . . . Munich." She slid her notepad across the desk to him. "There's the information," she said.

Misha glanced at it, then handed it back to her, looking into her heavily made-up eyes. "Listen, why don't you let the machine pick up for a while, Katya? Have a cup of coffee?"

"Do you want some, too?" she asked, smiling.

"Sure," Misha said.

Katya got up from behind the desk and headed for the kitchen.

Misha watched her go, taking pleasure in her movements. *She moves like a cat,* he thought. *A jungle cat, at that. Lithe, sensuous, and a little . . . predatory.*

He picked up her notepad and began flipping through it, looking at the list of this morning's calls. The telephone had been ringing off the hook for days, and Sonia had finally hired Katya Petrovna, a recent

Russian emigré she'd heard about through friends, to field calls. Agents, producers, recording company executives, entertainment lawyers, and promoters of every stripe had been relentless in their pursuit of Misha since the concert at Carnegie Recital Hall.

He tossed the notepad back on the desk again and walked to the kitchen, where Katya was making coffee. She looked up at him and smiled, holding up a hand and crooking a finger, summoning him to her. He walked over to her, and she put her arms around his waist, pulling him up against her.

"Ummm," she cooed, "you feel so nice, Misha."

He leaned down, kissing her neck, already aroused by her seductive wiles. He placed his hands on the kitchen counter, one to either side of her, virtually pinning her to the counter, pushing hard against her.

"Why don't we go upstairs?" he whispered, nibbling at her neck.

"We can't now," Katya said with a pout, pulling back from him. "Your mother will be home soon."

"Come on," Misha persisted, "we can hurry, like last time."

Suddenly Katya was all business. "No," she said, no longer teasing him. "I have to get back to work. You forget I need this job, and I don't want Sonia to be angry with me."

"Ah, shit," Misha swore, feeling the aching need in his groin.

"The coffee's ready," Katya said. "Let me go."

He pulled back, miffed with her for exciting him, and with himself for responding so quickly. He was even miffed with his mother for being due back home from her teaching duties at Julliard.

The buzzer sounded shrilly in the kitchen, startling them both, and Misha went to answer it while Katya poured their coffees.

"What is it, Sam?" he asked in an irritated voice while depressing the answer button.

"Visitor, Misha," the doorman answered. "It's Manny Cygelman."

"Send him on up," Misha said.

"You got it," Sam said.

Manny, along with Sasha, had become a fixture around the Levin household, but Sam never let even the most familiar face upstairs without first obtaining permission.

Misha turned and looked at Katya, but she seemed to be making a point of ignoring him. He sighed and went to the entry hall, where he unlocked the door and waited for Manny. He heard the elevator, and soon Manny stepped out of the car, dressed to the nines as usual.

"Well, old boy," he said in his most affected Etonian accent, "didn't catch you at a bad time, did I?"

"No, Manny," Misha said. "Come on in."

"I think you'll be glad I stopped by," Manny said.

"Where's Sasha?" Misha asked.

"He's at home, doing some paperwork for me," Manny said.

In the living room they sat on a couch, and Manny opened his brief-case and began riffling through papers. "I have some figures here that I want you to take a look at," he said.

Katya came in from the kitchen, two mugs of coffee in hand. "Hi, Manny," she said, greeting him like an old friend. He had been to the apartment nearly every day since she had begun working there. "Would you like some coffee?" she asked, handing Misha his.

"Please, Katya," he said, looking up. "That would be splendid."

"Lots of cream, two sugars?" she said.

"Lovely," Manny said, taking some papers out of the briefcase. He turned to Misha. "Look," he said. "Remember that recording deal I dis-cussed with you? About BBR? Brighton Beach Recordings?"

"Yes," Misha said. "What about it?"

"Take a look at these figures," Manny said. He handed Misha a sheet of paper with figures and notations carefully jotted down in black ink. "This," he said, putting his index finger on a heavily circled figure, "is the advance they're offering." He looked at Misha, a Cheshire cat's grin spreading across his lips.

Misha looked up at him, a surprised expression on his face. "You've got to be kidding," he said quietly.

Manny shook his head. "No," he said, "I'm not kidding."

"But this is fantastic!" Misha said excitedly, realization beginning to dawn. "More than I ever dreamed of!"

Katya came back in with Manny's coffee and handed it to him.

"Thanks, Katya," he said.

"You're welcome," she replied, and went back over to the desk, where she started playing messages back and taking notes.

"I think you'll like the royalty rate, too," Manny said smugly. He pointed at another circled figure.

"Manny!" Misha threw his arms around his friend's neck and hugged him, slapping him on the back. "You're hired!" he cried. "You're hired!"

"Ah, ah, God!" Manny gasped. "Let go, Misha! You're squeezing the life out of me! You'll make me spill my coffee!"

Misha slapped him on the back once more, then let him go. "This is fantastic! How did you do it?"

Manny set down his coffee, then straightened his tie and patted down the fringe of hair that circled his nearly bald pate. "Well, old boy," he said, recovering his dignity. "It wasn't easy, let me tell you. It wasn't easy. And I had a little help from old Sasha, you know."

They heard the front door open, and Sonia walked in, carrying a brief-case and a shopping bag. "Manny!" she said. "What a surprise! Or have you moved in?" She winked at him playfully.

"Hi, Sonia," he said, getting to his feet. They exchanged kisses on both cheeks, in the Continental fashion. "Just stopped by with some fig-ures for Misha to look at."

"Oh," she said, "so he's finally hired you to represent him?"

"Well," Manny said with a shrug, "not exactly. I mean, he hasn't signed on the dotted line or anything."

Sonia set down her briefcase and shopping bag, and sat down in an armchair, kicking off her shoes.

"Look, Mama," Misha said, getting up and going to her with Manny's figures in hand.

"What?" she said. "No kiss?"

Misha dutifully bent and gave her a peck on the cheek.

"That's better," she said, smiling. She took the proffered sheet of paper from him, then sat studying it for some time. Finally, she looked up at Manny, not her son, her face blank, impossible to read.

"How did you get these figures out of BBR if you don't even represent Misha?" she asked pointedly.

Manny's eyes fluttered and were downcast for a moment. "Well . . . I . . . I told them that . . . that he'd signed with me," he stuttered.

Sonia nodded. "I thought as much," she said. Then she turned her gaze on Misha. "You've had telephone calls from the most important agents in the world," she said, speaking as if Manny wasn't in the room. "They all want to represent you."

Misha nodded. "Yes," he said. "That's right."

"Have you made up your mind what you want to do?" she asked.

"I think so," he said, nodding again.

"And are you going to do what you discussed with your father and my-self last night?" she asked.

"Yes," Misha said, smiling now.

"Good," Sonia said, returning his smile. "I think you've made a very wise decision, Misha."

"I do, too, Mama," he said.

"Do you think perhaps it's time to make it public?" she asked.

"Yes," he said.

Misha turned to Manny, who had sat watching the two of them, a puzzled expression on his face.

"Manny," Misha said solemnly, "I want to sign on the dotted line. I want you to be my agent."

Manny made an effort to conceal his undiluted glee, wanting to appear to be accustomed to such victories, but he couldn't pull it off. His face lit up with a grin from ear to ear. He rose to his feet, walking over to Misha. Throwing his arms around him, he hugged him tightly. "You don't have to sign anything," he said. "Why don't we just shake on it?" He drew back and put out his plump hand.

Misha clasped it in his and shook it vigorously.

Sonia watched the two of them, tears of joy threatening to spill from her eyes. It gave her such joy to see the two of them together, so young, so earnest, so ambitious, and working toward a mutual goal. She rose to her feet, and they turned to her.

"Another kiss," she said. "Both of you." She held her arms out, and they went into them, kissing her and laughing.

"Ah!" she said, laughing with them. "You're good boys." Then she looked at Manny. "You were very clever to tell those record company people you already represented Misha, but I just want to know one more thing, Emmanuel Cygelman."

"What's that, Sonia?" he asked.

"What were you doing in that gym that day you met Misha?" She lightly patted Manny's ample belly with a hand.

Manny suddenly turned sheepish, and he swallowed. "I . . . I was . . . I was trying to meet Misha," he said.

"I knew it," she said. "I just knew it. You're every bit as smart as I thought you were."

Misha paced his bedroom, his face a constantly shifting mask of emotions as his thoughts shifted from argument to argument, weighing pros and cons, alternatives and approaches. He didn't yet know what he was going to do, but one thing he knew for certain: *I have to get out of this apartment,* he thought.

He tore off his sweatshirt and flung it to the floor, where it joined a pile of soiled athletic clothing. He pulled off his high-top Nikes and sweat socks, tossing them across the room, then got out of his sweatpants and jockstrap. Ditto.

His normally clean and ordered bedroom was clearly an indication of his frazzled frame of mind at the present. Rollerblades, sneakers, boots, shoes, socks, underwear, gym clothes, CDs, cassettes, books, magazines, music scores, helmets, knee pads, shin guards, wrist guards, gloves—all the necessities and amenities of daily life were strewn about the room in a chaotic mess, unsorted, dirty, and almost too overwhelming to deal with right now.

Sonia and Dmitri, God love them, he thought, were driving him to distraction. He knew that they loved him. He knew that they wanted what was best for him. *But,* he thought grimly, *but right now, all of that love, all those good intentions, mean nothing in light of the fact that their hovering presence is making me crazy!*

It was all too much. He felt that he had no privacy whatsoever, that he was intruded upon by their constant attention to his needs. Sometimes he felt as if he couldn't breathe, that he was being smothered by their unflagging devotion to him and his career.

In all fairness, he knew that their hovering over him had not always been so objectionable, that he had needed it, had appreciated it—still did, for that matter—but now he was a different person. A grown-up. An eighteen-year-old man embarking on a career of his own. An eighteen-year-old man embarking on a whole new life of his own. A life that included . . . sex.

And that was the crux of the problem as he saw it. Certainly, it posed the largest part of the problem he had with his parents.

I'm horny! he realized. *I'm horny and . . . loving it!*

And horny, he decided, most definitely did *not* fit well with Sonia and Dmitri and the large, comfortable two-bedroom apartment the three of them shared. No, indeed. In fact, Misha thought, there wasn't an apartment anywhere in the world that was big enough to contain the three of them.

What was the use of having the seductive and available Katya around if they constantly had to be on their guard because Dmitri or Sonia might return from work at any moment? Like the other day, when they'd both been naked, going at it like proverbial rabbits, lost in their lusty pursuit of pleasure, and what should happen?

Dmitri had waltzed in. Unannounced and unexpected. Miraculously, they'd somehow managed to throw on their clothes before he'd come knocking on Misha's door, but the look on Dmitri's face when the door had been opened and he faced the two of them standing there in embarrassed dishevelment had said everything. Shock, disappointment, disapproval, and—the most painful to see—hurt, all mixed into a single expression that Misha would not soon forget. Although there had been no further discussion of the matter, Misha knew that Dmitri was no fool.

He had to be aware of what was going on but had apparently decided, for the time being at least, not to mention the subject.

Now, of course, Katya was being difficult, making herself less available, because she was afraid that Sonia and Dmitri would dismiss her if they thought the sexcapades between her and Misha continued. Her new, cool demeanor toward Misha, whether his parents were there or not, was driving him to distraction. Having once tasted of that particular bit of forbidden fruit, Misha was hard put not to try to partake of its succulent flesh again and again, especially considering that Katya was an almost continuous presence in the apartment.

If his problems with Katya and his parents at home were driving him crazy, his difficulties with Vera were even worse. He was drawn to her as a moth to the flame, desiring her in ways he had never desired anyone else, enjoying her company as he had never enjoyed another's.

Vera, however, was herself a very complicated young lady, with an insightful intelligence that was a constant challenge to his own. Getting to know her, blunt as she could be, was like peeling the skin from an onion, layer by layer, constantly searching for the real Vera, trying to make sense of the bundle of contradictions, the multiplicity of thoughts and feelings, that she seemed to be.

Vera Bunim, he thought, was much more than a quick roll in the hay, unlike Katya, and despite that first night together—the night they had met—Misha was certain that it was not in Vera's nature to make casual sex a habit. That night had been a fluke. That night, she'd told him, had been different because they had been attracted to each other, of course, and even though they'd never met, they did have a history of sorts together. She'd known about the Russian prodigy her family was helping since he'd been six years old, and she'd followed the Levin family's progress all the way up to the night of his Carnegie Recital Hall debut, the night they'd first made love.

The night we first made love, he thought. *But was it love?*

Trying to clear his mind of these thoughts, Misha went into the bathroom, where he turned the shower on, adjusting the taps so that the water was refreshingly cool. He stepped in and lathered up, but he still couldn't stop thinking about Vera, try as he might.

God, it was all so complicated, he thought.

Even their lovemaking—the stolen moments they'd had since that first night—was an exercise in subterfuge, a constant test of their resourcefulness, their abilities to find ways, time, and places to meet.

While Dmitri and Sonia encouraged Misha to see Vera—were in fact delighted in what they suspected was a budding romance—they would not have thought a sexual relationship between the two of them was wise at this juncture in their lives. After all, Misha and Vera were only eighteen years old—too young and inexperienced to settle down, and they were both just embarking on careers. Vera, as far as they were concerned, would someday make the perfect daughter-in-law, but they saw that day but dimly, in the distant future, after Misha's name was made and his career flourished.

Ivan and Tatiana Bunim, on the other hand, had no objection to Vera and Misha becoming friends, but the idea of a romance between the two was repugnant. If their beautiful daughter wanted to have a sexual dalliance with the young emigré—if she thought of sex with him as one might think of an after-dinner mint—fine. But the Bunims would be shocked to learn of a budding romance between the two young people. For Misha Levin, with all his fine attributes, was, as far as they were concerned, not marriage material for their daughter.

Though he was a Jew of Russian extraction, he was straight off the boat, so to speak. They felt a powerful need to distance themselves as much as possible from the shtetls of Mother Russia. In the inevitable pecking order that was intrinsic to international society, Ivan and Tatiana had always known—indeed, much to their chagrin—that they didn't rank at the very top echelon and never would, no matter how hard they tried, no matter how much money they made and gave away. They were determined, however, that Vera would be accepted into this tier above them. In order for that to happen, she must marry exceedingly well.

If the groom-to-be was to be Jewish—and this was not a consideration of any importance to the Bunims—then it was imperative that he be a Jew of German extraction, and vastly rich. A Russian Jew would simply not do, looked down upon by Jews in international society as they were.

All of this and more Vera had gradually revealed to Misha during the last few weeks as they had become more and more familiar with each other, slowly becoming friends as well as lovers.

Vastly rich, Misha thought, rinsing his long black hair in the shower. That was, of course, the number one requirement for any prospective mate for Vera Bunim, regardless of religious background or country of origin.

He laughed aloud.

Rules me out, he thought. *I'll certainly never be rich enough, not the kind of money they're thinking about. And I'll never be anything but Russian.*

Well, he didn't really care right now. He turned the shower off and stepped out, grabbing a towel and starting to dry off.

It's all just as well, he thought, vigorously toweling his muscular legs. *They can have all their stupid social prejudices. Because I'm sure not ready to settle down yet. I want to experience everything there is out there before I commit myself to anyone. Even someone like Vera.*

His athletic body dry now, he dried his hair with the towel and shaved and brushed his teeth. Looking in the bathroom mirror, he liked what he saw reflected there and understood why women liked it, too. Vera included.

And, he thought, smiling at his image, *I'd like to have a whole lot more of that appreciative female attention before I get tied down with anybody.*

Walking back into the bedroom, he opened the closet door and began searching for just the right thing to wear for tonight's date. He liked to dress carefully for Vera, even if it was for the most casual occasion, because of his own innate sense of pride and vanity, and because Vera herself always made a special effort for him.

Besides, he thought, *there probably won't be too many more nights like this before I leave. Before I'm off touring the world, playing my music, meeting all kinds of women.*

He put on a lightweight white linen Armani shirt—it showed off his tanned and glowing skin—and well-worn but pristine Levi's, snug ones that accentuated his body in all the right places. No underwear or socks, he decided, just the brown suede Gucci loafers and brown Barry Kieselstein-Cord belt, all topped off with his navy blue double-breasted blazer made of featherweight pashmina.

He looked in the full-length bedroom mirror and decided he looked cool. Real cool. Cosmopolitan yet casual. Fine for an informal summer dinner at a trendy restaurant and . . . ?

He didn't yet know. It depended on whether or not they had a place to go.

With that thought he made a grimace of distaste. His mind had come full circle, right back to the issue that preoccupied his mind so much lately. He needed his own space, away from his parents, where he could do anything he pleased, when he pleased.

"Ah, shit," he said aloud, frowning now. *Maybe . . . maybe I should just bite the bullet and go ahead and broach the subject with Dad. And Mama, too. See what they have to say.*

He glanced at his watch. Almost seven o'clock. He had plenty of time to talk to them before meeting Vera at eight-thirty. He took a deep breath and closed his eyes.

Arkady, he prayed, putting his hands together in a prayerful gesture, *please be there for me tonight. Please, please, please! Be there for me now.*

He went downstairs to the living room, where he saw Dmitri, sitting, his feet up on an ottoman, reading the *New York Times*. Summer light, coming through the enormous windows, suffused the double-height room with a soft glow. Sonia was not there. She was most likely in the kitchen, he supposed.

"Misha," Dmitri said, looking up from his newspaper. "Are you going out, son? You look nice. Where're you off to tonight?"

"Vera and I are going out to dinner," Misha replied, "and maybe take in a movie or something."

"Good," Dmitri said. "You two must be having fun together, huh?"

"Yes," Misha said, somewhat resentful of the question. He'd really rather not discuss his friendship with Vera—or anyone else—with his father.

Sonia walked into the room, a dishtowel in hand. "I thought I heard you," she said. She looked at him. "All dressed up, I see," she said. "Or sort of," she amended. "No tie, old jeans. Oh, and no socks! Is this a trend?"

"I don't know," Misha replied somewhat sullenly. "But it's *me*."

"Okay, okay," Sonia demurred. "It's you. I meant no offense, Misha." She paused, studying her son's face. "Off to see Vera?" she asked finally.

"Yes," he said.

"How nice," Sonia said with a smile, "that the two of you have become friends."

"Yeah," Misha said, "it is." He stood there a moment longer, trying to decide what to do. *Broach the subject now or not?* Then he took a seat in a chair near his father. *Might as well get it over with,* he thought. *What's to lose?*

"I wanted to discuss something with the two of you," he said.

Sonia heard the earnest tone of his voice and immediately sat down on a couch, wondering what he needed to talk about. Was he in trouble of some sort? Could he be getting cold feet about performing? Whatever it was, it must be serious, she thought, because Misha hadn't been discussing much of anything with the two of them lately.

"We're listening, Misha," Dmitri said. "You know you can tell us anything, son."

Misha looked at his father, then his mother, and took a deep breath. "I don't know how to say this," he said, "but lately I've been feeling like . . . well, like . . . I don't have enough privacy. I'm eighteen now, and beginning a new life. You know I love you both very much and appreciate how wonderful you've been to me."

He paused a moment, hanging his head, as if embarrassed by his honest expression of his love for them, his hands folded together between his knees.

"I just . . . I just . . . feel . . . ," he began.

"You want a place of your own, don't you?" Sonia said in a matter-of-fact voice.

Misha's head jerked up, and he looked at her wide-eyed. "I . . . I guess . . . that's . . . what . . . I," he said.

Sonia rose to her feet and went to the chair in which he sat. She perched on its overstuffed arm, sliding an arm of hers around her son's shoulder and hugging him. She patted his back and mussed his hair, then leaned down and planted a kiss on his forehead.

"Misha, Misha," she said. "You mustn't underestimate your mama. Nor your dad. And you mustn't be afraid or nervous, *ever*, to talk to us."

He looked up at her with his dark eyes.

"Of course it's time you got your own place," Sonia continued. "As much as we hate to see you go, as much as we'll miss you sometimes."

Would this woman never fail to surprise him? "Do you really mean it, Mama?" he asked quietly, a look of wonder on his face.

"Yes," Sonia said. "Why else would I have talked to real estate agents already? Why else would I have already seen the perfect place for you in the Hotel des Artistes?"

"You've got to be kidding," he said in amazement.

"No," Sonia said. "Your father and I have been discussing it now for several weeks. We decided it will be affordable, and that . . . well, it's time, much as we hate to face it."

Misha looked at his father, who nodded his head. "She's right, Misha," he said, the glimmer of a smile on his lips.

"Then you really don't mind?" Misha said.

"Noooo," Sonia said, looking at him affectionately and squeezing his shoulder. "We really don't. But, please. Just promise me two things, if you will," she added.

"What?" Misha asked.

"That you'll show all of your friends," Sonia said, "the same respect that you've always shown us. Including your girlfriends. Especially your girlfriends."

Misha nodded and smiled. "What else?" he asked.

"That you'll be careful," she said, "and use protection."

"Protec . . . ?" Misha began, then slowly shut his mouth. He didn't know whether he should laugh or cry. How well these parents of his knew him! How understanding they were, and giving. And, of course, prying and intrusive also. Finally, he emitted a laugh, then was joined by Dmitri and Sonia, and the three of them laughed together, heartily, merrily, and as one.

Chapter Fifteen

Vera rolled over on her stomach and put an arm across Misha's hard, washboard stomach, looking up into his dark eyes. Her disheveled, pale hair hung loose, flowing just below her creamy shoulders.

Misha looked down at her and smiled.

They had been to dinner at Da Silvano in Greenwich Village, then had walked hand in hand to West Twentieth Street in Chelsea, where Priscilla Cavanaugh, a friend of Vera's, had a loft. Priscilla had let them borrow it, with a warning to be out by midnight.

"It feels so good to be with you," Misha said to her softly, stroking her hair as she stroked his chest.

"Likewise," Vera said, thinking what an understatement that was, for her at least. She'd never felt this happy, this content, *this right*, with anyone before. She was, in fact, astonished with her own feelings, never having experienced them before, and a little scared, if truth be told, because she didn't feel in control of her runaway emotions. She felt subjugated by them, at their mercy, and for Vera Bunim, the cool and intellectual woman that she was, that was truly frightening.

Misha continued stroking her hair. "What are you thinking about?" he asked.

"Ummm," she murmured. "Nothing, really."

"Come on," Misha said. "I know you better than that, and I know you've got something on your mind. Tell me."

"Oh," Vera said, "I was just thinking about how different this is. I mean, you and me."

"How?" Misha asked. "How different?"

"Just . . . well . . . it's more satisfying," Vera said, afraid to share with him the real depths of the emotions she was feeling. "It seems like it's more than just . . . more than just . . . sex." She looked up at him. "Do you know what I mean?"

Misha hugged her. "Yes," he said. "I don't feel like I've ever known

anybody as well as I know you. Or felt as comfortable with anybody else."
He laughed. "And the sex isn't bad, either!"

Vera joined in his laughter. "The sex is the best!" she said, tweaking
one of his nipples. Then in a softer, more serious voice, she said: "It's
never been like this for me before. Not even close."

Misha looked at her curiously. "What was it like?" he asked. "I mean
with the others? Before?"

Vera looked thoughtful for a moment, then shrugged. "The first few
times it was really awful," she said. "So fumbling and awkward. So messy!"
She giggled. "And the boy! Arrrgh! Terrible, poor thing!"

Misha laughed with her. "Who was he?" he asked.

"Jamie Croft-Milnes," she said. "Lord Rowlandseer, he was. The future
Earl of Something. I was about fifteen and so was he. It was at a big house
party at his family's estate in England. Kent. You know, a bunch of young
aristocrats and rich Americans, mostly. Experimenting with sex and drugs.
Neither one of us was sure exactly what to do." She laughed again. "It
was all so embarrassing."

"And then?" Misha asked. "Who else?"

"Antonio," Vera said. "An Italian guy I met in Gstaad on a skiing
trip."

"And was it good?" Misha asked.

Vera looked at him. "You're being awfully nosy," she said teasingly. "I
don't know if I should be telling you these things."

"Oh, come on," Misha said. "I want to know everything about you,
Vera."

"Well . . . ," she hesitated.

"I'll tell *you*," Misha said, grinning. "All about my own sordid past."

"Promise?" Vera asked.

"Promise," he said.

"Well, Antonio was fun," she said. "And experienced. Probably with
about every girl in Switzerland." She laughed. "He was very energetic,
but he was also gentle. He helped me overcome my fears and shyness and
to enjoy it." She looked at Misha. "But I knew it meant nothing with
him. It wasn't even a crush. It was just . . ."

"Fucking?" Misha supplied.

"Exactly," she said.

"And then?" he persisted.

"Well, I dated a lot of guys, but there was nobody serious," she said.
"The only other person I had a . . . well, a sort of a fling with was Simon.
A guy I dated in England." She turned suddenly quiet.

"Go on," Misha said. "What about this Simon?"

"Oh, we met at a party in London," she said with a sigh. "He's an artist. A painter. Studies at Slade. Very good-looking. Very intense. Very macho and *very* possessive. It was . . . interesting, at first. You know?"

Misha nodded. "I think so."

"It was all so new to me," she went on. "His sort of man, I mean. He had a motorcycle and a black leather jacket and all that," she said. "Sort of a rebel, I guess. But the macho attitude got to be unbearable, *and* the possessiveness. He went nuts if I so much as even looked at another man. I swore never again."

She looked up at him and shrugged again. "And that's really it," she said. "Till there was you."

Misha smiled and hugged her to him, kissing her on the forehead. "Till there was me," he said softly. "And you," he added, his lips brushing her eyes, her nose, and then her mouth.

Vera responded immediately, swept up on a tide of passion, of desire, of hunger for this man. "Oh," she whispered, "I'm going to miss you so much when you're on tour."

"I'll miss you, too," Misha said, his mouth moving down to her neck, where he licked and kissed her. "But I haven't left yet. We've got a little more time. Besides, I'll be able to see you in London, and I'll be coming back to New York regularly, so we won't be separated for too long."

His kisses became more urgent, and his hands went to her breasts, but then Vera jerked back. "Oh, Misha!" she exclaimed. "It's . . . it's so scary."

"What?" he asked. "What's so scary?"

"Just thinking about being separated from you," she said. "I know it hasn't been long, but I think . . . I think I'm in love with you." She looked into his eyes, afraid of what she would see there and already sorry that she had voiced such a revelation. The last thing she wanted to do was scare him off with what might appear to be a demand on his affections.

Misha looked thoughtfully off into the distance, his expression difficult to read. Finally, he hugged her and said, "I honestly don't know what I feel, Vera." He met her gaze. "I know you're a great friend, and I love being with you. But I really don't know what else to say."

"It's okay, Misha," she said softly.

He sighed. "Except I do know that I'm going to be putting my career before everything else for a while." He gave her a meaningful look.

"I understand," Vera said, nodding her head slightly. She hoped that her face didn't reflect the turmoil that she felt, the sadness that wrenched her heart in two.

If only he could have told me that he loves me, too, she thought miserably.

While she appreciated his being forthcoming with her, his honesty was little compensation for the profound sorrow she felt.

He kissed her tenderly, but she pulled away. "What?" he asked, reluctantly parting his lips from hers. "What is it?"

"What time is it?" she asked.

He looked at his wristwatch and grimaced. "Oh, God, no," he moaned. "Twenty of twelve."

"We're going to have to hurry," Vera said. "Before Priscilla gets back." She rolled away from him and sat up in bed. "She'll be furious if we're still here when she gets home. She's got some new boyfriend, and she plans on having quite a night with him."

"This is hell," Misha said. "Pure unadulterated hell."

She turned and looked at him. "Yes," she said gloomily, "it is." Then she brightened. "But just think, Misha! Soon you may have your own place. And I'll have one of my own in London, too."

"Not soon enough," he groused, sitting up beside her. Then he leaned over and kissed the pulsating artery on her neck. "Not soon enough."

They got out of bed and dressed quickly, then straightened the disheveled comforter on the bed. Misha took her in his arms and held her tightly.

Vera looked up at him and smiled. "You know what?" she said.

"What?" he asked.

"You didn't tell me about *your* sordid past," she said, tapping his nose with a fingertip.

"Next time," Misha said with a grin. "I promise."

"I'm going to hold you to it," Vera said. "I want to know everything there is to know about you, too."

"You will," he said. He kissed her passionately, then drew back. "I hate having to part this way," he said bitterly.

"We must," Vera said, "but only for now. It won't be for long."

I wish that we would never have to part, Vera thought. *I wish we could always be together.* But even as swept up in the emotional maelstrom that this love was for her, she knew that she could not have what she wanted. At least not now, when they were so young and inexperienced. Vera, however, felt certain that someday in the future, when the time was right, she would have what she wanted.

And that, of course, was Misha Levin.

Chapter Sixteen

London, 1990

Her flat in London's once bohemian but now highly fashionable and exclusive Chelsea district was in Cheyne Walk, inarguably one of London's most sought-after addresses. The house itself was a grand nineteenth-century limestone mansion that had been broken up into large, airy apartments at the turn of the century.

Although she would have preferred living in a younger, hipper neighborhood, like the trendy Notting Hill area, Vera did not want to appear to be ungrateful to her parents by complaining that the accommodations they had bought for her were ridiculously lavish for a student. She did, however, harbor a resentment toward their generosity, since it undeniably gave them a hold over her. Also, she found Angus, the live-in manservant they'd hired to see to her needs, an intrusion into her privacy. He was a powerfully built middle-aged man who, oddly, had been well trained as both a butler and a security expert.

Vera had laughingly told friends, "He knows how to serve a drink and cripple your best friend—all in one fell swoop!"

Though said jokingly, it was nevertheless true, and made her feel eerily uncomfortable.

Finally she'd resigned herself to her parents' well-meaning protective measures—and had reached a truce of sorts with Angus regarding her personal life. Through compromise she had enjoyed the last four years in London, first studying art history at the Corthault Institute, now getting a graduate diploma in fine and decorative arts from Christie's and the Royal Society of the Arts.

Seated in her library, a large room with antique mahogany floor-to-ceiling bookcases and walls covered in hunter green felt, Vera was working diligently on a paper that was soon due. Her desk, a George I yew and mahogany table, was piled high with books and papers, and faced the wall, a necessity as she became too easily distracted by window views or perspectives into her other rooms.

She put down her pen and rubbed her bleary eyes with her fingers. She'd been at it for about two hours already, and was tiring. As she glanced up at the wall, a welcoming pleasure suffused her with its warmth.

For above the desk hung a bulletin board, and pinned over its entirety were postcards from all over the world: Vienna, Prague, Budapest, Berlin, Copenhagen, Helsinki, Paris, Munich, Geneva, Rome, Venice, Madrid, Lisbon, Sydney, Capetown, Nairobi, Tokyo. Many of them were typical pictures of tourist attractions in the various cities—palaces, opera houses, performing arts centers, that sort of thing—but where possible, Misha had sent her rather risqué and sometimes downright silly cards. From Capetown, Nairobi, and Sydney there were photographs of copulating animals—frogs, hyenas, and zebras. From Paris there was a photograph of turn-of-the-century prostitutes, posing provocatively in antiquated-looking maillots, garters, and hose.

How like Misha! she thought with warm amusement. *Who else's taste runs the gamut from the grandest of palaces to the very sleazy all the way to unquestionably plain bad taste.*

But good taste or bad, she loved them all, especially the vulgar ones. In the last four years, since he had been on his world tours—playing the piano to great acclaim—the two of them had corresponded almost religiously, sending each other weekly, sometimes even daily, updates on their lives. Thus they chronicled their ups and downs, oftentimes divulged the quotidian details of their daily lives, the parties, the concerts, the people they met, and to some extent their emotional lives.

She reached out to an ivory-veneered box and opened the lid. Inside, it was stuffed full of letters. These letters and postcards had kept them in touch with each other, serving almost as a kind of therapy. When Misha grew lonely on the road, his notes to and from Vera helped fill the emptiness he often felt, especially during the long nights in anonymous hotel rooms. For Vera the notes served much the same purpose. She had found that in many of the social situations into which she was constantly being thrust by her family and friends, she sometimes became lonely. It didn't matter that she was being exposed to a constant stream of new and interesting people, many of whom wanted to become friends. She felt that her life was being misspent in some way, that she was wasting precious time. She knew the answer to this dilemma: she was without Misha.

She pushed her chair back from the table, deciding that she had done enough work on her paper today. Her work on the history of furniture and the decorative arts at Christie's and the Royal Society of the Arts was soon drawing to a close, and she was going to finish in the top of her class, no mean accomplishment. She could hardly wait to begin to apply some of the knowledge she had acquired, hopefully working for one of the major auction houses, either Sotheby's or Christie's in New York or London. Her father had assured her that she would have no trouble getting such a job, since he was a stockholder in one of the companies and a highly valued customer of them both. Besides, she was more than qualified.

At this point in time she had a powerful urge to get on with her life. Now that school was nearly over, she hoped that a job, whatever it turned out to be, would be fulfilling—and that a job *alone*, for a while at least, would be fulfilling for her. For she knew that Misha, despite their four-year, oftentimes long-distance friendship and the intimate sexual liaisons they scheduled whenever possible, was still not ready to make a commitment to her or—thank God!—to anyone else.

Vera knew now, more than ever, that she was still in love with him. Her love for him had only grown in the last four years. A part of her was waiting—and waiting, waiting, *waiting!*—for him to ultimately come to the decision that she was the one.

"Ma'am?"

Vera was startled from her reverie by Angus, who had appeared at the library door on whispery feet. *How does he do it?* she wondered for the thousandth time. *He's as big as a truck, but moves like a ballerina.*

She looked over at him, standing there waiting in such repose, such self-possession. "What is it, Angus?" she asked.

"There's a telephone call for you on line one," he said. "The young man."

She knew who he meant, and her heart jumped with excitement. "Thanks, Angus," she said. "I'll take it in here."

Angus turned and disappeared down the hallway, toward the kitchen.

She had all the telephones turned off while she worked, except for the one in the kitchen, which she couldn't hear, and Angus knew to interrupt her only if her father or mother, Misha, or Simon called.

She picked up the receiver on her desk. "Hello?" she said.

"Hey," the gravelly baritone answered. "You coming over tonight?"

"Yes," Vera said. "I'll probably leave here in about an hour. Okay?"

"See you then."

"Bye," Vera said, but the phone had already been hung up at the other end.

She replaced the receiver in its cradle and sat thinking, knowing that she should go upstairs and bathe and dress for her date—if that's what it could be called—but she wasn't quite ready to yet. She idly wondered if she really wanted to go out at all, asking herself if it wouldn't be smarter just to stay at home tonight. She often questioned if it was wise to be seeing this man.

She knew that Misha sometimes went out with other women, and he knew about her men as well. After all, his dates were chronicled in the gossip magazines and in society columns on both sides of the Atlantic, as were hers. They had often discussed some of the speculation written about them in the press, laughing, enjoying the often ridiculous assumptions made by the reporters. She'd found that they both had fallen into the habit of reassuring the other that the latest "love interest," as reported in the press, was no more than an acquaintance, someone just met, someone publicists had attempted to create a stir with; in short, never anyone to be concerned about.

"Oh, *her*," Misha had said just the other night. "Her father is a big patron of the arts in Italy, and Manny introduced me to her. He thought it would be smart to be seen out with her. You know. Stir up a lot of interest, since she's a big fashion model and all."

"She certainly is beautiful," Vera had said.

"Yes," Misha allowed, "but there's not much upstairs. You know what I mean?"

"Yes," Vera said, thinking that it often wasn't what was upstairs that interested men so much as what was downstairs.

"What about this Hugh . . . Whoever?" Misha had asked. "I saw your picture in *Hello* magazine with him. At some party."

"Oh, you know, Misha," Vera replied. "He owns an art gallery here in London. My family knows him. I go to parties with him sometimes when he needs a beard."

"Oh, so he's gay?" Misha asked.

"Yes," she said. "He's had the same boyfriend for years."

They'd had this conversation and so many like it over the years, she thought, that they both seemed to run on automatic pilot when the discussion veered this way.

Most of the time, Vera wasn't particularly concerned about these people they were both photographed with, but sometimes she did worry that one of the beautiful young women to whom he was constantly being introduced would finally steal Misha's heart away. That one of the inevitable one-night stands he had while on tour—and she was certain he must have them—would prove to be her nemesis. She was also certain that there were women he didn't tell her about in his notes, women who didn't appear in the pages of the international gossip reporters, somehow having escaped notice, closely as they followed him.

Secrets.

She smiled now, thinking of her own little secret, unmeaningful though he may be in the long run, certainly as far as Misha was concerned.

Simon Hampton.

Her rebel lover had been back in her life again for some time now, his possessive macho behavior tempered to some extent—chastened, she thought, by her refusal to see him for so long—but his demands as a lover were as rigorous, as energetic and creative, as they had always been.

Very simply put, she thought, *Simon is damn good sex, and he's always ready and willing.*

It was principally because of Simon that she had finally arrived at a sort of truce with Angus, the ever-present manservant. As they had come to know each other a little better and develop a degree of trust—and after a very long heart-to-heart talk—Angus had decided to look the other way when she disappeared for a few hours or perhaps the night, as long as she let him know that she would be at Simon's. She had offered Angus money for his silence, for she knew that he reported to her father, but Angus, mysterious sphinx that he was, had refused the cash. He would cooperate with her—and cover for her—as long as he knew where she was.

She was well aware that Angus did not like Simon, though they had met only briefly. She thought, in fact, that Angus disapproved of him. Yet he seemed to understand that Vera, whatever her reasons might be, must see the somewhat surly young man from time to time, and Angus saw that she came to no obvious harm as a result.

Had he asked Vera why she saw Simon, she could only have responded that he was sexually exciting. Simon was like the after-dinner mint that her mother often spoke of when she referred to certain men as sex toys, no more, certainly not marriageable. Vera's trysts with him were for her simply a release, a convenient arrangement whereby she could have most of her physical needs fulfilled without any strings attached, without the prying press knowing about it—and without Misha knowing. They always met at his seedy loft, and never went out in public, staying in, away from the glare of photographers' flashbulbs. She enjoyed these trysts, if truth be told, for Simon's intensity and his devotion to his painting—and his sensuality—never failed to remind her of Misha.

My *little secret*, she thought again, getting to her feet and walking upstairs to her bedroom to get ready. *I wish I didn't need him, but I do.*

Chapter Seventeen

❧

New York, 1992

Manny sat on the bed, sipping a gin and tonic, the telephone at his ear as Misha finished getting dressed.

"Look, Sol," Manny said with exasperation, putting his drink down on the bedside table, "if I've told you once, I've told you a thousand times. Misha is booked solid for that month. We've got commitments over two *years* down the road!"

Misha watched Manny's reflection through the mirror, where he stood putting in his shirt studs. Handsome solid gold knots that matched his cuff links. A gift from Vera a couple of years ago, when he'd played a concert in London at the Albert Hall. Finished, he put the gold cuff links on and tucked in his shirt, a white voile Gianfranco Ferré with elaborate but subtle white embroidery on the front. A gift from his parents. Taking one of his many black silk bow ties, he carefully tied it just so, in a perfect bow, the result of many years of practice, then stood back and studied his reflection.

Not bad, he thought. *Uh-oh. My cummerbund.*

He retrieved it from the mahogany valet where he had carefully draped it, and put it on, stepping up to the mirror again to make certain its black silk was centered perfectly.

There. Done. Or almost.

He turned around, looking at Manny, who was practically shouting into the telephone receiver at this point. His face was flushed beet red, and any pretense at sounding like an aristocratic Englishman was completely gone from his voice now. Misha never failed to find amusement in his voice's inevitable return to the streets of Brooklyn when he became excited.

He looked over at Sasha and grinned. Sasha returned it and shook his head, as if to indicate that nothing Manny said or did surprised him.

"How many times do I have to tell you, Sol! The answer is no. *N-o*," he spelled out. "I told you a long time ago that you'd have to commit by last spring. Last spring! Well, my friend, summer's here. It's too fucking late. *Capische!*"

He listened for a moment then slammed down the receiver without another word. He looked up at Misha. "What a schmuck," he cried. "He just won't listen!" He picked up his drink and took a long sip.

"Don't worry so much, Manny," Misha said. "You've got me booked for practically the rest of my life. I don't know how you do it, but whatever it is, it works."

Manny looked at him with a pleased expression on his face.

"Mama said she was in Tower Records the other day," Misha continued, "and they had my new CD displayed—guess where?"

"Where?" Manny asked, although he already knew the answer to the question.

"Between Madonna's new CD and the new one by the three tenors. At the counter and in special bins. Can you believe it?" Misha laughed. "I may have helped create a kind of mystique and a lady-killer image in the press. But the distribution deal you worked out with those people—whoever they are—is really fantastic. How the hell did you do it?"

Manny dismissed the question with an eloquent shrug. "Just leave all that to me," Manny said, exchanging a look with Sasha. "You don't have to worry about it."

"I'm just curious," Misha said. "It's amazing how little of the business end of things I know about. If something happened to you, I'd be lost. I wouldn't know anything."

"Well, nothing's going to happen to me," Manny said with an easy smile. "So forget about it. Even if it did, Sasha here could handle anything. Right, Sasha?"

Sasha nodded his head. "I know what's going on. I can deal with it. Don't forget, Misha, we're both failed classical pianists. So we do know a little bit about the business, even if we weren't good enough to play professionally."

"If you say so," Misha said.

"I say so," Manny retorted. "And Sasha's right. We may not have made it as concert pianists, but we know the business inside out."

Misha supposed he should listen to Manny. After all, money had been pouring in for the last four years, reaching a point now that he had never expected to achieve. Manny had set up his own record label, Brighton Beach, named for that section of Brooklyn that had become so heavily populated by Russian emigrés. Misha knew that Manny and Sasha had worked out some sort of a distribution deal with longtime Brighton

Beach acquaintances who were like them: young men of Russian descent on their way up. Idly, Misha wondered about them. He knew that there was an active Russian mob of some sort based in Brighton Beach, but he'd never really questioned Manny or Sasha about their business methods or their connections. He just took satisfaction in knowing that his recordings were in stores everywhere and were getting prime retail space.

Misha went to the closet and retrieved the black tuxedo jacket that matched his trousers. It was one of the double-breasted summer-weight ones made especially for him by Versace in Milan. He slipped it on and looked in the mirror.

"That looks capital," Manny enthused, recovered from his telephone battle, his British aplomb fully restored. "Even if it didn't come from Savile Row. I must say, Versace did a bang-up job, old chap."

"It does look good, doesn't it," Misha replied. He turned around. "What do you think, Sasha?"

"You look perfect," Sasha said.

"Well, you two about ready to go?" he asked.

"Yes," Manny said. "Whenever you are."

"Let's go downstairs," Misha said. "I think I'll have a drink, too, before we go."

"*You?*" Manny said, arching a brow. "Have a drink *before* the party?"

"Yes," Misha replied. "I think I'll need it tonight."

They left Misha's spacious balcony bedroom and walked downstairs to the living room, where Misha spread out on a sumptuous couch and Manny and Sasha sat opposite him in antique chairs. Over the years his apartment in the Hotel des Artistes had become a repository of the many purchases he'd made during his travels around the world. The double-height living room, much like the one in his parents' apartment a few blocks away, was dominated by the back-to-back ebony Steinway concert grand pianos, placed to take advantage of the light from the floor-to-ceiling windows. Suspended from the heights of the ceiling was a magnificent crystal chandelier he had bought in Venice, and on the floor was an antique Heriz rug, its once intense colors muted by years of wear and exposure to the light. Just the way he liked it. At one end of the room was a huge fireplace of carved stone, over which hung a heavily carved antique gilt mirror, also found in Venice. The chairs and couches were nearly all big and comfortable, covered in suedes, leathers, and tapestries, and antique occasional tables laden with bibelots and pictures were scattered about the room.

He had decorated the room himself, with Vera's advice from time to time about placement and her fine editorial eye, and he was immensely proud of it. It was chock full of antique furniture, objets d'art, and luxurious textiles, yet it was still a room that you could relax in, that you weren't afraid to put your feet up in. It also had an unmistakably masculine air about it, despite its treasures. Exquisite two-hundred-year-old neoclassical Italian chairs were covered in the softest leather as opposed to a silk brocade or damask, and the colors were dark and rich rather than soft pastels.

He got up and went to an Italian Empire console of fruitwood and gilt, and poured himself a scotch. He put in a few ice cubes from the silver bucket and poured in a dash of water, stirring it with a finger.

He turned to Manny and Sasha. "Do you two want more gin and tonic?" he asked.

"I'll get it," Manny said, heading for the table.

Misha sank onto a down-filled couch covered with soft chocolate-colored suede, kicked off his black-bowed, patent-leather slip-on shoes, and put his feet up on the heavy Giacometti glass-and-bronze coffee table.

The telephone bleated, and Misha sighed. "Jesus, not again," he complained.

"I'll get it," Manny said. He picked up the nearest receiver. "Hello?"

Misha looked over at Manny, who put his hand over the receiver. "It's Rachel," he said. "I'll just be a minute." Rachel was Manny and Sasha's very aggressive and very efficient secretary, one of the few people who had this number.

"Take your time," Misha said, waving a hand.

Sasha got up and went over to the drinks table, where he made gin and tonics for both himself and Manny. He set Manny's down beside him, then returned to his chair and sat sipping his drink silently.

Misha's eyes swept the room, relishing its opulent comfort and its quiet, only Manny's soft chatter in the background. It was good to be back in New York for the summer, after touring for months at a time. He'd hardly taken a break in the last four years, and he'd had Manny make certain that he would have the next three months almost completely free. He looked forward to a summer of solitary practice and simple relaxation, away from the hot stage lights, the grueling hours in recording studios, the adoring fans, the critics, and the incessant travel.

Manny was yelling into the telephone now. Wonder what's the matter? Misha mused. Rachel and Sasha, he knew, put up with it all the time. Manny seemed to be yelling more and more lately.

Trying to tune Manny out, he wished he didn't have to go out tonight but knew that he must. Tonight's engagement was far too important to beg off.

Vera had finished her studies in London and had just arrived back in New York, where she was now beginning a career as an employee of Christie's, the venerable auction house. She would be working in the Furniture and Decorative Arts Department of their New York branch. Tonight, her parents were giving a party in her honor at their lavish Fifth Avenue apartment. He certainly wouldn't go if not for Vera.

Vera.

He grimaced, then took a sip of his scotch.

What am I going to do about Vera?

He'd asked himself that question a million times at least and still had his doubts about the best tactic to use. But he'd finally made up his mind that they must talk about their future.

Tonight, he thought. *D-Day.*

Tonight's party might be in her honor, but he knew that they could easily disappear at some point and sneak away to her private terrace for a talk. He had thought about waiting, but after her last letter—and how wonderful those letters had been while he was on the road!—he'd decided that he would talk to her as soon as possible. So tonight it would be.

"Hey," Manny called, hanging up the telephone and walking over to the couch.

Misha looked over at him. "Hey, yourself," he said. "What is it? Office emergency?"

"No, just the usual," Manny said. "Diva breakdowns, conductor power trips, you know the story."

"Who is it now?" Sasha asked.

"Let's talk about it later," Manny said, giving him a meaningful look.

Manny looked at Misha with a grin on his face. "Rachel tells me that some girl, a Paola Something or Other, Italian, has been calling for you, old chap."

Misha grinned back at him but said nothing.

"As a matter of fact," Manny continued, "the aforementioned young damsel seems terribly distressed. She's been calling every hour, on the hour, every single day for the last two weeks. Says she lost your telephone number, and only has the office number."

Misha took a sip of his drink, then set it down on the coffee table. He looked up at Manny. "Rachel didn't give her this number, of course."

"Of course not, old boy," Manny said, "but Rachel is getting a mite perturbed, what with the constant interruptions, and the young lady's . . . shall we say . . . aggressive attitude and language?"

Misha shrugged. "Tell Rachel to tell her that I'm getting married," he said. "That'll get rid of her."

"No doubt," Manny said, "after she's nearly deafened poor Rachel with a string of highly inventive obscenities."

"I'll send Rachel some flowers," Misha said. "She'll forgive me."

Manny sat down and looked over at Misha. "Who is this Paola, old boy? Don't remember meeting her."

"Just a girl," Misha said. "You know. One of those girls who comes to a concert, hangs around backstage, follows you everywhere, won't leave you alone, won't give you a minute's peace, until you make her happy."

Manny took off his glasses and began furiously cleaning them with a pristine white linen handkerchief. "How young?" he asked.

"I don't know," Misha said, "but don't worry, Manny. She wasn't a kid, if that's what you mean. I don't go in for that, and you know it. She was at least eighteen. Probably more like twenty. A model, she said."

Manny momentarily paused with his handkerchief and looked at Misha. "Good," he said. "We certainly don't need a scandal, do we? And the way the press follows you around, well . . ."

"Manny," Misha said, "there is going to be no scandal. I hardly know the girl."

"That's exactly what I mean," Manny said. "You *don't* know her, but you can bet she knows nearly everything about you there is to know. You can also bet that there are thousands of them like her out there who would just love to slap a big paternity suit on you and part you from some of your hard-earned cash."

"Manny! *Jesus!*" Misha cried. "Would you quit worrying so much. I've been very careful. Nobody could *win* a paternity suit!"

"All the same," Manny countered, putting his glasses back on, "you don't need the hassle, the notoriety. The press is already calling you the rock and roll star of classical music."

"What do you want me to do, Manny?" Misha snarled. "Cut my god-damn hair?"

Sasha laughed. "I don't think that would be wise," he said.

"No, I don't either," Manny said equably. "Nothing so drastic as that, old chap. Just try to keep that thing in your pants." A huge smile spread his lips wide.

Misha laughed despite his anger. "Ah, Manny," he said "you're too much, you know that. Too much."

"Seriously, though," Manny said, "you can't be too careful in your position."

"I know," Misha said. "I live in a glass house now. I can't do anything without the whole world knowing about it." He sighed.

"Oh, well," Manny said, "things will change once Paola spreads the word that you're getting married."

Misha laughed again. "Are you about ready to head across town?"

"Anytime, old boy," Manny said. "I can't wait to see what the czarina, Tatiana Bunim, has had the serfs prepare for dinner."

Misha drank down the rest of his Scotch and set the empty glass on the table. "Then let's get a move on."

"My sentiments exactly, old boy," Manny said, getting to his feet. "My sentiments exactly."

Chapter Eighteen

Vaslav greeted Misha, Manny, and Sasha with the same cool demeanor with which he greeted everyone, regardless of their familiarity with the Bunims. Ushered into the drawing room, Misha's arrival caused an immediate stir in the room. After greeting Ivan and Tatiana Bunim, Misha, Manny, Sasha, and Vera all exchanged air kisses and pleasantries in front of her parents.

"It's so good to see all of you," Vera said, smiling serenely. "There's someone here who can't wait to see you."

"No," Misha said jokingly, "we refuse to speak to anyone else tonight. It's your night."

Vera laughed lightly. "Come with me," she said. She took Misha's arm, and Manny and Sasha followed along. She led them over to a French settee where Sonia and Dmitri were sitting, engrossed in conversation with people Misha didn't know.

Sonia looked up and could hardly control her cry of delight. "Misha! Oh, Misha!" She quickly got to her feet and threw her arms around him, peppering him with kisses.

"Oh, I'm so glad to see you, you naughty boy!" she said, finally letting go of him. "You haven't even called since you got back to New York."

Dmitri had gotten up and hugged his son, kissing both his cheeks. "Misha," he said. "It's so good to see you, son."

"And Manny and Sasha," Sonia cried. "I'm blessed with all my Russian boys tonight!" She grabbed first Manny and then Sasha in embraces, peppering them with kisses, too.

Vera watched, taking delight in their joy at seeing one another, and at the same time she was surprised to learn that Misha hadn't seen or called his parents since getting back to town. *I wonder what that's all about,* she asked herself. *Maybe he's just been too busy. But too busy to see Sonia and Dmitri? No, no way. He's been up to something.*

The dinner was a feast of Olympian proportions that delighted both the eye and the palate. Served at a table set for thirty in the main dining room, it was a setting indeed fit for the Romanovs, the Russian imperial family the Bunims were often compared with. Baroque solid silver chandeliers lit with candles hung over the long table, which was decorated with massive arrangements of fragrant pale pink peonies, Russian silver candelabra with beeswax candles, and antique imperial Russian china, silver, and crystal. The table was surrounded by walls of hand-painted murals that depicted fantastical pastoral views of the grand palaces in and around St. Petersburg. Draperies at the French windows were hung with raspberry silk panels, trimmed with a classical Greek border woven of pure gold.

Vera was toasted by her father, and then the dinner began. In this grand setting the guests were served Beluga Malossol caviar, smoked salmon, tiny quail, a risotto with truffles, paillards of veal, and a choice of dark chocolate mousse or, for those who had sworn off chocolate, strawberry and rhubarb cobbler with ginger ice cream. No less than six wines were served during the course of the meal, all of them of the finest and most expensive vintages, ending with a Château d'Yquem. Footmen in breeches and powdered wigs stood behind every chair to anticipate the needs of each guest.

Manny was in seventh heaven, being the epicurean that he was, the deliciousness of the food such that it made up for the *placement*. For he had been seated next to Delia, Countess Dardley, who was well known for her sharp and evil tongue, a reputation that Manny decided during dinner was well deserved. Despite her venerable lineage and obviously brilliant mind, he decided that her outlook was of such a bleak and negative blackness that five minutes of her conversation was surely suicide-inducing, even to the most sophisticated of her dinner partners.

Vera and Misha watched him with little smiles on their faces, occasionally catching his eye, giving him a quick, mischievous wink, sadistically relishing the torture they knew he must be enduring. They picked at their food, patiently sitting through the dinner, anxious for the ensuing after-dinner socializing with cigars and drinks and coffee to begin, because then they could steal away upstairs to be alone.

Their patience eventually paid off, and while the other guests mixed and mingled in the apartment's various public rooms, Vera led him upstairs to the private terrace off her bedroom. There they looked out over the city, as they had the first night they met, sipping champagne and talking quietly about their careers.

"I'll be researching and cataloging important French and Continental furniture," Vera said. "And some Old Masters paintings. But I'll also be trying to acquire furniture and paintings for the auction house to put on the block. With some of my family's friends, plus some of the people I've met in school over the years, I know quite a few people who have important collections or have inherited them."

"So you'll try to steer them to Christie's to put their collections on the market?" Misha asked.

"Exactly," she said. "In some cases it's easy. Either because the heirs hate the antiques and paintings and want to get rid of them, or they need the cash. Sometimes both."

"You'll be great at it," Misha said.

"I think so," Vera said. "I've learned a lot, and I love the work."

"And you're starting right away?" Misha asked.

She nodded. "Next week." She turned and looked at him. "But there aren't any auctions this summer, and things are a little slow. So I'll have plenty of free time. To do other things."

Misha returned her look. "That's good," he said.

Vera knew at once that he was holding out on her, that he wanted to tell her something but hadn't yet found the words—or the courage.

"Let's go sit for a while," she said, turning and walking to the couches under the awning. Misha followed her.

The scene of our first lovemaking, he remembered. *Six long years ago.*

They sat down, sipping their champagne in silence for a while. Finally, Misha set his flute down. "Vera," he said, "I wanted to talk about . . . well, our future."

She looked at him with a cool expression, which belied the turmoil she felt inside. "Go on, Misha," she said in a matter-of-fact voice. "What do you have to say?"

"Well, I don't know exactly how to put it," he said. "I want you to know that I love you." He looked into her icy blue eyes, such hard eyes to read, certainly in this light. "You're the best friend I've ever had, you know that?"

"I guess so, Misha," she said softly. "I know you're the best friend I've ever had."

"It's just that . . . well, remember when we talked before you went to London and I left to start touring? And I told you I was confused. That I didn't really know how I felt about you?"

"Yes," Vera said, nodding. "I remember every detail, Misha."

"Well," he said gently, taking a hand of hers in his. "I still feel pretty much the same way. I love you, Vera. As a friend. But I don't know if I'm *in* love with you. Do you understand that?"

"Yes," Vera said, hoping that he didn't hear the fear and the sorrow in her voice.

"I don't know what I want to do yet," he said. "I just don't feel like I'm ready to settle down. For the last six years I've worked like a maniac, playing concert after concert, hardly taking a break. I think what I want now is time alone, to think things through, to try to sort out the confusion in my head. Do you understand?"

Vera nodded, and looked up at him. "I do, Misha," she said. "Perfectly." She shrugged. "I guess it would be good for both of us to spend time alone, thinking about what we really want, where we really want our lives to go."

"Yes," Misha said. "I just don't want you to misunderstand me. I'll always love you. I love you like a . . . like a sister."

Vera's eyes bored into his for long moments, their iciness penetrating him with a chill. "Well," she finally said, "I hope you wouldn't fuck your sister, if you had one, like you did me."

Misha almost gasped, then he blurted a bark of a laugh.

Vera's icy demeanor didn't change. She sat staring at him with that unrelenting gaze. Then, gradually her face melted, and she began to laugh, too, her laughter building into an uproarious, joyful sound, joined by Misha's now carefree full-throated roar. They collapsed upon each other, hugging and kissing in their laughter, until finally Vera drew back, wiping the mirthful tears from her eyes.

"You're unbelievable!" Misha said, taking a hand of hers in his. "The greatest!"

"Well, do you want to have an old-fashioned roll in the hay before you say good-bye?" she asked in a playful voice. *Oh, God, I hope he doesn't hear the desperation in my voice,* she thought.

Misha froze. *That would only lead her on,* he thought, *giving her false hope. I can't do it. I've got to make the break now!* After a moment he shook his head. "I don't think it would be a good idea, Vera."

"Okay," she said. "Don't look so forlorn. I was only kidding." *If only,* she wanted to cry.

"I hope nothing else changes between us, Vera," Misha said. "I hope everything can be the same. I mean, that we can still be best friends and all."

Does that mean with or without the screwing? she wanted to scream.

"I hope so, too, Misha," she said. "I would like that very much. Anyway, you know where I am if you need me."

"Yes," he said. "And you know where I am." He squeezed her hand.

She looked into his eyes. "Why don't you go back down to the party now, Misha?" she said. "You've hardly seen your parents."

"What about you?" he asked.

"I think I'll stay up here a few more minutes," she said. "Have a little more of the bubbly. Alone." She patted his cheek with a hand. "You don't mind? I just need a few minutes of privacy."

"No," he said. "Not at all. You'll be down soon?"

"Yes," she said. "Now, off you go! Scat!"

Misha got to his feet and leaned over to kiss her. She turned a cheek to him, and he kissed it chastely. "Now, scat!" she said again, and he turned and went back inside.

The moment he passed through the French doors into her bedroom, her tears began to flow. They were profuse, unstopping, for she thought her heart had been wrenched in two and would never be whole again. She had never loved anyone like she had loved Misha, not from the moment that she first laid eyes on him. She couldn't explain it. It wasn't rational. But it had happened, nevertheless. And now she didn't see how she could ever be happy with anybody else.

But a voice somewhere in her mind told her not to give up, not to do anything rash. If she continued to wait, if she kept alive her undying love for Misha, then he would come back. He would sort out his confused feelings. He would decide he had to have her.

She got up and went into her bedroom and dried her tears, then went into the bathroom to check her makeup. Her eyes were a dead giveaway, but she could hide some of the damage with makeup. Ten minutes later, she had worked a magician's feat, repairing her face to its earlier serene and glowing perfection.

She looked at herself closely. *I've always had everything in the world that most people could want*, she thought. *And I've never had to work for it. I have worked at pleasing my parents, at keeping myself fit, at doing well in school, and I will work hard in my career. Now I must work hard, harder than I've ever worked in my life, to keep Misha. Or to get him back, if I ever had him.*

I am not going to play the grieving girlfriend. No. I am not going to make scenes or throw tantrums. No. Hurl accusations, place blame. No. Nor am I ever going to throw myself at him again.

What I am going to do, is be my cool, intelligent self, keeping busy, quietly waiting. Let him continue to sow his oats. Be there when he comes running back. Offer succor, not punishment.

Because I want him, Vera thought. *And I'm going to have him.*

She turned from the mirror and went back downstairs to the party in her honor, greeting her guests with poise, charming them all, her serene demeanor giving away nothing of what had just transpired.

No one noticed the broken heart that bled so copiously in her chest.

Chapter Nineteen

Misha closed the score of Beethoven's Piano Sonata No. 1, op. 11, the famous "Moonlight" portion, adagio sostenuto, which he had been practicing. He felt energized with adrenaline despite the long, grueling hours of work he had put in. Two three-hour shifts after a morning workout, with a brief break for lunch. Pushing back from the piano, he got up and stretched. That's when he remembered the telephone call he'd had earlier in the day.

Perfect timing, he thought with a smile.

He went to his desk, where he flipped through his black alligator date book, looking to see what, if anything, he had scheduled for tonight. He'd been so busy practicing during the day, learning new pieces and expanding his repertoire, then going out every night that he had to rely on his date book to keep his schedule straight.

Yelena had telephoned to say that she was coming into town, then right out again. So if he saw her, it would have to be tonight. She was going to be modeling during the day, doing a photo shoot for *Vogue.*

Looking at tonight's slot in his book, he saw that he'd penned in: *Christina. Late dinner. Life.* Christina was a beauty he'd met during intermission at the ballet. Life was the hottest dance club *du jour.*

Jesus, he thought. *What am I going to do?*

Christina was a bubbly dark-haired beauty, lots of fun, with a slightly roly-poly but voluptuous body that ought to be in pictures. Porno pictures maybe, not *Vogue.*

Yelena, on the other hand, was a very tall, skinny Russian model, with drop-dead bone structure, legs that didn't stop, and looks that literally stopped traffic. She also had the soul of a hit man.

Neither one of them was a brain surgeon exactly, Elton John being the only piano player they'd ever heard of. *But that doesn't always matter, does it?* Misha told himself.

So who is it to be?

Dance-with-her-till-she-drops, then fuck-her-till-she-screams Christina? Or the steel-thighed, kinky-minded Yelena?

Well, he reasoned, he could see Christina almost anytime. She lived down in Tribeca, was unattached, and was very much a free spirit. She went out nearly every night of the week, so she probably wouldn't be too upset if he canceled out on her. She would just pick up the telephone and call any number of readily available escorts.

Yelena, then. She would only be here tonight, and it had been months since their last date, a date that he didn't think he'd ever forget. The acrobatics had been exhausting but memorable.

He picked up the telephone and dialed the number she had left, some photographer's studio downtown where the shoot was taking place. When he finally got through to her, she told him to meet her at the Morgan Hotel on Madison Avenue, where she was staying. She'd probably be there by nine o'clock.

"I've got a surprise for you," he told her.

"Oh, and what's that?" she asked in her heavily accented English.

"You'll see," Misha said mysteriously. "But I think you're going to like it."

"Come on, Misha," she said, "tell me!"

"A new toy, that's all I'll say," he said. "See you at nine."

He hung up the receiver and looked at his watch. Six o'clock. Plenty of time to get cleaned up, dressed, and wow her with his surprise.

Misha strutted down the street to the garage, feeling like he had the world on a string. He was wearing tight Levi's, his new motorcycle jacket, and biker boots. Had his shiny new helmet in hand. A new breed of urban cowboy.

In the garage, he fired up his new Harley-Davidson soft-tail, all gleaming chrome and black paint. A recent purchase he'd kept secret from everyone. His parents and Manny and Vera would have been apoplectic had they known, envisioning his lifeless body on the roadside and a brilliant career gone down the drain.

Well, what they don't know won't hurt them, he told himself. *I'm twenty-four years old, and it's high time I had some real fun.*

Since he had time, he decided to head downtown on the West Side Highway, then cruise back uptown on the East Side to the Morgan. He headed west, across town, and hit the highway, going south, doing seventy miles an hour, exhilarated by the speed and the wind on his body. The mayor and his crackdown on speed could shove it! At West Twenty-third Street, he stopped at the light and decided to take a left and head straight across town to Madison Avenue. When he got the green arrow, he turned, and—

Jesus!

A car in the turn lane next to him—the same car that had been speeding down the West Side Highway alongside him—was veering into him. Headed straight for him.

What the—?

Misha opened the throttle and gave the bike gas, swerving to avoid the car, but he was too late. He saw the car veer closer, its side looming impossibly large in his visor, and he knew at that moment that he was going to be hit.

It was all over.

He gradually drifted up, up, up from under the thick, gauzy cloud that seemed to have a grip on his consciousness. First he heard sounds in the distance, not certain what they were, then slowly became aware of a faint, diffuse sort of light. In the beginning even its dimness was too bright for his unadjusted eyes, becoming bearable only after long minutes of trying to focus.

The world was a blur of cottony white, pale greens, and a yellowy beige, with indistinct definition. Then the sounds began to make sense: the glint of metal against metal, the squishing of rubber soles on tile, doors opening and closing, a PA system paging names he couldn't make out.

Struggling to think, to force himself up out of the lethargy that had him in its hold, he gradually became aware of his limbs and tried to move his arms.

A bolt of excruciating pain, like a charge of lightning, shot up his arm, and a subsequent throb in his head engulfed his entire skull in the white-hot heat of agony. His body broke out into a sweat so profuse that it soaked the bedsheets, and he gasped for air.

What's wrong? he wondered.

Where the hell am I?

The jolt of pain had brought him fully awake, if still a bit disoriented, and he moved only his eyes, searching his surroundings.

A hospital room. But where? What hospital? And why?

The door swished open, and he heard rubber soles squeaking on the tile. Suddenly a nurse loomed over him.

"We're awake, I see," she said, fiddling with IV lines at the side of his bed.

Misha could see that she had gray hair, cut very short, almost like a man's, with more than a hint of mustache to match. She looked like a woman who would not suffer fools gladly.

"Where. . . ?" he rasped, then tried to clear his throat. "Where am . . . I?" he finally managed.

"St. Vincent's," the nurse replied, removing the wrapper from a disposable thermometer.

"Where?" he asked again.

"St. Vincent's Hospital," she replied in a matter-of-fact voice. "In the Village. Greenwich Village. Here," she said, "open up for me." She held the thermometer positioned at his mouth.

Misha dutifully opened his lips to receive the thermometer, then closed them over it. *What the hell*, he wondered. *What am I doing in this place?*

The nurse removed the thermometer, looked at the digital readout, and made a note on a chart. "Welcome back to the world of the living," she said with a curious almost-smile. "You have visitors waiting to see you, so I'll send them on in now."

Visitors? His mind didn't quite seem to grasp the concept.

The nurse turned and left the room in a stream of squish-squishes, pulling the door shut quietly behind her. It almost instantly opened again, and Sonia, with Dmitri, Manny, and Sasha close behind her, inched tentatively into the room.

Misha watched as they slowly made their way to his bedside, aware of the worry and outright fear etched into their faces.

Sonia leaned over the bed and touched her fingertips to her lips, then very lightly brushed his forehead with them, choking back a sob. Dmitri had tears in his eyes, and appeared to be restraining himself from reaching out to Misha, afraid to touch him for fear of causing him pain. Manny, always in control of any situation, seemed genuinely at a loss. It was the first time Misha had ever seen him so distraught. Sasha's face was stony, but then it nearly always was.

Sonia drew herself up, tears coursing down her cheeks. "Oh, Misha, Misha," she wept quietly.

"What . . . why . . . why am I here?" Misha rasped, tears forming in his own eyes, seeing the tears of his mother and the distress of Dmitri and Manny.

"You were in an accident," Dmitri said. "You're very lucky to be alive, Misha."

An accident? he thought with surprise.

"A *motorcycle* accident," Sonia said, her emphasis on the word loaded with meaning, which was not lost on Misha. She wanted to smother him with love but couldn't conceal her anger, either.

Suddenly images of that night came flooding back into his memory. The motorcycle. He could remember going to the garage to get it out. He was going to see Yelena. Then he could remember leaving the garage on the bike. But the memory abruptly ended there.

"Am I . . . am I . . . okay?" he asked.

"It's going to be a long, hard road to recovery, son," Dmitri said. "A lot of physical therapy and—"

"What . . . what's wrong?" Misha burst out, fear in his voice.

"Your left leg is broken," Sonia said. "And . . ." She couldn't continue as tears threatened to spill from her eyes again.

"Your left arm is broken, Misha," Dmitri said in a hushed voice. "It was a bad break."

Misha's mind began to spin. "But my hands are okay?" he asked. "How bad is it? How long will it take to heal?"

"No need to panic," Manny said. "The doctor's prognosis is very good. Like your father said, with a bit of physical therapy it'll be as good as new in no time."

Misha riveted Manny with his dark eyes. "How long is no time?"

Manny shrugged. "It might be a few weeks," he said, "but . . . but more likely a few months. At least."

Misha sighed. "Ah, Jesus, Manny. My tour schedule! What am I going to do?"

"Don't worry about that, old chap," Manny said. "It's all taken care of."

"Your schedule is empty until you're completely healed and ready to play again," Sasha added.

"I don't know how you two work your magic," he said. "I really don't. It's really taken care of?"

"You bet," Manny said. "No problem. We've just got to get you well."

Misha moaned. "This can't be happening to me," he said.

"It is," Sonia said, "and all because of that foolish motorcycle. I don't want to lecture you while you're in pain, but the plain and simple truth, Misha, is that you were being reckless. Terribly reckless. And you know it."

Misha knew his mother was telling the truth. Suddenly he felt like a child again, and a wave of guilt washed over him, engulfing him in shame.

"Well, if it's any consolation," Dmitri interjected quickly, seeing the repentant look on his son's face, "the newspapers say that it was definitely not your fault. Several witnesses came forward, and they say it was a hit-and-run. The police are trying to find the guy who hit you."

Manny looked shocked. "When did you hear this, Dmitri?" he asked.

"Just before coming over," Dmitri said.

Misha sighed again. "Well, it doesn't matter now if they find him or not, does it? I can't play the piano."

"Oh, but you will, my boy, you will," Manny said, quickly recovering his composure.

The nurse came in and announced in an authoritative voice that the visitors would have to leave.

"There's a procedure we have to perform," she said, "and visiting hours are almost over anyway. Besides, we don't want to overtire the young man, do we?"

Sonia, Dmitri, Sacha, and Manny quickly said their good-byes and promised to see him at the next visiting time. Then they were gone.

I wish I could remember what happened, Misha thought. *I wish I could remember who did this to me. And why.*

Chapter Twenty

⸙

Vera paced the Aubusson carpet in the pale gray and gilt of her bedroom. There were tears in her eyes, and her body periodically trembled with fear and rage and shame. Shame was perhaps the worst of it, eating at her like some carnivorous animal, leaving her no peace, torturing her for her terrible misdeeds.

She stopped pacing abruptly and sat down on a chaise longue, picking up the newspaper again. She looked at the picture there on the front page once more and cried aloud.

Oh, God! she thought. *It's too much for anyone to have to bear!*

Violently wadding the paper up into a ball, she hurled it across the room, where it bounced off her desk and onto the floor, lying there, an ugly and mute testimony to her treachery.

What am I going to do? she asked herself for the hundredth time.

When she'd first picked up today's papers, she'd laughed at the headlines:

Hot Classical Pianist, Misha Levin
A Real Rock and Roller
Rock and Rolled off his Harley

Yet the humor of the ludicrous headline wore off very quickly. It seemed that the eyewitnesses to the accident had come up with a license number, and the police were tracking down the hit-and-run driver. The papers speculated that criminal charges would be filed.

Vera shuddered anew, thinking of the horror that she had unleashed on Misha, though unknowingly. For a moment she thought she was going to throw up. She dashed to the bathroom and spun the gold cold-water tap on the sink. She gulped down handfuls of the water and splattered her face with it, then stood up straight, looking into the mirror.

I have to come clean with the truth, she told her reflection. *No matter what the consequences are. I can't live with myself otherwise.*

With that decision made, she washed her face, which was puffy and red from crying, and quickly applied makeup and changed clothes for a trip downtown. Within minutes she was outside on Fifth Avenue, hailing a cab.

Misha smiled widely when he saw her come into the room. "I didn't expect to see you so soon again," he said. "The flowers are beautiful." He glanced at the enormous orchid plant, heavy with blossoms in full bloom.

Vera walked over to the bed and gave him a chaste kiss on the lips. "You seem to be doing a little better today," she said.

"Yeah," Misha said. "This sure helps." He pointed to the push-button device in his hand.

"What is it?" Vera asked.

"I just push the button, like so." Misha pushed the button, smiling up at her. "And give myself more painkiller."

Vera laughed, but it was not mirthful.

"I'll be out of here in no time, and back on the road again." He noticed the solemn look on Vera's face. "What's with you?" he asked.

Vera avoided his gaze. "I . . . oh, I . . . ," she began.

"What, Vera?" he asked. "What is it? I've never seen you like this before."

"I . . . I have to talk to you about something very important, Misha," she said.

"Then why don't you pull up a chair and sit?" he said. "You'll be a lot more comfortable than standing there looking so miserable."

Vera slid a chair over and sat down, looking over at him. "I don't know where to begin," she said.

"How about the beginning?" Misha said with amusement in his voice.

"Well . . . oh, Misha! This is so hard!" she cried. "The most difficult thing I've ever done!"

"Whatever it is, Vera," he said soothingly, "it's between you and me. So it's safe, okay?"

"Okay," she said. "I . . . I . . . you remember I told you about that guy . . . Simon, who I used to see in London?"

"Yeah," he said. "The *muy* macho, possessive motorcycle-maniac-artist."

"Yes," she said. "That's the one." She paused a moment, taking a deep breath, then finally gathered the courage to go on. "Well, the last few years while you've been touring, I saw Simon a few times, mostly in the last year."

"You've been holding out on me, Vera," Misha said. He felt a twinge of jealous anger, despite the agreement he and Vera had to see other people. "I thought you weren't going to see him anymore. You didn't like all that macho, possessive crap."

"I didn't," Vera said somewhat defensively, "but he seemed to have turned over a new leaf. You know, not being so possessive and all. Playing the good guy, respecting my privacy. I really believed him. I thought he just wanted to . . . you know . . . have some fun."

"Ah," Misha laughed. "The plot thickens."

"I'm afraid it's not very funny, Misha," she said softly. "Because . . . because Simon, of course, knew that I'd dated you. He knew . . . he knew how I . . . how I felt about you, and . . ." Tears welled up in her eyes, and she choked.

"Oh, Vera," Misha said, distressed. "Please don't cry. Please. You know I can't stand it when you cry."

"I'm sorry," she choked. "I just can't help it. Because what happened is . . . is so terrible!"

She caught her breath, then continued. "Simon came to New York this summer. He had a show at some gallery down in Chelsea. I knew about it, but I didn't see him. I swear."

"So? Big deal. Simon comes to New York. So do millions of other people," Misha said.

"Yes, but Simon didn't come for just the art show. He came with a purpose," Vera said.

Misha blinked, now very curious about where this was leading.

"Simon came to New York to try to kill you, Misha," she blurted out. "It was Simon who ran into your bike. Deliberately. He tried to kill you. He's still insanely jealous and possessive, and I should have known! It's all my fault!" She burst into tears again and couldn't continue.

Misha lay there stunned. Finally he found his tongue. "But how do you know all this, Vera? Are you sure?"

She nodded, then wiped her eyes with a hand. "He called me," she said. "Bragging about it. He said they'd never catch him. He was driving a stolen car. He's crazy! And even if they think it was just a hit-and-run, I know he was trying to kill you. He told me so. Oh . . . God! It's all my fault, Misha!" Her tears burst forth anew.

"Vera," Misha said, "you didn't know. It's not your fault. Don't be so upset."

"But I was keeping him a secret from you." She gasped a heavy sigh. "I knew that you were seeing other girls besides the ones we always talked about. And I . . . I decided to have Simon on the side, as a sort of way to get even, I guess. Telling myself that if you could do it, so could I."

She looked up at him, her face a sorrowful mask. "I feel so ashamed," she said. "My little secret has turned out to be a lot more dangerous than I'd ever imagined."

Misha felt another rush of jealousy. But then, he reminded himself, hadn't he behaved the same way? Hadn't there been lots of girls he hadn't told her about? But none of the girls he knew had tried to kill Vera!

He looked over at her tear-streaked face, her blond hair disheveled. He didn't like her deception, but he didn't want Vera to feel worse. He didn't want to punish her in any way, because he knew that in her heart she was punishing herself more than he ever could.

Nevertheless, when he spoke, his words were firm. "I think you ought to leave now, Vera," Misha said. "And I don't want you to tell anyone that you know anything about this. Certainly not the police. Neither one of us wants the kind of nasty publicity this would generate. This will be our secret. Just try to forget about it. And for God's sake, stay away from this . . . this Simon."

She looked at him in shock. "Never again will I *ever* see him!" she cried. "My father will make certain he never bothers me again."

"Fine," Misha said. "Now please, Vera, just go. And don't call me. I need time . . . I'll call you."

Vera sat for a moment longer, then rose to her feet and approached the bed, but Misha waved her away with his right hand.

"Please," he repeated, "just go."

Vera turned, tears in her eyes again, and left the hospital room.

I've lost him forever, she thought miserably. *And it's all my own fault.*

But she hadn't lost him forever.

It was only a matter of weeks before Misha was out of the hospital and on his feet, with the help of crutches, and calling her. Would Yelena or Christina or Valerie or Gigi or Vanka or any of the other mostly one-named beauties he knew take time out from their work and their habitual club crawling to minister to his needs? He knew better than to ask. When he thought about it, they had abandoned him while he was out of commission, not bothering to visit him in the hospital or send flowers or even a note.

Vera had dropped everything and rearranged her work schedule as much as possible, even skipping lunch, to accommodate his needs. And they were many. Helping him to and from his physical therapy sessions downtown, helping out around the apartment, sometimes even cooking and cleaning. Sonia, of course, would have relished taking care of her son, but Misha didn't want her hovering presence around. She always made him feel as if he were a child again. He could have hired someone, and did on occasion, to do the heavy cleaning and chores that Vera simply couldn't make the time for.

She devoted herself to him slavishly, making certain that one day soon Misha would once again stride across the concert stage and sit down at his piano and dazzle an assembled audience.

He was the love of her life, no matter what, and she would give him time to come to love her. Perhaps if she continued to lavish all of her love on him, he would begin to realize that he need not look elsewhere.

Chapter Twenty-one

≈≈≈

Brighton Beach, 1993

"The food is Russian, the music is Russian, and everybody speaks Russian," said Sonia with a disdainful air. "But I'm telling you, Misha. These are not our kind of people."

"Try to relax and enjoy yourself, Mama," Misha said, trying to humor her.

But Sonia was in no mood to be humored. "Look about you," she went on, her hand sweeping around with an elegant, if out-of-place stylish gesture. "These people are uncouth. The women with their garish makeup and bad bleach jobs. Those dresses! Straps all over the place, exposing nearly everything. And the men! They look like a bunch of gangsters!"

Misha laughed. "Don't let your imagination run away with you," he said.

"Oh, well," she said, "at least the blinis were almost like in the old country."

"That's more like it," he said, patting her on the back. But Misha himself was secretly wondering if she wasn't right on the mark. It *was* an uncouth crowd, and the men did indeed look like a bunch of gangsters who'd come here to party with their girlfriends or mistresses. He doubted that there were many wives in this club tonight.

If Manny and Sasha hadn't insisted on this celebration in Brighton Beach, none of them would be here, in this déclassé nightclub packed to the rafters with Russian emigrés. Misha didn't have anything against Brooklyn or the recently arrived Russians who'd flocked here to Brighton Beach, but these were not Russians or an aspect of Russian life that he knew much of anything about, or cared to learn about, for that matter. The cheap glitter and raucous, vodka-swilling crowd were as alien to him and his family as the predominately gutter-accented Russian they heard spoken around them.

Misha took a sip of the champagne that the fawning waiter had presented to them as a gift of the management. He looked over his glass at Manny, who was engrossed in conversation with Dmitri. His father, he noticed, looked as uncomfortable as Sonia, and Manny, if a bit more animated than usual, was as out of place here with his affected aristocratic airs and his Savile Row tailoring as they were. Why in the world did he and Sasha choose to have this celebration here? Misha wondered.

He knew, of course, that Manny and Sasha had grown up in this section of Brooklyn, that they had even named the recording label after it. But hadn't they worked triple-time to get themselves out of here, away from these reminders of their heavily ethnic and less than prosperous beginnings? But then, Misha supposed, this club and its crowd had certainly not been a part of their humble youth. The furs and jewels, the expensive suits and slicked-back hair, the thuggish-looking sentries stationed around the club and the stretch limousines parked out front, all the money being tossed around so recklessly for second-rate food and entertainment—all of these things were part of a new breed of Russian, and were surely not something that Manny and Sasha could identify with.

In any case, he hadn't wanted to disappoint Manny and Sasha when they'd broached the subject of a party. They had wanted to celebrate Misha's recovery from his injuries, Manny'd said, and give him a big send-off before his next world tour. Now, rather than embarrass his friends, Misha was simply trying to endure the gaudy spectacle around them instead of insisting that they leave.

"Penny for your thoughts," Vera said, nudging him on the arm with her elbow.

He turned to her and smiled. "To be honest," he said softly, not wanting to be overheard, "I was wondering why the hell Manny and Sasha chose this place for a party."

Vera shrugged her elegant shoulders and smiled. "Oh, I don't know," she said, her eyes glittering mischievously. "Maybe they thought the music would appeal to you."

"I think you know better than that," Misha said with a laugh. Vera was being an awfully good sport, he reflected. He knew that she must be cringing inside.

He reached over and squeezed her hand gently. "Actually," he said, "I was thinking that if I have to listen to just one more old Russian melody played on those infernal balalaikas, I'd get up and leave."

Vera smiled. "Maybe that's why everybody drinks so much," she said. "The music sounds better."

"That must be it," Misha replied. He leaned closer to her. "Thank

God, it's almost over. A little balalaika goes an awfully long way. I was thinking that after we leave here, maybe—"

"Mikhail Levin!"

The thundering baritone with its heavy Russian accent gave Misha a start. He and Vera turned to look up at a bear of a man towering over them at the table. He had salt-and-pepper hair, a thick brush of mustache on a jowly red face, and wore an expensive-looking suit, which looked odd on his beefy, broad-shouldered body. He put a thick mitt of a hand on Misha's shoulder, and extended the other for a shake.

"Yuri Durasov," he said, smiling hugely at Misha, exposing teeth that had been badly capped or bonded.

Misha started to rise as he shook the proffered hand, but Durasov quickly tapped his huge paw on Misha's shoulder. "Please, don't get up," he said. "I just wanted to say hello. I am one of the owners of the Club Moskva, and a big fan of yours."

"You are?" Misha said, hoping his voice didn't betray the doubts he had that this behemoth was truly a devotee of classical music. But he quickly decided that he mustn't allow himself to be fooled by appearances, and he certainly didn't want to be rude or ungracious. "Thank you very much," he said, "I'm glad that you enjoy my playing."

Durasov clapped him on the shoulder again. "Beautiful," he said. "Beautiful." His steely eyes swept over Vera, appraising her as if she were livestock at an auction.

"Your girlfriend?" he asked, his gray eyes still drinking in Vera's cool beauty, her elegant Mary McFadden cocktail suit and exquisite jewelry.

"Oh, sorry," Misha said. "This is my friend, Vera Bunim."

Vera extended a hand and smiled graciously. "How do you do, Mr. Durasov?" she said.

"It's a pleasure," he said, his gaze lingering on her a moment longer.

"This is my mother," Misha said quickly, indicating Sonia on his other side. "Sonia Levin."

Durasov extended a hand to her, and Sonia took it briefly and nodded politely before pointedly focusing her attention in the distance. She obviously had no desire to make conversation with Yuri Durasov.

"I hope you enjoyed your champagne and the dinner," Durosov said, his eyes on Misha again. "We are honored to have you here."

"The honor's ours," Misha said. "And thanks very much for the champagne."

Durasov clapped his shoulder again, and slowly lumbered around the table to Manny and Sasha, who quickly got to their feet and shook hands with him, then introduced Dmitri.

"Manny and Sasha seem to know him rather well," Vera said to Misha, watching the exchange across the table.

"It certainly looks like it," Misha said, his voice conveying an anxiety that hadn't been there before. Yuri Durasov had made him feel decidedly ill at ease. Despite the man's expensive clothing, meticulous grooming, and friendly air, there was something about him that gave Misha the creeps. He suspected that beneath what appeared to be a recently acquired veneer of polish and charm, there lurked a brute who was capable of extreme violence.

"Are you thinking what I'm thinking?" Vera asked.

Misha looked at her. "What's that?" he said. But before Vera could reply, Manny and Yuri Durasov came around the table to Misha. Sasha had kept his seat and was looking as stony as always.

"Misha," Manny said, his face a convivial mask that Misha had often seen. "Yuri wants to know if you would do the club the honor of playing a tune for them."

Misha looked up at him in surprise. Manny knew that he hated this sort of thing. Playing the piano was his *job*, for which he was paid, as he'd told him often enough. Seeing the hopeful look on Manny's face, however, he knew that he couldn't let him down. He certainly didn't care about Yuri Durasov or his club, but he could see that, for whatever reasons, his playing something was important to Manny.

"Well," he finally said, "I guess I could play . . . something." He could hear the irritation in his voice, and made a concerted effort to lighten up. "Sure, why not?"

Manny sighed with obvious relief. "Great!" he said. "You hear that, Yuri? He's going to play."

"This is a real honor," Yuri Durasov said. "A real honor. You want to come with me?" He extended an arm toward the small stage.

Misha rose to his feet, and Durasov led him to the front of the club, where he spoke briefly to one of the balalaika players. There were murmurs and curious glances around the dinner tables as the music died down and Durasov mounted the stage and took Misha to the piano. Durasov then turned to the microphone, and a hush fell over the club's guests.

"Ladies and gentlemen," he said. "We are greatly honored here at the Club Moskva tonight to have as our guest one of our very own. The great classical pianist from Russia, Mikhail Levin."

The audience burst into applause, and there were a few whistles. Misha wondered if any of these people had ever even heard of him, but he smiled at their response. Durasov turned to him and bowed, and after a few moments of concentration Misha began to play the instantly recognizable "Moonlight" movement, from Beethoven's Piano Sonata in C-sharp Minor. Though not Russian, its cry of unrequited love and its familiarity, he thought, would appeal to the club's rowdy crowd.

Misha played for a few minutes, guessing that the audience wouldn't want to hear much of this sort of music—it was certainly not what they'd come to the Club Moskva for—then improvised an ending, stood, and bowed. The audience's reaction was wildly enthusiastic, the deafening applause, whistles, and shouts no doubt fueled by the copious amounts of alcohol they were busily consuming.

Durasov rescued him from the stage, pumping his hand vigorously, and returned him to his seat at the dinner table. Misha sat down, and smiled tightly at Vera when she patted him reassuringly on the arm.

"That was very generous of you," she said.

Misha merely shrugged.

"Quite nice under the circumstances," Sonia leaned over and said. "But a complete waste of your talent," she added in a voice brimming with irritation.

Misha nodded curtly but didn't speak. He looked across the table at Manny. "I think it's time we left," Misha said.

"Right you are, old man," Manny replied. His manner was jovial, but the look on his face was sheepish. He placed his hands on the table and pushed himself up to his feet. "I'll be back in just a minute," he said. "Come on, Sasha," he added. Sasha got up, then the two of them turned and walked toward a long, darkened hallway, to what Misha assumed to be an office.

Durasov appeared at Misha's shoulder again, clapping a huge paw on him as before. "Thank you for playing," he said. "I hope you will return to our club and bring all of your friends. We like your kind of people."

Before Misha could respond, Sonia, who was looking up at Durasov with thinly veiled contempt, said: "I'm not so sure that *our* kind of people mix well with *your* kind of people, Mr. Durasov. Aren't you a gangster? And isn't this place one of those hangouts for the Russian mob?"

Yuri Durasov froze momentarily, and then the ingratiating expression on his face turned to one of stony fury. His gray eyes were colder than ice. He withdrew his hand from Misha's shoulder and snapped his thick fingers loudly.

"Out!" he said in a quiet but ferocious voice. "All of you. Get out! This instant!"

Three of the thuggish sentries appeared around the table. Sonia couldn't help feel a sense of unease; their thick-fingered hands were on the backs of the chairs they sat upon. *As though ready to pull them out from under us,* she thought.

"We don't need your help," she snapped, scraping her chair back and getting to her feet with dignity.

"Sonia, please," Dmitri said, coming around the table to her side. "Don't forget your manners. Mr. Durasov has been very nice to us—"

"Always the great peacemaker, aren't you!" she said coldly to her husband.

Misha and Vera rose to their feet. Vera surveyed the scene calmly, her expression inscrutable.

"Come on, Mama," Misha urged quietly. "Let's go." He took her arm, and Dmitri took Vera's. They started toward the club's entrance hall, where the woman in coat check already had their coats in a pile across the counter.

Manny, with Sasha trailing behind him, came rushing toward them from the hallway, a look of consternation on his face. "What—?"

Durasov grabbed him by the lapel of his jacket. "*You!*" he growled. "Come with me. You, too." He pointed at Sasha. He jerked Manny toward him, and led him back down the hallway again, toward the office, with Sasha, once again, trailing behind.

Misha stared after them as he helped his mother into her coat, then shrugged into his own while Dmitri helped Vera with hers. They'd started out the club's doors when Vera reached out and took Misha's arm.

"Maybe your parents should go on out to the car, Misha," she said coolly, "and we should wait here for Manny and Sasha." She gave Misha a significant look.

Misha eyed her thoughtfully, then nodded his assent. "Dad, take Mama on out to the car, will you?" he said. "We'll be right out."

"Sure, son," Dmitri replied. He took his wife's arm. "Let's go, Sonia," he said. "Quietly, please."

Sonia threw her shoulders back and held her head high, her bearing even more regal than usual. A smile of satisfaction fleetingly crossed her lips, but she didn't utter another word.

They exited through the heavy steel door that the mammoth doorman, silent and forbidding in a black leather trench coat, held open for them, his face expressionless.

Vera turned to Misha. "Do you think we ought to go look for them?" she asked, a worried look on her face.

"Maybe we should," Misha said. "But I really don't like this, Vera. Why don't you go on out to the car and wait there?"

"No," she answered with determination in her voice. "I'm staying with you. Let's go see—"

At that moment Manny and Sasha, unaware of them, hurried from out of the shadowy hallway. Manny's hands were clutched to his stomach, and his face shone with the sheen of perspiration. Sasha had a look of panic in his piercing gray eyes.

"What the hell, Manny?" Misha said.

Manny quickly dropped his hands and tried to plant a smile on his lips. His effort was feeble. He pulled a crisp white linen handkerchief from his trouser pocket and quickly began wiping the sweat from his face.

"Let's go," he said, his voice a breathy rasp. "Come on, Sasha." Then he and Sasha made a quick beeline for the door, not waiting for them.

Vera looked up at Misha, her eyebrows raised questioningly. He shrugged, his lips set in a grim line, then put an arm around Vera's shoulders. They followed Manny and Sasha out into the cold, dark Brooklyn night.

It's too late to ask any questions now, Misha thought. He certainly had no intention of grilling Manny and Sasha while his mother was still with them. Later, he thought. Yes. I'll ask them about this later, when we're alone.

But later didn't come. The next day the hectic activity surrounding his departure on the world tour became a whirlwind of preparation: scheduling and rescheduling, packing and repacking, endless telephone calls, tying up a hundred loose ends in Manhattan, and saying good-byes. It was easy to forget about the questions he'd wanted to ask Manny and Sasha, especially since he didn't really want to know the answers.

Chapter Twenty-two

Prague

Prague was a fairy-tale dream come true. It was like stepping centuries back in time, into a confection of a city complete with a turreted castle on a hill. Set on both sides of the Vltava River and linked by fifteen bridges, the city's beautiful center, with its domes and spires and steeples, gave Misha a thrill.

On the way in from Ruzyne Airport he had been sadly disappointed by the ugly gray stucco apartment blocks that lined the road in the out-skirts. They were utilitarian workers' flats that could have been trans-planted from that dreary section of Moscow where he and his parents had once been forced to live. What grim reminders, he thought, of the forty years of ruthless Communist rule here in the Czech Republic. But the city itself, he was delighted to see, had survived intact and was every bit as ravishing as he'd been told.

A young man named Karel had met him at the airport. He was an emissary sent by the Czech Philharmonic Orchestra to assist Misha. On the way into the city, Karel talked nonstop about the rebirth of Prague since the fall of the Berlin Wall and the "Velvet Revolution."

Misha checked into the beautifully refurbished Palace Hotel on Pan-ská, close to Wenceslas Square. He was pleasantly surprised to be offered a glass of complementary champagne.

"You have a message, Mr. Levin," the smiling receptionist told him.

"Thanks," Misha said, taking it from her. He glanced down at the piece of paper and saw that the message was from Manny. He had taken an earlier flight over here and was now engaged in a business meeting. Misha folded the message and stuck it in his pocket, then turned to Karel.

"Thanks for your help," he said, "but I think I can handle everything else on my own."

Karel looked crestfallen. An aspiring musician, he wanted to get to know the famous Mikhail Levin better. "But . . . an interpreter, a guide—?"

"Not necessary," Misha said firmly. "I've got a lot of work to do. But thanks." Well-meaning though he may be, Misha thought, I'll be able to concentrate on the tasks at hand a lot better without the constant commentary.

"It was a pleasure to meet you, Mr. Levin, and if I can be any further service to you, have the orchestra office contact me."

He turned to leave, and Misha called after him. "Karel?"

The young man turned back around.

"Please have the limousine and chauffeur remain here," Misha said. "I will definitely be needing them."

Karel smiled and nodded, then strode out the lobby door.

The chauffeured limousine would speed his getting around, Misha thought, and he had a lot to do in a very short period of time. First on his list was going to Dvořák Hall in the Rudolfinum. He would be performing there with the Czech Philharmonic Orchestra tomorrow night.

He was familiar with many of the world's concert halls at this point in his career, but he had never before played in Prague. Every concert hall has its idiosyncrasies, and he would have to familiarize himself with them before his performance. As always, his sound must be as perfect as possible.

He went up to his suite, tipped the friendly bellhop, and looked around. The suite had large rooms and comfortable amenities. Big, soft bath towels, hair dryers, and cable TV. They're making an effort to catch up with the West, he thought.

He quickly unpacked and showered, then slipped into his work clothes. A black turtleneck sweater, black slacks, and comfortable black loafers. He put on his long black cashmere overcoat and draped a scarf around his neck, then grabbed his gloves, pocketed his room key, and headed out.

Inside the limousine, Misha gazed out at the charming cobblestoned streets and squares and the beautiful architecture: Gothic, Renaissance, Baroque, and Rococo, with the occasional Art Nouveau masterpiece. They reached the Rudolfinum in Jan Palach Square within minutes. The grand neo-Renaissance building, named for the ill-fated crown prince of Mayerling fame, was decorated with a veritable army of elaborately executed statues of composers, sculptors, painters, and architects. No wonder it's called the Temple to Beauty, Misha mused. Its beauty was an inspiration to him.

In one of Dvořák Hall's splendid colonnades, he was besieged by a crowd. Administrators, musicians, conductors, and various minions flocked around him in appreciative awe. They enthusiastically welcomed him to Prague.

Misha was appreciative and gracious, but after the initial flurry of greetings, he set to work. First he checked out his favorite Steinway concert grand and talked to David Gregory, the tuner who had traveled with it. No problems there, thank God. One of his greatest fears was always that something would happen to his favorite piano and he would be forced to perform on an unfamiliar, or worse, inferior one. When David was finished with his fine-tuning, Misha did several sound tests, both alone and with the orchestra. Finally, there was a long rehearsal.

Several hours and countless cups of strong but delicious Czech coffee later, he was satisfied. Another rehearsal tomorrow, he felt, and he would be ready. He headed outside to the waiting limousine. It was dark and cold.

"The Palace Hotel," he told Jan, the chauffeur, as he settled into his seat. He was exhausted and couldn't wait to have a quick bite to eat. I'll risk the mercies of room service tonight, he thought. Then I'll crawl straight into bed.

But it was not to be.

In the hotel lobby, Manny hurried over to him. "Well, well, old man," he said enthusiastically, clapping him on the shoulder. "How did it go at the Rudolfinum?"

"Okay," Misha said in a tired voice. "I think everything will be ready for the concert. Where's Sasha? Didn't he come?"

"No," Manny said, "he had too much work to do in New York. I don't know. Contracts and stuff. Whatever. Anyway," Manny added, "you're free tonight?"

"I'm exhausted, Manny," he said. "I'm going to call room service for a snack and go straight to bed."

Manny's face dropped, but only momentarily. "Look, Misha, there's someone here you absolutely must meet," he said.

"Who might that be?" Misha asked, not really curious but deciding to hear Manny out.

"Remember when we were talking about getting a really top-notch photographer to do pictures for the new CD covers and publicity shots?"

"Yes," Misha said matter-of-factly, wondering what was up.

"Well, guess what, old man?" Manny enthused, rubbing his hands together vigorously. "The most extraordinary coincidence!" His bright eyes locked on Misha's.

"What is it, Manny?" Misha asked with tired exasperation. "Get to the point. I'm bushed and want to go to bed. Remember?"

"Staying right here in this very hotel," Manny said, "is none other than Serena Gibbons. *The* Serena Gibbons. You know, the photographer. She's here doing a fashion shoot."

Misha nodded. He'd heard of her, of course—who hadn't?—and he recalled having seen some of her celebrity photos in magazines. As he remembered, they were good, but he knew nothing about her.

"And naturally," Manny continued excitedly, "yours truly has gotten to know her. I think she's just the person to do the pictures of you. In fact, I know she is. She's brilliant, Misha, and . . . beau-ti-ful. You're going to . . . love her!"

"Not tonight, Manny," Misha begged off. "Not tonight."

"But she's right upstairs waiting for us!" Manny cried.

Misha stared at Manny. He'd really like to choke him at times like this. But he had to admit his enthusiasm was infectious.

"Only for a quick drink," Manny cajoled. "Just one quick quaff. Then off to bed with you. She knows you have a concert tomorrow and doesn't expect a long visit. Come on, sport! Ten minutes max. For *me?*"

Misha expelled a sigh. "You won't give me any peace, will you, Manny?"

"Ten measly *minutos?* That's all I ask."

Misha sighed again, then reluctantly nodded. "Okay, Manny, but ten minutes," he said, wagging an admonishing finger in the air. "And not one single minute more."

"Great, old sport," Manny cried. "I promise, you won't be sorry."

Misha was anything but sorry.

Serena Gibbons was the most striking and enchanting woman he'd ever had the privilege of laying eyes on. And a privilege it was, he thought. If he'd seen her on the street, he'd have taken bets that she was a high-fashion model, not an accomplished photographer who worked on the other side of the camera.

Nearly six feet tall in heels, she had a long torso and long but shapely legs. Her lustrous, raven black hair fell below her shoulders and contrasted dramatically with her flawless, lightly tanned skin. Huge hazel eyes that seemed to change color continuously, shifting from brown to gray shot through with blues and greens, were alert, mischievous, and imbued with a lively curiosity. Her full, sensual lips, high forehead, and swan's neck were complemented by exquisite bone structure: high, prominent cheekbones, a long, straight nose, and perfect chin. Surprisingly, she wore very little makeup, at least not that he could detect.

Unlike so many beautiful women, Misha perceived that hers was a careless beauty, one she wore easily and comfortably. She seemed not to work at it, and perhaps was not even completely aware of how truly dazzling she was. As he watched her move about the suite making their drinks, Misha wondered if she'd been a tomboy growing up. Her stride was long and purposeful, her movements quick and efficient. She wasn't dainty, or girlish.

The most striking—and decidedly disturbing—quality about Serena Gibbons, however, was something he couldn't quite put his finger on. He knew that it had to do with an aura that surrounded her, an almost palpable sensuality that was combined, very unusually, with an innate elegance.

During the course of the evening—an evening that stretched from ten minutes to more than two hours—he quickly discovered other, more surprising, qualities about Serena Gibbons. They were characteristics he would never have suspected in a woman so utterly beautiful—*and* accomplished, he reminded himself.

She was completely down to earth, humble even. The pretentiousness he'd seen in so many beautiful women seemed alien to her. But most surprising of all, Serena seemed to be totally honest, both with herself and others, a characteristic that Misha found rare in anyone. He found it both refreshing and alluring. *Like everything else about her,* he thought.

He wasn't surprised that she was a much sought-after photographer. She seemed to have an extraordinary inner eye—part of that innate elegance, he supposed—through which she viewed the world around her. She'd made it clear that she was poorly educated, but Misha could see that she was possessed of a native intelligence that was daunting. Classical music, she'd told him, was something she knew next to nothing about, but she was anxious to learn what she could.

"If I get the commission to photograph you," she said in her smoky, alluring voice, "then you'll have to educate me a bit." She took a sip of her drink, a green tea with ginseng and honey.

"How?" Misha asked, his eyes glued to hers.

"Well, for starters, I'll want to hear you play," Serena said. Then she added in a soft voice: "I'm ashamed to say that I haven't."

"That's okay, Serena," Misha said with a smile. "Not everybody's a classical music fan."

"I'm glad you feel that way," she said. "Anyway, I'll want to know which composers you prefer. The type of music you favor. You know, like Bach or Bernstein? Your favorite musical places. I mean, like your favorite concert halls, or places that are important to the history of music."

"But why would you want to know all those things?" Misha asked, still

entranced by her hypnotic eyes. "All you'd be doing is taking a few pictures." He picked up his scotch and water and took a sip.

Serena smiled, exposing her perfect white teeth. "It's obvious," she
replied. "To get to know more about *you*. It's the only way I can take a
really great photograph. The better I know you, the better the picture's
going to be. At least that's been my experience."

Misha nodded. "I guess it makes sense," he allowed. "But it sure is a
lot more complicated than showing up at a studio and sitting down in
front of a camera and smiling." He grinned, then mugged a frown. "Or
brooding or trying to look mysterious," he added.

Serena laughed. It was the most beautiful laugh he'd ever heard, deep,
throaty, sexy, and *stirring*.

"Yes," she said, "it's a lot more complicated than that. If you want
really great photographs, not the merely good."

She paused, looking at his nearly empty glass. "Oh, here," she said,
"let me make you another drink. I'm ready, too." She turned to Manny.
"You ready, Manny?"

"No, thanks, Serena," he said.

Misha watched her get to her feet, pick up his glass, then take long
strides to the minibar. She was wearing tight black kidskin trousers that
clung provocatively to her firm buttocks and a black sweater that hinted
at breasts which, if not exactly voluptuous, would certainly be more than
ample. Despite her tall, fit thinness, Misha observed, she had curves in all
the right places. Oh, yes, indeed.

Manny caught Misha's eye and winked lewdly. The sexual vibrations
between Serena and Misha had certainly not been lost on him.

Misha ignored him, his gaze returning to Serena. "Can I help you with
anything?" he asked her.

"I've got it under control—" she began. Then: "*Shit!*" She laughed
again, that same smoky, sexy laugh. "I've spilt the scotch."

Misha quickly got to his feet and crossed to the minibar. He grabbed a
towel and squatted down to wipe up the puddle on the carpeting.

"Oh, here, let me," Serena said. "I did it."

"It's okay," Misha said, scrubbing the rug vigorously. After a minute,
he stopped and examined the spill.

"Gone," he announced, getting back to his feet. "It's as good as new."

As he handed the towel to Serena, his long tapered fingers brushed
hers, and Serena jerked involuntarily. Misha looked at her with a startled expression, and saw that her face, beneath its healthy tan, was
flushed bright red.

She must have felt the same jolt that I felt, he thought. *The same rush, the same thrill, the same precursor to . . . ?*

He wasn't sure what, but he knew what he wanted. She had drawn him to her like a siren from the moment he had first seen her, and he felt like a helpless victim who had fallen under her spell. It was a physical reaction—a chemical reaction, he thought—that he had never before experienced. Not with anyone.

As they sat back down, Manny looked over at Misha, stifling a yawn. "Excuse me," he said sleepily. "I'm a bit knackered and have an early morning meeting, you know." He began getting to his feet.

"Serena," he said, proffering his hand. "It was a delight to meet you and get to know you better."

"It was great to get to know you, too, Manny," Serena said, starting to get back up again.

"No, no," Manny said. "Please keep your seat. I can show myself out." He turned to Misha. "Why don't you two carry on the discussion?" he said. "I'd better hit the sack. Long day tomorrow."

Misha looked up at him, then turned to Serena. She smiled at him knowingly.

"Fine," he said, his dark eyes still on Serena. "Get a good night's sleep, Manny."

Manny let himself out, quietly pulling the door shut behind him.

Misha got up and walked over to the couch where Serena sat, watching him with her huge hazel eyes. He stood before her, his tall, muscular body towering over her.

"Do you mind?" he asked, indicating the cushion next to her.

"Please," Serena said, patting it with her hand.

Misha sat down, sliding an arm across the back of the couch, behind her. He turned his face to hers. "I'm glad we're alone," he said softly. He could smell her intoxicating scent and hear her quickening breath.

Serena nodded. "Yes," she said. "I am, too."

Misha saw the expectant expression on her face and brought his arm around her shoulders. He pulled her very gently, closer to him, looking into her eyes.

Serena responded immediately, drawing herself toward him, her eyes never leaving his as their lips met. They began kissing, slowly at first, then with more urgency, beginning to devour each other passionately. After that first taste, which had been so long awaited, their hunger was all the more ravenous, consuming them with its need.

It seemed like a lifetime of anticipation but was only moments before they were disrobing each other in the bedroom of her suite. Quickly,

recklessly, intent on feasting upon each other after the hours of tantalizing yearning, they tossed their clothing to the floor, where it lay scattered
harum-scarum. Finally naked, they stood drinking in the magnificence
of each other's bodies, but their overwhelming desire made lingering impossible. They tumbled onto the bed, their hands and lips all over each
other, stroking, patting, prodding, kissing, licking.

Misha entered her quickly but gently, and Serena gasped with pleasure, pulling him to her. As he plunged deeper and faster, he heard her
moan in ecstasy, and a torrent began to rise within him. He felt omnipo-
tent and thrust with all his might. His was the power to give pleasure, to
conquer, to possess this exquisite creature.

Serena began to tremble, then convulsions seized her, and she began
to writhe wildly from side to side.

"Oh, Misha," she cried. "Oh, Misha . . . I . . . I . . . *ahhhhhh—*!"

He plunged in with a bellow, his seed joining her sweet nectar, then
collapsed atop her, smothering her face with kisses. He hugged her to him
tightly, as if he never wanted to let her go.

Later, after their breathing had returned to normal, they lay facing
each other in the dim light. Misha's long fingers roved over her beautiful
flesh, stroking, patting, his lips tenderly planting kisses in her hair, on her
face, her neck, her breasts.

Serena didn't think she'd ever felt so wanted, so appreciated, and she
knew that she had never felt such desire for anyone as she did for Misha.
She ran her hands through his long black hair, over his handsome features, and down his powerful shoulders and chest, returning his sweet
kisses, inhaling his masculine scent.

She looked into the dark pools that were his eyes. "I think that was
like a mazurka," she said with a smile.

"Prestissimo?" he replied.

"Something like that. Very fast. Almost over before it started."

"Disappointed?" he asked quietly, squeezing her shoulder. He knew
with a certain knowledge that she wasn't. She had been as driven by her
own lusty appetites as he had been.

"Oh, no," Serena said. "Anything but that. It was wonderful, Misha."
Her hand moved slowly down his stomach to the prize of his manhood.
"Wonderful," she repeated.

He looked into her hazel eyes. Even in the dim light, they shone
bright with lust. "I think it should be much slower this time," he said, his
fingers lightly thrumming her nipples, feeling them become erect. "Much,
much slower."

His mouth went to one breast, kissing, licking, and sucking it ever so slowly. Then he looked up at her. "Adagio, I think." Then his mouth went to the other breast.

Serena moaned with pleasure, and felt his cock come to life in her hand. "Oh, yes," she whispered. "Oh, yes, Misha. Yes, yes, yes."

The eternal dance began again, more leisurely this time, as they explored each other's bodies, becoming more familiar, relishing their newly found intimacy until the wee hours of the morning.

When they lay sated at last, their bodies suffused with a glorious tiredness, Misha held her in his arms, and they talked and laughed. In this magical afterglow of their lovemaking, they began to explore on another level, gradually coming to know more about each other's professional lives, their families and friends, their likes and dislikes.

Before they finally drifted off into a peaceful slumber, Serena said: "You've played my body like an instrument."

"Oh?" Misha said with amusement, kissing her on the ear. "And what instrument are you?"

"I don't know," she replied huskily, "but you're a master musician." She rubbed the tip of his nose playfully with a finger.

"And you, Serena Gibbons, are the finest instrument ever made," he said, taking her finger and kissing it.

Serena looked into his eyes. "Just remember," she said, "mazurkas are great. Adagio is fabulous. But I don't like nocturnes. So please, don't play any nocturnes? They make me sad."

"Nocturnes," Misha promised, and hugged her tightly. "I promise you, I won't ever play you a nocturne."

Misha's concert at Dvořák Hall was a smash success. Critics and concertgoers praised him to the skies. Personally, he felt that he had never before played with such unabashed passion. Although he'd planned upon returning to New York before his next performance, he changed his mind and decided to remain in Prague. And celebrate with Serena.

Through lovers' eyes, the old city took on even more of a fairy-tale aspect. They strolled its cobbled streets from Wenceslas Square to Old Town.

There, in the very heart of the city, they stopped to watch the Town Hall's famous fifteenth-century astronomical clock strike the hour. From its two windows Christ and the Apostles emerged one by one, then disappeared as the skeleton of death inverted an hourglass. Finally, a cock flapped its wings and crowed.

Serena looked at Misha and made a face. "Creepy, isn't it?"

Misha laughed. "Not a happy reminder, that's for sure."

Calories be damned. They stopped at one of the famous coffee shops and indulged in a taste-fest of delicious pastries.

"I've got to walk this off," Serena said, guilty after happily stuffing herself.

"A very good idea," Misha agreed, taking her hand in his.

They crossed the Charles Bridge with its many statues and walked up to Prague Castle, where they feasted their eyes on the splendor of St. Vitus's Cathedral, myriad chapels, royal apartments, courtyards, and picture galleries.

"It's all like a giant movie set, isn't it?" Serena said.

"And you look like the star of the movie," Misha replied sincerely.

Serena smiled self-consciously but was immensely pleased. She believed the compliment was heartfelt coming from him, unlike so many men she'd known in the past.

Finally exhausted from the walking and the constant visual stimulation, she turned to Misha. "What would you say to going back to the hotel for a drink and maybe a shower before dinner?"

"I thought you'd never ask," he said, and kissed her on the forehead.

At the hotel Misha called room service and ordered champagne. They took their first sips in the sitting room, then took the bottle and their glasses to the bedroom. Quickly undressing, they lay naked in bed, entwined in each other's arms, the champagne losing its sparkle as they feasted instead on each other for the remainder of the afternoon.

That evening, they went to U Maliru Restaurant, one of Prague's best, where they dined on venison pâté with lingonberries, smoked trout, rack of lamb, and a rich strudel with ice cream.

"I shouldn't be eating like this," Serena said, sighing with contentment. "But it's absolutely wonderful."

"We can both go on diets tomorrow," Misha answered, smiling.

Serena suddenly frowned. *Tomorrow.* She didn't want to think about tomorrow, because the next morning they had to part company. Misha had to get back to New York before the next leg of his tour, and she had to leave for another fashion shoot, this one in Paris.

He saw the expression on her face and reached over and took her hand. "What's wrong, Serena?" he asked.

She sighed. "Oh, Misha, I . . . I just hate to think about leaving," she said, studying their hands, joined there on the table as they were.

"We have the rest of the night together," Misha said, giving her hand a squeeze. Her disappointment touched him deeply.

"I know," she said, "and believe me, I'm glad. But I can't help but think about . . . about . . . afterward." Her gaze shifted from their hands up to his face. "You know. After we've both gone back to work."

The look on her face was almost imploring, Misha thought. He could see that she was truly distraught about being separated from him, and while he certainly didn't want to see her unhappy, he couldn't help the thrilling sensation that passed through him. *She feels the same way I do.* He put an arm around her shoulder and pulled her to him.

"We'll be able to see each other," he said with confidence, looking into her eyes. "We'll *make* the time, Serena. Somehow. Whether it's in New York when we're between trips, or meeting up on the road."

"We'll be like ships passing in the night," she said. "We're both on the go so much."

"Look," Misha said, "we can work it out. I know we can, Serena. Don't you see? If you're in London and I'm in Paris, one of us can make a quick hop over to see the other."

"I hope so," she said.

"I know so," he said, chucking her under the chin. "So put a smile back on that gorgeous face of yours."

She did smile, and dazzlingly, her eyes brightening with possibilities. His reassurances made her feel with more certainty that she wasn't simply a passing fancy that he would soon forget.

"Just think," he said softly. "You and I, Serena. We can make love all over the world."

The wake-up call was a shrill, unwelcome end to the short sleep they had managed after a night of lusty acrobatics. Their lovemaking had been all the more frenzied, knowing that they would have to part come morning. They knew the early call was coming, of course, but they couldn't control the overwhelming sexual pull they had on each other. It was almost as if they had become enslaved to their desires.

"Do you want to take a quick shower?" Misha asked, half-awake, his arms wrapped around her.

"No," Serena said, shaking her head. Then she whispered into his ear: "I want to smell you on me all the way to Paris."

He grinned conspiratorially. "Then I won't either."

After they had dressed, Misha insisted on taking her to Ruzyne Airport to catch her flight to Paris.

"You don't have to do that, Misha," she protested.

"I won't have it any other way," he asserted. "I want to spend every minute with you possible."

She hugged him fiercely. "You're almost too good to be true," she said.

"So are you, Serena," he replied solemnly.

They made it to the airport, and her flight was announced almost immediately.

"I'd better board," she said, reluctant to let go of his hand.

"Good-bye, Serena," he said. "I'll see you very soon."

Serena laughed mirthlessly. "It'd better be."

He leaned over and kissed her chastely on the lips. "I love you," he whispered.

"I love you, too," she said breathlessly. Then she turned and disappeared into the tunnel of the jetway quickly, so he couldn't see the tears that were beginning to form in her eyes.

Misha stared after her long, lithe body until she was gone from his sight, then turned and left the airport. On the ride back in to Prague, he looked out through the limousine's windows unseeingly, so preoccupied with thoughts of Serena was he. He already felt her loss like a great emptiness inside him, a monstrous hunger that he somehow knew wouldn't go away. But how could that be? he wondered. For it suddenly occurred to him that he'd known her for only two days.

Two days, he marveled. *Only two short days, but it seems like I've known her all my life.* And it was with a sense of wonderment that he realized: *We're already planning a future together. We're lovers.*

Misha was packed and ready to leave on the night flight to New York, but he had one more stop he wanted to make before heading out to the airport once again. He gave the chauffeur his instructions, and Jan drove the limousine toward the Prague Ghetto. Misha had thought about taking Serena there yesterday but had decided that this was one visit he wanted to make alone.

In the ghetto, he gazed out the car window at the buildings along Siroka Street, Červená, Maiselova, Jachymova, and Dusni. He peered with curiosity at the house where Rabbi Löw, the famed and much-storied golem maker, had once lived. He saw the Gothic Old-New Synagogue, Maisel Synagogue, and the High Synagogue.

At the Old Jewish Cemetery he had Jan pull over and stop. Misha slid out of the limousine and stood, looking around in amazement at the ancient graveyard, where headstones—over twelve thousand of them—were scattered helter-skelter in the small space, some atop others, many falling down, more than a few in disrepair.

He took a few steps into the cemetery, then stopped, reluctant to go any farther. He had traveled the world and seen many things, but he didn't know if he had ever seen anyplace that was as overwhelming, as *haunting*, as this.

As his heart swelled with sadness, his mind was suddenly aswirl with memories, and his thoughts turned, inevitably, to Mariya and Arkady, his old friends in Moscow. They were now long gone, and he wondered about their graves, if anyone ever visited them and if they were well kept. He then had the shameful realization that he hadn't thought about them—those precious and revered friends of his youth—for a very long time.

His career, his pursuit of fame and glory in the world of classical music, and his tireless nighttime pursuit of pleasure—his work and play—had obsessed him for so long that he had virtually forgotten his old mentors. He felt a wave of guilt wash over him, remembering that for a long time he had failed to even notice, much less stroke or kiss, the mezuzah he'd bought to replace the old one that Arkady had entrusted to him.

He walked farther into the cemetery, then stopped again. Tears were beginning to form in his large dark eyes. He bowed his head.

Arkady, he intoned as if in prayer, forgive me for failing to think of you. For neglecting your memory, and Mariya's. I am back now, beside you, and I need your blessings more than ever. And your help, Arkady. For I have found a woman. *The* woman, Arkady. And I must have her. She must be mine.

Chapter Twenty-three

❧

"How many times have I told you, Manny?" Misha stormed thunderously. His brows were knit in fury, and his lips were curled into an ugly snarl.

He jumped to his feet and flung the musical score he'd been studying behind him. It struck the piano, then fluttered to the jewel-toned Persian rug at his feet.

When Manny didn't respond immediately, Misha lashed out again, his voice even louder and harsher. "I will *not* perform in Moscow! Not *ever*! I will not perform *anywhere* in Russia!" He glared at his agent, his body quivering with rage.

Sasha sat in a corner, observing the scene quietly, seemingly unperturbed by Misha's reaction.

Manny pulled a crisp white linen handkerchief from his rear trouser pocket and began nervously polishing the lenses of his tortoiseshell glasses. His pudgy fingers moved jerkily, ineffectively, but he continued nevertheless, displacing his anxiety onto his expensive glasses.

"I . . . I just thought . . . ," he stammered.

"You thought *what*?" Misha shouted.

Before Manny could reply, Misha lasered him with his dark eyes and lashed out again. "I'll tell you what! Nothing! That's what you thought! Nothing! Zero! Zilch!"

He began pacing, an accusatory finger pointed at Manny punctuating his words. "You know why? Because you weren't *thinking*! If you had been, you wouldn't even have mentioned the *possibility* of me playing in Russia!"

Manny stood, hands folded behind his back, observing Misha's theatrical pacing. He had been shamefaced at first, but now he was becoming increasingly angry as the abuse continued to be heaped on him. Nor did he like Sasha seeing him upbraided like this. At the same time, he realized that he had to do everything in his power to placate his star client. Oh, yes. He had to be very careful in the way he handled the primary source of his bread and butter. Failed pianists, he reminded himself for the umpteenth time, can make a good living off of successful ones.

"Misha," he finally managed in a calm, even tone. "I did think about it. And I thought that perhaps after all this time you might have changed your mind. It'll soon be twenty years since you left Russia."

Misha flopped down onto a suede-upholstered couch, sinking amid its antique silk-embroidered Turkish pillows. He put his head in his hands, shaking it from side to side.

"Manny," he said, looking up at him. His voice was quieter now, and his eyes looked weary. "I've told you how they took our home away from us. *And* everything in it. I've told you how they put us in a rundown project full of the worst kinds of people. Bums and whores and drunks. How they took all the privileges away from my parents. How they wouldn't let me study with the best instructors at the Moscow Conservatory. How they wouldn't let us emigrate for two years."

He paused, staring into Manny's eyes.

Manny sat down in a chair opposite him and folded his hands in his lap. "Yes, Misha," he replied. "You've told me all that many times, and I can understand the pain and suffering it caused you and your family. But don't you think it's time to let bygones be bygones? There's a whole new regime over there. The Wall's come down."

"I don't care," Misha said. "They treated my family like dirt. And I'm not going to perform in Russia, homeland or not!"

"But . . . but think of all the money they're offering," Manny sputtered. "Jesus, Misha! You just don't turn down that kind of money."

Misha shot him a hard, level stare. "Maybe you don't, Manny, but *I* do."

"But . . . but . . . you'd get a *hero's* welcome," Manny continued excitedly. "Can't you see it? Former Russian citizen, mistreated by the Communists, welcomed back with open arms. It'd be great publicity. An international event. You couldn't buy publicity like that."

"I'm not going to be used as a poster boy for the new Russia," Misha replied. "So forget it, Manny. No way. Case closed."

Manny fidgeted in his chair. "Aw, Misha. I . . . I just don't . . . see—"

"Case *closed*," Misha roared, and slapped his hand down on the couch. He was glaring at Manny once again, his eyes wide, the veins in his forehead distended.

"Okay, okay," Manny said, backing down. He knew that he'd pushed too hard, and if he hoped to ever succeed, he'd better drop the subject quickly.

He pushed himself to his feet. "Sorry, Misha. I'm really sorry for upsetting you," he said. "I won't bring it up again."

"Don't!" Misha said.

"Well, we'd better be off," Manny said, injecting a jovial tone in his voice and glancing toward Sasha, who immediately got to his feet and stood ready to leave. Manny rubbed his hands together with anticipation. "Have some pressing business we need to take care of."

Misha made no movement to get up. "You can see yourself out," he said.

"Right," Manny said. "Well, cheerio, then, old chap. Later." He and Sasha turned and left the room.

Misha heard the apartment door close behind them. He sighed and stretched, then kicked off his shoes and put his feet up on the couch, spreading out lengthwise. He stared up at the high ceiling, lost in thought.

Why is he pushing a Russian tour so hard? he wondered. Why won't he just give it up? He's been at me about it for the last four years, ever since the Berlin Wall came down.

He expelled a sign as his gaze swept over the heights of the room. He could see from the changing light on the ceiling that the sun was beginning its descent in the west. I've soon got to get up and get ready to go see the folks, he realized.

As he climbed the stairs to his bedroom, though, he couldn't shake the feeling that there was something strangely off-kilter about the pressure Manny was putting on him to perform in Moscow. There's something very fishy about it, he decided. Yes. Something definitely stinks. But what the hell is it?

Then, as if a magic wand had been waved across his path, he reached his bedroom, and his thoughts immediately turned to Serena. Manny, Sasha, and the Russian tour were completely forgotten as he remembered that she would be in New York tomorrow.

He nearly ached with anticipation when he looked at his bed, thinking that in twenty-four hours or less he and Serena would be curled up together there. His mind flashed on the enthralling beauty of her body, its elegant perfection and erotic possibilities. He felt the hunger for her again, that long raven hair, her generous lips and creamy breasts, her strong thighs and tight buttocks, and that glorious mound. He was shocked that his body became aroused at the mere thought of her.

He wondered if she ached with the same desire he did, if she still wanted him as much as she thought she had amid Prague's fairy-tale beauty. Then he remembered how they had whispered that they loved each other.

He slowly undressed, enjoying his body's arousal, wondering if what they felt for each other was *really* love or just a powerful chemical pull that was some sort of animal lust. As he stepped into the shower, he decided he didn't care what it was called. He would give himself up to it willingly, joyously, knowing that he had never felt anything like it before.

Sonia couldn't help smiling as she witnessed the scene across the dinner table. Misha and Vera sat side by side, engrossed in conversation, the rest of the world excluded from their intimate familiarity. They laughed with each other like children. Like the oldest and dearest of friends, Sonia thought. And maybe—dare she think?—maybe like lovers? Ah, if only, she told herself. For they were the most perfect young couple she had ever seen. Ideal for each other in every way.

She saw that Dmitri, too, had been observing them, if a bit less obviously, stealing a glance from time to time over his glass of wine. She knew that he shared her sentiments, for hadn't they discussed Misha and Vera often enough? But Dmitri would invariably point out that Misha and Vera had known each other for seven long years. Seven years during which their relationship had seemed to run hot and cold, and sometimes, perhaps more dangerously, lukewarm.

Lately, he'd pointed out that now they both had successful careers, plenty of money, and nothing that he could see to stand in the way of their marriage. He reasoned, therefore, that something was simply not clicking between them.

Sonia was nothing if not practical, and she knew that Dmitri was right on the mark. For her part, she felt certain that the only obstacle in the way of their perfect union was Misha's wandering eye. Her son wanted to sow his wild oats before settling down. But, she asked herself, how many wild oats could a young man have?

"Mama?" Misha was looking across the table at her with a grin.

Sonia suddenly became aware of his attention focused on her. "Yes, Misha," she said. "What is it?"

"Have we lost you?" he asked with amusement. He hadn't failed to notice his mother's smiling approval as she watched Vera and himself. And he knew exactly what was on her mind. Hadn't she made enough little hints over the years? She'd tried to be subtle, but subtlety was not Sonia's strong suit.

"No, no," Sonia replied. "I was just thinking, Misha."

"What about?" he asked mischievously.

"Just . . . things," she said evasively. Then she abruptly changed the subject. "Where're Manny and Sasha, by the way?" she asked. "I thought they were coming tonight. Then the secretary called and canceled for them."

"I don't know," Misha said, her question deflating his good humor. "I don't know what they're up to." There was a note of irritation in his voice.

"You sound a little unhappy with the dapper Mr. Cygelman," Vera said. "And his Arctic sidekick. What've they done now?"

"Yes," Sonia interjected. "What *have* they done?"

"It's not that they've done anything," Misha replied. "It's just that they keep harping on me about doing a tour in Russia. Working with some promoters they know over there. At least I think they're over there."

Sonia set her fork down on her plate with a clatter. "With Manny and that Sasha, who can tell?" she said derisively. "For all you know, it might be some of those awful gangsters we saw out in Brighton Beach. Have you thought about that?"

"Not really," Misha said. "How am I supposed to concentrate on my music and worry about the business end of things, too? Anyway, whoever these guys are, they're willing to pay an enormous amount of money to get me to do a Russian tour."

Sonia stared at her son, her brows knit together in concentration. "Misha, I haven't wanted to discuss this with you, but I think it's time you considered searching for a new agent. I think that Manny might be mixed up with—"

"Mama!" Misha broke in. "I think you have a vivid imagination. Manny and Sasha have done a fantastic job for me so far. I get booked into the best concert halls. I get dates playing with the greatest orchestras. I play the best festivals. And besides, the music company is flourishing. It's phenomenal. My CDs are selling like hotcakes, the distribution is fantastic, the publicity is first-rate. What more could I ask for?"

"I've wondered about all that," Vera said matter-of-factly.

"What do you mean?" Misha asked, turning to her.

"Well, it seems almost too perfect, Misha," Vera said, choosing her words carefully. "How do Manny and Sasha always, and I mean always, manage to book you into the best concert halls? Everybody in the music world knows that some of the places you play are hell to book. Top stars are kept waiting or even have to settle for less. And why are your CDs distributed better than nearly anyone else's? Why do they get the most prominent retail space in the stores? I'm not saying they don't deserve it. I'm just saying that it's very curious that from the very beginning this upstart company of Manny's and Sasha's has done what even major, well-established companies sometimes can't do for their artists."

"You should listen to Vera," Sonia said, nodding her head. "I can tell that she's been thinking along the same lines that I have."

Misha laughed. "Maybe the two of you have some special female intuition that men don't have." He was trying to make light of what they'd said, but in actuality he was afraid that they were zeroing in on potentially bothersome problems that had been worrying him as well. He simply hadn't wanted to think about them.

"I don't think female intuition has anything to do with it," Dmitri said, speaking up for the first time.

Everybody at the table turned to look at him.

"What are you saying, Dad?" Misha asked.

Dmitri cleared his throat, then spoke. "I agree with your mother, Misha. I think it's time that you looked for a new agent. Something is beginning to tell me that Manny and Sasha may not be altogether trustworthy."

"Are you saying this because of that one stupid dinner in Brighton Beach?" Misha asked. "Or is it because you think Manny and Sasha are lovers or something."

"No," Dmitri said, shaking his head. "Definitely not. I don't care if they're lovers, but I certainly don't like to think that Manny and Sasha are involved in any way with those people. Because"—he paused and looked into his son's eyes—"that involves you by association."

"I don't even know any of those people!" Misha countered defensively.

"You don't have to, son," Dmitri said. "At least for people to associate you with them in their minds." He cleared his throat again. "In any case, I'm not denying that Manny and Sasha have done a good job for you so far. But I think they've been awfully secretive, particularly regarding the recording business. Every time I broach the subject or try to ask questions, they brush me off. The long and short of it is, I smell a rat."

Misha looked at his father thoughtfully. "I'll talk to them about it," he promised. "But I'm not going to fire them now. They've been with me since the beginning, and I owe them my allegiance."

Sonia emitted an audible sigh. "So what are you going to do about this Russian tour?" she asked.

"I'm not going to do it," Misha said.

"Well, it's up to you, Misha," she said. "You know we'll back you up whatever your decision is."

"Thanks, Mama," he said.

"But I do hope you'll give a new agent some thought," she added.

"You're not going to give up, are you?" Misha said.

"Not on your life, young man," she said.

After dinner, Misha hailed a taxi on Central Park South, and he and Vera slid in. He gave the driver Vera's address, and the taxi sped off toward the East Side.

"You want to come in for a nightcap?" Vera asked.

Misha was looking out the window distractedly and didn't answer her for a moment. "I don't think so, Vera," he finally replied. "I . . . I—"

She patted his arm. "Misha, you don't have to explain yourself to me. It's Vera, remember?"

He drew his gaze in and smiled at her. "I know," he said. "And I'm really glad to see you. You know, your letters and telephone calls practically keep me alive while I'm on tour."

"Yours make a big difference to me, too," she said. *But they don't replace you*, she thought.

"We'll have to get together *alone*," he said, "before I leave again."

"That would be great, Misha," Vera said. "If you've got the time."

"I'm just sort of bushed tonight," he said. "I want to hit the sack." *I've got to get ready for Serena's arrival tomorrow*, he thought.

"You just need a good night's rest," Vera said. *He never has to go to bed early if there's something he really wants to do*, she thought. *I wonder what's really up?*

"I guess so," he replied.

The driver pulled up in front of the town house where Vera's apartment was, and Misha started to get out.

"I can get inside safely, Misha," Vera said.

"No," he insisted. "I'll walk you to the door." He turned to the driver. "Wait here, please. I'll just be a minute."

He walked Vera to the door. She took her key out and turned to him. "Good night, Misha," she said. "Call if you get a chance." *I can't push him*, she thought, *or he'll run away*.

"I will," he promised. He leaned over and kissed her chastely on the cheek. "Talk to you later." He turned and rushed back to the waiting taxi.

If only I could talk to her, he thought. *If only I could tell her about Serena. Tell her about the love of my life.*

He suddenly realized that Vera was the best friend he had, but she was the last person in the world he could tell about Serena.

Chapter Twenty-four

When Misha saw Serena emerge from the Customs area, he could swear that his heart skipped a beat. He had never known what that meant. Nor would he have even believed such a physical manifestation of romantic anticipation was possible. His body's response to the sight of Serena, however—her long black hair, dark glasses, chic trim black pants suit and high-heeled boots—had made him a firm believer.

She didn't see him, and he called to her. "Serena! Over here!"

She turned her elegant head toward him and took off her dark glasses. Misha was gratified to see her generous lips immediately spread into a smile as genuine as his own.

"Misha!" she called back, heading in his direction.

He held his arms out, and she went into them, returning his hug. He thrilled at the touch of her and her unique scent, an exotic blend of musk and citrus and the mysterious Far East.

She kissed him on both cheeks, airily, he thought, as if they were friends, not lovers. But he soon knew why.

"Misha," she said, drawing away from him, "this is Coral Randolph, my agent."

Misha looked over and saw a painfully thin woman somewhere in her middle years, her age difficult to ascertain. She had shiny jet black hair, like shoe polish, he thought, parted down the middle and severely cut in a short page boy. It contrasted almost grotesquely with her white-powdered skin and plum-hued lipstick. Her eyebrows were plucked to thin arches, if not entirely penciled on.

"How do you do?" Misha said to her, extending a hand. He had expected Serena to be alone and was disappointed that this strange woman was with her, but he tried not to let his feelings show.

Coral Randolph took his proffered hand and shook it with surprising strength. He noticed that hers was very long and thin, her nails perfectly manicured and lacquered the same plum shade as her lips. She wore an enormous pearl set in gold on one finger.

She looked him directly in the eye. Her gaze was intense and appraising and, he thought, absolutely fearless.

"It's a pleasure, Misha," Coral said in an eastern boarding school voice. "Serena's told me so much about you, and of course I know your beautiful playing quite well."

"Thank you," Misha said.

"Look," Serena said excitedly. "There's Sal!"

Misha looked over to see a young lady approaching them. Her hair was cut like a man's, and she wore a expensive-looking man-tailored suit, complete with a tie.

"Sally Parker, Misha Levin," Coral said quickly, by way of introduction. "Sally's my assistant."

Sally nodded but ignored Misha's extended hand. "Hey, guys," she said. "Let's get a move on. I'm double-parked."

She had the voice and manner of John Wayne, Misha thought.

Serena and Coral turned and started to follow her.

"But . . . ," Misha began.

"What is it?" Serena asked, smiling.

"I thought you'd ride back in with me," he said. "I have a limo waiting."

"Oh, God!" Serena said. "I didn't think. Sal always picks us up. Why don't you ride with us? Just get rid of your driver."

"It won't take a minute," Misha said. "I'll meet you right out front. Okay?" *Damn*, he thought, *no necking on the way back into the city.*

"Shake a leg," Sally/Sal said.

Misha rushed out of the terminal and down to the curb where his limousine was parked. He quickly paid the driver, tipping him generously, and dismissed him, then rushed back up the sidewalk to where the three women stood waiting for him.

"What about your luggage?" Misha asked.

"Oh, we Fed Exed everything from Paris," Serena said. "It's so much easier that way. Ready?"

"Yes," Misha said.

"Let's get in," Serena said.

The car was a vintage Phantom V Rolls-Royce, an immense, shining black presence at the curbside.

"My God, it's magnificent," Misha enthused.

"It's Coral's," Serena said, opening the door and sliding onto the backseat's luxurious and aromatic black leather. Coral slid in after her, and Misha got in next to Serena on the other side.

"So it's yours, Coral," Misha said, his eyes sweeping the interior of the car appreciatively.

"By default," Coral said. "Actually, it was my step-grandmother's. My grandfather gave it to her, and the old dear left it to me."

"All set?" Sally/Sal asked from the driver's seat.

"Yes," Coral said. "And Sal?"

"Yeah?"

"Please don't drive *too* fast on the way into the city. Okay?"

"You got it," Sally/Sal said.

As they drove into Manhattan, Misha found it difficult to keep his hands off Serena. He gathered from her somewhat ladylike distance that this was not the time or the place for any touchy-feely games. *With Coral, the vampire, on the other side, and John Wayne in the driver's seat,* he thought, *I guess I'd better restrain my natural impulse to ravage Serena here on the backseat.*

Sally/Sal dropped Coral off at her apartment building in the east Sixties at Fifth Avenue. Just the sort of address she would have, Misha thought, at least from the looks of her. World-class shopper, world-class breeding and taste, and probably a patient of world-class plastic surgeons, psychiatrists, nutritionists, and personal trainers.

They rolled majestically down Fifth Avenue to Fourteenth Street, then went crosstown and rolled down Seventh Avenue, eventually pulling up in front of Serena's SoHo loft building.

"See ya, Sal," Serena said as they slid out of the Rolls-Royce.

"Yeah," Sally/Sal said. "See ya later, Serena."

As the big car rolled away, Serena and Misha entered the lobby of her building. It had obviously been expensively renovated, but there was no doorman.

In the elevator, Misha turned to her, and they fell into each other's arms, kissing passionately, hungrily, desperately, making up for the torturous wait while driving into the city. When the elevator car stopped at Serena's floor, they were in a clinch and didn't part for a few moments.

They finally entered Serena's vast loft, which was both her photography studio and home, and made a beeline for the bedroom. Without preamble they rapidly undressed, tossing their clothes on the floor. They fell onto the bed, devouring each other with an urgency and need born of long absence.

Later, much later, they lay entwined in each other's arms, whispering in the near-darkness, sipping glasses of wine that Serena had gotten in the kitchen.

"How long are you here for?" Misha asked her.

"Two days," Serena said. "Two days of back-to-back meetings. Then I'm off to Helsinki for a shoot. Three or four days shooting models in furs."

"Damn," Misha said.

"What?" she asked.

"I'm going to be here the rest of the week, then I'm off to Berlin for a performance," he said.

"Well, maybe . . . ," she said teasingly, "maybe I can fit you in between meetings tomorrow and the next day. Huh? What do you say?"

Misha laughed. "You need to ask?" He pulled her closer, hugging her tightly. "You couldn't cancel some meetings while I'm here? So we could spend more time together?"

Serena pulled away from him. "No way," she said in a firm voice.

Misha saw the cross look on her face. "Okay, Serena," he said. "I just wondered."

"Remember one thing, Misha," she said. "My career takes precedence over everything else. I don't miss meetings or assignments. There are lots and lots of photographers out there waiting in line to take my place."

"I understand," he said.

"Good," she said, "because that's the way it is."

He leaned over and kissed her forehead. "Don't worry," he said. "My career's the same way. I really do understand."

"I hope you do," she said mildly. Then more playfully: "We'll have the next two nights, Misha. Just think! Just you and me."

The next two nights were perhaps, Misha thought, the loneliest and most miserable he'd ever spent. On Thursday, they were to have met at her loft at nine, after her day was finished. Serena telephoned him around eight to tell him she probably wouldn't be through work before midnight. It was a model emergency, she said. About eleven, she had called to say it would be more like two or three in the morning before she could get home. He hadn't questioned her or argued with her, but she heard the disappointment in his voice.

"I hate this, too," she said. "But there's nothing I can do about it. Tamara and Justine, two of the models for the fur shoot, have vanished into thin air. We're finding replacements."

"Vanished?" he replied.

"Well," Serena said flippantly, "they've probably run off to St. Bart's with some coked-up rich guys."

Friday was a replay of Thursday. He waited on pins and needles to see

her, then ultimately gave up in the middle of the night. Their last conversation was at 2:30 A.M. Friday morning.

"Sal's taking me to Kennedy at seven, so you go to bed," Serena
had said.

"I can take you," he insisted.

"That's ridiculous," Serena said. "You need your rest."

"You haven't gotten any yourself," he said testily.

"I can sleep in the car on the way out to the airport and on the plane,"
she said.

"I *hate* this," Misha said.

"I told you there would be times like this," Serena said evenly. "I can't
help it, Misha. It's part of the job."

"I know," he said with weary resignation.

"Listen," she said, "we'll be together again soon. And I can hardly
wait."

"Me, either, Serena," he said.

When they finally hung up, he was sorely dissatisfied. At the same
time, he began to fantasize about the next time he would see her, would
hold her in his arms, would inhale her intoxicating perfume. It wouldn't
be too long.

"Manny," Misha said, "I wanted to have a little talk before I leave for
Berlin." They were seated in Misha's sumptuous living room, drinking
freshly brewed coffee that Misha had brought in from the kitchen.

"What's going on, old chap?" Manny asked. He was in a particularly
expansive mood today. Several new suits had arrived from his tailors in
London this morning, and to top it off, the Jaguar XJ6 convertible he'd
had on order had been delivered just before he came over to Misha's.
British racing green with a tan rag top. Just the ticket. It would look appropriately sporty, sitting alongside the more sedate black Mercedes in
the garage beneath the apartment building where he'd bought the penthouse, complete with wraparound terraces and views of the entire city
and New Jersey and Long Island beyond.

"Well, you know I don't know very much about Brighton Beach Recordings, Inc.," Misha said. "And I think it's time for you to give me a
brief on it."

"A brief?" Manny said, somewhat startled. "But you have copies of all
your contracts, and I drew them up myself, so you know they're kosher,
Misha. And you're getting very handsome advances and royalty rates—as
stipulated in the contracts."

Manny paused and took a sip of his coffee, looking at Misha over his tortoiseshell glasses. Misha was studying him intently, but Manny couldn't read his expression.

"You've also got copies of your royalty statements for the last few years," Manny continued, "and if I say so myself, I don't think anybody could have made more money for you than Brighton Beach."

He sat with a pleased expression that Misha recognized as a cover-up for the discomfort that he was actually feeling.

"It's not the money so much," Misha said, "or the contracts and royalty statements. My father has had all of those examined by an independent entertainment attorney." Misha noticed that a flicker of alarm crossed Manny's features, but it was quickly replaced by a mask, this one of the indulgent listener. "Anyway, Elliot Lufkin went through everything, and he assures Dad that everything is in order there."

Manny nodded. "I'm gratified that so famous an attorney would think so," he said, "but I still don't understand why you . . . or your father went to the trouble. Don't you trust me, Misha? Or Sasha?"

Misha was silent for a moment, then answered Manny with a question. "What about distribution, Manny?" he asked. "I'm in the dark there. And what about your phenomenal booking abilities? Brighton Beach seems to be able to book me anywhere, anytime. I'm in the dark there, too. I'd like a rundown—"

Misha's private telephone line bleeped, and he reached over and picked it up.

"Hello?" he said, not really listening.

"It's me," Serena said at the other end.

Misha's face broke out into a wide smile. "Hi, you," he said. "Where are you?" As usual his heart gave a leap at the sound of her voice, and his body was aroused, anxious to touch her, hold her, fulfill her every need.

"Helsinki," she said. "I only have a second, but I wanted to call and tell you that I miss you."

"I miss you, too," he said.

"I thought that since you're coming to Berlin that maybe we could meet for a night in Copenhagen or Stockholm."

"Oh, my God, that would be great, Serena!" he said excitedly. "When could you manage it?"

"This coming weekend," she said.

"Sunday?" Misha asked. "I could be in Copenhagen for a few hours on Sunday."

"Yes . . . Sunday's fine," she replied.

"I'll call you back when I know what time I can be there," he said, "and I'll make hotel reservations. Okay?"

"Fabulous!" Serena said.

"Where can I reach you?" he asked.

Serena read off a telephone number.

"I'll call you back pronto," Misha said.

"Gotta run," Serena said. "See you in Copenhagen." She hung up.

Misha replaced the telephone in its cradle and sat smiling into space, Manny observing him.

"Serena?" he finally ventured.

"Yes," Misha replied, looking over at him.

"Mind if I'm a tad personal?" Manny asked.

"What is it?" Misha said.

"Are you in love?" Manny asked in a serious voice.

"Yes . . . no . . . I don't really know," Misha answered honestly. "I know that I've never been as attracted to anyone, ever, as I am to Serena. I've never had such sex in my life. It's wild! It's like there's some chemical pull between us. You know what I mean?"

"I think so, old boy," Manny said. "Although I must admit, I myself have never experienced anything quite like that."

Misha looked at him curiously for a moment. Weren't he and Sasha an item? It was odd, he thought, that they'd never broached the subject. "Anyway, it's as if fate or destiny had thrown us togther," Misha went on, "and we *must* have each other. It's like it's meant to be."

Misha paused, looking into the distance, lost in thought. "We come from different worlds and have such different interests," he said. "But at the same time, we're both involved in the arts. Our lifestyles are totally different, but very much alike. We're both career-driven and travel almost constantly."

"Maybe somebody like her's just what you need, old boy," Manny said. "Someone more like you, creative and all."

"You mean as opposed to Vera, who isn't?" Misha said.

"Well . . . I mean, Vera's fabulous in her own way, but . . . you know . . . she's very much the marrying and settling-down type. She'll probably give up her job at Christie's, raise a family. Not terribly creative."

"She certainly is around the house," Misha said in her defense. "She creates fantastic environments with furniture and pictures. She makes a place elegant and comfortable and her food is always the best."

Manny quickly backpedaled. "Oh, yes, I know. I didn't mean to belittle her obvious talents, old boy. She's a whiz at all those things."

"I'm going to see her tonight," Misha said, suddenly distracted. "Listen, Manny, why don't you run along? We can talk later. I have a lot to do. Getting ready for Berlin. Scheduling Copenhagen. And going over to Vera's new apartment tonight."

Manny was already on his feet and headed toward the door, grateful that this conversation was at an end. The less he and Misha discussed Brighton Beach Recordings, the better, as far as he was concerned. He was also glad for the opportunity to steer Misha clear of Vera. She was, he thought, far too overprotective of Misha and smart as hell. He didn't need her nosing into the business. He would be glad to see the back side of her one day soon.

Manny left the apartment, resolving that he would certainly do everything in his power to promote Serena Gibbons's star in Misha's galaxy. Yes, he thought, she was just exactly the sort of girlfriend Misha needed. She would never give a thought to Misha's career.

Chapter Twenty-five

After toiling in her overheated, closet-size kitchen, Vera rushed into her tiny bathroom to repair her makeup. Misha would soon be here, and she wanted to look her best for him. She quickly brushed her pale blond hair, then pulled it back and tied it with a ribbon at the base of her neck. Nothing could be simpler, she thought, but she knew it showed off her fine-boned features to perfection. She put on a dab of palest pink lipstick, blotted it, then brushed on the merest hint of blusher.

She stood back and eyed her reflection critically. She really didn't particularly like wearing makeup and resented taking the time to apply it, but with her natural coloring being so pale, she thought that she looked ghostly without a bit of added color. Giving her face a final inspection in the mottled mirror, she decided that she looked fine. Considering that she'd been up since six o'clock, gone to the gym, put in a hectic day at the auction house, grocery shopped, and cooked.

Cooking in her minute kitchen was a trial, and she hoped that Misha would appreciate her efforts. She had poached a salmon and made a fresh dill sauce to go with it. She would serve it with tiny new potatoes roasted with fresh rosemary, fresh green beans with mushrooms, and a mesclun salad with a garlic vinaigrette. For dessert she had bought homemade ginger ice cream and fresh strawberries.

It was, she realized, a simple, straightforward meal, uncomplicated and not too rich. She knew that Misha grew tired of the calorie-laden, fancy foods served at so many of the hotels and at the dinner parties he was required to attend. She quickly strode about her apartment to make certain that everything looked neat and clean, stopping to rearrange the fresh flowers she'd placed in the living room and on the dining room table, then stood, surveying her realm with pride. She had moved out of her parents' palatial thirty-six rooms on Fifth Avenue and taken this apartment on East Seventy-fifth Street. Her father had bought the apartment for her, but Vera had insisted on signing a note, promising to pay him back in full, plus the going interest rate, as she rose in the ranks and her professional career became more rewarding financially. She was determined to stand on her own two feet as much as possible.

The apartment had once been the parlor floor of a beautiful limestone town house, now split up into five floor-through apartments. Hers was not enormous, but she loved the proportions of its large living and dining rooms with their high ceilings, elaborately carved moldings, and fireplaces. The single bedroom was small but cozy, and the kitchen and bath were tiny but serviceable.

She had lavished attention on the apartment's decoration, and it now resembled the pied-à-terre of an eccentric but wealthy collector with its mixture of furniture, art, and bibelots of various styles and periods. With the exception of her most prized books, she had brought almost nothing here from her parents' apartment. She had purchased nearly everything herself, some of it from the auction house, where she was always on the lookout for treasures that others bypassed, and some of it from auctions and antique stores out in the country.

Much of the furniture was worn, with chips and nicks, and ancient fabric, and some of the paintings desperately needed restoration. Vera, however, liked the lived-in look of faded grandeur. She wanted to avoid the museum look, in which everything was glowing perfection, like the apartment she had grown up in. Here, you weren't afraid to put your feet up, and spilling a glass of wine wasn't a tragedy. Comfort ruled.

Satisfied that everything looked warm and inviting, she went to her bedroom to change clothes. She discarded her jeans and sweatshirt, and put on a pale fawn cashmere sweater and matching cashmere trousers, then slipped into pale pink ballerina slippers. They were so comfortable after heels all days. She still wore the single strand of pearls around her neck and pearl studs in her ears, and decided they looked perfect with her casual outfit.

The buzzer sounded, and she quickly dabbed perfume at her ears, throat, and wrists. A concoction Caron in Paris had made especially for her, it had distinctive but subtle notes of tuberose. She hurried to the kitchen and pressed the talk button on the intercom.

"Who is it?" she asked.

"Misha."

She took a deep breath and pushed the button to release the outside door lock. She rushed to her door and opened it. He stood there, his dark eyes dancing, his raven hair shining, his sensuous lips set in that irresistible smile.

"You look beautiful," he said, kissing her on the cheek.

"And you look better than ever," Vera replied, inhaling his masculine scent. She ushered him from the small entry foyer into the living room.

Misha stopped and stood in the large, gracious room and looked around him. "My God, Vera," he said with awe in his voice. "This looks fantastic."

"It's a beginning," Vera said modestly.

He turned and looked at her. "You know better than that," he said. "It's really fantastic. Really special."

"Thanks, Misha," she said.

"I should have known," he said, "especially after all the help you gave me."

"Have a look around at the rest, if you want to, and I'll get us something to drink. White wine okay?"

"Yes," he replied. "That'd be great."

Vera went to the kitchen while Misha slowly toured the living and dining rooms, then the bedroom, examining the furniture and paintings, the bibelots and photographs, the books and drawings. He noticed a photograph of himself clustered with several family pictures on a desk in the bedroom.

"Cheers," Vera said from the bedroom doorway, holding their wineglasses.

Misha turned around and looked at her. She looked so ethereally beautiful, like the very first time he had seen her, all those years ago. He took the wine from her, and they clinked glasses.

"Cheers," he said, taking a sip.

"Let's sit in the living room," Vera said.

Misha followed her out, and they both sat on the big, comfortable couch in front of the fireplace.

"It's strange," Misha said, looking about him, "how much our tastes are alike. I mean, this place is lighter and airier than mine, but in many ways it's the same. We both like Old World art and antiques, worn-out stuff a lot of people laugh at."

"I know," Vera said, smiling, "but I think yours is much more dramatic and interesting."

"Maybe more dramatic with all the color," Misha conceded, "but not more interesting."

They discussed his upcoming concert dates and her work at the auction house, his family and hers, their mutual friends, and finally ate dinner by candlelight in the dining room.

"I can't believe you did all this yourself," Misha declared after finishing the last of his dessert. "It was really wonderful, Vera. Do you have any idea what a treat this was after all the fancy, rich stuff that's forced on me?"

"I'm glad you liked it," she said. Her heart soared, and she felt foolish at being so pleased by his compliment. "Would you like coffee?" she asked.

"Sure," he said, "if you're going to have some."

"Why don't we have it in the living room?" Vera said. "Go get comfortable, and I'll bring it in."

Misha kicked off his shoes and sprawled on the couch, feeling contented. The apartment was just right, he thought. And the food. Everything done to just the right turn. So civilized yet homey.

Vera came through the dining room with their coffee on a small tray. Misha started to sit up when he saw her.

"No," she said. "Spread back out and make yourself comfortable." She put the tray down on the coffee table, and sat on the floor next to the couch, then handed Misha his cup of coffee.

"Thanks," he said, taking a sip, then putting the cup back down. He propped his head up on pillows, and lay there looking at Vera.

She sipped quietly at her coffee and looked over at him. "What is it?" she asked.

Misha smiled. "Nothing," he said. "I was just thinking how wonderful you look, how great this evening's been."

"I'm glad you've enjoyed it," she said. "I have. It's not often we can get together these days."

"No," Misha said, "it's not." He looked at her again, thoughtfully, then asked: "Are you seeing anybody now?"

Vera put her coffee down. "Not really, Misha," she said. "I go out a lot, socialize a lot. You know. See friends. Go to work functions, a few society parties, things like that. But I'm not really seeing anybody."

"Then who are these guys I see you coupled up with in the social columns?" he asked lightly.

Vera laughed. "This is like old times," she said, "when we used to compare notes about who the press reported we'd been seen with."

"You don't have any secrets anymore, then?" he asked, teasing her about Simon Hampton.

"No," Vera said emphatically. She shivered involuntarily and rubbed her hands up and down her arms. "And that's not funny, Misha," she said.

"I'm sorry," he said. "I shouldn't have been so flippant about it."

"That's okay," she said.

"Still," he said, "I find it hard to believe that you're not seeing *somebody* at least half seriously."

Vera looked at him and shrugged. "Well, I'm not."

"How's that possible, Vera?" he asked. "I mean, you have everything in the world to offer some guy."

She looked away, feeling very uncomfortable. How could she tell him that no other man on earth interested her? How could she tell him that she had no desire to become involved with those men who had been genuinely interested in her over the years?

"I just haven't met the right person, Misha," she finally said.

He reached out a hand and stroked her hair gently. "You will, Vera," he said. "I'm sure of it." Then he leaned over and kissed her forehead.

Vera looked into his eyes, and Misha saw the sadness and the desire there in their pale watery blueness. Inexplicably, he would afterward think, he pulled her to him, caressing her, tenderly peppering her face and neck and ears with kisses, inhaling her sweet fragrance.

Vera held onto him as if for dear life, before abruptly pulling back. "No, Misha," she whispered. "Please, I don't want your pity."

He drew her to him with a much more considerable force, kissing her more passionately, his tongue darting between her lips hungrily, his hands stroking her hair, her back, her shoulders, then, inevitably, her breasts.

Vera gasped and began to shake her head from side to side.

"Shhh," he whispered, moving his lips to her ear. "This has nothing to do with pity, Vera. Nothing at all. It's me, Misha. Remember? Just let yourself enjoy it. Let us both enjoy it."

He began again, gently, tenderly, lovingly, until they were both swept up in a tide of passion, of need, of urgency, that ultimately led them to her bedroom and sweet, sweet release.

Jesus! he later thought, getting dressed. I wanted to tell her about Serena, and look at what's happened. He experienced a strange sensation, unlike guilt, unlike shame, but unfamiliar and worrisome. He didn't feel that what he'd done with Vera was wrong. How could it be? he asked himself. It had somehow felt so right. It was a coupling, he thought, of familiarity, between friends.

Vera was like a safe harbor, a very loving one, and very exciting in her own way. What then was Serena? And why was he so drawn to her? Could he love them both, in different ways? He didn't know, and was genuinely confused. Only a short time ago he had been convinced that Serena was the only woman in the world who mattered to him. And now?

What's wrong with me? he wondered. What am I going to do?

Vera let him out, then returned to her bedroom. The evening couldn't have worked out more perfectly, she thought, even if she hadn't planned it that way. She was glad that she hadn't tried to seduce Misha, for she knew with dead certainty that that would be the worst mistake she could possibly make.

She shut her eyes and hugged her arms around herself tightly. Maybe . . . just maybe, she thought, he'll finally realize that no one else can possibly love him like I do. And maybe someday, he'll come to love me, too.

Chapter Twenty-six

Misha rolled over in bed and put his hands behind his head. He sighed with postcoital contentment and stared up at the bedroom's white ceiling and the ugly exposed pipes. Even in the bedroom's dim lighting, he could see them crisscrossing above him. When he'd first seen Serena's loft in SoHo, he'd been enthralled with its vast proportions, its high ceilings and huge windows, the drama of its cutting-edge modernity and minimal decoration. Over the last few weeks he had spent many nights here—every night when they'd both been in New York City—yet by now he found that his initial enthusiasm had changed to a kind of boredom, if not active dislike.

The loft's vast whiteness now seemed sterile and somehow inhuman, its modernity uncomfortable, institutional even. Serena was too much on the go, he reflected, to do anything to make it more livable.

The furniture was all horrendously expensive and beautifully designed but hard-edged and cold. On the walls hung a few pieces of contemporary art, most of it in varying shades of black and by artists he was unfamiliar with. None of it inspired him. A few of Serena's photographs hung in the only bedroom and a hallway—all high-fashion shots, very well done, but like the rest of the loft, cold and unfriendly. There were very few bibelots, almost nothing to indicate that she had traveled the world over in her work. Most peculiar of all, he thought, was that there was not a single photograph of family or friends.

Even the kitchen, usually the coziest gathering place in these expensive downtown aeries, was a temple to the industrial. The industrial stoves and refrigerators, the cabinetry and counters—nearly everything glass and steel and granite—gave Misha more the impression of a surgery than a welcoming hearth where friends cooked and ate and drank together, talking and laughing. It looked as if it had never been used, and indeed Serena said that she almost never had.

At first Misha thought that she was surely exaggerating, but he had come to believe her. Every night he'd come down after his daily piano practice, they'd ordered food in: Chinese, Japanese, Burmese, Thai, Vietnamese. The few times they'd gone out, Serena had insisted they go to chic, overpriced restaurants, the sort of fashionable and trendy restaurants where one went not for the food, but to see and be seen.

Mornings at the loft were always the same: coffee. Period. Gulped down quickly as Serena geared up for the day's business, usually placing and receiving telephone calls as she made and drank the coffee, often on more than one line at a time. Stylists, models, publishers, photo editors, art directors, fashion designers, advertisers, ad agencies, assistants, and her agent—the telephone never seemed to stop. And his being there never stopped her from answering it.

He smiled, thinking how adept Serena was amid this beehive of activity. How she handled a million details with such orderliness and aplomb. He would be half-crazed, he thought, if he lived in the incessant whirlwind she did. His own life was so different, so much more isolated, revolving as it did around the piano and the music in front of him.

He realized that in some ways they hardly knew each other at all, despite their many nights of intimacy together. *We both work such long, hard hours,* he thought, *and the work and travel make it very difficult to have a relationship that's more than sexual.* Sometimes he felt they weren't a couple at all, but strangers repeating an erotically charged one-night stand over and over.

Even sojourns, like their few hours in Copenhagen together a few weeks ago, as much fun as they had been, had begun to lose their luster. Perhaps, he thought, the novelty had simply worn off, but he suspected it was more than that.

He heard Serena shut off the shower in the adjoining bathroom and waited for her to appear in the doorway as he knew she would, a towel wrapped around her head like a turban, her resplendent body blushed pink by the hot shower. When she did, surrounded by a halo of light, he looked at her intently, wondering who she really was, what lay beneath the beautiful, polished exterior.

She saw the expression on his face and looked at him questioningly. "What is it?" she asked.

He smiled. "I was just wondering about some things," he said.

"What things?" she asked, walking over to the bed and sitting down on the side next to him.

He reached a hand up and ran a finger down her spine. "Oh, about you. Who you are. Where you're from. Things like that."

Serena expelled a sigh and turned to face him. "I'm Serena Gibbons," she said wearily. "I grew up in Florida. Can't that be enough for you?"

Misha shook his head. "I can't help but be curious," he said. "You know everything about me, Serena, and I want to know everything there is to know about you."

"I've told you before, Misha," Serena replied, a note of irritation in her voice. "I don't like to talk about the past. There's nothing to know." She began drying her hair with the towel, rubbing it slowly.

"I find that hard to believe," Misha replied.

"Try," she said, toweling her hair with more vigor.

"I have," Misha said. "For several weeks. I think it's pretty amazing that so far I've found out more about you from an article in *Vanity Fair* magazine than you've ever told me."

Serena put the towel down and slumped. She turned to look at him again. "What is it you want to know?" she asked in an exasperated voice.

"Come on, Serena. You know," he said. "The things lovers tell each other." He gently pushed strands of wet hair from out of her eyes. "About your family, about growing up, your friends and dreams and ambitions. All those things that tell me about *you*."

She looked into his eyes, her own glinting bright and hard in the dim light. "If I tell you once and for all, will you promise not to ask me anything about the past again? Ever?"

Misha nodded. "I promise," he vowed. He pulled her to him and kissed her tenderly.

Serena pulled back and wrapped her hair in the towel again. Then she got under the covers next to him. She stared straight ahead. "You know what you read in the magazine article," she said. "That I was born in Florida."

"Yes," Misha said.

"Well, I was," she said. "Only it isn't the Florida that most people know. It was in a tiny, dilapidated cracker shack near the Gulf coast. Way out in the boonies near Crystal River."

Misha listened, watching her beautiful face, and saw the faraway look in her eyes. He was afraid that if he interrupted her to ask questions, she wouldn't continue.

"My father, if you could call him that," she said harshly, "was a fishing guide. When he wasn't too drunk. My mother was what some people would call a housewife. When *she* wasn't too drunk." She paused and looked down, studying her fingernails, as if the rest of her story lay hidden in them.

"I had two older brothers who I don't remember much about," she finally continued. "At least not until I was about ten years old." Her voice became hushed, and her eyes dimmed with sadness. "That's about the time they started messing around with me."

Misha gently put a hand on her arm, but she brushed it away.

"When it wasn't them, it was my father," she said. "And when I told my mother, she beat the shit out of me for leading them on. For tempting them, as she put it." She turned and glanced at Misha. "So there was no way I could win." She paused again, and looked away.

Misha wanted to reach out and touch her, to hold her, to give her comfort, but he was afraid she would push him away again.

"Anyway, I started running away from home when I was about twelve," she went on. "Then finally, when I was fifteen, I ran away for good. And I haven't been back to that hellhole since," she said with vehemence.

She turned and looked at Misha again. "I became a rock band groupie, hanging out with the guys, traveling all over the country with them, doing gigs. They gave me food and shelter and booze and drugs." She looked away again. "And I gave them anything they wanted. And I do mean anything."

She was quiet for a while, studying her fingernails again. She seemed reluctant to finish her story, but finally took a deep breath and went on. "I started taking pictures of the band and the groupies. Onstage, while the band was performing, and backstage while they were gearing up. Then at the parties in hotel rooms, motel rooms. It was an accident really. Just something to pass the time. Have fun."

She looked over at him again and shrugged. "Anyway, you know the rest. Magazine editors saw some of my pictures when they were interviewing the band, and my career got started. They were snapshots really. The early ones, I mean. Candid shots that were hard to come by, but I got them. I had the access. When I realized what I had, I used that as a stepping-stone, learning as I went along. Then I met Coral Randolph, my agent, and the rest, as they say, is history."

"You've come a long way," Misha ventured.

"Yes," she said. "I've come a long, long way. And I've never looked back. And I never will, either."

"I'm glad you've told me, Serena," Misha said, taking her hand in his.

"So there you have it," she said, extracting her hand. "I don't want to talk about it anymore, Misha. Can you understand that?" She looked into his eyes.

"Yes," he said. "I do now. I won't ask you about it again."

"Don't," she said. She got back out of bed and padded toward the bathroom, toweling her hair again. "Not ever."

Misha watched her disappear into the bathroom, his mind swirling with what she had told him. No wonder there were no family photographs sprinkled about the apartment, he thought sadly. No wonder she never mentioned her past. It dawned on him that Serena was probably afraid of true intimacy and that she most likely didn't trust anyone. Not surprising, considering her childhood.

He wondered if he could ever penetrate that beautiful, polished exterior. The sex is so fantastic, he thought. But will it ever go beyond that? Will she allow it to?

He supposed that her own terrible experiences explained why she had no desire to meet his parents. He had been so anxious to show her off to them, but she had resisted so far, making any number of transparent excuses. Could it also explain why she never wanted to spend the night at his place? She had made jokes about his richly decorated and lived-in apartment, calling it an Aladdin's den of treasures. Was she intimidated by its being more of a real home, a place where he lived with many of the things he loved? Or was she afraid of him in his own lair, on his own turf?

He didn't know the answer to any of these questions, but there were a few things he did know now. Serena, for all her beauty and talent and accomplishments, was somehow damaged. That he knew with a certainty. At her core, he decided, was an insecurity and a fear that seemed to color her every action. But most frightening of all, he thought, was a certain poverty of spirit.

Serena was a fighter and a survivor, that was clear, but could she ever really learn to give of herself without fear? And to accept what's offered her on trust?

Will she ever let me really love her? he wondered.

Chapter Twenty-seven

❧

Serena was in Kenya, photographing models cavorting about in couture gowns at a wildlife preserve.

Misha was in Tokyo, playing for a packed house.

Serena was on an *estancia* outside Buenos Aires, taking pictures of muscle-bound male models, strutting about the stables, dressed in the latest "macho-man-meets-nancy-boy" looks from London designers.

Misha was climbing pyramids in Teotihuacán after his performance thrilled critics and audience alike in Mexico City.

Serena was somewhere in the Indian Ocean on one of the Maldive Islands, taking an extended vacation with Coral and Sal/Sally—"Sorry, ladies only, Misha!"—after a particularly grueling and trouble-fraught fashion shoot in the wilds of Rajasthan.

They really were like ships passing in the night.

Misha, back in New York, was lonely and a little angry with Serena. He was utterly bored with the beautiful models who wanted to go club crawling every night, more often than not high on drugs.

He decided to call Vera to see if she would like to go antiquing upstate over the weekend. She was thrilled at the chance, and they sped off together in his little silver-blue BMW sports car, the top down, their hair blowing in the wind. Up the Taconic State Parkway they went, searching for treasures in off-the-beaten-track places.

In Hudson, they found two magnificent lead garden urns, a matched pair. Just the thing to place on pedestals, one in each of Vera's parlor windows. Down the street they found a massive four-poster Italian Renaissance bed, beautifully carved and canopied. Precisely the piece Misha had been searching for to replace the bed in his apartment.

They dined at the Charleston Restaurant, enjoying its excellent cuisine, then spent the night at a romantic little bed and breakfast in the nearby Berkshires.

Returning to New York, they glowed with the happiness of their new acquisitions, which would soon be sent to them. Though they weren't necessarily bargains, they'd had fun searching for them. More important, they relished their rediscovery of each other's company.

Sunday night Vera insisted on cooking in rather than going out, as so many weekenders did on returning to the city. At Misha's apartment, in his large, well-equipped kitchen, she threw together a delicious pasta with artichoke hearts, scallions, and cayenne pepper, while he made a salad of arugula and tomatoes with an olive oil and balsamic vinaigrette.

They drank wine and talked and talked and talked. Vera occasionally got up to move one of his treasures here or there for greater effect, making suggestions about rehanging some of his pictures, helping him decide how to place the new bed in his bedroom. They discussed which of the ancient fabrics they both collected would make the best hangings for it, Vera telling him about her old crewel work that she might be willing to part with.

It was very late before they finally ascended the stairs to his bedroom for the last time that night, hand in hand, smiles of contentment on their faces. They were already pleasantly tired by their mutual enjoyment of the weekend and the pure delight they took in each other, but invigorated at the same time. It was a night of sweet and leisurely lovemaking, ending in heavy, reenergizing sleep.

Misha's private telephone line began a persistent, shrill ring early Monday morning. He rolled over and turned the offensive instrument off, noticing that Vera had already gotten up and gone off to work.

Later, after coffee, juice, and toast, he listened to his messages. All from Serena, as he suspected they would be. He knew that she was due back in New York this morning. He decided he would call her back, although he was still miffed that she hadn't found the time to fit him into her hectic schedule. He knew from his own experience that with some effort—and desire—she could have done so.

He picked up the receiver and dialed her number.

After three rings her telephone was answered. "Yeah?" It was the gruff John Wayne voice.

"Sal . . . Sally?" Misha asked.

"Who wants to know?"

"It's Misha Levin," he said. "I was calling for Serena."

"Hold on."

He heard the receiver bang loudly against something, as if Sal had deliberately let it drop. After a moment Serena's voice came on the line.

"Hi!" she said cheerfully. "I tried to get you earlier but didn't get an answer."

"I had the phones off," he said. "I was sleeping late." The enthusiasm in her voice mollified his anger to some extent, but he still wasn't ready to forgive her.

"Aha!" she said. "What've you been up to?"

"This and that," he said, unwilling to be forthcoming. "A guy has to amuse himself when he's been left in the lurch. You know?"

"Are you pissed?" Serena asked.

"I guess you could put it that way," he allowed.

"Misha," she said firmly, "we've been seeing each other for months, and I would think that by now you would've gotten used to my crazy schedule. You know how it is. I can't drop everything like some bored little housewifey and run every time you say run."

"I know that," he said heatedly, "and you know very well that I hardly expect that."

"Look," Serena said mildly, "I've got the day free. Why don't you come on down here and we'll talk? Okay?"

"Would you like to come up here?" he asked, knowing that she would say no. "There'd be fewer distractions."

"No," she said, as predicted. "Better here. I'm expecting some important telephone calls."

"Of course," he said with a tinge of sarcasm. "The all-important telephone calls. That all-important umbilical cord. You could bring your cell phone up here, you know."

"That won't work," she said. "There may be some deliveries, and there won't be anybody here but me." She sighed. "Look, Misha," she added, "I just can't help it. Please come on down here."

"Give me about an hour," he said, unable to resist her allure, the seemingly magnetic pull that she held for him.

He hung up the receiver, staring off into space. "Damn!" he exclaimed. And he thought, *How much longer can I go on like this, her running hot for me one minute, then cutting me off completely?*

The elevator bobbed to a halt on Serena's floor, and Misha got out. John Wayne stood there, legs spread wide in a particularly butch pose, waiting for the elevator.

"Hi, Sal," he said brightly.

She eyed him with suspicion, then nodded, grudgingly, he thought. She got into the elevator with a swagger and slammed the button with a fist.

He rang the second intercom—there was one in the lobby as well as one at the loft's door, for added security—and Serena buzzed him in. He stepped into the mammoth loft, and Serena called to him.

"Misha," she cried. "Back here. In the studio."

He headed off to the right, toward the vast space that adjoined her living quarters. It contained her photographic studio, complete with bathrooms, changing rooms, wardrobes, storage facilities, and dark room. She was standing, almost hidden, by huge trunks filled with lighting equipment, cameras, and countless accessories, as well as several rolling racks of clothing and boxes piled high with shoes, boots, hats, and who knew what else.

She looked up at him and smiled widely, her raven hair framing her lightly tanned face. "Hi," she said.

At that moment, she looked, he thought, like a Madonna. Exquisite and innocent. Pure and—

Then he saw what she was wearing.

"What in the world?" he gasped. Then he laughed lightly.

Serena grinned. "I'm trying on clothes for a photo shoot," she said. "A magazine in London is doing a big feature article about *me*! Imagine! And they sent down *tons* of outfits to try. I have approval—with their input—as to what to wear in the photo spread."

She did a pirouette, then stood looking at him. "What do you think?" she asked.

Misha was momentarily at a loss as to what to say. "Well, I think it makes you look like a hooker," he blurted. "A hooker with a specialty," he added with amusement.

Serena laughed. "You don't think black leather hot pants with skull studs all over them are *moi*? How about the matching bustier? Oh, wait," she said, looking in the mirror. "It *doesn't* match. It's studded with crossed bones."

"It makes your breasts look huge," he said, eyeing them appreciatively.

"And the boots!" she said. "Practical, no? Stiletto heels and thigh high. Nice for a day of shopping."

"Yes," Misha said, laughing. "I can just see it. You'd clear the store out wearing those. All the customers would go running."

"Come here," she said, stamping one of her heels.

He walked over and took her into his arms, kissing her deeply. She responded immediately, throwing her arms around him, matching his desire with her own.

"I think you like these big breasts," she said, drawing back and looking mischievous.

"I like *you*," he said.

"And the big breasts?" she said teasingly.

"Maybe those, too."

"Let's go to the bedroom," Serena said, taking him by the hand and leading the way.

Misha followed, glancing at her firm buttocks, tightly molded by the shiny leather. He found himself excited by the bizarre outfit.

In the bedroom, the sexual high jinks were quick, boisterous, and explosive, both of them hungrier than ever for each other. Not only had it been a long time, but they also found that her fetishistic clothing was erotic and arousing.

Afterward, they lay naked and spent upon the bed, then finally began to talk.

"So," Serena said, staring up at the ceiling. "Are you still mad at me?"

Misha turned his head and looked at her long and hard. "I have to confess that I find it very difficult to be angry with you, Serena. Especially when I'm with you. But believe me, I was angry. When you were away."

"Well, you may as well get over it," she said a little imperiously. "Because this is the way I am. This is me. This is my life."

"I understand," he said, "but did you have to cut me out of your vacation entirely? We could've done something together. I had free time, and so did you. And you knew it. It seems like—"

She jerked up off the pillow, staring daggers at him. "Don't *ever* expect me to do something like that," she burst out. "To give up something special for you. I was with my agent, Coral, who is vital to my career."

She paused for a moment, and some of the anger seemed to drain out of her eyes. "Besides, we didn't want any men around. It was a girl thing."

She ran her fingers through her long black hair, looked over at him, and shrugged. "Don't you ever do that?" she asked. "Hang out with the guys, I mean?"

"Not really," Misha replied. "I guess I'm sort of past all that. I did it in school some, sure. But nowadays I guess I'm not much into male bonding."

Serena groaned aloud. "God, Misha!" she said. "I can just see you encroaching more and more on my independence. Gradually making more and more demands. Eating up my time. Eating *me* up in the process."

Misha was stunned. What the hell was she talking about? Ever since he'd known her, she'd done everything she wanted to do. Though at times he'd been hurt and angry, and, yes, sometimes he'd complained, he had certainly not "encroached" on her independence, as she put it.

"Do you really feel that way?" he asked, when the initial shock had worn off.

"Absolutely," she said without hesitation. "And," she added, "I won't put up with it from anybody."

"What if I were your husband?"

She turned the full force of her bewitching hazel eyes on him and then stared at him.

He thought that for a moment at least, she had suppressed a laugh or a smile, but he couldn't be certain.

"Husband!" she exclaimed at last. "Husband!"

She paused a moment, and the wonder on her face was replaced by a serious expression.

"*If* I ever marry, Misha—and that is a very big if—it will not change my life one iota." She stabbed the air with a finger. "Not marriage to you"—her fingers stabbed the air again —"or anybody else."

Then she dramatically slammed a fist into the palm of her hand. "No compromises! None!"

He hung his head under the weight of her ruthless gaze. Whatever dreams he had nourished were all now dashed onto a rocky shore.

After a bout of silence he ventured another supposition. "So . . . ," he began, then cleared his throat, before continuing. "So . . . I guess it's safe to say that you'd never cut back on the travel for a . . . family."

Serena looked at him a moment, then laughed uproariously. "I'm sorry," she finally sputtered. "I . . . I just don't believe I'm hearing this. You don't have a fucking clue, Misha, do you?"

He rose abruptly to his feet, and began gathering up his clothing and putting it on. He wanted to get away from her and this place as fast as possible. He didn't like her mocking him now, and he was very disturbed by the ugliness in her character that it showed.

Serena watched him dress. "You don't have to leave, Misha," she said.

He buckled his belt and zipped up his trousers, then looked down at her, his face full of sorrow.

"Oh, yes, Serena," he said. "I think I do." He slid into his jacket. "Good-bye, Serena," he added in a whisper.

"See ya later," she said, reaching for a nail file on the nightstand.

Back down on the street, Misha felt aimless, like a boat adrift. He simply didn't know what to do next, where to go, how to make sense of what had just transpired.

What do I do now? he asked himself.

He had always known that he would have to see her on her terms. But was she truly unwilling to compromise at all? Did she truly have no more feeling for him than that? Was she truly unwilling to make changes for a husband? And a family?

After what she'd been though growing up, he'd imagined that she would welcome the opportunity to show a child or children that the world wasn't necessarily the bleak and monstrous place she had experienced. That the world could be nurturing, bountiful, and loving.

He supposed that her family was Coral Randolph and Sally Parker. Nothing wrong with that, he thought. And, of course, there were all the models and stylists and assistants and their inevitable hangers-on who peopled her life, celebrated ups with her, helped her through the downs, no doubt. So many of them were cocaine-snorting, amphetamine-popping, pot-smoking wastrels, he thought. Often not the best sort of brothers and sisters, mothers and fathers.

That won't do for me, he thought. Absolutely not. I want a wife. And children. I want a real family of my own. To share my life with.

Unbidden tears formed in his eyes. I am lost, he thought. So lost. And I don't know what to do or where to go.

Then he began to walk. He walked and walked and walked, aimlessly, paying no attention to where he was going. Time had failed to exist for him, and he felt as if he were in a dimension outside it. He had no idea how long this wandering went on.

When he finally looked up, to avoid a pedestrian in his way, he looked around. He realized that he'd walked all the way from SoHo to Midtown and beyond. The east Sixties.

Then it came to him. As if a lightning bolt had struck him and un-leashed from his confused mind an idea that had been there all along, just waiting to be discovered.

Misha knew what he would do. Yes! He knew with a certainty he had never felt before. He looked about him again. The city seemed to have taken on a clarity that he'd never seen before. Then, with a confident, self-assured stride, he picked up his pace, headed in the direction of his solution, no longer aimless, no longer lost.

I know exactly what to do. Exactly where to go, he thought. And he marveled: *I've found myself at last. I know my heart's desire.*

Chapter Twenty-eight

"Misha, I want you to think about this," she said. "At least for a few days, if not longer." She eyed him warily across the table. "You should be absolutely certain in your own mind that this is what you really want to do."

Misha nodded and his dark eyes flashed. "I don't have to think about it," he said in an earnest voice. "I've already thought about it. Make no mistake about that. This is definitely what I want to do."

His eyes, she thought, had never sparkled with such determination, and that handsome square jaw of his had never looked more assertive. Still, she felt that she must make certain that his decision wasn't a snap one, made in the heat of anger or in desperation. And she knew that it might very well be.

She took a deep, fortifying breath. "Misha," she said, as evenly as she could. "I just want to clear up one thing first."

"Anything," he said. "What is it? You can ask me anything."

"I . . . I hope," she said, choosing her words carefully, "that you're not making this decision on . . . on . . . the rebound."

Misha returned her gaze. "On the rebound?" he repeated. "Why would you think that?"

"If there's one time in our lives when we've got to be absolutely honest with each other," she said, "then that time is surely now."

He readily nodded in agreement.

"And I expect you to be as honest with me as I am with you," she went on. "So tell me the truth, Misha. Are you doing this . . ." She paused and took another deep breath, then hurried on, rushing her words while she had the courage to use them. ". . . because you're angry with her? Have you come running to me just to get back at her?"

Misha's face reddened, and his eyes strayed from hers, off into the distance. Then he heaved a sigh, and his eyes shifted back to hers.

"You knew," he said.

"Yes," she said, nodding.

"How long have you known?" he asked.

She shrugged. "I don't know. Well . . . for a long time. Since the beginning, I guess."

Misha was stunned. "How?" he asked. "How did you know?"

"It doesn't really matter, does it?" she said. "I'd heard rumors," she said. "After all, we do know some of the same people."

He looked at her. "You never said a thing," he said in a sad voice. "Not a single word."

She remained silent.

"All this time," he said, "and you carried on valiantly, like there was nothing to worry about, as if everything was as it should be."

He reached over the table and took one of her hands in his. "You're even more wonderful than I'd thought," he said. "And that's why I want to marry you, Vera. Not because I'm angry with her. And not to get back at her. I decided that I've loved you all along. All these years."

Tears of joy crept into the corners of Vera's eyes and began to spill unchecked down her cheeks. She wasn't certain that she believed him, but she wanted to. Oh, how she wanted to!

"I just didn't know it, Vera," he continued. "I guess I was too blind, too stupid, too self-absorbed to recognize it for what it was." He paused, and his voice softened. "To see that I loved you all the time. That you're the only woman I ever really wanted."

He reached over and gently wiped the tears from her face with a fingertip.

"You . . . you're really sure about this?" she finally managed to whisper.

"Oh, yes," he said, bringing her hand to his lips and tenderly kissing it. "I want to marry you. I want us to have children and be a family. Please say yes, Vera."

Vera saw the plea in his eyes, unconcealed and vulnerable. Her mind was reeling with a thousand unexpressed emotions, but she forced herself to utter her prevailing sentiment: "Yes," she said. "Oh, yes, Misha. I *will* marry you. Yes, yes, yes!"

Later, back at her office, Vera realized that she didn't even know the name of the nondescript little restaurant where Misha had proposed to her. He had come rushing in just as she was getting ready to leave for lunch. Then he'd taken her arm and rushed her off, mumbling mysteriously that they must talk, at once. Now, she didn't even think she could remember what block it was on.

But it didn't matter. Nothing else mattered to her right now. Not even the beautiful Serena Gibbons, who she knew had held such a spell over

Misha. For Vera finally, after years of patient waiting, had just what she wanted: Misha Levin.

She wanted to shout it from the rooftops, to let the whole world know that Mikhail Levin loved her, Vera Bunim, and that she and Misha were going to be husband and wife. But she went about her work dutifully and with her usual poise, containing for the time being her utter joy.

Life will be perfect now, she thought. *No matter what happens, with Misha at my side, nothing in life can defeat or hurt me.*

Vera let herself into her apartment. She dropped her keys in a silver bowl on the commode in the foyer and put her shoulder bag on a chair.

"Home, sweet home," she said aloud, expelling a sigh of gratified relief. "Home at long last."

Vera was exhausted. The wedding was but a little more than a week away, and helping her mother with the myriad wedding details—plus keeping up with her heavy workload at the same time—were taking their toll.

The apartment was oddly silent because, unlike nearly every evening for the last few weeks, Misha was not here. That, too, filled her with a sense of relief. As much as she missed his company, she was glad that he was busy tonight.

Tonight. What *was* tonight. . . ?

Oh, right. The dinner and a long business meeting with Manny and Sasha. So he would be staying across town at his own apartment.

If he were here, she thought, our evening would just be beginning. We would be up half the night . . . Cooking together. Eating together. Talking together. Planning things together. And, of course, making love together.

Together. That was the magic word.

Tonight, she'd taken advantage of his absence and stayed late at her office, catching up on work, nibbling on a tuna sandwich she'd called out for. *So much for dinner!* she thought. But it didn't matter, because she couldn't wait to crawl between the sheets. She headed straight for her bedroom, where she undressed and slipped into an old T-shirt, smiling with secret delight as she did so: it was one of Misha's, and her very favorite thing to sleep in.

She padded into the tiny bathroom, loosening her pale blond hair from the silk Chanel scarf casually tied at the base of her neck as she went. At the old pedestal sink she flossed and brushed her teeth and washed and dried her face, then flipped off the light and made a beeline for her bed.

Sliding beneath the covers, she savored the feel of the crisp linen sheets against her. *This is truly heaven,* she thought. *Just what the doctor ordered for my overworked bones.* Just then the telephone jangled in her ear, startling her at first.

She reached over and grabbed the receiver. "Hello?" she said.

For a moment she heard only breathing, a clearly audible respiration that sent a chill up her spine.

"Who . . . who is it?" she asked, slightly unnerved.

There was no answer.

The breathing continued, rhythmic and . . . threatening.

Vera shivered, then thought: *Don't be silly. It's only a stupid prank.* She started to slam down the receiver, but at that exact moment she heard her name.

"Veeeerrr-rrraaaaa."

It was a low, gravelly voice, her name drawled out eerily. The voice was unmistakably British, and instantly recognizable: Simon Hampton.

Oh, my God, she wondered, *what's he doing calling me after all this time?* A call from Simon could mean only one thing: trouble. She made an effort to control her pounding heart and the rising fear that held her in its thrall. "Simon," she said, despising the quaver of apprehension she heard in her voice.

"You've been seeing that fag musician again," Simon said in a mocking tone.

Oh, my God! He's . . . he's been following me!

The realization was like a powerful physical blow, and Vera thought for a moment that she would surely be sick. *This can't be happening to me!* She felt an involuntary tremor run through her, and she nearly dropped the receiver.

"You shouldn't be seeing him, Vera," Simon said in a singsong, as if he were chastising a naughty child. "It might be very dangerous for him if you do."

"You wouldn't dare," Vera cried, fear—now mixed with anger—consuming her. "I'll report you to the police," she said. "I'll tell them that you're the person who tried—"

"Shut up!" Simon snarled. "I can get to your precious faggot before the police can. I'm right around the corner from him."

"You're lying, you bastard," Vera cried.

"Now, now, Vera," he said in the mocking singsong. "We want to watch our language." Then his voice became even more threatening as he reverted to his normal baritone. "The piano player's gone downstairs to a café. Having a nightcap with that fat manager of his. I can *see* them, Vera."

Vera choked back a sob. *Is it possible?* she wondered with horror. *Can he really see Misha? Or is he bluffing? Just trying to scare me?*

What can I do? she agonized.

Her mind reeled with possibilities, but she couldn't sort through them, couldn't make sense of them.

"Meet me," he said in a demanding voice.

"Meet you?" she nearly whimpered.

"Yeah," he said. "Down in the Village. It'll be like old times. Just you and me, Vera. We'll have a drink. Go for a walk."

Vera was both revolted and terrified at the very idea of seeing Simon now. Was he completely crazy? Would he try to hurt her? To pay her back for seeing Misha?

Oh, my God! What if he knows we're getting married? What will he do then? She felt a knot of fear such as she had never known form in her stomach, wrenching it into a tight fist.

What am I to do? she asked herself again. But she knew what she must do.

Her head spinning, her stomach lurching into her throat, she took a deep breath and finally spoke: "Okay, Simon," she said, with as calm a voice as she could muster. "Where do you want to meet?"

"A little café on West Street," he said. "At the foot of Christopher Street, head north. You'll see it. It's a sidewalk café."

"I'll be there," she said, "but it'll take me a while to get dressed and get down there in a taxi."

"*Ciao*," he said. The line went dead.

Vera replaced the receiver in its cradle and sat still as a stone, thinking. After several minutes, she slid out of bed and got busy.

She went to her closet and pulled out an old pair of jeans, a black T-shirt, and black sneakers. She put them on, then searched until she found an old baseball cap. She put her hair up in it and pulled it low over her brow.

In a dresser drawer she rummaged through neatly folded underclothes until she found the gift her father had given her several years ago. She threw it and her wallet in her black leather shoulder bag, then grabbed her keys and dashed out of the apartment in search of a taxi.

Vera sipped the chilled chablis in her glass, eyeing Simon across the table. He had been throwing back generous amounts of bourbon and water, and she saw that he was beginning to get sloshed. The café was deserted and had been ever since she'd arrived. It was a Wednesday night, and the sidewalks had been virtually empty, only the occasional pedestrian hurrying by. The incessant stream of traffic on the West Side Highway was beginning to thin out.

She had been very wary at first, seeing Simon seated there, his long blond hair dirty and windblown, his big blue eyes sparkling, his tall, muscular body at ease, sprawled at a sidewalk table. Oddly enough, they hadn't discussed the telephone call or Misha. Simon didn't seem to want to, and Vera was anxious not to provoke his wrath. He seemed content merely to be in her company, acting as if nothing was out of the ordinary. He had talked about his latest show at a small gallery in London, and the painting projects he was working on now.

Maybe this will satisfy him, she thought hopefully. *Maybe I'll be able to simply get up, leave him here, and go straight to Misha's. Then we'll alert the police. Maybe . . . maybe I won't be forced to do anything crazy.* But she had no way of knowing what Simon was going to do next and didn't want to take any chances.

"Do you still want to take that walk?" Vera finally asked.

"Yeah, sure," Simon said, smiling over at her. "Are you ready?"

"Whenever you are," she said evenly, trying not to betray the nervousness she felt.

He asked for the check, and the waiter brought it, disappearing back inside. Simon looked at the bill and counted out some cash. Then he placed his glass atop both and got to his feet, stretching his arms.

Vera looked up at him. *Oh my God,* she thought miserably. *I'd forgotten how big he is. How tall and muscular. How will I ever do it, if I have to?* She quickly rose to her feet and walked over to him.

Simon put one of his powerful arms around her shoulders. "Let's walk over to the piers," he said, pointing across the West Side Highway toward the Hudson River.

"Whatever you'd like," Vera said, attempting a smile.

He hugged her to him closely, and they crossed the highway, then walked along the promenade. There was chain-link fencing along the shore side of the piers, put there to keep people from wandering out onto them.

"Look," Simon said, pointing at a gap in the fence. "We can climb through here and go all the way out to the end of the pier."

"Do you think that's safe?" Vera asked.

"Yeah," Simon said. "I've seen people out there."

He helped her climb through the gap, then followed close behind her. They strolled all the way out to the very end, far out into the darkness of the Hudson River. At the pier's edge, they stood, gazing over toward the distant lights of New Jersey.

"It's strangely beautiful," Vera said, "isn't it?"

"Yeah," Simon said. "It is."

The sky was overcast, and they could see no stars. It was virtually dark out here, eerie with only the sounds of the powerful wind and the distant traffic. No one else was about, at least not that Vera could see.

She shivered, and Simon drew her closer, stroking her arm with his. But it wasn't the wind that chilled her. No. It was knowing what she might have to do. *And this,* she thought grimly, *is the perfect place to do it.*

Simon turned to her, and she could see his eyes gleaming in the near-darkness. "You're going to marry him," he said quietly. "Aren't you?" His grip on her shoulder became suddenly painful.

For the second time that evening, Vera thought she would surely be sick. The pressure of his powerful arm and hand gripped like a vise, and the gleam in his eye was one of utter madness. *I'm trapped and helpless, and he's going to kill me!* She struggled to find the words to answer him.

"I . . . I came here . . . to . . . to meet you . . . didn't I, Simon?" she stammered. "Just like you wanted me to."

"You didn't answer my question, Vera," he said. He looked at her with a strange sort of triumph in his eyes. "But you don't have to, because I know. Everybody in London knows."

"You're hurting me, Simon!" she cried. "Please let me go!"

He shook his head slowly, looking into her eyes. "I don't think so," he said calmly. "If I can't have you, Vera, then nobody's going to."

Vera struggled to escape his grasp, but it was impossible.

Simon began to laugh, then said: "You'll come up a lovely floater, Vera."

She suddenly went white-hot with a combination of fury and fear, struggling more urgently, then kicking wildly at him with her feet.

Simon laughed again, then loosened his grip slightly and started to push her over the edge of the pier.

Vera saw her chance and swung around, bringing her knee up into his crotch with all her might, slamming it home with a grunt.

Simon gasped in pain, his eyes momentarily focusing on her with shock. He released her instantly and grabbed his crotch. When he did, Vera saw him lose his footing, one boot slipping over the edge of the pier. His arms flailed at the air as he fell sideways, like a broken puppet, off the pier.

Vera looked on, her eyes wide with horror. She heard a loud thunk, and could swear that she could feel its impact in the boards beneath her feet. Then there was a muffled splash, barely perceptible above the sound of the wind.

For a moment Vera didn't move. She could hear the sound of her own labored breathing, coming in loud gasps. Then, gingerly she looked down, over the edge of the pier. In the near-darkness the first thing that caught her eye was an enormous iron bolt projecting from a half-rotten piling. Beneath it she could see nothing but the blackness of the water, slapping gently against the pier.

Oh, my God, she thought. *Oh, my God!*

She began to heave uncontrollably, her tuna sandwich cascading down into the darkness. Tears began to run from her eyes, but she forced herself to keep searching for any sign of Simon.

The water continued lapping gently against the pilings, unbroken, undisturbed.

She finally got to her feet, backing carefully from the pier's edge. Tremors began to run through her entire body, and she choked on the bile in her throat. *Get a grip,* she told herself. *It's over, and you've got to get out of here!*

She brought a hand first to her eyes, then to her mouth, wiping it on her jeans. Taking a deep breath, she turned and started back to the landside of the pier, moving quickly but not running. When she got to the fence, she found the gap and crawled through, then made her way across the highway and up back streets to Eighth Avenue, where she hailed a taxi back uptown.

In the safety of her apartment, she took the snub-nose Smith & Wesson from her shoulder bag and replaced it in the dresser where she kept it.

Thank God, she prayed, *that I didn't have to use it!*

She began to tremble, and tears began to flow from her eyes. *But I would have done it,* she thought. *I was prepared to commit murder to protect Misha.* She began to sob. *What kind of a woman am I? What kind of a monster?*

Chapter Twenty-nine

❧

The wedding was celebrated at the Fifth Avenue Synagogue and was, everyone agreed, an extravaganza rarely seen among even the rich and important society crowd and the cultivated music and art world denizens who attended.

Everyone is here, Vera thought. *At least two members of the president's cabinet, two senators, the governor and mayor, financiers from everywhere, several titled Europeans and New York bluebloods, along with famous conductors, composers, musicians, and artists.*

Sonia and Dmitri Levin, teary-eyed at the ceremony, were thrilled that their son had finally come to his senses. Even Ivan and Tatiana Bunim, who had always objected to their daughter's romantic interest in Misha, had given their blessings to the marriage.

They had often discussed Vera's reluctance to develop a relationship with any of the appropriate young men who had been interested in her, and they knew the reason. They also knew very well how stubborn and single-minded their beautiful daughter could be. Although they had hoped she would form an alliance with a scion of one of the legendary Jewish families of great wealth, they realized that Mikail Levin was an excellent catch for any young woman.

In the candlelit synagogue, Vera's beauty drew gasps of awe and appreciation. Her dress was designed by Catherine Walker, the famous London designer who had fashioned many of the Princess of Wales's gowns. A princess line with a round neckline and short sleeves, its bodice was intricately beaded with Venetian pearls, and a long silk faille train swept grandly behind her. Her silk tulle veil was held in place by a diadem made of diamonds, emeralds, and rubies. It had been worn by her mother on her wedding day. Diamond drop earrings and a diamond necklace, gifts from Misha, sparkled in the candlelight. She carried a simple nosegay of full-blown pink roses.

Vera's only attendant was her lifelong friend Priscilla Cavanaugh, who had once loaned her loft to Misha and Vera to make love. She wore an Empire-style dress in pale pink silk chiffon.

Misha was attended by his father, both of them resplendent in white tie and tails, as was Ivan Bunim, who gave his daughter away.

After the traditional ceremony, the reception was held in the Bunims' Fifth Avenue apartment. Jacques Ravenal, renowned the world over for his incomparable party planning, was flown in from Paris to decorate for the ceremony and the reception. And if the guests thought the ceremony was beautiful, the reception and dinner were unparalleled in their elegance and sumptuousness.

The flowers alone cost thousands of dollars, and like the guests, came from all over the world. Masses of roses, peonies, lilies of the valley, hydrangeas, and Madagascar stephanotis—all in whites and the palest of pink—were flown in to decorate the synagogue and the Bunim apartment's thirty-six rooms.

A string quartet played in the entrance gallery as guests arrived and during dinner. In the Venetian-style ballroom a society orchestra played later in the evening for dancing the night away. Dinner was served in the ballroom at tables draped with ivory Venetian damask and centered with five-foot-tall candelabra decorated with masses of peonies, with vines trailing down to the tables. Antique Russian silver and imperial china gleamed, and Baccarat crystal dazzled the eye. Waiters in tuxedos and white gloves made certain that the crystal was kept filled with Dom Pérignon and Louis Roederer Cristal champagne. The dinner was delicious, and Vera was justifiably proud. She had decided on the menu herself: Beluga caviar, buckwheat blinis, crème fraîche, whole roasted boneless quail with a lemon stuffing, spring peas, wild rice with grapes and orange zest, baby field greens, and toasted bleu de Bresse on Crouton.

The wedding cake was a ten-layered, six-foot-tall creation, artfully decorated with a realistic-looking spiral of pink and white roses creeping up its latticework. It was served as dessert, along with lavender sorbet. Coffee and silver dragées followed.

Vera and Misha were toasted by many of the guests, including a senator, the governor, and a member of the Romanov family.

After all the merriment, the jovial conversation, the eating, drinking, and dancing, Vera and Misha were exhausted but exhilarated at the same time. They repeatedly tore themselves away from their parents, from Manny and Sasha and Priscilla, and a host of well-wishing friends, only to become involved in yet another conversation, another dance, another tearful embrace among the flowers and candles.

Late in the evening, Misha danced Vera into a far corner of the ballroom and whispered into her ear: "Why don't we make our escape now, Mrs. Levin?"

"I think that's the best idea you've had all night, Mr. Levin," she replied.

They quickly exited through a hidden jib door, painted to look as if it were part of the room's grand murals, and dashed laughing down the hall-way to the elevator, which would take them upstairs. At the door to Vera's bedroom, Misha took her into his arms and kissed her passionately. Vera returned his ardor, then pulled away.

"We're never going to get away if we don't hurry," she said.

"I'll give you ten minutes to get ready," Misha said, a mischievous smile on his lips. "Or I'm leaving without you, Mrs. Levin."

She tapped him on the cheek. "Just try it, Mr. Levin," she said.

She turned and went into her old bedroom to change clothes, and Misha went down the hall to a guest room, where he would change his.

Less than fifteen minutes later, he knocked on her door.

"Misha?" she asked.

"Yes," he said. "May I come in?"

"Yes," she said.

He opened the door and saw her, standing at a dresser. She looked beautiful in a white Chanel suit with gold buttons and blue trim. It was the same blue as her eyes, Misha noticed.

"I'm just about ready," she said, eyeing herself in the mirror. She blot-ted her lips, then turned to him. "You look so handsome," she said.

"Thank you," Misha said, preening in his fashionably cut Armani suit. "And you look ravishing." He took her into his arms and kissed her. "Now, let's get out of here," he said.

"One more thing," she said. "I have to throw my bouquet first."

"Then let's get it over with," he said. "Okay?"

"I'm ready," she said. She picked up the beautiful nosegay of roses from the bed, and they headed for the elevator, hand in hand.

In the ballroom, the guests began to applaud as they realized that the newlyweds had appeared in their going-away clothes. Vera, with Misha at her side, made her way to the platform where the band was set up. There was more applause and laughter as several of the single women rushed in the same direction. The orchestra conductor silenced the musicians, and without further ado, Vera lifted the bouquet high into the air. She threw it almost straight up over the heads of the guests below her.

The bouquet fell, fell, fell.

Straight into the hands of Manny Cygelman, who looked at it with bemused surprise for a moment. Then he joined in the laughter and applause around him.

Misha pointed at him. "You're next, Manny," he said. "Who's she going to be?"

"I don't have a clue, old man," his agent said, with a laugh. Then he turned and graciously handed the nosegay to Priscilla Cavanaugh, who stood at his side. Sasha watched the spectacle with a smug expression.

Vera took Misha's arm, and they started waving good-byes all around, slowly making their way through the guests, headed toward the entrance gallery and a final escape. Their parents awaited them at the elevator, teary-eyed once again. After hugs and kisses all around, Vera and Misha left. A car would be waiting downstairs to take them to the airport, where a chartered Gulfstream V would whisk them off on a nonstop flight to their honeymoon destination.

Perched high atop a hill near Ubud, in central Bali, the house overlooked the spectacular Ayung River Gorge, volcanic mountains, and terraced rice paddies. It appeared to be part of the tropical forest in which it was set, being made almost entirely of ironwood beams, teak, and coconut palms. Many of its rooms were entirely open to the elements, while others were surrounded with glass French doors that took advantage of the dramatic views but offered refuge from the weather.

The air carried with it the sounds of wind chimes, cicadas, and bullfrogs. The sweet scents of a profusion of flowering trees and plants commingled to form an intoxicating perfume that suffused the house with its headiness.

It was here, in this house, on an enormous teak bed swathed in draperies of pristine white mosquito netting, that Vera conceived her first child.

Night after night, day after day, she and Misha made love in that giant bed, the smell of their sex charging the air, blending with the scented breezes, driving them to heights of erotic passion that were unfamiliar to Vera, so powerful and compelling was their thirst for each other. Their lovemaking had always been full of wonder for her, but it had taken on a new dimension, one almost of carnal obsession.

The overcrowded beaches with their tourist hotels were far away, the way Misha and Vera had planned it. Here alone, except for the efficient and discreet servants, they had settled in for a honeymoon stay of quiet reading, listening to music, and taking walks. All without a care in the world.

After several days of little else but eating, sleeping, and making love—

days that had seemed to merge seamlessly into one with their single-minded activity—Vera lay in the huge bed, Misha asleep at her side. She pondered the mystery and miracle of their love.

Her body literally ached from their lovemaking, something that had never happened to her before, and she felt immensely fulfilled in a way she had never known was possible. She had believed that Misha loved her, but she had never thought that he would find her as sexually exciting as he did.

No matter how faithful, no woman has ever been more loved, Vera thought. *What have I ever done to deserve such love?* she asked herself. *To be so desired?* Then she wondered: *Am I worthy of such love?*

Unsolicited, the memory of that horrifying night before the wedding sprang into her mind, twisting its way into her consciousness like a poisonous snake, flicking its hideous tongue at her, accusing her.

She had tried to rationalize her actions that night, telling herself over and over that what she'd set out to do was out of necessity. She told herself repeatedly that she hadn't, after all, killed anybody. But the guilt still ate at her, insinuating that her intentions mattered, and that those intentions had been murderous.

I was going to murder him, she thought. *I went there with every intention of killing him if I had to. I must be some kind of . . . monster!*

She covered her face with her hands, as if to block out the vision of Simon reeling off the pier, his hands flailing at the air, grasping for a hold that wasn't there. Then she heard the horrible thud when he hit the giant bolt, the barely perceptible splash as he hit the water. She looked into the blackness of the filthy water that lapped so gently against the pilings and saw—Vera almost mewled in terror—Simon's evil eyes looking up at her from under the water, his mouth a twisted rictus, accusing her of murder.

She began to pant, gasping for air, as a sheen of cold sweat covered her face. Her hands shook, and she moaned. Grasping a pillow, she covered her face with it, trying to still her agonizing pain.

She would never tell Misha what had happened. Never. She couldn't let anything spoil the perfect love that they felt for each other.

She slowly removed the pillow from her face and laid it at her side. Her breathing returned to normal, and she began to relax. Perhaps, she thought sensibly, these horrible visions and the debilitating guilt will eventually dissipate. Perhaps I can even learn to like myself again. After all, Simon intended to kill me . . .

She was jerked out of her reverie by Misha's voice.

"What are you thinking about?" he asked sleepily.

She looked at him, conjuring up a smile. It was surprisingly easy when she looked at his handsome face wreathed by his disheveled raven hair. "Oh," she said calmly, "you and me. How great it's going to be moving into your apartment. And what a great honeymoon this is."

Misha grinned and reached over and pulled her closer to him. He nibbled on her ear playfully. "Do you really think so?" he asked.

"Yes, I really think so," Vera replied, the dark thoughts of only moments before already receding from her mind.

"Let's make it even better," Misha said, running one of his hands over her breasts, lightly flicking her nipples. He lowered his mouth to one of them, almost reverently, she thought, then began licking and kissing her there.

Vera gasped in pleasure and ran her hands over his hard, muscled chest, down to his tight stomach, and on down to the thicket between his legs. He gasped as she encircled his turgid cock with her hand. She delighted in its power, its ability to give pleasure, and its life-giving seed.

They made love, once again leaving her sated and, unknown to them both, pregnant.

When they left for New York days later, they were exhilarated and refreshed. They had become much more than the loving friends who'd experimented with sex before their marriage. They had become true lovers.

May it always be like this, Vera prayed. *May we always love each other the way we have these last weeks. Please, God. Never let it change.*

Part Three

TOMORROW

Manhattan Beach, Brooklyn

The house was expensive. Outrageously expensive. And ugly. Monstrously ugly. Or so the young man thought as he pulled up to the curb in his outrageously expensive but tasteful car. He sat on the buttery soft leather upholstery for a moment, studying the offensive edifice. He didn't think he'd ever seen so much money put to such contemptible use.

The gargantuan pile was such a pastiche of stylistic elements from different periods, of building materials of every conceivable kind, that he could only assume that the designer and owner had worked very hard to make certain that no period of history had been neglected and no expensive specimen of wood or stone had been ignored in its building.

It's no distance at all between Brighton Beach and Manhattan Beach, but it was light-years away in every other respect. Brighton Beach was a somewhat down-at-the-heels community of Russian emigrés. Manhattan Beach was quickly becoming an extraordinarily expensive enclave of very successful Russian emigrés, many of whom, like the man he was about to see, had their business virtually around the corner in Brighton Beach.

The young man turned off the engine and took a deep breath. He wasn't looking forward to his meeting with the older man. The Russian Neanderthal of the appalling bad manners. Which went so well with the appallingly ugly house he'd had built for himself and his garish, equally uncouth wife.

He got out of the car and walked up to the house's entrance. A videocamera was mounted above the door, as at the club. He rang the bell and waited. After a moment the door was opened wide by the older man's wife, a bleached blonde who wore lots of badly applied makeup and a skintight sweater with skintight pants. She was smoking a cigarette.

She looked the young man up and down, then blew a plume of smoke toward him. She had about her a superior air that the young man found laughable. "Come in," she said with a Russian accent.

"Thanks," he said.

"He's in his den," she said. "Follow me." Her high heels click-clacked on the entrance hall's marble floor as she led the way.

The young man looked around. The house was hideously decorated—a lot of cheap faux Baroque glittery golds and silvers, with whites and reds—but immaculate, unlike the club, for which he was grateful. They probably have an army of emigrés straight off the boat to clean for nearly nothing, *he thought, eyeing the abundance of artificial flowers and plants with distaste.*

She led him down a short flight of stairs with white carpeting to a lower level, where he followed her down a short hallway to a door. She opened it and stood back. "In here," she said, nodding her big bleached hair toward the room.

"Thanks," the young man said again. He entered the room, and she closed the door behind him.

The older man's office had shiny jet black pile carpeting and hideous black and white leather-upholstered chairs and sofa, a gigantic black and glass desk. Out of the corner of his eye, he saw a familiar-looking goon sprawled on the sofa. In a white leather chair nearby sat his counterpart, flexing his fists on the chair's arms. On the wall above him was a painting of a nude woman, posed provocatively, one finger between her pouty red lips, another between her thighs.

He approached the desk, where the older Russian sat, a cell phone attached to his ear as usual. He didn't acknowledge the young man but eyed him as he continued to talk.

The waiting game again, the young man thought with irritation. And there wasn't a chair placed in front of the desk where he could sit and wait. Another one of their ridiculous tactics. You don't just keep them waiting, you keep them standing as well.

After what seemed like an interminable length of time, the older man finished his telephone call, snapped the cell phone shut, and carefully placed it on the desk to the right of him. He then placed his meaty paws on the desk, in the very center, intertwining his sausage fingers. He looked up at the young man with his wolf's eyes, then slowly began shaking his head from side to side.

"You are becoming a great disappointment to me," he said at last. "A great disappointment." He tapped the desktop with a thick finger, his malevolent gaze riveted to the young man.

The younger man stood silently, knowing that nothing irritated the older Russian more than his silence, but he didn't really care. Two can play his stupid waiting game, *he thought, returning the man's stare.*

The older Russian finally exploded in anger, spittle flying. "What do you have to say for yourself?" His face had turned beet red, and the veins stood out in bas relief on his face and neck.

"I have nothing to say," the young man replied in a self-assured voice, "except that he has thus far refused to listen to reason. As you well know."

"Nothing to say!" the older man echoed in a thunderous baritone. "Refused to listen to reason!" He glowered at the younger man as if he couldn't believe his ears. "You're going to end up in a fucking body bag, and you don't have anything to say for yourself?"

The young man just stared back, his confidence not in the least bit affected. He knew, and the older Russian knew, that Misha Levin was an extremely difficult man to even get to, much less get close to. To convince him to sign any kind of performance and recording contract—to unknowingly become a part of their evil empire—would be a feat well worth waiting for. If these hooligans stood any chance at all of succeeding, they knew, and the young man knew, that he was not only their best chance but their only chance.

The older man reached into a rear trouser pocket and pulled out a handkerchief, then proceeded to wipe beads of sweat off his flushed face and from around his thick neck. When he'd finished, he reached around and stuffed the handkerchief back down into his trouser pocket. His breathing was an audible wheeze.

He looked up at the young man and shook his head again. "You've got till the end of the year," he said in an even tone, making an effort to check his explosive temper. "If you haven't gotten him to sign on the dotted line by then, you're both in trouble. Got that?"

"I've got it," the young man said with a nod.

The older Russian began scratching out something on a pad of paper. When he was finished, he ripped the sheet of paper off of the pad and held it out.

The young man took it from him and looked down. He could barely restrain a smile. He's upping the offer, he thought with amusement. He'll pay almost anything to get Misha Levin to sign a contract with his production company.

"This is the final offer," the older man said. "Make that clear to Levin, but don't make any threats." He looked over at the goons, who had sat silently watching the exchange. "We'll do that if and when the time comes."

The behemoths half smiled, as if in anticipation of being able to exert their brute force.

The older man returned his gaze to the young man. "We want Levin's willing cooperation if at all possible. That's the ideal situation, and that's your department. Leave the rest to us."

The young man smiled evilly. "It would give me great pleasure to convince Misha Levin that he must sign with you," he said. "I have immediate access to him, his wife, his child, anyone, and I could be very, ah . . . convincing."

The older man eyed him shrewdly. He knew the young man was a brilliant manipulator. But it hadn't occurred to him that he might actually be capable of anything physical. Now he thought he recognized a kindred spirit of sorts. A man who would use any means possible to get what he wanted.

"Just do as we say for the time being," the older man said. "If and when the time comes, I'll decide how we'll go about convincing Misha Levin that he must cooperate with us."

The young man nodded.

"And keep in mind that time is becoming increasingly important," the older Russian said. "There are political and economic changes in Russia every day, so go to work on him."

The young man nodded again.

"Now get out of here," the older Russian said. "And don't miss any Saturday night calls."

The young man turned on his heel and started toward the door. He nodded to the goons, who had been watching him with indolent expressions. One of them cracked his knuckles and his lips became a smirk.

The young man restrained a smile once again. They think they're in control. Well, let them think it. I'll show them who has control. Who knows how to get things done. They don't have a clue who or what they're dealing with here.

Chapter Thirty

❧

New York City, April 1999

"Look, Grandma!" Nicky cried. "Look!" When he was certain that he had her undivided attention, he carefully positioned his foot over a bright red balloon, then gave it a gleeful stomp. It burst with a loud pop!

Sonia's eyes widened in a semblance of alarm, and she threw her hands to her heart, as if mortally wounded. "Ah! I'm shot!" she wailed. "Your poor old grandmother is shot!" She slumped to her side, and her eyes fluttered shut.

Nicky shrieked with laughter and tore off in search of more mischief. Sonia opened her eyes and straightened up in her chair, a smile on her face as she surveyed the chaotic scene before her.

Hundreds of balloons, all in colors that bobbed about the apartment's high ceilings, their long streamers dangling temptingly. Their deflated counterparts, victims of innocent child play, lay mute on the floor after loud and startling explosions. The apartment's spacious rooms were still filled with the squeals of laughter. She heard the encouragement or admonishment of several doting parents, and saw that Olga, Nicky's efficient nanny, was busily searching out the missing in action.

Birthday cake and ice cream were generously smeared on faces and clothes. Nor had some of the furniture and rugs been spared, Sonia noticed. But it didn't matter, she thought, judging that no irreparable harm had been done. Besides, it was Nicky's fourth birthday, and the party, to her and Vera's immense satisfaction, had been a boisterous, messy, and completely delightful affair—and, thankfully, was drawing to a close. Clivo the Clown had come and gone, after enchanting some of the children while simultaneously terrifying others with his age-old slapstick shenanigans. Manuel the Magician, his tatty old cloak and Hispanic accent notwithstanding, had departed to pleas of "More! More! More!"

Now parents, nannies, and au pairs were arriving to pick up the little ones, and between good-byes she'd decided to get off her tired feet.

The explosive pop! of yet another balloon meeting its end gave her a start, and she saw that Nicky was the culprit. She looked at her grandson with unabashed pride.

He's so much like his father was at that age, she thought. The same raven black hair framed his angelic face, and the same beguiling eyes, so dark brown they appeared to be black, begged for your attention. Even in his child's plump little face, she was certain that she could discern his father's handsome features slowly emerging. *He's going to be a heartbreaker*, she surmised. *And that, too, is just like his father.*

"It's been a wonderful party, hasn't it?" Vera said, patting her mother-in-law on the shoulder and sitting down next to her.

"Oh, yes, Vera," Sonia replied, "it's been a fabulous party. Nicky and all the children have had such a good time." She looked at Vera with a wistful smile on her face. "I was just thinking how like his father Nicky is," she said. "Of course, you've heard that a million times, and not just from me."

"Oh, yes," Vera said with a laugh. Her alert blue eyes shifted to her son. He was racing about the room in a frenzy of youthful delight, grasping at the balloon streamers within his reach. "But it's true," she said. "He's so like Misha, it's uncanny. And he idolizes his father."

"Where *is* Misha?" Sonia asked. "I thought he was going to stop by for the party."

"So did I," Vera said. She sighed and shifted uneasily in her chair. "I don't know what's held him up." She gazed off into the distance a moment, as if searching for an answer, and unconsciously began nudging her wedding band and engagement ring around her finger with a thumb.

She turned to Sonia. "I'm just glad that he made a big production out of Nicky's birthday this morning," she said, "and gave him his present after breakfast."

Sonia knew her daughter-in-law extremely well, and she could see that Vera was annoyed with Misha. Even though she was making an effort to conceal it, her beautiful daughter-in-law was obviously nervous. She had a strong suspicion that it was more than Misha's missing the birthday party that had upset her.

What could it be? she wondered, wishing that she could ask Vera what was troubling her. *They have everything*, she told herself. *A beautiful home, successful careers, and plenty of money. Best of all, they have each other and an extraordinary child.* But something was definitely amiss. She didn't want to pry, however. Vera, she knew, felt free to discuss her problems with her and would talk to her when and if she needed to.

It's strange, she thought. *Vera comes to me, but never goes to her own* mother. But then Tatiana Bunim, for all her good qualities, was hardly the type of woman that one would feel comfortable confiding in. She wasn't even motherly, Sonia thought, let alone grandmotherly.

She turned to Vera and gave her a gentle pat on the arm. "Maybe," Sonia ventured, "our Misha will still make it." She didn't herself believe it, not now that the party was virtually over, but she wanted to do what she could to bolster up Vera's flagging spirits.

"Probably not." Vera smiled ruefully. "But I appreciate your efforts to make me feel better," she added.

Misha's failure to show up was just one in what was becoming a very long string of more and more frequent absences. After their marriage and during the first six months of her pregnancy, she'd traveled with Misha to almost every performance, be it far-off Tokyo or nearby Pittsburgh. Then, after Nicky's birth, she'd quite naturally stayed in New York for the first few months, running the household and helping raise their son. She hadn't quit her job altogether, but had worked out an arrangement with the auction house whereby she acted as a consultant and worked on special events. That way she could work at home and would be free to travel with Misha at almost any time. Theoretically, at least.

It hadn't worked out that way however. The demands on her time in New York made traveling with him more difficult than either of them had imagined. Should Nicky be sick, for example, she wouldn't even consider leaving him at home alone with Olga, no matter how efficient she might be. Then, too, her job required that she entertain very important clients, a responsibility that Vera didn't take lightly. As a result, Misha often traveled alone nowadays.

She'd long since grown accustomed to his being away. These were necessary absences, after all. But what disturbed Vera was Misha's behavior when he was home. He was increasingly aloof and restless, preoccupied and distracted.

It's as if he's absent when he's actually here, she thought.

When she'd tried to broach the subject, Misha lightly told her that she was imagining things, or worse, he retreated into himself, closing up and refusing to discuss it.

As much as she hated to think it, Vera was beginning to fear that he was disenchanted with their marriage and family life.

With Nicky, his own son, and me.

She could remember Nicky's first two birthdays as if they were yesterday. Misha had planned and executed extravagant celebrations, not leaving anything to chance, insisting on doing nearly everything himself. He'd been a lively and attentive presence for his son. Then, last year, when Nicky turned three, Misha had left everything up to her. She hadn't minded at all but was surprised. When she asked him about it, he'd merely shrugged and said he was too busy. She knew that if he'd wanted to, he could have found the time. At least, she thought, he'd made the effort to put in an appearance at the party.

And now this year. Not even showing up.

What's happened? she asked herself. *What's going on?*

She'd told herself that she wouldn't agonize about it today, but she couldn't help but reflect back on the last five years of their marriage. During the first two years or so he'd been the picture of a doting father and husband. When she went into labor with Nicky, Misha had had sympathetic labor pains. When she gave birth, he'd insisted on being there with her. Later, despite the nanny and household help, he'd wanted to learn to change Nicky's diapers and to feed him. He'd tucked the baby into his perambulator and taken him for long walks, proudly showing him off to the entire neighborhood.

Vera didn't doubt for a minute that Misha loved his son with all his heart. But in the last year Misha had begun to show less and less interest in Nicky.

And me, she reflected painfully.

Something she couldn't yet put her finger on had slowly pulled her husband away from her and Nicky. For a while she'd thought that it had started after their trip to Vienna. It was the last trip they'd taken together, and she'd looked forward to it, only to be disappointed by his inattentiveness. That old enthusiasm he used to have when she was along for the trip was missing. After she'd given it some thought, however, she began to realize that it had started long before the trip to Vienna, a year or two at least. The trip had simply marked a turning point in the downhill slide of their relationship. Since then his attention had been increasingly drawn elsewhere, and she'd begun to seriously ask herself why.

Was it mere boredom? she wondered. Disenchantment? If not, what? Or, she trembled to think, *who?* Had he actually met someone to replace her in his affections?

Vera didn't know, but she made up her mind to find out, one way or another. She loved Misha, and nothing—or *nobody*—was going to take him away from her.

Through the open window of Serena's loft, a truck rumbling and banging along Vestry Street added percussion to Mabel Mercer's soft rendition of "Honeysuckle Rose." Neither she nor Misha heard a thing. All they had eyes and ears for was each other.

Their clothes, tossed haphazardly about the room, were a testament to their haste to relish each other's bodies unencumbered. In the subdued lighting of her bedroom, they lay absorbed in the satisfaction of shared desire.

Serena's fingers were tangled in his hair. "Ahhh!" she moaned, giving herself up to his ministrations. "That's soooo good, Misha." She relished the feel of his hot breath on her there, his tongue caressing her. "Oh, it's so . . . goooood!"

From down between her long, firm thighs, he looked up at her. Her head was thrown back against the pillow, but he could see that her face was set in a look of euphoric determination. He knew that she was close, very close, which only served to make his urgency all the greater. He couldn't wait a second longer. He rose up, his weight on his hands to either side of her, then quickly mounted her, plunging in to the hilt.

Serena gasped and threw her arms around his back, clutching him with all her might. "Oh, yes, Misha," she cried. "Yes! Oh, my God. Yes!"

They began to move together in a rhythmic frenzy, their desire for each other overwhelming them, and it was only moments before she cried out in ecstasy, her nails digging into his back. He felt her body arch against him, and then she began to tremble from head to toe.

Misha let himself go then, in a final, powerful lunge, and groaned with pleasure as he released all his pent-up passion in a lusty explosion. His body shuddered mightily, and he collapsed atop her. He peppered her face with kisses, holding her to him tightly as he gasped for air.

They lay catching their breath, their bodies, coated in a fine sheen of perspiration, heaving one against the other.

"That was . . . so fantastic," Misha finally managed to rasp, looking into her eyes.

Serena smiled. "Y . . . yes," she panted. "It . . . it was the best, Misha." She ran her fingers through his hair lovingly. "The . . . the very, very best."

He kissed her lips, then slowly rolled off onto his side, his breath gradually returning to normal. He slid an arm under her shoulders. Serena turned onto her side and snuggled close against him, expelling an immense sigh of utter contentment.

"Oh, God, Serena," he said. "I'm so glad you're back." He gently stroked long tendrils of raven black hair away from her face.

"Me, too," Serena breathed. "I knew I'd missed this—missed *you*—but I didn't know how much."

"I missed you, too," Misha said. "I swear I literally ached for you night and day. I couldn't stop thinking about you."

"I know exactly what you're talking about," she said. "I've felt exactly the same way." She kissed his lips and looked into his dark eyes. Then her voice dropped to an impassioned whisper. "I wish we could be like this forever. Here, together. You and me."

Misha's breath caught in his throat. He looked at her, his eyes widening. "Do you mean that?" he asked. "Are you really serious?"

"Yes." Serena nodded. "I really do mean it, Misha."

"Oh, my God, Serena," he said, almost moaning in rapture. He hugged her and kissed her urgently, deeply, suddenly swept up in a tidal wave of passion by what amounted to a protestation of love from Serena.

When he finally willed himself to stop, he drew back. "I never thought I'd hear you say anything like that, Serena," he whispered, searching her face, as if he could find there confirmation for the truth of her words. "You're sure it isn't just the sex?" he asked, still disbelieving.

"Oh, yes," she said, her voice earnest. "I feel that way, Misha. It's not just the sex, although I love that, too."

Her face took on a serious expression. "I've done a lot of soul searching since we ran into each other in Vienna," she finally continued in the same tone, "and I've come to the conclusion that I really want . . . to be with you. That I really . . . I really love you, Misha." With that said, she looked at him, a tentative smile hovering on her lips.

Misha returned her look, then hugged her again, as if by holding her she couldn't take back what she'd said. "Oh, my God," he moaned again. "You do mean it, don't you." Then he reverently kissed her hair, her forehead and eyes, her nose and each cheek, her chin, and finally her lips.

"I'm the luckiest man alive," he said in a whisper.

Serena laughed lightly. "You didn't believe me in Vienna, did you?" she said. "When I told you that I love you."

"I didn't really know," Misha said honestly. "It was all so new and sudden and exciting after all those years. And we were both so . . . so—"

"In a state of lust," Serena provided with a smile.

"Yes," he said, smiling back at her. "Definitely in a state of lust. So I wasn't sure what to believe. I wasn't certain about anything." He paused a moment, his eyes studying her face again.

Serena thought that he had never looked more like a happy puppy, so adoring, so obliging. So ready to offer his unconditional love. "But you're certain now?" she asked, ruffling his hair with her fingers.

"Yes," Misha said, his eyes brightening. "Oh, yes, Serena. I believe you really do love me, and I *know* I love you."

He pulled her closer again and began kissing her deeply. Serena responded with ardor, as ravenous for him as he was for her. It was only moments before they were savoring the delights of each other again. In that same rhythmic dance, only at a more leisurely pace this time, they lingered over the exquisite sensations they aroused in each other until ultimately, sated for the time being at least, they lay spent and exhausted on the bed.

The sun had begun its afternoon descent in the sky, and the light in Serena's bedroom had slowly shifted with it. Misha lay on his back, with Serena nestled next to him, her head on his shoulder, an arm thrown over his chest. They were quiet for a while, each in his own world, but at the same time very much aware of each other.

"What are you thinking about?" Misha asked her, stroking her back with his hand.

"How happy I am," she said softly. "How fulfilled and completely contented I feel. How . . . alive."

Misha kissed her forehead. "You took the words right out of my mouth," he said quietly. "This has been one of the best afternoons in my life."

"Me, too," Serena said. "I don't want it to end."

"Neither do I," Misha said.

"Do you want to stay for dinner?" she asked. "We can call out for something or go—"

"Dinner?" Misha asked, a sudden look of alarm on his face.

"Yes, I thought—"

"What time is it, Serena?" he asked, his voice anxious. He sat up.

"Just a minute," she said. She rolled over and grabbed her watch off the nightstand on her side of the bed, then sat up and looked at it. "It's about five o'clock," she said.

"Oh, Jesus!" Misha groaned. "Oh, *Jesus!*"

"What is it, Misha?" she asked, a worried look on her face.

He slammed his fists down on the bed with all his might. "I missed my son's birthday party."

Chapter Thirty-one

Vera paced the floor, arms folded across her chest, fingers nervously tapping her elbows. She had come straight from a meeting and was wearing a delft blue Chanel suit that harmonized with her eyes, an oyster silk blouse that matched the black and oyster braid trim on her jacket, and black Manolo Blahnik heels. Her necklace was a single strand of pearls that matched her earrings. A bracelet of thick gold links was on one wrist, her gold watch on the other.

From the couch, Sonia watched her daughter-in-law closely. Her face, she observed, was set in an expression that was at once thoughtful and tortured. *Every waking moment for her is an agony,* Sonia thought. *She's living in utter hell, the poor child.*

She cleared her throat. "Are you absolutely certain," she ventured, "that it's not something else?"

Vera abruptly stopped pacing and turned to her mother-in-law. Sonia's white hair shone lustrously in the sun that poured through the double-height windows of the beautiful Central Park South apartment. Her posture, Vera noted, was as erect and regal as always. At seventy years of age. Sonia was still a striking woman, self-assured, strong, and wise.

"I'm certain that's it, Sonia," she finally said. "I don't have any real proof," she added, "but all the indications point to it." She thought, but didn't say, *another woman.* She walked over to one of the big comfortable armchairs near the couch and sank down into it.

"I . . . I really hate to talk to you about this," she went on in an anguished voice. "I feel so . . . so . . . guilty about it. I mean, Misha is your son." She paused and looked over at Sonia. "But you're . . . well, you're the best friend I've got, Sonia. You've been like a mother to me."

Sonia rose to her feet and took the few steps to where Vera was seated. Leaning down, she put her arms around her shoulders and hugged her reassuringly. "Darling, don't ever be afraid to bring your troubles to me," she said. "Problems with my son included."

Vera began to weep, heaving quietly against Sonia. "I'm . . . I'm . . . just so . . . so . . . *sorry*," she said through her tears.

Sonia gently stroked her back, as if she were a child. "You have nothing to be sorry for, darling," she said soothingly. "Nothing at all. I'm glad that you came to me." She continued holding her, trying to console her, until Vera had regained her composure.

"Oh, God!" Vera exclaimed. "I swore I wouldn't cry. I must be a mess. Let me get a Kleenex out of my bag."

Sonia straightened up and watched as Vera retrieved her black shoulder bag from the floor next to the chair. She rummaged in it until she found the Kleenex, then wiped her eyes and blew her nose.

"Please, Sonia," she said. "I'm all right now. Sit back down."

"Are you sure you don't want some coffee or tea?" Sonia asked. "It's no trouble, darling."

"Maybe just some water," Vera said. "I had too much coffee at the auction house meeting."

Sonia went to the kitchen to get the water, and Vera kicked off her heels and lay back in the chair, staring thoughtfully at the high ceiling. She'd been reluctant to discuss this problem with Sonia, but she didn't really have anyone else to talk to. After going down a mental checklist of friends, she'd ticked off one after the other, deciding there wasn't a single one she could trust with this secret. Besides, she could well imagine their advice.

There would be the Get Even Group, those who would tell her to try to get the "goods" on Misha, then run straight to the best divorce lawyers in New York and stick it to him royally, in court. Revenge, they would happily inform her, is the best medicine.

The Pyschobabble Bunch would tell her to discuss it with her analyst. She did have one, didn't she? Then, talk to a good marriage counselor. Get Misha to go with her, and try to work it out.

Then there would be the Boy Toy Bunch, that brittle, sophisticated set who would laugh it off and tell her she was lucky he had an outside interest—to get one for herself. Preferably young and hot and horny. Didn't everybody nowadays?

Sonia returned from the kitchen with a small tray. On it were two glasses of ice and a bottle of San Pelligrino. She set it down on the coffee table and filled both the glasses, then handed Vera one.

"Here, darling," she said. "A little sparkling water. Is that okay?"

"That's perfect," Vera said, taking the glass from her. "Thanks, Sonia."

Sonia took one for herself and sat back down. "Do you want to talk about it?" she asked, looking at Vera.

Vera took a sip of the water, then set her glass down. "I don't know where to begin," she said, "but I'll try." She took a deep breath, then gave Sonia a quick rundown on Misha's increasing restlessness and inattentiveness. She told her how it had been going on for a long time, and was getting much worse lately.

"Missing Nicky's birthday party was a good example," Vera said. "He didn't even bother making excuses. He just said he'd been tied up."

Sonia nodded thoughtfully. "Have other things like that happened?" she asked. "Since then?"

"Oh, yes," Vera said. "It's getting a lot worse. It happens all the time now, in fact. He'll be practicing, then suddenly get up and say he has to go over to Manny's. He'll be gone all afternoon, and Manny will call for him while he's gone."

"Stupid man!" Sonia said. "That's so sloppy! Not even covering his bases!"

Vera couldn't help but laugh. "Not very clever," she agreed. "If I ask him about it, he'll say he got waylaid. Be very vague. Then sometimes he'll be late for dinner or miss dinner entirely. He'll make really lame excuses or he won't even bother. It's as if he doesn't care."

"This does *not* sound good," Sonia conceded. "It . . . it reminds me of the way he used to behave when he was defying us for some reason or other. Or"—Sonia looked at her daughter-in-law—"keeping guilty secrets from us."

"Exactly," Vera said. "That's the way it seems to me, and that's what has me so worried. He's never been like this before."

Vera took a sip of water and cleared her throat before continuing. "Another highly suspicious thing is the way he'll sometimes lavish attention on Nicky and me. Suddenly. From out of the blue. For absolutely no reason." She shrugged. "It's as if he were trying to make up for something."

"Uh-oh," Sonia said, arching an all-knowing brow. "I smell a fish. Yes. I most definitely smell a fish."

Vera looked at her mother-in-law, then began twisting her wedding band and engagement ring around her finger, an unconscious nervous tic Sonia recognized all too well. She took a deep breath and expelled a heavy sigh. "But the worst thing," she finally said, "is that he . . . he doesn't want me anymore. Not . . . sexually." She looked down at her hands for a moment, then back up at Sonia. Her face was etched with grief. "That's so hard to live with," she said miserably.

"Oh, darling," Sonia said, "that must be truly humiliating for you. You must be devastated."

"Yes," Vera said calmly, "I am. I feel utterly abandoned and . . . unloved." Her voice choked. "It . . . it makes me feel like a failure, Sonia. I'm *flooded* with a sense of failure." Tears came into her eyes again, and she wiped them away with a Kleenex.

"Vera," Sonia said. "Come here." She patted the couch with her hand. "Sit next to me."

Vera got to her feet and did as Sonia asked, sitting on the cushion next to her. Sonia took Vera's hands in her own and looked directly into her eyes.

"Listen to me," she said in a stern but caring voice. "And you listen hard. No matter what's going on, whether all of your suspicions are right on the mark or not, you must *not* think of yourself as a failure, Vera. Under no circumstances. You have done nothing wrong here. You've been as good a mother and wife as I've ever seen."

"But I—I—" Vera began.

"Let me finish, Vera!" Sonia said emphatically. "Nicky alone is proof of what a wonderful mother you've been. You haven't let your job or Misha's work interfere with raising him. As far as Misha goes, you've made him extremely happy in the past, Vera. You've traveled with him, sometimes at the drop of a hat, and you've made a marvelous social life for him. His work—his whole life!—has been greatly enriched by you. All of our lives have been."

She gave Vera's hands a gentle squeeze, and Vera started to speak again.

"Sonia, I—"

"Hear me out!" her mother-in-law said. "You work wonders for the auction house. You work on committees and boards. And even with all that going on, you run the household extraordinarily well. Everybody knows that. Dmitri knows that. Your parents know that. *I* know that better than anyone."

Sonia paused and took a deep breath, then leaned forward and kissed Vera on the cheek and released her hands. "Now," she said, "I've had my say."

Vera, though teary-eyed, smiled at her formidable mother-in-law. "Thanks, Sonia," she said softly. "I really do appreciate your vote of confidence, and I guess what you're saying is true. But still . . . I feel like I must be doing something very, very . . . wrong. Don't you see?"

"No, I don't see!" Sonia snapped in exasperation. "I don't think you've done anything wrong. But I strongly suspect that Misha has!" She sighed heavily. "He could never keep it in his pants."

Vera didn't know whether to laugh or cry. She looked at Sonia in surprise, even though she knew the truth of her words. Her mother-in-law, she thought, always seemed to hit the nail on the head.

"You're right," she said calmly. "I've always known that. I guess I just hoped that . . . that all that would end when we got married." Her face looked stricken, and her voice acquired an edge of panic. "If I only knew what to do," she cried.

Sonia took hold of her hands again. "If he keeps behaving this way, there'll come a point, I think, when you'll have to confront him one way or the other." She sighed again. "Oh, darling, I wish I could be of more help. You know I'll do anything I can. I'll certainly keep my eyes and ears open. In the meantime, try to make the best of it—easier said than done, I know. But try to stick with it. Act like nothing is out of the ordinary. Maybe that would be the best policy right now. For Nicky's sake—and your marriage. Do you think you can do that?"

"I honestly don't know," Vera said. "I'm very busy and that helps. But I . . . I feel . . . abandoned." She looked into her mother-in-law's eyes. "Oh, Sonia," she said, her voice cracking, "without him I'm so . . . lonely."

"You're a worse fool than I thought," Coral said harshly. She was seated rigidly in a chrome and black leather Le Corbusier chair, eyes flashing emerald fury. "No. Scratch that," she snapped. "You are, bar none, the *biggest* fool I know."

"Oh, Coral," Serena said, her voice almost a little-girl whine, "I just can't help it!" She flopped down on the Le Corbusier chair's matching sofa, stretching out her long, shapely legs. She glanced over at her furious agent, her eyes expressing the bewilderment she felt. "I love him, Coral," she said softly. "I really love him."

For a moment Coral looked like she was going to be sick on the new loft's expensively finished floors. Even beneath her mask of ghostly white powder, Serena thought she could detect the blood draining from Coral's face. She quickly regained her composure, however.

"Love?" she spat. "What on earth do you know about love, Serena?"

"I know what I feel," Serena said defensively. "And I really believe it's love. I've never had feelings like this before, Coral."

"Feelings!" Coral glared at her with imperious hauteur, and her words came in a staccato torrent. "Don't make me laugh! It was *feelings* that got you hooked up with that lowlife rock and roll star, Rick . . . Rick . . . Whoever! The one who liked to beat up on you for his amusement. It was *feelings*, young lady, that got you mixed up with that stoned-out drummer who liked passing you around to his friends! Or was he the one that liked to tie you up? Who remembers? They're only two in a long line of major creeps. Your *feelings*, as you call them, Serena, have taken you to some pretty awful places. I think I would be just a little bit leery about trusting them if I were you."

"Oh, Jesus!" Serena groaned. She leapt to her feet and made a beeline for the glass and steel drinks table, where she splashed a generous portion of Jack Daniel's into a glass. "Do you want something, Coral?" she asked petulantly.

"No, thank you," Coral said, watching her. Then she added: "I thought you were laying off the booze with this new diet of yours."

"I was," Serena said, tossing two ice cubes in the glass. She gulped down half the drink in one large swallow, then shuddered from its fiery passage down her throat. She walked back to the couch and sat down, placing the drink on the coffee table.

"Why do you always have to bring up all that old shit, Coral? It's ancient history, and you know it." She glanced at her agent, who was drumming her fingernails on the armchair, as if she were impatiently indulging a wayward child.

"I'm a different person now," Serena claimed in a strident voice. "I've done a lot of growing up since then. Hell, I'm thirty years old."

"Then try to act it," Coral said. She looked at Serena quizzically. "Don't you see a pattern in your behavior, Serena? It's as plain as the nose on that beautiful face of yours."

"What?" Serena asked.

"You've gone from one impossible relationship to another," Coral said. "From one abusive man to another."

"Misha is not abusive," Serena said angrily. "He's gentle and kind and—"

"And *married*!" Coral said with emphasis. "Married! With a child, for God's sake! Have you given that any thought?"

Serena took a sip of her drink, then stretched out on the couch again, holding the drink on her stomach and staring up at the ceiling.

Yes! she wanted to scream at Coral. *Of course I've thought about it. And I've decided that I don't really give a damn. If somebody gets hurt, too bad. This is my chance for love, and I'm going to take it. I blew it once before, and I'm not going to make that mistake again.*

She didn't think it was wise to share these thoughts with Coral, however.

"Yes," she said, "I've thought about it. I've thought about it a lot, as a matter of fact." She sat back up and placed her drink on the table. "Listen," she said evenly, looking over at Coral again. "Misha is really miserable in his marriage and has been for a long time. He married her on the rebound from me, you know. I think he was actually trying to get back at me by marrying her."

Coral emitted an audible sigh. "That's what he's told you?" she asked.

"That he's unhappily married? Yes. That he married her on the rebound? Yes." Serena nodded. "He didn't exactly tell me he'd married her to get back at me, but that's what I think."

"So it was all just a little mistake," Coral said sarcastically. "Marrying her and fathering a child."

"Yes!" Serena said angrily. "It was!"

"And where does the child fit into all of this?" Coral asked. "Or has he even mentioned the little bundle of joy?"

"Jesus, Coral," Serena cried. "He adores his son. Of course he's mentioned him."

"And he's willing to virtually give up this son he adores so much so he can be with you. Yes?" Coral's eyes glittered malevolently.

Serena shrugged. "I—I don't know," she stammered. "We haven't really discussed that."

"Perhaps you should," she said. "Perhaps you'll take this innocent child into account the next time you and Misha Levin get cozy," she said.

"Oh, hell," Serena lashed out. "What do you know about these things anyway? You don't even like men!"

Coral digested this comment in silence. When she finally spoke, her voice was soft. "I thought you were a little sick of them yourself," she said. "I know there was a time when you were." She gave Serena a knowing look.

Serena tossed her long, raven hair and looked away, ignoring Coral and remaining silent.

"But I think that's beside the point really," Coral went on. "What we're talking about here is a relationship, and I do know a bit about them, even if I'm not involved with a man. Brandi and I have been together for over twenty years, and it hasn't always been easy, believe me. Love is great, wonderful. But it's taken work to make a go of it, and a lot of it. And that's without the complications of a divorce or a child entering the picture."

"I know," Serena said contritely. "I'm sorry I said what I did, Coral. That was a low blow."

"That's okay, Serena," she replied. "You're angry with me, and I can understand that. But you've got to remember that I'm thinking about *you*. I really believe that you've got some very serious soul-searching to do, Serena. Getting involved with somebody like Misha Levin is entirely different from having a little fling with one of the celebrities you photograph."

"I know it is," Serena said, nodding.

"You were terribly hurt by him once," Coral said, "and I hate to see you get hurt again."

"I appreciate your concern," Serena said, meaning it, "but that's not going to happen again."

"How can you be so certain?" Coral asked. "Don't forget that Misha Levin had quite a reputation before he got married. It was a different girl every few weeks, and from what I heard at the time, a lot of one-night stands thrown in for good measure."

"That was years ago," Serena said in his defense.

"Yes," Coral conceded. "About five or six years ago. Hardly ancient history, Serena. What I'm saying is, he has a history of playing around. Not only that, but his life is much more complicated now than it was the last time you two got involved. He wasn't married then, and didn't have a child."

"I know all that," Serena said, sighing wearily.

"And what about your career?" Coral asked. "Have you given that any thought? You've signed a contract for loads of money, and you're going to be under a lot of pressure to produce. You're going to be extremely busy." Coral waited for a response, but Serena sat mutely, staring at the floor.

"How's Misha Levin going to like it when you have to be gone half the time?" Coral persisted. "That was the problem the last time, if I remember correctly, and that hasn't changed. Are you willing to give up your career for him?"

"I would never do that," Serena said, her eyes bright with determination. "Besides, he wouldn't want me to. Misha's proud of my work, and somehow, I just know we can work it out."

She turned her hazel eyes on Coral. Her face was etched with an anguish that Coral hadn't seen there before. "We've just *got* to work it out," Serena said in a near whisper. "Because I meant what I said, Coral." Her voice broke then, and tears came into her eyes. "I'm really in love with him."

Jaded though she was, Coral's heart melted, and she looked at Serena tenderly. She rose to her feet and walked to the couch, her high heels click-clacking on the floor. She sat down next to Serena and took her in her arms.

Serena laid her head on Coral's shoulder and wept, Coral stroking her hair, whispering, "It'll be all right, darling. It'll be all right."

She wished she believed that her words were true. She did know that despite all her good advice, there was nothing more she could do to convince Serena that she was making a terrible mistake. Whether it was truly love or not didn't matter, Coral realized, because Serena *believed* she was in love and *believed* that Misha loved her.

How could she tell Serena what she really thought? she wondered. She couldn't, she decided. It was as simple as that. The truth was too cruel and would simply be too much for Serena to cope with on top of everything else.

Coral was convinced that Serena Gibbons had experienced so little real love in her life, so little nurturing, that she wouldn't recognize love if she was shown it or she herself felt it. She had never known anything but abuse, Coral reasoned, first from her family, then from the men she became involved with. And she was so starved for affection that when she'd been shown any degree of attention, she'd usually responded inappropriately, confusing even the basest lust with something infinitely more complicated and rewarding.

I think I'm probably the only person who's ever really loved Serena, she thought sadly.

At the same time, Coral was extremely worried because she also knew that Serena was quite capable of being extraordinarily insensitive to others, doling out the same kind of abuse she'd always received. Something fundamental, she had come to believe, had been so damaged by abuse and neglect that she wondered if Serena would ever heal.

"There, there," she whispered calmly, still stroking Serena's hair. "It'll be all right, darling."

Serena abruptly lifted her head and looked at Coral. Her eyes were red and puffy. "Oh, Coral," she said, sniffling, "I don't know what I'd do without you. Even if you do make me mad as all hell sometimes." Then she laughed and, pulling away, sat up straight.

"There's some Kleenex in my handbag," Coral said. "I'll get it." She got to her feet and retrieved her big Hermés Kelly bag. She found the packet of Kleenex and handed it to Serena.

Serena took it and wiped her eyes, then blew her nose. "Thanks, Coral," she said.

Coral stood watching her a moment, then crossed back to the chair and sat down. "Do you want to come uptown with me and go out to dinner?" she said. "Or we could order in, if you like."

"No." Serena shook her head. "I've got to start packing for the trip to England. Jason and Bennett are coming over to help." And she thought: *I've got to be here to talk to Misha when he calls.* She hadn't told Coral that they were meeting in England, and she had no intention of doing so now.

"Good," Coral said. "How are Jason and Bennett?"

"They're great," Serena said. "No tantrums, very efficient. And they're loads of fun to work with."

"I'm sure you could use some fun tonight," Coral said lightly. Then her voice suddenly became serious. "I'm really sorry I've upset you, Serena. I—"

"Forget it, Coral," Serena interjected. "I know you're trying to do what you think's right for me."

"Yes," Coral said. "I am. I know these are things you don't want to hear, but I care enough about you to say them. Just remember one thing, Serena. No matter what happens, I'm on your side, and I'll do whatever I can to help you." She didn't want to add that she had a strong feeling Serena was going to be needing her more than ever in the coming weeks.

Serena looked over at her. "Thanks, Coral," she said. "I really appreciate it." She got to her feet and stretched. "Now, why don't you go on? I know you want to get back uptown, and I'm okay."

"You're sure?" Coral asked.

"Yes," Serena said. "I'm sure."

Coral reached for her handbag and rose to her feet. She kissed Serena on the cheek, and Serena kissed her back.

"I'll walk you to the elevator," Serena said.

Arm in arm, they crossed the living room's huge expanse to the loft's entrance hall, where Serena pushed the button for the elevator. It opened immediately.

"Call me before you leave," Coral said, getting in the car.

"Oh, I will," Serena said. "Sometime tomorrow for sure. Bye." She waved.

"Good-bye, Serena," Coral said as the doors closed on her.

Serena turned and slumped against the wall. *Jesus,* she thought. *Thank God she's gone.*

Coral, she knew, meant well, but she simply couldn't get it through her head that Serena was in love. She walked back to the living room and picked up the glass of Jack Daniel's, then walked to the kitchen and threw the drink out in the sink.

What Coral doesn't realize, Serena thought, *is that I'm going to have Misha Levin come hell or high water.*

Misha replaced the telephone receiver in its cradle and looked thoughtfully toward the French doors, which led out to the wraparound terrace. He didn't see them, however, or the beautifully planted terrace that lay beyond them, with its spectacular view of Manhattan's twinkling night-time lights.

What he did envision was Serena, standing tall, slender, and magnificently nude. Her long black hair hung loose about her face, and her creamy naked breasts and firm thighs beckoned him to her, offering her body's rich delights and secret pleasures. He sat transfixed, reveling in her siren's call and his own heightened state of arousal, marveling that his merely speaking to her on the telephone still had such an effect on him.

Even after all these months, he reflected, since running into her in Vienna. It seemed like yesterday, that chance meeting, yet at the same time, like a million years ago. Their relationship had evolved into something so intense, and their lovemaking had become so familiar—yet always *fresh*, he thought.

"Everything okay, old boy?" Manny, fastidiously dressed and groomed as always, abruptly entered Misha's field of vision as he stepped through the terrace doors into the living room, a crystal balloon of brandy in hand. Sasha, aloof as always, remained out on the terrace.

Misha reluctantly relinquished the erotic specter that held him in its thrall and forced himself to return to the present reality. In this case, Manny and Shasha's lavishly decorated penthouse high above the West Side near Lincoln Center.

"What did you say?" Misha asked, swirling the scotch and water around in his glass before taking a sip.

"Everything okay?" Manny asked again.

"Yes," Misha said. "Everything's fine, Manny."

"So you two are getting together in London, I take it?" Manny asked, seating himself in a Jean-Michel Frank chair. Its bone leather upholstery squeaked under his weight.

"No," Misha said, "not London." He looked over at Manny and smiled conspiratorially. "But we *are* going to meet out in the country. At this place where Serena's going to be shooting. A big country house. She says it's really spectacular, practically a palace."

"And I assume," Manny said, "that this hanky-panky isn't going to interfere with your schedule?" He looked over at Misha through his thick tortoiseshell glasses.

"Has it ever?" Misha asked somewhat heatedly.

"No, no," Manny quickly replied. "I didn't mean—"

"I don't care what you meant," Misha snapped. "Don't ask me stupid questions." He shifted his weight on the shagreen daybed where he was seated and eyed Manny crossly.

"Jesus, Misha," Manny said, his face reddening. "Sorry!" *Prick!* he thought. *What the hell's got his goat, anyway? He thinks he's so fucking superior?*

Misha took another sip of his drink, then set the glass down on the rosewood Eugène Printz table next to him, noticing that it, like everything else in Manny's luxurious penthouse, was a pristine original. He looked up then and saw the hurt expression on Manny's face. He immediately felt contrite for snapping at him.

"Christ," he said, "I'm sorry, Manny. I didn't mean to jump down your throat."

"It's okay, Misha," Manny said. "Forget it." He shrugged, then took a sip of his brandy, savoring its fiery taste on his palate. "You're not yourself tonight. What's bugging you, old boy?"

Misha looked at him for a moment, then sighed. "To be honest, Manny, I don't like the way you used 'hanky-panky' to describe the relationship that Serena and I have."

"I—I'm sorry," Manny said, looking at Misha with surprise. *If it's not hanky-panky,* he thought, *what the fuck would you call it, then?*

"It's much more than that, Manny," Misha said, as if he'd read Manny's mind. His face was set in a solemn expression and his tone was serious. "In fact, it's not like that at all. This is serious, Manny. Real serious."

Manny returned his gaze. "So you're sure this isn't just a passing fancy?" he asked.

"Anything but, Manny." Misha shook his head, and ran his long fingers through his hair. "I'm in love with her. Head over heels in love."

Manny could hardly restrain himself from clapping his hands in glee. Nothing could make him happier, for he had come to loathe Vera Levin and her unwavering attention to Misha's business. She was always asking questions. Always going through Misha's royalty statements with a fine-tooth comb. She'd made it quite clear that she didn't trust him or Sasha.

Manny cleared his throat. "Uh-oh," he said.

"Uh-oh, indeed," Misha responded.

"And she's in love with you, I take it?" Manny said.

Misha nodded. "Yes."

"What are you going to do about it?" Manny asked. "I mean, are you—"

"I don't know," Misha answered truthfully. "I don't know what to do. But I do know that it can't go on like this much longer. Sneaking down to her loft like some kind of criminal or trying to meet if we're traveling in the same part of the world—it's not enough. It's making us both a little crazy."

Misha paused and took a sip of his scotch and water. "I hate the subterfuge," he said with a scowl. "It makes me feel dirty. It makes what Serena and I do—what we have with each other—seem sordid. And it's not, Manny. It's anything but. It's beautiful and wonderful and pure." He looked at Manny, his eyes burning bright with conviction.

Manny simply nodded, and thought: *Whoa! This gets better and better. He really believes he and Serena are involved in some kind of great and noble love affair instead of a good old-fashioned fuckfest.*

"But having to sneak around and tell lies taints everything," Misha added. He heaved a sigh. "I hate the deceit and the furtiveness. But I guess most of all I hate the . . . the unfaithfulness."

"Are you going to tell Vera about it?" Manny asked.

"I'm going to have to, and soon," Misha replied. "It just can't go on like this."

"I'd say the sooner the better," Manny suggested. "Then you won't have to lie or sneak around. You'll feel a whole lot better about yourself."

"I wish it were that easy," Misha said. "I guess I'm being a real chicken, but I know that Vera's going to be crushed. She hasn't really done anything to deserve this, you know? She's going to be hurt. Really hurt. And Nicky . . . well . . . I—"

Misha's voice suddenly broke, and he looked at Manny with his big, dark eyes. They were immensely sad with the knowledge of the pain he would inflict on his wife and his son.

"I think Nicky's still too young to know what's going on," Manny said quickly. "And no matter what happens, you'd see a lot of him. Vera's not unreasonable. She'll be hurt of course, but we both know that Vera's strong and resilient, Misha. She'll get over it. Probably quicker than you think."

"Why do you say that?" Misha asked.

"Just look at her, Misha," Manny said. "She's young and beautiful and rich in her own right. She knows a lot of people. Believe me, she won't be on the loose long."

"You almost make it sound like I'd be doing her a favor," Misha said.

Manny shrugged. "Well, better she's free to start a new life of her own—you, too, for that matter—than both of you live in a marriage that's not working. Right?"

"I—I guess so," Misha said thoughtfully. Then: "Yes, you're right, of course. I'm just so . . . so uncertain about things right now. Except Serena." He looked at Manny. "I know I really love her and want to be with her."

"If you're certain about that," Manny said, "then all the rest follows. You know what you have to do if you want to be with her."

Misha sighed again. "Yes. I know exactly what I have to do. I guess I'm just putting off the inevitable, aren't I?"

Manny nodded. "I'd say so, old boy." He took another sip of his brandy, relishing thoughts of Vera's face when she got the news. He couldn't wait to tell Sasha the news. "What does Serena have to say about all this?" he asked.

"She is impatient," Misha said, "but she understands."

"She's a spectacular lady," Manny said. "Beautiful and talented. Extremely creative. You two are a lot alike. You have a lot in common."

"We do, don't we?" Misha said, as if the thought had never occurred to him before. Then he smiled, somewhat ruefully. "Well, I have you to thank for introducing us."

"Guilty as charged," Manny replied. *And little did I know that eventually it would work out so perfectly,* he thought.

Misha sipped the last of his drink and set the glass down. "I'd better get going," he said.

"You sure you won't have another drink?" Manny asked.

"No, thanks," Misha answered. "I've got to finish packing for London." He got up and stretched, then turned to Manny. "Thanks for listening, Manny," he said, "and everything else. You've been a real friend."

Manny pushed himself to his feet. "Don't worry about it, Misha," he said. "I'm only too glad."

They started toward the entrance hall, then Misha suddenly stopped, looking in the direction of the fireplace. "Is that a Delvaux?" he asked with awe in his voice.

"Yes," Manny said. Then he quickly added: "I got it for nothing, old boy! A fire sale!"

"You're kidding," Misha said, walking over for a closer look at the painting. A large canvas painted in tones of putty, grays, blues, and browns, it depicted four female nudes standing in a bedroom. On the bed, was sprawled a fifth.

Misha silently studied it for a moment then turned to Manny. "I can't believe I didn't even notice it before," he said. "It's really beautiful."

"Hmm," Manny said. "Got it cheap from a friend of a friend of Sasha's in Los Angeles. You know. Desperate for money in a hurry. Sasha seems to know a lot of that type." He took off his glasses and began nervously cleaning them with a handkerchief.

"How sad," Misha said. He took a last look, then turned and headed toward the entrance hall again. "I'd better hurry home." At the door, he turned to Manny. "Thanks again, Manny," he said. "You've been a lot of help. I guess I'm just a little scared. Of my feelings and all."

"You have to remember you're an artist, Misha." Manny clapped him on the shoulder. "And you have to follow your heart."

"I guess you're right," Misha said with a bewildered look.

"I know I am," Manny replied, opening the door.

"Well, 'night." Misha turned and left.

Manny closed the door behind him and walked back into the living room. He picked up his balloon of brandy, took a large swallow, then sat down. *Poor lovesick Misha!* he thought. *Follow your heart, indeed! If I play my cards right,* he thought, *the Delvaux is only the beginning.*

Chapter Thirty-two

London's September sky was gray, but the rain, an almost daily event this time of year, had temporarily let up. Misha, umbrella in hand and Burberry thrown across his arm, got into the limousine awaiting him on Kensington Gore and instructed the driver to take him back to his hotel. He glanced back at the huge dark brick pile of the Royal Albert Hall with its enormous glass-and-iron dome. The rehearsal had gone without a hitch, but he was glad to be going back to the hotel. He was ready for a nap before tonight's performance.

As the driver slowly negotiated the big car through the heavy traffic from Knightsbridge to South Kensington, Misha reflected on his upcoming performances. The Royal Albert Hall would certainly never have been his first choice as a venue in London. It was huge, seating at least thirty-five hundred people, and for the annual Proms—a series of serious concerts by top classical musicians—the seats in the pit were taken out and over six thousand people were accommodated. Misha's popularity as a performer, however, had made filling up the vast space two nights in a row an easy matter. Both nights were sold out.

Misha preferred more intimate settings. Unlike most musicians, he wasn't intimidated by enormous spaces like the Royal Albert Hall and Avery Fisher Hall in New York's Lincoln Center, but they did pose problems. The majority of piano music had been composed for performing in intimate spaces. In this case Misha had solved this problem brilliantly by choosing an all-Liszt program. The Liszt pieces had all been composed to be performed in large, public halls and were thus perfectly suited to the Royal Albert. He would begin with the Sonata in B Minor, play a ballade, a consolation, a *funérailles*, and wind it up with the Mephisto Waltz no. 1. It was an utterly romantic repertoire, which suited his mood perfectly: he had privately dedicated tonight's performance to Serena.

Too bad she couldn't be here for the concert, he thought. At least he was certain that his sound would be as good as possible in the vast hall. At one time the Royal Albert had a double echo caused by the huge glass-and-iron dome. Sir Thomas Beecham had joked that if a musician wanted a second performance of his music, he had only to play it in the Royal Albert. In the 1960s the problem had been solved by putting huge saucer-shaped discs in the dome. While the sound was now beautiful, it certainly didn't equal the supreme acoustics of Carnegie Hall's wood and plaster. So today Misha had worked for hours doing more sound tests than usual, finally satisfying himself with the results.

The limousine pulled to a stop at 33 Roland Gardens, rousing Misha from his reverie. He looked out at Blakes, his home away from home in London. Set in a somber mansion block in South Kensington, Blakes was a small hotel with only sixty rooms, but it was very chic, an oasis of quiet favored by a well-heeled clientele. The rich and famous could come and go without fear of reporters and their flashbulbs invading their privacy.

The endlessly talented Anouska Hempel, an erstwhile actress turned designer, known more formally as Lady Weinberg, had created in Blakes a *folie de grandeur par excellence*. While its decoration might be considered eccentric by some, Misha found its theatrical elegance and opulent luxury to his taste.

The driver opened his door, and Misha slid out of the big car. He dismissed the driver for the time being and headed for his room. It had faux tortoiseshell walls hung with prints of Asian costumes and faux marble mirrors. The room was dominated by a huge four-poster bed complete with a canopy draped in dark red silk damask lined with black velvet. Its headboard was appliqued in gold, and the draping was held by tasseled ropes as thick as hawsers. The bed's posts were wrapped in red and black in the Venetian manner.

He couldn't wait to pull back its opulent silk damask spread and slide between the antique linen sheets. There he could clear his mind of all extraneous concerns but the music, and then nap before tonight's performance.

It was not to be, however.

In the lobby, perched on an Asian-inspired settee next to a lovebird's cage, sat Coral Randolph. She looked for all the world like a raptor, he thought, a peregrine falcon perhaps, poised to descend on its prey. Her jet black hair, magnolia skin, and glittering emerald eyes seemed somehow appropriate to this setting, as did her black cashmere suit with its Russian sable-lined cape. Coral Randolph was opulence personified.

As he approached her, passing the piazza-style market umbrella, she stood on very high Gucci heels. She held a black leather Hermés handbag and elbow-length black leather gloves in one hand. He couldn't help but notice the extraordinary cabochon emeralds at her ears and throat, as well as those set into a gold cuff at her wrist and the one huge perfect one set in a gold ring on one of her fingers. Her nails and mouth were painted a cognac.

"Why, Ms. Randolph," Misha intoned with as much charm as he could muster. "What a surprise seeing you here."

"Coral, please," she said, extending her free hand.

Misha took her hand in his and bowed over it in the Continental fashion, bringing it to his lips but not touching it. He straightened up and looked at her. "And it's Misha," he said. He could smell her perfume. Its aroma was powerful and expensive.

"Very well, Misha," Coral said. "I realize that this isn't the best time, but I must have a few words with you. Immediately."

She was the picture of politeness, Misha thought, but there was a command in her voice that dared one to defy her.

"I could spare a few minutes," he said. "You know I have a performance tonight, and I have to rest beforehand."

"Yes," Coral said, with a barely perceptible nod. "Perhaps in your room, then. Right away."

"Not in the restaurant?" Misha asked.

"No," Coral said firmly, with a slight shake of her head. "Privacy is essential."

"Very well," Misha said. "It's this way."

Once in the dark grandeur of his room, he turned to Coral. "Please have a seat," he said. "Make yourself comfortable."

"Thank you," Coral said, and seated herself on an Asian chair of inlaid black lacquer.

"I'm going to call down for a drink," Misha said. "What would you like?"

"Champagne with a bit of Campari in it," Coral said without hesitation.

Misha called down their order, then turned to Coral. "Would you like to hang up your cape?" he asked.

"No, thank you," Coral said. "I freeze in London at this time of year."

Misha hung his Burberry in the closet, then sat down on a chair. He started to take off his Gucci loafers, then stopped. "Do you mind?" he asked, looking over at Coral. "I've been at it for hours."

"No," Coral said, "of course not."

Misha finished, then wiggled his toes and got to his feet. He sat on the bed, then leaned back against the sea of pillows, and spread out his long legs. "Are you staying here?" he asked.

"No," Coral replied, "I'm at the Ritz."

"How did you know I was here?" he asked.

Coral looked at him. "Serena, of course," she said.

"I guess I know what you've come to discuss with me," he said.

There was a tap at the door, and Misha got off the bed and answered it. A waiter brought their drinks in on a silver tray and set it down on a table, then turned and left.

Misha handed Coral her champagne and Campari.

"Thank you," she said.

He took his scotch and water back to the bed with him, where he spread out against the pillows again. He raised his glass. "Cheers," he said.

Coral raised hers. "Cheers," she repeated with a slight smile, and took a sip of her drink. Then she set the crystal flute down and turned to Misha.

"I might as well get to the point," she said.

"Yes," Misha said, smiling. "Might as well."

Coral cleared her throat. "Serena doesn't know I've come to see you, and I'd rather she didn't."

"I can keep a secret," Misha said.

"I know about your involvement with Serena, of course," Coral said, "and I don't like it, to be perfectly honest. She thinks the two of you are in love."

"We are," Misha said.

"I don't know whether I believe that or not," Coral said. "But it's beside the point really. What I have to say is this. Serena is a very fragile young woman. She's been terribly abused in the past and was deeply hurt the last time the two of you were involved."

"Yes, but—"

"Please, Misha," Coral said, "let me finish what I have to say so that I can leave and you can have your nap."

"Okay." Misha shrugged.

"The situation is infinitely more complicated this time because you have a wife and child," Coral continued. "But all the complications aside, Serena is determined that the two of you will be together. That you will eventually marry." She looked at Misha to see what his reaction, if any, would be to that statement.

She was not disappointed.

"I want more than anything in the world to marry her," Misha said ardently, sitting up in the bed. "I really love Serena, Coral. With all my heart."

"I see," Coral said. "Well, this affair has been going on now for nearly a year. Since Vienna. And Serena is becoming increasing anxious and impatient. So much so that I'm afraid it will affect her work."

She took a sip of her drink before continuing. "I find it regrettable that your wife and child may be harmed by whatever happens, but my primary interest here is Serena, of course. She's been practically like a daughter to me, and there is no one else to watch out for her interests."

She looked over at Misha, her emerald eyes sparkling. "My point is, I want you to either marry Serena," she said evenly and calmly, "or I want you to break it off with her immediately."

Misha was taken aback. He had been fully prepared for Coral to tell him to stay away from Serena, but not to suggest marriage as an alternative.

"So you're saying it's all or nothing, in other words," Misha said.

"Exactly," Coral said, nodding.

"Well, it's quite obvious that I can't marry her yet," Misha said, "and I'm certainly not going to stop seeing her until I can."

"Then I suggest that if you want to continue seeing her," Coral said, "you should start plans to marry her right away."

"But that means—"

"Misha," Coral interjected, "we both know precisely what it means. You're going to have to get a divorce from Vera." She used a cognac-colored nail to brush an imaginary wisp of hair from her eyes, then turned the full power of her gaze on him, looking directly into his eyes. "If you don't start divorce proceedings immediately," she said, "then I'll go to Vera myself."

"You'll what!" Misha said, his deep baritone resonating powerfully in the room.

"You heard me," Coral said succinctly. "You either leave Serena now— and I mean now, tonight—or you start divorce proceedings. If you don't do one or the other, then I'll personally visit Vera and tell her everything. And I mean *everything*."

"You're a monster," Misha said, his voice low and menacing.

"Perhaps," Coral conceded calmly. "But no more so than a man who virtually abandons his devoted wife and son to satisfy his basest desires with another woman. A highly inappropriate woman, I might add."

"What do you mean?" Misha spat angrily.

"Don't be a fool," Coral said harshly. "Serena may be beautiful and talented, but she's no match for you. Do you think she understands your music or even gives it so much as a thought? No. Of course not. Nor will she be at your concert tonight."

"No," Misha said defensively. "She's got her own work to do."

"Yes," Coral said sweetly. "She'll be nightclubbing with her assistants,

Jason and Bennett. Probably a brief dinner at Annabel's to mix with the upper crust, from there to gay and lesbian dance clubs, then on to those dreary sex clubs in the far-off hinterlands of the East End."

Misha digested this news in silence for a moment. "Well, she has to live her own life," he finally said. "I don't expect her to be at my beck and call. To be at my concerts all the time."

"That's wise of you," Coral said, "because Serena could give a fuck about your concerts."

Misha nearly leapt off the bed, so enraged was he by Coral's remarks. "Why don't you leave now?" he said angrily. "I've got your message."

Coral rose to her feet with dignity. "Good. I was hoping you would. Just remember," she said, "either you talk to Vera or I will."

That said, she went to the door. She opened it, then turned back to Misha: "I'll give you until Thanksgiving to leave Vera. I don't want to see Serena spending it alone."

She closed the door and was gone, her perfume, like a malodorous cloud of evil, lingering in her wake.

Misha wanted to run after her and throttle her skinny neck between his hands, but he slumped back down onto the bed, his head in his hands. *What am I going to do?* he agonized. He knew that there was a lot of truth in what Coral had to say, but he needed time. He wanted to tell Vera in his own good time. In his own way. Two months. The bitch had given him about two months.

He picked up the telephone and dialed Manny's number at Claridges, but there was no answer. He didn't bother leaving a message.

God, help me, he thought. *What am I going to do?*

Chapter Thirty-three

Serena, wearing only a white terry cloth bathrobe, sat studying her reflection in the ancient, mottled mirror that rested atop the fancily skirted and swagged dressing table. Its Baroque sterling silver frame was heavily carved, with the family's coat of arms emblazoned at the top like an ornate crown. But for all its grandeur, she mused, it was one of the lousiest excuses for a makeup mirror she'd ever tried to use. She could hardly make out her reflection for all the spots.

Thank God the makeup crew has trunkloads of its own equipment, she thought. *If they'd relied on the facilities in this old dump, they'd be up a creek.*

She sighed with frustration. *It's like everything else around this place,* she told herself. Big and old and grand and virtually useless. When she'd gotten the assignment—shooting spring couture clothes on young English aristocrats—she'd been excited. What could be more appropriate than photographing some of the world's most expensive clothes on rich, titled, young people as if they were having a house party at Mummy's and Daddy's place in the country? In this case, one of the largest homes in all of England, where the whole crew—the young men and women serving as models, herself, her assistants, the stylists, hairdressers, and makeup staff—would all be staying as guests for the duration of the shoot. Anywhere from three to five days. It would be a voyeuristic look at what a house party of the *jeunesse dorée* was like.

Sounds great, she'd said. Only it hadn't worked out exactly like that.

There'd been no end of problems. Some of them had been easily solved, if time-consuming. Like the electrical problems. She'd decided the place had been wired when they started building it, sometime in the 1300s. Then there'd been the weather. Rain, rain, and more rain. Shooting outdoors had been virtually impossible. Also easily solved—shoot indoors only—but annoying nevertheless, as she'd planned to use the formal gardens with their ancient statuary and pools to advantage.

Then there'd been the problems with the so-called models. Professionals they weren't. Spoiled, overly confident, often arrogant, horny young aristocrats they most decidedly were. With more interest in playing hide the salami, drinking, and poking powder up their noses than posing for hours on end in change after change of clothing. The poor dears seemed to have had no idea it would actually involve a bit of work.

Then, there'd been the squabbles over the clothes they were told to wear. India thought that the Christian Lacroix gown Lucretia was wearing would look ever so much more suitable on her than the tacky Versace she'd been assigned in one scene. Rupert sniffed that one of his outfits looked like something for a "poofter," so give it to Desmond, if you please. Desmond, in turn, proceeded to put out Rupert's lights, grabbing one of the countless precious *objets* lying at hand. In this case a priceless piece of Chinese Export porcelain. Malvise had even accused Septimus of pocketing her "everyday" pearls, a gift from her grandmummy, the duchess of So and So.

To top it off, Serena found the stately home too big, too cold, too damp, too tattered, and a bit moldy. With a staff that could be described in the same terms. Plus, said staff watched them constantly to make certain that none of the house's much faded glory was further helped along the road to disintegration by their being there. Besides which, the food was absolutely unendurable. Serena had never before seen veggies cooked beyond the point of recognition or been served food that had long gone from hot to cold. But then, she supposed, it was such a long way from the kitchen to the dining room that there was little choice.

She couldn't believe that people paid through the nose for the privilege of staying in this old pile, perhaps on the off-chance that they would get to have a drink and rub noses with the present lord and lady—who were, thank God, traveling on the Continent at present.

What the hell would Misha think? she asked herself. She'd thought it would be so romantic, so idyllic.

Ah, well, she told herself, *the rain has let up, the shoot will soon be over, and Misha is on his way. Somehow or other they would grin and bear it.*

With a finger she deftly dabbed a bit more of the purplish currant blusher to her cheekbones, then began carefully spreading it out with her fingertips, thinning it toward the edges just so, not too much. She sat back, then leaned forward, her eyes concentrating on her reflection once again.

That'll do it, she thought. Now, just a bit more of that new port-colored lipstick. She found the golden tube among a pile of cosmetics on the dresser, and carefully brushed it across her generous lips, then blotted, and studied them in the mirror.

"Purr . . . fect," she told her reflection.

"So you're so desperate you're talking to yourself now?" said a voice from behind her.

Serena jerked around. "Jason!" she cried. "You're an angel from heaven. Just in time to help me pick out something to wear tonight."

"So Magic Fingers is descending upon us, I take it," Jason said. He flipped his nearly waist-length dark brown hair with its bold blond skunk stripes out of his eyes.

"Yes," Serena said. "He's supposed to be here in time for dinner."

"I got the *Times* and the *Daily Telegraph*," Jason said. "They both have fabu reviews of his concerts. You'd think he was the second coming." He flapped the newspapers against the black leather jeans he seemed to live in.

"Oh, Jason, you're a sweetheart," Serena said. "I'd forgotten all about the papers. You'll have to tell me what they say." She giggled. "Misha'll think I'm really keeping up."

"Should I read them to you?" Jason asked.

"Skim," Serena said. "The highlights. You know." She fumbled through the multitude of bottles on the dressing table until she found the one that contained her magic potion—a perfume made especially for her with lots of vetiver, various citrus notes, a hint of floral. It was an exotic scent that she knew Misha was crazy about. She began dabbing it generously around her ears, down her throat, at her wrists, between her breasts and thighs.

Jason sat down on the worn Turkish carpet, crossing his big logger boots in the lotus position, and riffled through the *Times* until he found the review there. He cleared his throat.

" 'The Liszt Sonata in B Minor,' " he began, " 'has never been played more diabolically or erotically than in Mikhail Levin's brilliant interpretation of it the last two evenings in the Royal Albert Hall.' "

"Diabolical! Erotic!" Serena cried with delight. She slapped a hand against the dresser and laughed. "Oh, Misha will love that, won't he?"

"I guess so," Jason said. He grinned. "If he plays like he looks, then it's got to be hot."

"Read, you naughty boy," Serena said as she began brushing her hair.

Jason continued. " 'Levin has exposed everything imaginable in this virtual autobiography of Liszt—' "

"What the hell does that mean?" Serena asked.

"I don't have a clue," Jason said, laughing. He squinted in the dim light as he continued skimming the article. "Whoa! Get this shit! 'Levin is the embodiment of the Romantic, a Byronic superman.' "

Serena squealed. "I don't believe it! My little Misha!"

"I bet he's not so little," Jason quipped.

"Skim!" Serena said.

Jason went on. " 'He cuts a proud, irresistible figure and represents the epitome in behavior, looks, and achievement of the true Romantic hero.' "

Jason stopped and looked up at Serena. "This is too much." Jason laughed. "I think *I'm* falling in love with him." He pushed the sleeves of his sweater up above his elbows, and the tattoos that covered his arms undulated as he moved the newspaper about.

"He's off-limits," Serena teased, brushing her hair in long, even strokes. "Keep skimming."

" 'The Faustian theme—' " Jason began.

"Oh, God, Jason," Serena cried. "Spare me. That's enough. That's already more than I want to know. I don't need to know any of the boring details."

"What about the *Daily Telegraph*?" Jason asked.

"Forget it," Serena said. "Where's Bennett, by the way?" she asked.

"The last I saw him," Jason replied, "he was sneaking out to the stables with one of the models."

"You're kidding?" Serena said. "Going for a ride, maybe?"

"Ride one of the stable boys is more like it," Jason said.

"Naughty, naughty," Serena said. "I thought all these boys and girls would be pretty straight arrows. Coming from such stuffy, rich old families and all."

"No way," Jason said. "The boys have all gone to those fancy schools where they diddle each other till they're in college. A couple of them hit on me. I don't know about the girls, but nearly all of them—boys and girls—do a lot of drugs."

Serena got up from the dressing table and walked over to the huge armoire where she had hung most of her clothes. She swung its doors open wide. "Look," she said. "Go through there and see what you think."

Jason began pushing hangers, glancing through the large selection of beautiful dresses and gowns. Suddenly he stopped. "This is fabu!" he said excitedly. "This is it!"

He jerked the gown out of the armoire and held it up in front of Serena with a flourish.

"Oh, one of the Galliano's from Dior," Serena said. "Do you think so, Jason?"

"Definitely," he said with a nod. "It's just the thing. Magic Fingers will love it."

Serena looked at the dress. She took it from Jason and held it up against her body, eyeing herself in the big cheval mirror in the corner. What a fabulous concoction, she thought. It had a silk brocade jacket that was made almost like a doublet, cinched in very tight at the waist and flared out around the hips. It was a creamy white with pinkish flowers and gold-green foliage. A hood attached to the jacket was lined with nutria dyed a royal blue and decorated with silk flowers in various shades of blue. Worn under the jacket was a ribbed rayon turtleneck that glimmered gold. The skirt was a gold lamé bias mermaid cut that was embossed with flowers.

"If you get cold at dinner," Jason said, "you can wear the hood."

Serena laughed. "Not a bad idea," she said. Then she looked at him. "You're sure that Misha would like it?"

"You out of your mind, girl?" Jason said. "Of course he will."

"That's settled, then," Serena said. "Thank God."

"Thank God what?" a mellifluous baritone asked from behind the two of them.

Serena turned around and saw Misha standing there, suitcase and garment bag in hand, watching them with a smile of amusement.

"You're here already," she squealed. She dropped the dress to the floor and rushed into his arms.

"Yes," he said, setting down his suitcase and laying his garment bag across it. He eagerly embraced her, reveling in the feel of her body against his. He kissed her with abandon, ignoring Jason for the moment, then drew back, looking into her eyes.

"I'm so glad to see you," he said, gently squeezing her shoulders.

"You can't be happier than I am," Serena breathed excitedly.

Misha looked over her shoulder and saw Jason, rescued dress in hand, watching them. The young man's face was flushed with embarrassment, witnessing their intimacy. He quickly averted his eyes and hung the dress on the armoire's open door.

"Hi, Jason," Misha said. He gave Serena a peck on the lips, then went over and shook hands with Jason. "How's the shoot been going?" he asked.

"I think I'd better let the boss lady fill you in," Jason said.

"Ah-ha," Misha said, taking Serena's hand in his as she joined them. "That bad?"

"Not really," Jason said. "Anyway, I'll leave you two alone. I've got to start setting up for tonight." He started toward the bedroom door.

"See you later," Serena said. "And Jason?"

He turned at the door and looked at her. "Thanks a lot. For everything."

"No problem," he said, grinning. He turned back around and left, quietly closing the bedroom door behind him.

"He's a nice kid," Misha said.

"Yeah," Serena said, "he is." She put an arm around his waist and snuggled close to him.

With a finger Misha tilted her chin up and looked into her eyes. His expression was solemn. "We've got to talk," he said.

Serena frowned. "You look so . . . so grim," she said. "What's wrong?"

"Nothing's wrong," he said, reassuringly. "There's just some things we need to discuss. Let's get comfy, okay?"

"Sure," Serena said. She sat down on the edge of the huge canopied bed, then scooted back against the pillows, watching Misha take off his jacket and shoes. He joined her, taking one of her hands in his.

"You're making me nervous, Misha," she said anxiously. "What's this all about?"

He looked at her. "I've asked you before, but I want to know for certain now." He took her other hand now, covering both of hers with his. "Do you really want to be with me all the time, Serena?" he asked. "Do you really want to get married?"

Serena's breath caught in her throat, and for a moment she couldn't respond. Then she slowly began to nod. "Y-yes, Misha," she stuttered. "I—I really do."

"One last time," he said. "You're absolutely certain?"

She nodded again. "Yes," she said with more conviction. "Yes, Misha. Yes, *yes!*"

He pulled her to him then and kissed her passionately, overjoyed with her words. "Oh, Serena, you can't imagine what this means to me," he said breathlessly. "It makes me the happiest man in the world to know that you love me."

"And I do, Misha," she said. "I do love you, and I want to marry you. This is not a game. You're the only man who's ever made me feel like a woman. You're the only man . . . well, the only man whose children I've ever wanted to have."

Tears sprang into Misha's eyes, and he hugged her again. He could hardly believe his ears. *To think that this sublime creature loves me! And to think that she wants to have my children!*

He began to smother her with kisses, pulling her bathrobe from her exquisite body in a frenzy of desire. Within moments they both lay naked on the bed, frantically kissing, licking, stroking, probing as he mounted her, their desire for each other so profound and all-consuming that they reached that ultimate wave of ecstasy almost instantly, their cries of pleasure mingling with the juices of their love.

Later, cuddled next to each other, Misha didn't think that he had ever felt so fulfilled, so wanted or needed, or as . . . *powerful*. It was a power derived from the love that she felt for him, a power that meant he had conquered this exotic, independent, sublimely beautiful woman.

He turned to Serena. "Next week, when I go back to New York," he whispered, "I'm going to ask Vera to start divorce proceedings."

Serena stared at him. "You're sure about that?" she asked.

"Yes," he said, nodding. "Next week. I don't know how long it will take, and I don't know what kind of a fight she'll put up, if any. But I'm definitely going to tell her next week."

Serena kissed him tenderly. "You won't lose your nerve?" she asked.

"No," Misha said, "not now. Now that I'm sure of the way you feel, and the way I feel."

"If you get cold feet," Serena said, "just think of me. Waiting for you." She ran a fingertip around his face delicately, lovingly.

"I will," he said, smiling.

"I don't want to move from this spot," Serena said. "From you. But we'd better start getting dressed for dinner."

She sat up in bed and leaned over, reaching for her bathrobe on the floor. Then she slid out from under the covers, got out of bed, and shrugged into the robe.

"Wish we could skip dinner," Misha said, still lying back against the pillows.

"No can do," Serena said. "And we'd better hurry. Really."

"Okay," Misha said, getting out of bed. "Black tie, right?"

"Yes," Serena said.

Misha picked up his suitcase and put it on the bench at the foot of the bed, then laid the garment bag across the bed. He caught a glimpse of the newspapers on the Turkish carpet where Jason had left them.

"Were you two looking at the reviews by any chance?" he asked Serena.

"Oh, yes," Serena said, slipping out of her bathrobe and taking the gown off its heavily padded hanger. "They were fantastic, Misha. Jason and I got a big kick out of one of the critics saying your playing was diabolical and erotic. And all that stuff about you being a Romantic hero. Wow!" She giggled. "I didn't know I was going with Byron!"

Misha looked at her curiously. She had never shown quite this much interest in his concerts before. In fact, she seemed to have very little curiosity about his professional life at all. Perhaps that wretched vampire, Coral Randolph, had been wrong. Maybe Serena really was becoming interested in his career.

He began slowly dressing, watching Serena as she got into her bra and panty hose. Then he remembered something else the vampire had said.

"Did you get into London at all?" he asked Serena in a casual manner.

"What?" she asked.

"Did you manage to get into London at all?" he repeated.

"Yeah," she said. "The night of your first concert." She turned and looked at him, then shrugged. "But there was no way I could get to it. I had the whole troupe with me. The models, assistants, and so on. It was a night out for us to get to know one another a little bit. You know, break the ice so the shoot would be easier. Theoretically, anyway."

"What did you do?" he asked, putting on his heavily starched white tux shirt.

"Went to Annabel's for din-din, then went dancing at some gay bars. The kind of discos where they let straights in. Then we ended up at these really sleazy sort of sex clubs way off the beaten track that some of the kids knew about. You know. The kind of place where you see every kind of freak on earth. It was a blast." She giggled. "We did have fun, but I was dead the next morning."

Just like the old vampire said, he thought. *But at least Serena told me about it. So where's the harm?*

Misha adjusted his cummerbund, then slipped on his dinner jacket. Finally he put on his black patent leather shoes with the grosgrain bows. He turned to Serena. "Will I do?" he asked.

"You look positively . . . Byronic!" she said, laughing. "Oh, you look so handsome." She gave him a kiss on the lips. "I'll just be a second."

She pulled on the glittering turtleneck, then slipped into the gold, embossed lamé skirt.

"Wow!" Misha said. "Beautiful!"

"Wait till you see the rest," she said. She got the creamy silk brocade jacket with its hood from the back of a chair and slipped into it, cinching it at the waist. "What do you think?" she asked.

Misha looked at her long and hard. She was a vision, he thought. She had never looked more beautiful or more sophisticated. There was absolutely nothing of the girl raised in the swamps or the runaway about this divine, ethereal creature.

"You're magnificent," he said simply. "Magnificent."

"Thank you, sir," she said. "Ready, then?" she asked.

"Ready."

"Shall we?" She held out an arm, he took it, and they swept out of the stately bedroom, and began the long, long walk through hallway after hallway to the dining room.

"That was a *hoot*," Misha exclaimed as he and Serena stumbled into the bedroom, both of them intoxicated by the evening, the wine, and each other.

"A hoot?" Serena echoed, swirling around in her Galliano gown, enjoying its silken movement against her body. "That's what you really thought?"

It was after two in the morning, and the dinner and after-dinner drinks and conversation were finally over.

"Ah, yes!" Misha enthused, untying his bow tie and dropping it into his suitcase with a flourish. "An extraordinary hoot at that. It was wonderful!" He laughed and took Serena into his arms.

"It reminded me of the dinners with some of the dotty old European aristocrats I have to go to a lot. These kids are just younger versions of the same people. Their children or grandchildren. But at the fancy dinners I go to, they don't usually pass around a vial of coke or whatever to snort, along with the food."

Serena laughed. "No, I bet they don't." She freed herself from the silk brocade hooded jacket and laid it on a chair, then began sliding off the gold lamé embossed skirt.

Then he became more serious. "You know what though, Serena?"

"What?" she said, sliding her panty hose down her long, trim legs.

"It was a beautiful evening. Extraordinarily beautiful," Misha said, his voice wistful. "The fabulous couture clothes, the candlelit chandeliers and candelabra, the flowers from the greenhouses, all the old table linens and family china and silver and crystal. It was magnificent, really."

"Yeah," Serena said. "Too bad the food sucked."

Misha looked at her with an irritable expression. "Well, the food was typically English," he said. "I expected nothing more or less. But what a room to serve it in! The family dining room is phenomenally beautiful. The carved moldings and doors and those gigantic carved marble fireplaces. All that precious gold silk damask on the walls, with paintings, one on top of the other!"

"Yeah, I guess so," Serena allowed, shrugging into her bathrobe. "But did you see how there're tears in the silk? Even in the curtains. This whole joint is coming apart at the seams."

"I think that's part of its charm," Misha said. "All the shabby grandeur. The wear and tear of the centuries has given everything a patina that only time can."

"They can keep it, if you ask me," Serena said.

"You love all your glass and steel and chrome better, don't you?" Misha said.

"You bet," Serena said. "If I had this old dump I'd get rid of it."

"Serena!" Misha said with surprise in his voice. "You're talking about one of the most historically important houses in all of the United Kingdom. You ate dinner surrounded by exquisite paintings of some of the greatest Englishmen and women of the past."

"Well, I'd get rid of them, too," she said emphatically.

"A lot of those paintings are very fine," Misha protested. "Some of them are Van Dycks."

"I don't care what they are. They're ugly, if you ask me," Serena said. "No wonder this country lost its empire. It's so wrapped up in the past."

Misha felt an angry impatience rising within him. He checked himself before he snapped at her, but he really didn't like her attitude one bit. A Van Dyck painting ugly? How could she say such a thing? Was this grand house nothing more to her than a "set" that had served as a chic backdrop in a fashion shoot?

He supposed so. He reminded himself that she'd wanted to wipe out her own past, so it made sense that she had no respect for the past in general. Could she not see that this evening had been a truly magical one, set amidst all this beauty and history? He suddenly felt saddened by the disdain she held for what had to him been romantic and inspirational in its beauty.

"I'll be back in a minute," Serena said, heading for the adjoining bathroom.

As Misha slipped into his bathrobe, the newspapers, now neatly folded and placed on a table, caught his eye. The maid had straightened up. He picked them up and made himself comfortable on the big canopied bed. First, he began thumbing through the *Times*, looking for the review of his performances at the Royal Albert Hall.

Suddenly a familiar name jumped off the page. He felt a flutter in his chest, and his hand trembled slightly. Like a ghastly flashback to a terrifying nightmare, the name riveted his attention.

Can it be? he wondered, all thoughts of the review forgotten. With dread he began to read.

SIMON CURZON HAMPTON RETROSPECTIVE

FREDERICA EBERLY GALLERY

Curator Peregrine Lavery-Blunt has assembled an impressive collection of the post-modern paintings by the late Simon Curzon Hampton. The paintings—and there are a large number of canvases—were executed primarily in the early 1990s, before the artist's untimely and bizarre death.

Hampton, a graduate of Eton and the Slade School of Fine Art, is represented in many private collections, including the Saatchi Collection in London. His estate is represented here by the Frederica Eberly Gallery exclusively.

The current retrospective was assembled with the assistance of the artist's family and various well-known collectors. His brother, Mitchell James Hampton, a sometime race car driver, provided five works, and his father, the well-known sports figure, Curzon Cavendar Hampton, of Hastings Lodge, Castledown, Surrey, supplied several others. His mother, Lady Isabel Etherington-Hawkes, has said that none of his works are in her possession because she finds them "too depressing." She resides in Buenos Aires and caused a scandal among the social set in 1972, when she deserted her husband and sons for the well-known South American polo player, Enrique Gomez-Rodriquez.

At the time of his mysterious death five years ago—he was found drowned near the Verrazano Narrows Bridge in New York City—Hampton was in New York City for a show of his paintings at the Schulman Lazare Gallery.

"Good God," Misha whispered as he finished reading the article. "What is it?" Serena asked, emerging from the bathroom. Misha looked up. She saw the troubled expression on his face. "This article," he said, stabbing the paper with a finger. "It's about somebody Vera used to know. Used to date, in fact. He . . . well, he was a troublemaker." Misha, for some reason, decided on the spur of the moment that he wouldn't tell Serena about Simon Hampton trying to kill him.

"You're kidding," Serena said. "Somebody Vera used to date?" She snuggled next to him in bed. "Here, let me see."

Misha absentmindedly handed her the newspaper. He became lost in thought, wondering if Vera knew about this. If she knew Simon was dead. An involuntary shiver ran through him. Simon's long-ago attack on him, coupled with finding out about his strange death after all these years, left him with an uneasy feeling.

"Wow!" Serena said. "Weird."

"Here," Misha said, snapping out of his reverie. He took the newspaper from her, folded it, and placed it on the bedside table. He looked at her and smiled. "Let's try to forget about that, okay?"

"Sure," she said.

"Why the solemn look all of a sudden," he asked. "Is it the article?"

"God, no!" she said. "I didn't know him! It's . . . it's nothing."

"Come on, Serena," Misha cajoled. "What's going on in that beautiful head of yours?"

"Oh, I was just thinking," she said. "In the bathroom. I'm . . . I'm really sick of these assignments."

"You mean like this one?" he asked. "Fashion shoots?"

"Exactly like this one," she said harshly. "I'm starting to really hate them."

"Was it just this shoot?" he asked.

"No, Misha," she replied. "A lot of the others, too. I've been thinking about this for a very long time. I'm sick and tired of taking pictures of celebrities, no matter who they are, and I'm sick of fashion shoots. It's getting to be old hat. The same old thing over and over. Nothing new. Besides, I want some respect for my work."

"Serena," he said, "everybody likes your work. Why else would you have such a huge contract?"

"I know that," she said. "But it's not those people I want to please anymore. It's a different crowd I'm after."

"You mean the critics?" Misha asked.

"I guess so," she said. "I want to start doing some serious photography. The kind of stuff that'll get me gallery shows and reviews."

"But there've been shows of your work," Misha pointed out.

"Yeah," she said, "but at places like the Fashion Institute of Technology. I'm talking about something completely different, Misha." She looked at him. "I want to do serious pictures that'll be bought by museums and collectors. Like that guy that Vera knew. His paintings. I want to go in that direction. You see what I mean?"

Misha looked at her and expelled a deep breath. "You're talking about switching from commercial to art photography," he said.

"Right," Serena said, looking at him with a smile.

"Are you certain about this?" he asked.

"Yes," Serena answered, "and I'm going to have a confab with Coral about it. I want to start taking some serious pictures."

"That's going to be quite a switch," he said. "And a huge challenge. You know, the critics will be gunning for you because you've been so successful commercially."

"I know all that," she said. "And I'll just have to take that chance."

"Do you have anything in mind?" Misha asked.

Serena shook her head. "Nothing definite yet," she said. "But I've been giving it a lot of thought."

"And what have you thought?" he asked, tenderly brushing a strand of hair from her face with his fingertips.

"Oh, just that maybe next month when I'm in the Far East on *another* fashion shoot"—she turned to him with a grimace on her face—"I might make some side trips. Go to Vietnam, Cambodia. Like that. See what I can get."

"You're absolutely serious?" he asked.

"Yes," she nodded. "You know. Things like, what's Hanoi like now? The killing fields? Pol Pot's successors? There's a lot of stuff there that's open now, stuff that I know I could get to. Pol Pot's prisons and all. It might be really interesting. And serious. It might get me some respect as a photographer."

"This sort of thing might keep you on the road a lot more than what you do now," Misha pointed out. "And it might be a bit depressing to boot."

She nodded. "I know. I've thought about that, too," she said. "I know I can handle the . . . unpleasantness of some of it. And I figure that if you really love me, you'll put up with it. I might be gone a lot for long periods of time." She studied his face.

Misha sighed. He didn't like hearing this. He had envisioned her eventually scaling back some of her commercial work so that they could have more of a home life, a family life—and children.

"I hadn't expected this," he confessed in as neutral a tone as he could muster.

"No," Serena said. "But it's the direction I'm definitely going in, so I had to tell you."

"But what about being with me?" Misha said with mild exasperation. "And what about those children you said you wanted?"

"Oh, Misha, please." She scowled and slapped the bed with a hand. "There's plenty of time for all that kind of stuff."

He stared straight ahead. *This is almost like déjà vu,* he thought. *Like all those years ago when she refused to budge an inch, career-wise, so that we could have more time together. But then neither did I.*

"Misha," she cajoled, "this is very important to me. Please, don't be angry."

He turned to her. She looked like a lost child, vulnerable and afraid. He pulled her to him and stroked her hair. "I'm not angry, Serena," he said.

"Thank God," she said, snuggling closer. She ran a hand down his chest, then unknotted his bathrobe and ran her hand down between his thighs.

Misha immediately responded, leaning down to kiss her. "How could I be angry with you?" he whispered, already forgetting his worries and irritations, already swept up in an overpowering hunger for her.

Chapter Thirty-four

⤜✺⤛

Candles. Dozens of beeswax candles.

Chandeliers in the living and dining rooms and candelabra placed strategically about the apartment glimmered iridescently, their Old World luminescence suffusing the apartment with an air of mystery and romance.

On the deserted dining table, the shifting light of tapers, now burning low, glinted off the imperial silver and china. It danced against antique Russian crystal, casting prismatic shards of color about the room.

Flowers, hundreds of them, all old-fashioned full-blown English roses— palest pink Abraham Darby, fading red Othello, creamy ivory Heritage, and pale yellow Thomas Graham—were stuffed blossom to blossom in silver mint julep cups that ran the length of the dining table. Fragrant nosegays of them were placed throughout the rooms, their combined aromas imbuing the air with a sweet intoxication.

Vera had gone all out to make the evening a truly memorable one for everyone. Sonia and Dmitri had officially retired from their full-time positions at Julliard, and Vera wanted to mark the occasion with a very special dinner.

Misha had offered to take them all out for a lavishly expensive dinner—Le Bernardin, La Chanterelle, Petroussian, anywhere—but Vera had insisted that they have a family dinner at home. Sonia and Dmitri were thrilled with her thoughtfulness, but had told Vera to go to no trouble, knowing that she had so many responsibilities. Vera, however, was determined that no one—not even her richest and most important international clients at the auction house—would ever have a more beautiful dinner party than that which she would give for her beloved in-laws.

Sonia was now seventy years old and Dmitri seventy-two, and although they would continue to teach a handful of talented students at home, their public professional careers were at an end. It was a big transition for them, Vera realized, and while they were both in good health, she could also see that they were beginning to slow down considerably.

There was a bit less spring in their steps, a bit less of that indefatigable energy that had propelled them so very far in life.

From the dining room Vera peered unseen into the vast living room's flickering light and couldn't help but smile with pleasure. She loved watching Misha interact with his parents, especially when he was in an expansive mood. Tonight he had been at his most ebullient—the old Misha, she thought wistfully—happily jabbering and gesticulating, animated and engaging and—loving.

The interplay between the three of them was both heartwarming and inspiring. She had always hoped that the relationship between herself and Misha and Nicky could be like that. It was at times like these— simple, small moments, most people would call them—that she realized the importance of family, its awesome capacity for warmth and goodness and love.

Oh, how I wish it could always be this way, she thought. *That tonight would never end.*

But she knew that her wishes were futile. Tonight was exceptional in more ways than one. Misha's gregarious mood would inevitably dissipate into withdrawal and quietude, casting a cloud of gloom over the house, and she and Nicky would be excluded from his world, as if they were strangers. Sonia and Dmitri would suffer the same alienation, if at a distance, because Misha would undoubtedly neglect seeing them for weeks at a time when he withdrew into his other, exclusionary world. And in this other world, she was certain, Misha was not lonely, like her. No. It was a world he shared with—

"Vera, tonight was really lovely," a voice from behind her said.

Vera turned around, her reverie interrupted by the familiar voice. Manny stood watching her, a crooked smile on his face. *Almost a smirk*, she thought. *Or am I imagining it?* He was slightly flushed from the copious amounts of wine he had drunk.

"Thank you, Manny," she said. "I'm glad you enjoyed it, and I'm glad you and Sasha came. He's worked for you such a long time, and I feel like we got to know him a little better tonight."

"He loved it," Manny said. "The food was exceptional. I can't believe you did all this yourself and didn't have it catered."

Vera smiled. "I try," she said. She looked at him. "Can I get you something?"

"No, no," Manny said quickly. "I was just . . . just upstairs using the bathroom. Sasha was in the powder room down here. We're going to be going in a bit."

"So soon?" Vera said.

"Yes," Manny said. "Early morning, you see."

"Don't leave without a good night kiss," Vera said. "I'm just seeing to a couple of things here and will be back in the living room in a minute."

"Right you are," Manny replied. He turned to leave, then stopped. "Vera?" he said.

"Yes?" she replied, looking at him questioningly. "What is it?"

"I know I shouldn't be asking this of you," he said haltingly, "but . . . but I wondered if you might try to convince Misha that doing the tour of Russia would be a good idea."

"He's already said no to that," she said. "Yet again. I know Sasha talked to him about it earlier this evening."

"Oh, I know," he said. "But I mean have him think about the future. Because the opportunity is always there. And it is golden, you know."

Vera looked at him with curiosity. *Why is he suddenly trying to conspire with me?* she wondered. "I know it's a golden opportunity, Manny," she said. "And I think it's high time Misha let go of all those resentments he's harbored for so long against Russia. But he still feels very strongly about it."

"I know, Vera, but—" he began.

"Manny," she interjected, "I'll try to talk to him about it again. I have before, but I don't know how much good I can do."

"Well, thanks, Vera," he said.

"You're welcome," she replied.

Manny turned and crossed the dining room and disappeared through the arches into the flickering light of the double-height living room.

Vera picked up a silver candle snuffer and began putting out the low-burning tapers on the dining table. *How odd,* she thought, *that as Misha has grown apart from us—from Sonia and Dmitri and Nicky and me—he has grown closer and closer to Manny. They seem to have become practically inseparable. Misha always seems to be over at Manny and Sasha's. Or going somewhere with them.*

She hadn't particularly wanted Manny and Sasha here tonight, but Misha had insisted. Then she herself had decided it was a good idea to have them, remembering that old adage: *Keep your enemy close.*

She was certain that she knew what this new closeness was all about. It was simple, really. Misha had found allies in Manny and Sasha. Allies in the battle he was having to extricate himself from his wife and son. Because Manny detests me, and always has. She could imagine the sorts of conversations they must have. Misha pouring his heart out in confession. Manny listening attentively, telling Misha that it was all right, that it wasn't really *his* fault. He must do whatever he felt because he was an artist.

Artist! What shit! she thought. *It doesn't matter if you're a coal miner or the greatest painter alive. Infidelity is infidelity. Neglecting your child is neglecting your child.*

She snuffed out the last of the guttering candles with an especially emphatic tap, splattering tallow with satisfaction, then replaced the silver snuffer on the sideboard. She stood back and looked at her reflection in the ornate Venetian mirror above it. She was wearing a long, body-hugging, corseted dress by Dolce & Gabbana, with sliplike shoulder straps. It had been delicately hand-painted with flowers in yellows, reds, whites, and purples, their wispy greenery trailing the length of the gown. It was truly beautiful, she thought.

But was it a good choice? she wondered, smoothing it down at her hips. Then suddenly she decided she didn't want to play that game. She refused to think that her appearance could be the cause of her husband's disaffection. She wasn't going to start agonizing over every choice of dress and makeup and hairstyle, hoping that her decisions pleased him.

Squaring her shoulders, she turned and walked elegantly back into the candlelit living room. She was surprised to see that everyone was getting ready to leave.

"There you are!" Sonia said. "I thought maybe Nicky had waked up. Is he all right?"

"Oh, yes. He's sleeping soundly," Vera said. "Are you already leaving?"

"It's getting late," Dmitri said, "and Manny and Sasha have offered us a lift home. So we're taking advantage of it."

"It's been really lovely, Vera," Sasha gushed, which was totally unlike him. His pale blond hair shone in the candlelight, and his ever watchful gray eyes seemed sincere.

"You must both come again," Vera said, accepting a kiss on the cheek from Manny.

"The apartment looks so beautiful, it's hard to leave," Sonia said. "Darling, we'll never forget tonight. The food, the flowers, everything! It was perfect, and we appreciate it so much."

"Thanks, Sonia," Vera said. "It was for very special people."

They exchanged kisses, then Dmitri hugged and kissed his daughter-in-law. "We love you like our own," he said.

"And I love you," Vera said.

"You are the luckiest man alive," Sonia said pointedly, looking at Misha. "The luckiest man alive!" She kissed his cheek.

"Y-yes," Misha said haltingly. "I suppose I am." He began walking them toward the entrance hall.

Sonia, trailing behind, took Vera's hand. "Patience, darling," she whispered into her ear. "Patience."

Vera simply nodded.

"And call me if you need anything," Sonia added. "Anything at all."

"I will," Vera promised. "But I think it'll be okay."

The candles had all been extinguished, the music turned off, and Anna, the maid, had finished cleaning up after the party. The apartment was quiet. Misha, undressing in the bedroom, reflected on the evening. It had all been so convivial, he thought, so warm, and stimulating, and though he hadn't looked forward to the dinner party, his participation hadn't been anything other than genuine. He hadn't had to force himself to participate in the lively conversation, to indulge in Vera's superb cooking and the excellent wines. But deep down inside he'd felt a gnawing emptiness, a need that the company of his attentive wife, loving parents, and doting friends couldn't provide. It wasn't the first time he'd felt this way—being surrounded by such loving, caring people, yet feeling so empty, so alone and sad—but for some reason in the aftermath of tonight's celebration he felt particularly heavy of heart.

Expelling a loud sigh, he neatly hung his trousers in the closet. Perhaps, he thought, it was knowing that evenings like this one were soon to end altogether. At least in this beautiful setting, with this cast of characters assembled together. He would see everyone that had been here, of course, but it would never be the same.

He'd planned to have a talk with Vera this evening—and still planned to—but the dinner party made his task much more difficult. Celebrating with the only family he'd ever known had only served to emphasize the enormity of what he was about to do.

And it is enormous, he thought. For he realized that while he and Serena certainly had a close relationship, an intimacy that was fresh and lusty and joyful, it was not always comfortable or easy. Sometimes, in fact, Serena seemed like an enigma to him. *How well do I really know her?* he asked himself.

He slipped into his bathrobe and padded into his bathroom. He began brushing his teeth, looking in the mirror over the sink but seeing, instead of his own reflection there, the ravishing creature he so desperately wanted to be with. *Oh, God*, he thought, *she is so beautiful and so desirable, yet . . . yet does what I'm about to do make sense? Is it what I really want?*

He suddenly thought of Nicky and his little boy's excitement tonight, getting to eat with the grown-ups and stay up late with his grandparents. He could see his chubby, pink cheeks and his raven black hair, could see the glee in his dark eyes and hear his contagious laughter.

Serena had said that she eventually wanted a family and some semblance of a home life, but did she really mean it? For that matter, did she even know her own heart? Certainly, she knew what she wanted career-wise, and that seemed to take precedence over everything else. *It always has, hasn't it?* he told himself. *Would that ever really change?*

Finished in the bathroom, he went back to the bedroom, where he spread out, still thoughtful, on the bed. He reached over for the small balloon of Armagnac on his bedside table and took a sip. He'd promised himself that he would confront Vera, but now the mere thought filled him with a mixture of dread and sorrow. The Armagnac, normally so soothing, tasted fiery and vile on his palate tonight.

What rotten timing, he thought. Just before the holidays. Could he have possibly timed it worse? Vera and Nicky would have both his parents and hers, so they wouldn't have to be alone. And of course, he would be with Serena or *would* he? Come to think of it, Serena hadn't even mentioned the holidays. She'd only seemed interested in meeting him somewhere in the Far East while he was performing there. It would be convenient for them both, since she was dead set on going to Cambodia to take photographs. His trip would fall between Thanksgiving and Christmas, so maybe they could work something out. She would surely make it a point to be back for Christmas, wouldn't she?

Vera came into the bedroom then, and he looked up at her. She had looked beautiful tonight in her new dress, and she looked no less so in her cream silk robe with its lace trim. Her pale blond hair was down, just sweeping her shoulders, and her Dresden blue eyes looked serene and content.

"Where were you?" he asked.

"Just checking on Nicky," she said, smiling. "I thought I heard him coughing, but I guess I was imagining it."

"You don't want to spoil him," Misha said, thinking that she spent an awfully lot of time seeing to Nicky.

"I hardly think that checking on him at my bedtime is going to spoil him, Misha," Vera said coolly. "Sometimes I enjoy just watching him sleep."

Misha suddenly felt annoyed with her, and at the same time knew that it was an irrational feeling. He resented her being the perfect mother and wife. It made his own self-absorption seem that much more odious to him.

She took off her robe, laying it on a chair, and slid out of her slippers. Then turning, she looked at him. "Aren't you going to bed?" she asked.

"In a while," he said, taking another sip of his brandy.

Vera pulled back the covers and got into bed beside him. "I think tonight went very well, don't you?" she asked, making conversation.

"Yes," Misha said matter-of-factly. "It was very nice."

"I hope next week's dinner party goes as well," Vera said.

He looked at her. "Next week's?"

"Yes," Vera replied, looking at him in alarm. "Don't tell me you've forgotten, Misha."

"Forgotten what?" he asked with puzzlement.

"You promised me you'd be here for the Caprioli-Fontini dinner. You know how important it is," she said, trying to keep the frustration out of her voice.

He grunted noncommittally.

"I'm trying to get their art collection for the auction house to sell," she went on. "I'll get a huge fee if I pull it off."

"You always manage, Vera," he said nonchalantly, "with or without me."

"But . . . but you promised!" she said with exasperation. "They're big fans of classical music and of *yours*, Misha. I told them you would be here because you're not on tour. You *promised* me," she repeated. She ran a hand through her hair nervously and sighed.

"Well, perhaps you should have taken me out of the quotient," Misha snapped. "Your job has nothing to do with me!" He glared at her. "I don't understand why you make all of these social obligations anyway, and then try to involve me. I bet you've got parties and dinners lined up from now through the New Year."

"As a matter of fact, I do," Vera said in a slightly miffed tone. "But this is the only one that was supposed to involve you other than family functions. I deliberately planned this around your tour dates. And I did ask you about it beforehand, Misha. When you told me you definitely had decided not to do the Russian tour, I scheduled this."

She searched his face for a reaction, but he sat mutely, staring straight ahead, holding the balloon of Armagnac with both hands at his waist, pointedly ignoring her. *He's like a pouting child,* she thought disgruntedly. *I'd better try another tack. Try to rescue the situation.*

"Misha," she said softly, "I know you need lots of time to yourself these days, and I understand—"

"Just drop it, Vera," he snapped harshly, turning angrily to her. "Haven't you done enough to complicate matters for me? You are *not* running my life, and you *don't* understand a fucking thing!"

Vera felt a powerful anger blooming deep down inside her, then growing until it burst through her normally cool facade. Her patience snapped.

I don't deserve this, she thought. *I've done nothing to deserve being treated like this.*

She turned to face him. "Why are you acting like this, Misha?" she said firmly. "Why are you treating me this way? There was a time when you would've gladly gone out of your way to be here for something like the Caprioli-Fontini dinner. You would have been proud of me and wanted to help."

Then, despite her attempt at self-control, her voice choked, and she caught her breath before going on. "What's happening, Misha?" she finally cried. "What's happening to us?"

His eyes flitted across her face; then he quickly averted his gaze from her again. *Oh, God,* he thought, *why does it have to be like this?*

"I . . . I . . . I don't know," he finally said almost plaintively. "I just . . ." He paused, gritting his teeth, then took a swallow of the Armagnac.

Vera saw that his face was etched with anguish. It was a tortured expression she'd never seen on his handsome features before. Suddenly she realized that he wanted to tell her everything, to tell her about his affair. He was struggling to find the right words to use, to soften the blow, she assumed, but he was having trouble doing it. That, she told herself, explains his overreaction tonight, his testiness. It was a result of his own emotional turmoil, that battle he was waging within himself over her and . . . the other woman.

She looked at him. He sat staring silently into his glass of Armagnac. "It's because of the affair you're having, isn't it?" she said in a very quiet voice. "That's what this is all really about, isn't it?"

Misha jerked slightly and then looked over at her, returning her stare. But he remained silent. *How can I lie to her?* he wondered, seeing the look of compassion in her eyes. *Yet . . . how can I tell her the truth?*

"I know you're having an affair, Misha," she continued, her voice almost a whisper. "And if I must accommodate it, then so be it. But your cooperation would be helpful."

"How do you know I'm having an affair?" he asked quietly. He wondered whether or not she really did know, and if so, how.

"It's obvious," Vera said matter-of-factly. "You don't want me anymore. You are less and less interested in Nicky—"

"That's *not* true," he interjected with an edge of anger in his voice.

"Well, you spend less and less time with him," she amended. "And you spend less and less time at home these days. I would have to be stupid not to realize that something is going on, Misha."

He hung his head. "I guess so," he said at last, not looking up at her.

"Then why don't we talk about it, Misha," she said gently. "It's time to get it out in the open, and get past it or . . . whatever. Deal with it in any case."

"I . . . I don't know what to say, Vera," he said.

"How about the truth?" she replied. "We've always shared everything, Misha. This shouldn't be so different."

He looked up at her. Vera had always been there for him, and he knew deep down inside that she would be now.

He nodded again and closed his eyes a moment. When he opened them, he said, "Yes, I've been seeing someone."

Vera cringed inside and felt deathly sick for a moment. For even though she'd known the truth for a long time, hearing him confess it made her physically ill. She wanted to scream louder than she'd ever screamed in her life, and at the same time she wanted to lash out at him with both her fists. Instead, she sat, breathing deeply, trying to control herself. Lashing out at him would accomplish nothing except perhaps drive him away. When she could finally trust herself to speak reasonably, she asked: "Is it serious, Misha?"

He looked into his nearly empty glass. "Yes . . . no." He sighed. "I don't *know*. I guess . . . I guess so." He looked up at her.

"Do you know what you want to do about it?" she asked.

"No," Misha said. "I'm . . . I'm very confused right now. I don't know what to do."

Vera suddenly felt deflated. *It must be very serious,* she thought, *if he's this undecided about what to do. If it was a mere flirtation, he would've said so immediately.*

"I . . . I hope," she said, "that you'll know soon, because I don't think I can go on living this way much longer."

"I can't either," Misha said disgustedly. He looked over at her. "You know, you're not the only person who's suffering in this situation, Vera," he said.

"I didn't mean to imply that I was," she retorted. "But I am the one forced into this situation, Misha. I haven't chosen it, like you."

He suddenly leapt off the bed and began pacing the floor, guilt and self-loathing fueling his anger with her.

"You can be awfully self-righteous," he said.

"Misha, I'm simply trying to—" she began.

"You're trying to make me feel worse than I already do!" he snapped unreasonably.

"That's not true!" Vera cried. "I'm—"

He stopped pacing and glared at her. "Oh, I know you too well," he interjected again before she could finish, "and you're not the perfect little angel that everybody seems to think you are." He pointed an accusatory finger at her.

"I know that the perfect little Miss Vera used to get a little on the side with nasty Simon Hampton, didn't you?"

"Misha, you're being—" she began to no avail.

"I'm being what?" he roared. "I'm being realistic. Because you were screwing around with the creep before we married and for all I know you could be screwing around now!"

Vera looked at him with a mixture of astonishment, horror, and fury. "Simon Hampton is dead," she said from between gritted teeth. "Dead!"

Misha looked at her with surprise. "Dead?" he said. How did she know? One of her friends in London could have called her with the news, he guessed, or it might even have been in the New York papers, though he doubted it.

"Yes!" Vera said miserably. "Dead!"

"When was this?" Misha asked. "When?" he repeated when she didn't immediately answer.

"Right before our wedding," Vera finally said.

"What happened to him?" he asked, trying to find out what she knew.

Suddenly Vera realized they were in treacherous waters, and she didn't know what to say.

"Well?" Misha taunted. "What?"

"He drowned off one of the piers in the Hudson River," Vera said quietly.

Misha looked at her curiously. How on earth would she know that? he wondered. The papers—if she saw them—said he'd been found drowned near the Verrazano Narrows Bridge. He could have floated there from anywhere in the New York Bay. *What the hell's going on here?* he asked himself.

"How do you know that?" he finally asked her.

Vera began twisting her wedding band nervously, round and round her finger, trying to think what to say, her mind reeling with possibilities and implications.

"He ... I ... I don't remember," she sputtered at last, knowing it was a lame response at best.

"You don't remember?" Misha asked sarcastically.

Vera looked away and didn't speak.

"You claim he drowned out on the piers. But he was found down by the Verrazano Narrows Bridge. How do you know where he died?" He paused, studying her troubled features. "Why don't you tell me the truth? You always lied about Simon Hampton, didn't you? Why don't you try to tell me the truth now? Huh?"

Vera sat mutely, her misery and turmoil clearly evident on her elegant face. How in the name of God did the conversation take this turn? she asked herself. How could I have let this happen?

"Come on, Vera," Misha cajoled nastily. "Out with it. How did you know about Simon Hampton's drowning?"

"Because I was there!" she cried at last. "Because I saw it happen!"

Misha looked at her in stunned disbelief. "You were there?" he said. "You saw it?"

Vera nodded. "That's what I said, Misha," she said quietly.

His mind whirled with a million questions, and for a moment he couldn't focus on one. Finally he asked, "Why, Vera? Why were you seeing Simon Hampton right before our wedding? Were you two still seeing each other?"

"Oh, Jesus," Vera said. "You think it was a sexual tryst or something? It wasn't that at all."

"Then what was it?" Misha continued relentlessly. "What in God's name were you doing with him?"

"I was trying to keep him from killing you," Vera finally said.

"Killing me? Again?"

Vera merely nodded again as tears began to fill her eyes and spill onto her cheeks.

Misha's heart lurched at the sight of her tears, and he sat down on the bed and gently took one of her hands in his. "Tell me about it, Vera," he said softly. "Please tell me everything."

And she did, telling him exactly what had transpired that horrible evening over five years ago, a night she had hoped to bury forever.

Misha listened without interrupting her, alternately fascinated, revolted, and ultimately convinced that no one else had ever loved him enough to make that sort of self-sacrifice for him.

When she finished her story, she looked up at him, tears still in her eyes. Misha slowly took her in his arms and held her there, stroking her head and her back, while fresh tears, prompted by his simple loving act, began to flow unchecked down her cheeks once again. She cried and cried until she'd cried herself out, for the time being at least, feeling a great burden lifted from her heart. The secret she had for so long carried was finally out, and she felt its weight lifted, giving her a sense of freedom from its heavy guilt and shame.

She reluctantly drew back from the comfort of his arms and reached over to the bedside table for a Kleenex. She wiped her eyes and blew her nose.

Looking at Misha, she smiled ruefully. "I suppose there's some sort of irony in all this somewhere."

Misha cocked his head. "What's that?"

"We were always going to be open and honest with each other," Vera replied, "and now I'm finally telling you my last ugly little secret on the very night you've finally chosen to tell me that you're having an affair with Serena Gibbons and most likely want a divorce."

Misha, who'd been watching her so placidly, jerked involuntarily at the sound of Serena's name. A flush immediately reddened his face. He was momentarily nonplused.

This revelation, tripping so easily off her lips, made him a little angry: she had known but never breathed a word to him. How foolish he'd been to think that he could hide anything from her. At the same time, like Vera, he felt a vast sense of relief that his secret, too, was at last revealed. There would be no more subterfuge, and for that he felt, also like Vera, a new freedom.

"So you knew," he said simply.

Vera nodded.

"For a long time?" he asked.

Vera nodded again.

"How did you know it was her?"

"I caught a glimpse of her in Vienna when we were there together," she said. "At the Hofburg. And that's when everything started to change." She shrugged and looked at him. "It's simple. I put two and two together."

Misha sighed. "And you never said a word."

Vera shook her head. "I . . . I just hoped you'd finally get her out of your system."

He sat staring at her, her delft blue eyes puffy and red from crying, her nose pink. *She truly loves me,* he thought. *Like no one else.* Then: *What the hell am I going to do?* For the revelations tonight hadn't solved his dilemma. There was no sense in trying to fool himself. He was still drawn to Serena. She was truly a bewitching siren whose call to him could not be denied.

What the hell am I going to do? he wondered anew.

"I know you need time," Vera said softly. "And I know this isn't easy for you. I just want you to know that I'll do my best to accommodate this, but I don't want Nicky hurt." She heaved a sigh. "But that's inevitable. What I mean to say is, I want him hurt as little as possible."

She looked up at him, pinning him with her gaze. "If you want a divorce, I'll give it to you."

She saw the look of confusion in his eyes. *He's still uncertain about what he wants to do,* she thought. *Perhaps our marriage does stand a chance. Perhaps someday we can once more be a family.*

Misha reached over and took one of her hands again. "I was going to ask you for a divorce tonight," he said honestly. "But I don't know if that's what I really want."

Vera reached over with her free hand and gently stroked his hair away from his handsome features. "We'll see," she said. "Give it some time."

Misha impulsively took her into his arms and clasped her to him. His heart swelled with gratitude that she could be so magnanimous. His hands tenderly brushed through her pale blond hair, down her back and her arms. Then he tucked a hand under her chin, lifting her face to his, and began kissing her there, softly touching lips to forehead, eyes, cheeks, nose, and mouth, so tenderly at first but more and more hungrily as the feel of her and the scent of her fueled his desire.

Vera responded immediately, relishing the intimacy she had so long been denied and at the same time thinking she must be a fool to let him have his way. But she wanted him as much as she ever had, wanted him, if it was possible, more desperately than ever.

In moments they were naked, flesh against flesh, and that familiar, comfortable lovemaking of the past was now intensified by their long separation and a new intimacy as a result of their revelations tonight. Feverishly and inexorably they moved toward a release at once ecstatic and poignant and ultimately fell into heavy sleep in each other's arms.

Chapter Thirty-five

⌘

"I think this is the most reckless thing you've ever done," Coral said harshly. "But since there seems to be no changing your mind, I've made all the arrangements that I can at this end."

"Thanks, Coral," Serena said distractedly. She hadn't really been listening to what her agent had to say, but she'd caught the gist. Enough to know that she would be having it her way, as she'd always known she would. She continued sorting through camera equipment, paring down the possibilities to a bare minimum. She was going to be traveling light on this trip.

"I've told the magazine editors that you're working on a super secret project," Coral went on, "so hush-hush I can't breathe a word. And that you won't be able to do anything until after New Year's. That'll keep them satisfied for the time being, more or less, *and* intrigued with what it is you're up to."

Coral paused, pleased with herself, and waited for a response. Then she realized that Serena hadn't been paying any attention. She was contentedly sitting cross-legged on the floor, examining camera lenses and filters and such. Coral frowned and took a deep breath, silently counting to ten, determined not to start a scene with Serena tonight. This irresponsible, ungrateful, willful, and very talented young lady was, she reminded herself, an artist *and* her prize moneymaker. And as ill-advised in some ways as Coral thought this trip to Cambodia was, her business instincts told her that she and Serena might very well turn the resulting photographs into a gold mine. It could, in fact, be the beginning of a whole new career direction in which prints of Serena's work would command thousands of dollars more than the considerable prices they already fetched in galleries. Photography collectors would be lining up for prints. Then, of course, there would be the inevitable coffee-table books of her work, another source of income—and prestige.

Thus, Coral had convinced herself that she should overlook the political unrest and other dangers inherent in Serena's undertaking this project. After all, Pol Pot was dead, and the country was opening up to outsiders—even his wretched prisons were being exposed for what they were. Plus, Jason would be with Serena, she told herself, and if nothing else his appearance would frighten the natives half to death.

Her concerns for Serena, however, weren't merely monetary. Coral harbored a genuine affection—once infatuation—for the prize of her stable and felt a responsibility to her that was a mixture of the professional and, she supposed, the maternal. She tried to protect Serena from herself—her instincts could go awfully awry—and the world at large, including predators like Misha Levin.

The thought of the dashing and famous pianist reminded her of an unanswered question or two she had forgotten to ask Serena. She cleared her throat.

"Serena," she ventured, "why are you planning the stopover in Kyoto?"

Serena looked up from her sorting, her large dark eyes sparkling. "I'm going to meet Misha there," she said. There was a determination in her voice that barred all discussion.

"I see," Coral said in as neutral a tone as she could muster. "He's performing there?"

"Yes," Serena said. She dropped the equipment she held in one hand and sat up, looking into Coral's eyes. "I think he's going to ask me to marry him, Coral. He's asking his wife for a divorce."

Coral did not like hearing this bit of news, not one single little bit, but she controlled herself. I've done all I can do in that department, she told herself. She won't listen to a word I have to say about it anyway.

"Well," she said mildly, "I hope you'll keep me posted."

"I promise to check in regularly," Serena said. She glanced at Coral out of the corner of her eye. *What?* she thought. *No lecture about meeting Misha in Kyoto? Will wonders never cease?*

Coral rose to her feet. "I'd best get back uptown," she said. "Brandi and I have plans so I won't see you again before you leave, but Sally will be taking you to Kennedy as usual. Give me a kiss before I go?"

Serena, sitting amid piles of equipment, looked up and smiled. "Of course," she said. She got up from the floor and hugged Coral tightly, then kissed her on both cheeks and stood back. "Don't worry, Coral," she said. "It'll be fine. I'm sure of it."

"I hope so," Coral said, oddly feeling teary-eyed, a rare phenomenon in the pantheon of her emotional responses. She threw her shoulders back and picked up her handbag. "I'll see myself out," she said. "You go on with your sorting."

"Okay," Serena said. "I've got tons to do to get ready."

Coral turned and walked toward the giant loft's entry hall. She looks older somehow, Serena thought, and lonely. Suddenly she went after her, coming up behind her and putting an arm around Coral's waist. Coral gazed up at her with a perplexed but grateful expression.

At the elevator, Serena kissed her again, on the lips this time. Then the doors closed and Coral disappeared from sight.

Misha closed the last of his suitcases with a loud snap, spun the locks, then placed it on the floor alongside the others. He slumped down onto the bed, staring at the luggage, lined up in a neat row like soldiers. He sighed, thinking about the upcoming tour. He had decidedly mixed feelings about this trip to Japan. On the one hand, he looked forward to it. Although he had played in both Tokyo and Kyoto before, he'd hardly had time to do more than perform, eat, and sleep, and had seen almost nothing of the country. This trip would be different, however, since he was allowing himself time to explore the local culture, which had always intrigued him.

On the other hand, his enthusiasm was tempered somewhat by his meeting with Serena in Kyoto. He was leaving ahead of schedule to meet her there. He didn't quite know how he felt about that. He did know that the instant he laid eyes on her, he would want her as desperately as always, but beyond that—beyond the mutual lusty fulfilling of their physical desires—did he really want more?

God, he thought miserably, *how did I get myself into this mess?* He knew that Serena expected him to announce that he'd asked Vera for a divorce. Hadn't he told her as much himself? Hadn't he convinced himself that that was what he wanted and that that was what he was going to do? His emotions were more in a state of confusion than ever, feeling a powerful attraction and desire for Serena, yet at the same time feeling a profound need and, yes, he thought, love, for Vera.

"Are you ready, old man?" Manny said as he stepped into the bedroom, his custom-made Lobb shoes silent on the antique silk Tabriz rug.

Misha turned and looked at him in surprise. "Yes, all set. What about you?"

"Sasha's finishing up for both of us," Manny said. "We've got time, since we're not leaving until day after tomorrow."

"I didn't expect to see you tonight," Misha said.

"I called and Vera said you were about finished packing," Manny replied, "so I strolled on over. I wanted to have a word with you before you leave, if you don't mind."

"No," Misha said, looking at Manny with a curious expression. He wondered what could be so urgent that Manny hadn't simply called him. "Why don't we have a drink in my study?"

"Great, old man, great," Manny enthused.

Misha got up and led the way to his small book-lined study, where he went straight to the drinks table. "What'll you have, Manny?"

"A couple of fingers of scotch," he replied. "A whisper of water. Hold the ice."

Misha made the drink and handed it to him.

"Thanks, old man," Manny said.

Misha poured himself a small scotch and added ice cubes and a splash of water.

"Here's to Japan," Manny said. He lifted his glass, and Misha followed suit.

"To Japan," Misha echoed unenthusiastically.

They sipped at their drinks and took seats in comfortable Edwardian chairs, which were upholstered in worn old leather, on either side of the fireplace. Light danced across their features from the log fire that flickered in the grate.

"What's on your mind, Manny?" Misha asked.

Manny shifted uncomfortably in his chair, and looked over at Misha through the thick lenses of his tortoiseshell glasses. "Well," he began slowly, "I wanted to broach the subject of Russia again."

Misha's face froze, but his eyes glittered in the light of the fire. Manny had no doubt that he'd struck that familiar nerve in Misha which positively vibrated with his intense hatred of his homeland.

"I know I'm upsetting you by bringing this up," Manny rushed on, before Misha could tell him to drop the subject. "But it's something that I've absolutely got to discuss with you, Misha." His voice was uncharacteristically earnest. "Please listen to me. *Please*. Just hear me out before you fly off the handle and tell me to get lost." He looked at Misha with a pleading expression, a rarity for Manny Cygelman.

Misha acquiesced with a barely perceptible nod of his head but remained silent, his body assuming a pose of stiff formality.

Manny took a sip of his scotch, set the crystal old-fashioned glass down, then launched into his well-rehearsed speech. "Your CD sales are fine," Manny said, "and your concert bookings are great. They both have been phenomenal since the very beginning, all those years ago. *But*"—he looked Misha in the eye—"how long will sales and bookings continue at this rate?" He shrugged. "We don't know, do we? The whole bottom could fall out of everything. CD sales could drop, and concert bookings could shrivel. Nobody can really predict that sort of thing."

Misha eyed him shrewdly. "Why would my career suddenly take a nose-dive if I continue to play as I do now, Manny?" he asked. "Why would people suddenly stop going to my concerts? Why would they suddenly stop buying my CDs? It makes no sense, Manny. You're grasping at straws. You and Sasha both. Desperately trying to get me to do a Russian tour. Again."

Misha allowed his body to relax in the chair, sitting back. He took a sip of his drink, idly waiting to hear how his very inventive agent would respond. *Manny's machinations!* he thought with amusement. *The gears in that Byzantine mind of his never stop turning.*

Manny cleared his throat. "You're right," he conceded. "Fans and classical music lovers aren't suddenly going to stop buying your CDs or going to your concerts. Not suddenly. But, and this is a big 'but,' as new talent comes along, some of your fans are inevitably going to drop you for somebody new to the scene. Somebody fresh. Somebody different. Let's face it, Misha, you're not the young prodigy you once were, and that aspect of your drawing power is coming to a close. No matter how beautifully you play."

Manny paused and took another sip of his scotch, hoping that he hadn't offended Misha and at the same time hoping that Misha was digesting what he'd said.

And he was. Misha knew that there was a degree of truth in what Manny said, especially if a performer overexposed himself, no matter how rare and wondrous his talent. Discovering where that fine line lay— between too much exposure and not enough—was a very difficult task, if not impossible. He also knew that a lot of his fans were as mercurial as butterflies, fed by the buzz and hype of music critics, the press, and the recording industry. Many of them would drop him in an instant, any allegiance to him forgotten as they took up with the next boy wonder to come down the road.

Yet Misha didn't worry about such matters. He was still extremely popular and in constant demand. He had no doubts about his own abilities—his playing had never been better, he believed—and there was a contingent of faithful music lovers who would never desert him, as long as he could play as well as he played now. These music lovers looked for quality, and weren't slaves to all the hype and buzz. As for the long range . . . *Well,* he thought, *I'll deal with that when the time comes.*

"There's a brilliant way to deal with this situation," Manny rushed on. "Before it becomes a real problem. I think one way to generate new excitement—a way to punch up your career—is to do this Russian thing. Now, listen carefully."

Manny looked over at Misha to see if he was paying attention. Satisfied that he was, he quickly continued, his words tripping over one another in his mounting excitement.

"I've told you before how it could be built up as a grand gesture on your part," he said. "Picture it, Misha! A return to your homeland for the first time since you were a child. Back to your roots, since that evil Wall has finally come down. I can see the newspapers now: 'Misha Levin forgives Russia at last for the cruelties that were perpetrated against him and his family.' "

Manny paused briefly, looking at Misha intensely, waiting for a response. When it didn't come, he hurried on again. "A move like that would receive *international attention*," he said with emphasis. "Just think of the press. And even if you don't care about the press, think of the money."

Misha waved a hand at him, as if it were not worth mentioning.

"They're offering a fortune, Misha! A fortune!" Manny cried. "They want to do a five-year deal. Two concerts a year. That's all. You'd play Moscow and St. Petersburg. That's it! Half the money up front!"

Misha held a hand up in an effort to halt Manny's swift and ebullient flow of words, but Manny was so caught up in the excitement of the moment, he paid no attention.

"Wait, wait, *wait*, Misha!" Manny exclaimed. "Think of the proceeds from the Russian CD recordings. It would give us a whole new marketing approach. For five years running. People will be waiting with bated breath for the latest Misha Levin in Moscow. Misha Levin in St. Petersburg! Then we'll box an entire set at the end of the five years. It's a gold mine. More money than you've ever made!"

Manny dramatically slapped his right fist into his left hand, then threw both hands wide. His eyes were huge with his excitement about the possibilities, and his breath was coming in audible gasps.

Misha looked at him and smiled. "Manny," he said calmly, "have you and the producers you've talked to about this—*whoever* they are—considered the dire state of the economy in Russia? Have you asked yourselves where all this money in Russia is coming from? For that matter, who are these Russians that can afford to pay the ticket prices that they'll have to ask to fill up the concert halls?"

Manny waved off the questions. "The country may be broke, Misha," he said, "but believe me, there's still plenty of money floating around Russia. Tons of money. Sasha and I'll fill those concert halls to bursting with people with their money, their custom-made suits and couture gowns and expensive jewelry. Make no mistake about that, old man."

Misha looked at him thoughtfully for a moment, his hands at his chin, two fingers steepled. Then, he reached over and picked up his scotch, took the last sip, and set the glass back down.

"Manny," he said, "you know who these people are, don't you?" It wasn't a question but a declaration of certainty. "You know that they're mobsters and hooligans who've stolen everything they can get their greedy hands on. They're men who are bleeding the country dry, letting the poor starve, taking everything they can get. The Palace Hotel in St. Moritz is full of them. Monte Carlo is full of them. The best restaurants all over the world are full of them. Spending all that stolen money."

Manny's excitement had slowly ebbed as Misha spoke, and he now wore an unhappy expression on his plump face. "What you say may be true to some extent, Misha, but they've got the money to fill those halls and make those recordings possible, nevertheless. Besides, some of them aren't hooligans. Some of them have simply taken advantage of the opportunities that arose with the fall of communism."

"Spare me, Manny," Misha said. "Would you *want* me to play for a crowd like that?" he asked. "Would you want me to give them some kind of legitimacy because I'd played for them?"

Manny shifted uncomfortably in his chair again. "Well, I don't think . . ."

"Maybe," Misha said with emphasis, "maybe someday I will go back and play there." He paused and took a breath. "But not for people like that. Not for mobsters."

Manny, his head hanging in defeat, looked up. "That's your final word?" he asked.

Misha nodded. "That's my final word. Now, go home and help Sasha finish getting ready for our trip. I want to be alone for a while."

Manny pushed himself to his feet. He looked over at Misha. "See you later," he said.

"See you later," Misha echoed.

Manny turned and left the room, his stomach churning with the bile of defeat.

Vera was seated at the big antique pine table in the kitchen, sipping her morning coffee, her appointment book and a scattering of various lists at her side. She'd already seen Nicky off to his kindergarten, and was double-checking her appointment book for today's meetings and making a list of the telephone calls she should return.

When Misha walked in, she looked up. "Manny called," she said. "The limo will be here in a few minutes. Mario's already been up and taken your luggage down to the lobby." She looked back down at her appointment book, where she was jotting down a note, hoping that Misha wouldn't notice that she was troubled by his leaving.

"Thanks," Misha said. She's always so busy, he thought. Running the household, keeping up with her job at the auction house, caring for Nicky. And caring for me. All without complaint.

He pulled out a chair and sat down. "Vera . . ." he began.

She looked over at him questioningly, a slight smile on her face. "Hmm?" she murmured, trying to appear to be somewhat distracted.

"I'm glad we've talked," he said, "and I want you to know that . . . well, I'll try to straighten out the mess I've made . . . somehow."

Vera took a sip of her coffee and set the cup back down. "Whatever you decide to do, Misha," she replied in a soft voice, "let's both try to go about it in a civilized manner." She twisted her wedding band nervously. "You know where I stand. I . . . I . . . love you regardless, and I will be here for you. But I want to be treated fairly."

Misha nodded. He wanted to say he loved her, too, but he felt that the words would have no meaning for Vera right now.

Before he could respond, the intercom buzzer rang, signaling that the limousine had arrived to take him to Kennedy and his flight to Japan.

"You'd better go," Vera said. "Don't keep the driver waiting." She rose to her feet.

Misha got up and stood by his chair for a moment, then abruptly went around the table and put his hands on her shoulders. He leaned down and kissed her on the lips, then drew back and looked at her.

Vera returned his gaze, looking into his dark, troubled eyes. She desperately wanted to hold him and to be held, but she didn't want to push too far.

Misha gave her a squeeze, then turned and was gone.

Vera stood, staring at the empty kitchen doorway, tears welling up in her eyes. *Please,* she prayed, *come back to me. Please come back to me and Nicky.*

In the private elevator foyer, Misha punched the button for the lobby. Waiting for the elevator car to arrive, he twisted around on his feet in nervous anticipation. Out of the corner of his eye, he caught sight of the mezuzah on the door frame. The same one that he had himself nailed there years ago. The mezuzah he had bought to replace the one old Arkady had given him in Moscow long ago.

Misha reached over and brushed the cold metal with his fingertips, thinking about Arkady, his loving mentor, and his wise and benevolent guidance and advice. He realized that he hadn't thought of Arkady in a long, long time.

I wonder what Arkady would have to say about my life now? Misha asked himself. But he felt fairly certain that he knew the answer to that question: *Not much. No, not much at all.* Arkady would tell him that he'd let his passions run away with him. At the expense of his virtue.

Oh, Arkady, forgive me, he prayed. *And help me. Please help me to know what to do. I'm lost, Arkady. Lost.*

Misha leaned over and reverentially brushed the mezuzah with his lips. He heard the elevator car arriving and quickly turned back around, fingering the tears from his eyes. When the doors opened, he stepped in and was gone.

Part Four

NOW
Fall 1999

Upper West Side, Manhattan

The older Russian stepped from the apartment's entrance hall into its vast living room, his sycophantic younger muscle, in their trademark twin black leather trench coats and lizard-skin cowboy boots, at his heels. He planted his feet on the deep plush-pile carpeting and looked around, taking in the huge room with its expensive-looking modern furniture and its paintings and sculpture. Through the French doors in the distance he could glimpse the lush retreat of the wrap-around terrace and its evergreen plantings, here high above ordinary mortals and the noise and grime of the city streets.

One of his goons let out a low whistle, nodding as his eyes swept the circumference of the luxurious space. "This what they call culture, huh?" he said in his thick Russian accent.

"Great fuck pad," his buddy said, rocking on his boot heels.

"Stay here," the older Russian said, ignoring their remarks. He walked the length of the living room to the French doors and went out onto the terrace. Pausing at the balustrade, he looked out over the city and beyond. It was a cold but crystal clear day, and he could see north to the George Washington Bridge and the Palisades of New Jersey.

Some people know how to live, he reflected. Know how to spend their money. And some of it's thanks to me.

He was genuinely appreciative of what he vaguely recognized as good taste and sophistication, but he was also envious and resentful. These kinds of people, he thought, acted superior to him and didn't give him the respect that was his due.

I'm sick and tired of stupid excuses from the smart-ass, he decided. I'm sick of the whole business, in fact. He took a deep breath and shifted his gaze south, to the World Trade Center and out to the Verrazano Narrows. It's time for results.

That was why he'd come here today. He'd made a final offer—an enormous offer—but not exorbitant in terms of the benefits he and his organization *would reap. If Michail Levin accepted it. With Michail Levin's name, they would have no trouble packing concert halls, selling CDs, setting up distribution deals, and signing up other music-world luminaries. As it was, everything was in place.*

What they needed now was a big name to get the ball rolling. He was going to get the answer today—here on a piece of the younger Russian's own turf. He knew the young man would return soon, and he wanted to be here to surprise him, give him a scare. If the young man had finally convinced Levin, there wouldn't be any need for any further action. If that was not the case, however, then . . . well, he would see.

Levin, after all, was virtually defenseless. He had a wife, a kid, and a mistress—which could all easily be used to get him to cooperate.

He knew, of course, that Levin had left for Japan today. Kyoto. That his management was leaving tomorrow. For Tokyo. A perfect situation, he thought. Levin and his girlfriend in Kyoto. His "friends" in Tokyo. His wife and kid in New York.

He turned and walked back into the apartment, where one of his goons was giving the furnishings and art closer inspection while the other was sprawled on a sofa, thumbing through a book.

"This is some weird shit," the goon with the book said, holding it up. "Look at this. Buncha naked fags or something."

The older man paid no attention to him but walked over to the drinks table, where he poured some club soda into a crystal old-fashioned glass and drank it down in one swallow. He poured another one, took a sip, then set it down on the table when he heard the front door opening. He walked to the middle of the room and stood there, his feet planted wide, waiting for the young man to appear.

The young man came through the arched entry into the living room, a briefcase and keys in hand. He saw the older Russian and stopped in his tracks. His face instantly drained of color, and for a moment he could only stare in disbelief.

"What the fuck are you doing here?" he asked angrily after recovering from his initial shock. "And how the fuck did you get in?"

"Never mind how," the older Russian said.

He looked over at the goons. "Put that book back where you found it," he snapped at the one who sat on a couch. The goon slammed the book shut and banged it down on the coffee table.

The young man placed his briefcase on a chair and put his keys down on top of it. Then he turned to the older Russian. "What do you want?" he asked in a calmer tone of voice.

"An answer," the older man said.

The young man didn't answer for a moment. "The answer's no," *he fi-nally said.*

The older Russian's expression didn't change, but he was not happy to hear this news. "You're certain about that," *he said.*

"Absolutely," *the younger man said.* "He won't do it. He thinks the deal reeks of scum like you."

The goons looked up at their boss, and their bodies seemed to spring to life, all rippling muscle and tension just waiting to pounce.

The older Russian stood staring at the young man. The little cocksucker's a lot braver than I'd thought, *he decided.* He sure as hell isn't afraid of us. Maybe he's the one who ought to have a go at Levin. Like he wanted.

"Follow me," *he said to the young man.* "Let's have a little talk."

The young man wasn't sure it was a good idea for him to be out on the ter-race with the older Russian. Then he realized that they still needed him, perhaps more than ever.

He smiled confidently at the goons, who sat watching him, then squared his shoulders and walked over to the French doors and out onto the terrace.

Chapter Thirty-six

Misha had fallen in love with Kyoto, Japan's former imperial city, and Serena, if not precisely in love, was an enthusiastic sight-seer and voracious shopper.

Magnificent Buddhist temples—over sixteen hundred of them—Shinto shrines, Zen monasteries, and Amida temples beckoned from every neighborhood. Palaces, gardens, and pleasure pavilions abounded with their delights. The city's sensitivity to beauty was evident in so many ways that Misha understood easily why it was always flooded with pilgrims, come to pay their respects.

In its eleven centuries Kyoto had endured earthquakes, fires, and the desecration of war, always to rebuild with reverence for its past. Despite its urban sprawl and twentieth-century high-rises, it was the center of traditional culture in Japan, and its residents had worked to protect its precious cultural artifacts from ruthless modernization.

Misha loved the old wood and plaster row houses, which had all but disappeared elsewhere in Japan, particularly the *ochaya*, the traditionally styled two-story wooden teahouses where geishas entertained. When strolling through the Gion district he and Serena caught their first glimpses of a geisha and her apprentices, *maiko*, on their way to appointments at the teahouses. At the Minami-za, Japan's oldest theater, they were intrigued by the Kabuki drama, and the solemn chanting and masks of the No play they saw at the Kanze Kaikan No Theater left them no less dazzled.

On Shinmonzen-dori they shopped for antique pottery and lacquerware. On Imadegawa-dori, Misha bought Serena a beautiful silk kimono. At the famous To-ji, a flea market, Serena found exquisite old silk obi and *furoshiki*—silk for gift wrapping—which she gave to Misha for having pillow covers made. They stopped for unidentifiable but delicious grilled fish in an open-air market, and at Rakusho, a tea shop in a former villa, they had a frothy *matcha*, the tea reserved for the tea ceremony.

Misha decided that what he loved most about this ancient city was its devotion to the spirit, as evidenced by its many temples and shrines, and the flesh, as seen in its districts set aside for physical pleasure. One could worship in so many ways in Kyoto, he thought with a secret smile. Yet he saw that there was an artistic blending of both flesh and spirit in everything.

And I'm certainly not immune, he reflected as he and Serena strolled, exhausted after a full day of sightseeing, back to the Tawaraya, the ancient inn where they were staying.

He had come to Kyoto determined that the first thing he and Serena would do was sit down and have a talk. He still wasn't sure that he knew his own heart, and he knew even less of hers. Yet when he'd arrived at the Tawaraya, Kyoto's most famous *ryokan,* Serena was waiting for him in their antique-furnished room. She'd welcomed him wearing a *yukata,* a simple cotton kimono, open down the front—and nothing else. Her body, resplendent in all its beautiful curves and angles, had beckoned to him as always. He'd needed no further coaxing to arouse his desire for her, to forget that he had wanted to talk to her.

They'd made love on the immaculate futon, a passionate and satisfying experience. Yet he'd felt that something was missing, that they were both holding back in some indefinable way. He hadn't had a chance to think about it, however. Afterward, they'd immediately headed out to begin sightseeing.

Now, as they took off their shoes at the doorway to the *ryokan* and put on the slippers provided by the inn, he reflected that their activity, while pleasurable, had been a delaying tactic. Holding off the inevitable discussion they both knew was coming. While Serena had been convivial and engaging, interested in what they were doing, she had nevertheless seemed distracted. Perhaps, he thought, she's simply preoccupied by thoughts of her trip to Cambodia.

He sighed as they made their way to their room, immune to the serene beauty of the ancient inn, still lost in thought. Her ambition he could understand. Wasn't he consumed by his own? Yet . . . yet he realized that, unfair as it might be, he didn't want to be secondary to her ambition.

At the door to their room, they removed their slippers and padded onto the tatami-matted floor with bare feet. Tonight they would be served dinner here in their room. Misha knew that it would be exquisitely presented on beautiful porcelain and lacquerware, course after course. There would be *shabu-shabu,* a dish of thinly sliced beef; *suppon,* a turtle dish; *tsukemono,* assorted pickled vegetables. Dish after dish, on and on. Suddenly he wasn't looking forward to it.

Serena began undressing, throwing her clothes on a chair. She slipped into the *yukata* and turned to face him.

"Don't you want to get comfortable?" she asked.

Misha hesitated a moment before answering. "I . . . I guess so," he finally said, and began stripping off his clothes.

Serena eyed him with a quizzical expression. "What's wrong, Misha?" she asked. "You were awfully quiet coming back to the inn."

He shook his head. "Nothing, really," he said. "But I thought the same thing. That you were being awfully quiet."

Serena sat down and tossed her raven black hair out of her eyes. She held her hands out in front of her and examined her long, BrazenBerry-polished fingernails. She seemed absorbed in them, ignoring his response to her, as if her expensive manicure was the most important thing in the world.

Misha silently folded his clothes and slipped into his *yukata*, then sat down in front of her and took her long, tapering hands in his. "Talk to me, Serena," he said. "We've been having fun, but you're at least as preoccupied as I am. What is it, huh?"

She looked at him and sighed. "I guess I'm just anxious to get going," she said. "You know. To Cambodia. It's just yours truly and Jason this trip. I've got a lot of work to do, and I need to get to it."

"Jason's here?" he asked.

She nodded. "Yeah," she said. "Didn't I tell you? He's staying in a little inn hidden away over in Gion."

"Maybe we should invite him to dinner," Misha said.

"No," Serena said, shaking her head. "He'd be bored stiff. He's probably already out exploring the bars anyway."

"I guess so," Misha said. He squeezed her hands lightly. "So," he said. "You're anxious to get going. And that's all? I mean, that's the only reason you're so . . . well, a little distant?"

"Yes," Serena said, looking at him. "I guess so. I'm glad we could meet, Misha, but I guess it was just bad timing."

For a moment he didn't believe his ears. This stopover was "bad timing"? Hadn't she expected him to tell her that he was getting a divorce? Didn't she expect him to ask her to marry him? Hadn't they reached a turning point in their relationship? Perhaps they had. Only it wasn't the turning point he'd thought.

Serena, however, dispelled this notion with her next comment. "Besides, Misha," she said, her hazel eyes looking into him, "I've been waiting for you to tell me that you're getting a divorce and that we're going to get married." There was a hint of a smile on her lips.

So she had been thinking about it. But now that the subject was out on the table, his mind went blank. "I . . . I don't know what to say," he said. "I . . . I talked to Vera, but . . ."

"But what?" Serena asked. She jerked her hands out of his. "But what?" she repeated.

"We talked about a divorce," Misha said, "but we didn't come to any definite conclusion."

Serena sighed. "Lame," she said. "That is so lame."

"Call it what you will," Misha retorted, "but that's the way we left it."

" 'We'!" Serena spat. "What's 'we' got to do with it? It's simple. You're supposed to be getting rid of her!"

Misha cringed. He could understand her anger and disappointment, but he couldn't handle her insensitivity toward Vera and their marriage.

"Serena," he said. "Vera and I've known each other for a very long time. You don't just unceremoniously dump somebody that you've known and . . . and . . . loved for that long. You should know that."

Serena looked at him with a pouting expression. "What about me?" she asked.

Misha looked at her thoughtfully. "Do you really love me, Serena?" he asked gently. "Do you really want to marry me and have children? Do you want to have a family with me? Ask yourself. Deep down inside, do you? Are you absolutely certain?"

Serena shrugged. "You know I love you, Misha. As much as I can. As much as I know how. Isn't that enough?"

"I don't know," he replied. "I don't know if love is enough." He shook his head. "You've told me about your relationships in the past and how sometimes you thought you were in love but weren't, as it turned out. Sometimes I wonder if that's what's happening now."

"I don't think so," she said. "I know I have problems with . . . with intimacy. My parents . . . my family were so . . . unloving."

"I know that, Serena," Misha said. "And you know it. Do you think you can ever get beyond what your parents did to you? Do you think you can ever get over your fears and really give yourself to somebody?"

"I don't like this conversation," Serena said angrily. "I don't like it at all. I just know that I do love you, Misha, and that's that." She looked at him with widened eyes.

Misha was silent for a moment, digesting her words. "I love you, too," he said at last.

"But," Serena said. "It sounds like there's a definite *but* coming."

Misha nodded. "I don't know if I can give up my family for you. I love my family. I want a family. I need a family. And I don't really believe you do. I think the most important thing to you is your career."

Serena ran her fingers through her long raven hair and laughed nervously. "How many times do we have to discuss my career?" she asked. "What about yours? Are you willing to give it up for a family? Huh?"

"No," Misha said, "and I've never meant that you would have to give yours up for a family. But for God's sake, look at what you're doing now. Going off to Cambodia for weeks, leaving me alone for the holidays. Is that love?"

"Holidays!" Serena snapped. Then she laughed. "Who cares? I've got pictures to take." She shook a finger at him. "And I bet if you had a big concert to play during a holiday, you wouldn't hesitate to leave your wife and kid at home."

Misha hung his head. "Maybe you're right," he muttered.

"I know I am," Serena said. "We're like two peas in a pod, Misha. We're artists, and we live for our art. That's what's important. Not family." She paused and took a deep breath, exhaling noisily. "Let's forget it, okay? Let's forget marriage and all that business right now. What's the hurry? I like the way we've been meeting, even if we've had problems. We can both do our own thing and still have a great time together."

She took his long, slender hands in hers and squeezed them. "We don't have much time, Misha, so let's have fun. Forget all this other stuff, okay?"

He didn't respond immediately, and Serena took his hands. "Come on, what do you say? Friends and lovers? Tonight and tomorrow until I leave?"

Misha slowly nodded and looked up into her eyes. *She's like a little girl,* he thought. *A sad little girl who wants to be loved so desperately. And who wants to return it the best—the only—way she knows how.* His heart melted for her, but at the same time he realized with a feeling, deep down in his gut, that it was over for him. Serena could never give him what he wanted. She was incapable of giving him what he wanted. It simply wasn't in her. At the same time he realized that the reverse was true. He could never give her the freedom and independence she wanted, that she had to have. Not genuinely, he couldn't. No, he wanted something different.

He had a sudden longing for the comfortable familiarity of Vera, for her perfumed embrace, so sweet and uncomplicated, so tender and unconditional. For the noisy, joyous flinging of his son's arms about his neck. For the warmth of their home. He felt a wistful need to see Sonia and Dimitri and tell them that he loved them, that he appreciated the nurturing, loving home they had always provided for him, no matter the circumstances.

His eyes misted over. He looked over at Serena and nodded. "Friends and lovers," he said. "Tonight and tomorrow. But I don't know beyond that, Serena."

Chapter Thirty-seven

The young man adjusted the knot of his yellow silk tie, making certain in the mirror that it was perfect. Always a fastidious dresser, he felt a special need to appear so now. In the mirror he saw the young woman light a cigarette and blow a plume of smoke toward the ceiling.

She was still sprawled out on the bed, though she had dressed again. In head to toe shiny black vinyl, including thigh-high, stiletto-heeled boots. The outfit, heavy makeup, and bleached streaks in her jet black hair—the bleach a certain sign of a renegade soul in Japan—no longer appealed as they had before he had satisfied himself with her.

He patted the hair at the sides of his head with his hands. He wanted to get out of this love-by-the-hour hotel. He hated this sort of place—afterwards—but what choice had he had? He'd left the luxurious hotel where Misha had put them up, off to seek adventure in Shinjuku's Kabuki-cho, home to Tokyo's wildest nightlife. And he'd found it, but he couldn't possibly take her back to the Four Seasons Hotel Chinzan-so.

He snapped his fingers at the girl. "Let's go," he said, nodding his head toward the door.

The girl took a drag off her cigarette, then eased her booted legs off the bed, taking her time to get up. When she stood, she wavered slightly, still drunk or stoned or both.

Jesus, he thought. *You can almost smell the viruses.*

He took her arm and unceremoniously pushed her toward the door, which he opened with his other hand. *Misha Levin,* he thought. *Rich, famous, handsome, successful Misha Levin. It's his fault I have to put up with shit like this.*

He deserves whatever he gets. Whatever I have to give him.

Vera closed the novel she'd been trying without much success to read. She'd caught herself reading the same sentences time and again, without their meaning registering in her whirling mind. She stowed the paperback novel in the compartment on the back of the seat in front of her and stretched her legs as far as she could, wiggling her toes. She'd long since kicked off her Chanel heels.

Turning her head to the jet's porthole, she looked out into the pitch black night. *I must be crazy,* she thought. *Or maybe I'm doing the first sane thing I've done ever since I knew Misha was having this affair.*

She had finally decided that she was going to fight to keep her husband. She was sick and tired of being the patient, understanding wife, willing to keep the home fires burning while her husband did whatever he pleased. Nobody was going to take him away without a fight.

That was why she was on this flight to Tokyo. She'd left Nicky with Sonia and Dmitri. Sonia had wished her the best of luck. She was going to attend Misha's concerts whether he liked it or not, and she was going to do everything in her power to lure him back. To lure him away from Serena Gibbons. Misha would probably be appalled, but she didn't care anymore.

So here I am, she thought. *Alone, on a crazy adventure, facing I don't know what. But I've got to do it. What can I lose? Everything and nothing.*

With that thought, she reached up and switched off the reading light above her seat. *I've got to get some sleep,* she thought, closing her eyes. *I have to be sharp for the next couple of days. I've got to save all my energy to save—us.*

Chapter Thirty-eight

The young man returned to his room at the Four Seasons Hotel Chinzan-so with his recent purchases, all neatly wrapped and placed in a single shopping bag. He set the bag down and started to hang up his expensive overcoat, then thought better of it.

It'll be useful, he decided. *Yes, indeed, it's just what the doctor ordered, in fact.* A smile crossed his lips.

He took the coat on into his room and threw it over the back of a chair, then he headed straight to the table where he'd earlier placed a bottle of exorbitantly expensive whiskey. It was perched enticingly on a small lacquered tray with glasses and a bottle of mineral water. He poured a stiff drink, at least three inches, in one glass, then recapped the whiskey and set it back down. Then he picked up the bottle of water and filled another glass with it. A chaser. Taking a deep breath first, he downed the whiskey in a single long swallow, shivering as it went down his throat and hit his stomach. Quickly picking up the glass of water, he downed it on top of the whiskey.

"Awww," he exclaimed, almost gagging. He shivered once again, then stood still for a moment, letting the whiskey and water settle in his stomach. He didn't normally drink like this, but today he'd decided he could use a good belt of whiskey to screw up his courage.

Gradually feeling much better—in fact, pretty damn good, he thought—he rose to his feet and retraced his steps to the entry, where he retrieved his shopping bag.

He set the bag down on the chair where he'd put his overcoat, then reached in it and pulled out a small package. He quickly tore open the box and extracted his first purchase. A pair of handcuffs, complete with keys. He'd bought them in a shop full of sex toys. He practiced opening and closing them. *Child's play,* he thought. He eyed them proudly for a moment, then slipped them into one of the capacious pockets of his overcoat.

He dipped into the shopping bag again and took out a small paper bag.

A typical hardware store bag, and indeed that's where he'd found this purchase. He examined it closely. It was a simple sledgehammer, small variety, the kind with a wooden handle about six inches long and a heavy steel head about five inches long.

It could batter someone's brains out, he thought. *Or smash a hand to pieces.*

He slipped it into the other large pocket of his overcoat, then held the coat up for inspection. There was a slight bulge, but nothing that would draw undue attention. He smiled with satisfaction.

Finally he extracted a small roll of duct tape. *Good for shutting someone up,* he thought. He tossed it into the pocket with the handcuffs, and held his overcoat up once again. A little bulge as before, but nothing to be worried about.

He laid the coat back down and walked into the bathroom, where he took a small bottle of pills out of his fine black leather shaving kit. He held the bottle up to the light. Ketamine. It hadn't taken any effort to get these heavy-duty animal anesthetics. After all, Ketamine was very popular in the downtown clubs these days and easy to get hold of. Ketamine would do the trick.

Only I won't be taking the pills. Misha Levin will.

Walking out of the bathroom, his cell phone bleeped, distracting him. *Jesus!* he thought. *The fucking thing bleeped half the night and all day long.* Well, he wasn't going to answer it. He didn't want to talk to the only people who had the number for this particular phone. *This is my business now,* he thought. *They can go fuck themselves.* He grabbed it from the table and unceremoniously threw the phone across the room. It bounced off the wall and fell to the floor.

He headed toward the bathroom again. *Time to pour all my pills into one big capsule,* he thought. *Then it's to the elevator after that's done. It's just upstairs a few floors to Misha Levin, world-famous classical pianist and world-class prick.*

There was a detached smile on his face, and his eyes burned right with anticipation.

Misha, laden with shopping bags, stepped into his suite at the Four Seasons Hotel Chinzan-so and closed the door behind him. Mr. Hara, his publicity agent in Tokyo, had politely offered to help him with his load, but Misha had declined the offer. He wanted to be alone right now. Setting down the cumbersome bags, he shrugged out of his black cashmere overcoat and hung it up. Manny and Sasha had teased him about looking like a ninja here in Tokyo. He was wearing his customary working outfit:

black turtleneck sweater, black trousers, and comfortable black Mephisto sneakers.

He'd spent part of the afternoon going through the usual pre-concert procedures: testing the acoustics in the concert hall, positioning and fine-tuning the piano with his assistant, and rehearsal. The afternoon had gone swimmingly, he thought. The acoustics in the Tokyo Opera City Concert Hall, the result of a great deal of research and vast expenditures of money, were as near perfect as could be, so his job had been relatively simple.

He picked up his shopping bags and carried them out to the suite's private garden patio—he had one of the hotel's coveted Conservatory Suites—where he set them down to go through later. First a drink, he thought. Retracing his steps to the sitting room, he made himself a scotch and water. Swirling the ice around, he took it back out to the patio and sat down in a comfortable chair, sipping his drink and idly glancing at the shopping bags.

He smiled with contentment. This morning he'd gotten up early and ventured out alone to buy souvenirs and gifts. Now, he thought, I'll have another look at the booty. He set his drink down and scooted one of the bags over to his side and began rummaging around in it.

First, he pulled out the oiled paper umbrella he'd bought for Vera. Removing the beautiful tissue paper it was wrapped in, he opened it and looked at the exquisite cherry blossoms, which had been hand-painted all around it. He'd been told the umbrellas were actually quite effective in the rain. *That doesn't really matter*, he thought. *It's so beautiful, who cares if it works? Vera certainly won't. She'll love its delicate colors and design.* He closed it and placed it on the coffee table.

Next, he took out the first gift he'd bought this morning. The box was long and heavy. He opened it to reveal an ornately engraved replica of a Samurai sword. For Nicky. It was, he realized, a touristy sort of gift to purchase, as was the umbrella, but he also knew that Nicky would be thrilled to death with it. Nicky, like most little boys, loved weapons.

Misha took the sword from its niche in the box and examined the length of steel closely, surprised at its weight. Running his thumb along the edge, he quickly jerked it away. It was very sharp. Jesus, he thought. I could have sliced my thumb. Not good for a performance. He carefully placed the sword back in its fitted niche and looked at it.

Well, he decided, not good for a kid, either. Nicky will just have to admire it on the wall until he's older and can appreciate the fact that it's more than a mere toy.

He placed it next to the umbrella on the table and slid another shopping bag over to him, taking out a large box, this one also very heavy. He opened it and removed the paper from around an antique porcelain charger, about two feet in diameter. It had been made in Arita, on Kyushu, and was elaborately decorated with birds and flowers. He knew that Vera would love it as much as he did. After admiring it, he carefully placed it on the table with his other purchases, then sat looking at them, taking immense satisfaction in the fact that they were going to give so much pleasure to those he loved most. There were more gifts, quite a few more—handmade writing papers, lengths of exquisite silk, several small pieces of porcelain—but he would look at the rest of them later.

He stood and sipped his drink, gazing out the patio windows. The hotel was beautifully situated in what had once been an imperial garden, and as he surveyed the scene before him, the events of the last few days began to unfold in his mind like a movie reel, superimposing themselves on the city's landscape.

He had seen Serena and Jason off in Kyoto. There had been no tears, only smiles, and for that he was grateful. Despite his discussion with Serena—telling her that he didn't think he should leave his wife and son for her—they had parted, if not friends exactly, then in a friendly, civilized manner. He thought that Serena had seemed almost relieved. It was hard for him to tell. She was so excited by her trip that nothing else seemed to matter.

"I'll let you know when I get back," she'd said, "but don't worry, I won't bug you." She'd smiled hugely, thinking: *You're sweet, Misha, but you're right. It would never work.* Only she didn't want to tell him that.

"I'll be too damned busy with the thousands of pictures I'm going to take to think about anything else," she'd said, laughing. "Including you." She'd given him a kiss on the cheek and looked into his eyes. For a moment there was a wistful expression on her face, but it was replaced quickly by a look of determination. "Bye," she'd said. Then she turned and was gone.

She'd been like a joyful little girl, he thought, setting out on a new adventure. He knew now that they would probably never see each other again. It was far too dangerous. The fires within them might not have been fully extinguished, and any encouragement to reignite them would inevitably lead only to heartbreak for one or both of them. *And others*, he thought.

Now he felt a powerful need to be with his wife and son, to restore—perhaps reinvent—the loving relationship they'd once had. He knew that there was work to do, and healing, but deep down inside he knew that they could make a go of it.

Suddenly there was a knock at the door. Misha jerked. *Who on earth?* he wondered. *Everybody knows I'm not to be disturbed before a concert.*

He set his drink down and went to the door, disgruntlement on his face. He didn't like this, not one little bit.

I'll get rid of whoever it is, he thought. *In double-time.*

"You ready, Jason?" Serena asked.

"Yep," he replied. "Whenever you are."

"Let's go," she said, turning and smiling at him.

"Don't you think we really ought to, like, you know, take that guide with us, Serena?" Jason asked.

She shook her head. "No," she said. "He'll just get in the way. We can get back without him. Besides, he's stretched out asleep on the ground. Let's leave him be."

"If you say so," Jason said doubtfully.

Serena took another look around and shivered. This place gave her the heebie-jeebies. Bad vibes seemed to emanate from the walls, even the ground on which the place was built. It was almost as if the walls could speak, and what they had to say was so obscene she didn't think she could stand hearing much more of it.

They'd been shooting pictures for hours in one of Pol Pot's former detention camps. It was a prison such as Serena and Jason had never seen. The walls were now covered with photographs of Cambodians who'd been horribly tortured and killed here. There'd been thousands.

Thousands, she thought. Just in this one place. Millions all over the country. And nobody cared. She wanted to change that. She'd been talking to survivors, with the help of a translator, and photographing them. There was so much to do, so much to learn, so much more to see and document.

She flung her long raven hair out of her eyes. *How could I have become so distracted by Misha?* she wondered. *Or any other man, for that matter. I should have been here weeks or even months ago, working on this project. It's like I've finally found something that really means something to me.*

Despite the creepiness of the place, the sense of horror that lingered in the air like a miasma, she felt extraordinarily happy. She was in her element, shooting pictures.

Now, she and Jason were calling it a day and going back to the fleabag that called itself a hotel. Their guide, who demanded more money at every bend in the road, had wandered off to sleep while they worked. *Well,* she thought, *getting back to the hotel is easy. A long bicycle ride but easy to find.*

She started out ahead of Jason, both of them loaded down with equipment in backpacks, peddling through the brush, taking a shortcut back to the main road. Her eyes scanned the treetops and bits of sky above her. It was a clear day, beautiful really, as dusk fast approached. She turned her head, looking back at Jason. "I'll beat you back to the hotel," she cried, a huge smile on her face, at once beguiling and joyful.

Suddenly there was an explosion.

Jason, bringing up the rear, was thrown off his bicycle. When he finally scrabbled to his feet, he looked up ahead, reorienting himself, then threw his hands over his face for a moment. When he removed them, he began to scream. And scream.

Misha opened the door and stood back in surprise. "I thought you two were going shopping," he said.

"We did," the young man said. "But I'm finished and just thought if you had a few minutes we could have a drink and talk over a few things."

Misha didn't hide his irritation, but he opened the door wide. "Come on in," he said.

"I know this isn't good timing," the young man said, "but I really need to talk to you."

"Sure, sure," Misha said, walking back out to the garden patio. "It's not a problem as long as I can take my nap."

His nap! the young man thought. *The world could come crumbling down around him, and all he'd think about would be his nap! Or his rehearsal! Or his cock!*

"I won't be long, Misha," the young man said. "I promise."

"Want a drink?" Misha asked.

"I'll make it," the young man said, seeing the bottle of scotch on a table in the sitting room. "Want yours freshened up?"

"Why not?" Misha said, sitting back down in the comfortable chair he'd just left. "But only a splash of scotch. I've got to be in top form tonight."

"Goes without saying," the young man said. He went into the conservatory and picked up Misha's drink, then walked back to the table in the sitting room. He turned his back to Misha and mixed himself a scotch and water, humming tunelessly all the while. That done, he took the capsule of Ketamine from his overcoat pocket, opened it, and poured the powder into Misha's nearly empty glass. He then splashed some scotch in the glass, filled it with water and ice, and stirred it vigorously, making certain the powder was completely dissolved.

When he finished, he turned to Misha, who sat waiting patiently for him in the conservatory. *"Voilà,"* he said, walking back to Misha with the appropriate drink extended in one hand. "You'll have a very nice nap now."

Misha smiled. "Thanks," he said, taking the proffered drink. He held it in his hand, swirling the ice around, then took a large swallow. *The sooner I finish this, the sooner he'll feel compelled to leave,* he thought. "What's on your mind?" he asked.

The young man stood sipping his drink, looking out at the Tokyo skyline. "This is some view," he said. "These Conservatory Suites are fantastic."

"They are, aren't they," Misha said, looking at the young man. "Why don't you take off your coat and sit down?" he asked. *Damn, just get on with it,* he thought. *I'm tired and need my rest.*

"I'm fine," the young man said, looking at Misha. "Here's to tonight's performance, by the way," he said, lifting his glass ceremoniously, then taking a sip.

"Tonight," Misha said, politely lifting his glass and taking another large swallow.

The young man walked toward the end of the conservatory and stood looking out again. "The reason I came by," he said, his back turned to Misha, "is that I wanted to let you know what's happened with this Russian thing. The tour."

"I don't really care what's happened," Misha said, scowling. Suddenly he felt a little woozy. *I'm more tired than I realized,* he thought.

"Well, you'd better start caring," the young man said, his back still turned. "Because these people are very upset with you. They don't like taking no for an answer."

There was an unusually aggressive tone in his voice, and Misha laughed, despite being annoyed. "I don't think I have anything to be afraid of," he said. He took another swallow of his drink. *Almost gone,* he thought. *Then politeness will force him to leave when I refuse another.*

"I wouldn't be so sure," the young man said. "These are dangerous people." He turned to face Misha. "They're capable of hurting you. Or Vera. Or Nicky." He paused dramatically for effect. "Even Serena," he added.

Misha started to rise to his feet in outrage. *I will not listen to any more of this kind of talk,* he thought. He shifted his weight to his feet to get up, but it was as if his body wasn't quite getting the message from his brain. The effort was suddenly too much.

What the hell? he wondered, puzzled by his sluggish reactions. He set his drink down on the table next to him, almost spilling it as he did so. *What the hell?* Then it dawned on him.

The son of a bitch has drugged me! he thought.

"You ... you've ... drugged me," he said, staring quizzically at the young man.

"Yes, Misha," the young man said, walking toward him. "I have indeed." Then, with lightning speed he withdrew the handcuffs from his overcoat pocket and slammed them around Misha's wrists, snapping them closed with a loud metallic clank!

Misha didn't comprehend what had transpired, the movement had been so swift, and when he finally did, he coughed a short laugh. "Ri-*dic*-u-lous," he slurred.

When the young man continued to stand and stare at him, smugly smiling, Misha began to think that perhaps this wasn't a joke after all. "What the hell—" he began, panic slowly beginning to seize him. *My hands!* he thought. *My hands! I need my hands!*

The young man had taken the small roll of duct tape out of his pocket, and now peeled off a length and slapped it unceremoniously across Misha's mouth, pushing it hard against his lips with both hands.

Misha's hands moved up toward his mouth but dropped down again, as if the effort was too much. He eyes, however, were wide with rising terror.

The roll of tape dangled at the end of the strip across his mouth until the young man roughly ripped it off. Then he calmly peeled off another length, this one much longer, and wrapped it once around Misha's head, placing a second layer of tape across his mouth. Finally, taking the roll, he got down on his knees and wrapped the tape around Misha's legs, pinning them to the chair legs.

He stood back up, finished, admiring his handiwork. "You never looked better, Misha," he said sarcastically, wiping beads of sweat from his brow. His breathing came in labored gasps from his exertions. "Never."

He shook his head from side to side and wiped his brow again. "Now you're going to listen to me, aren't you?" He barked a laugh and walked back into the sitting room, where he poured himself another scotch and water. Then he returned to the conservatory and stood in front of Misha, sipping the drink.

"How does it feel to be on the bottom?" he asked in a malicious tone of voice. "Well, for once in your life, you can't answer, can you? You have to listen to *me. I'm* the boss. Now you know how I've felt all these years, having to do whatever you told me to do, having to be at your beck and call. Having to ride on your coattails because I wasn't good enough to make it on my own."

He paused and took another sip of his drink, still staring at Misha. "I didn't have the talent or the *looks*—and that's part of your success, you know, your pretty face—so I had to kowtow to you, taking a tiny percentage of your huge income. Now comes along a chance for me to make a big wad of cash—this Russian deal—and you? You just won't do it, will you? Because of your fucking principles."

He took the small sledgehammer from the pocket of his overcoat and began to swing it loosely in his hand, getting used to its heft, strutting back and forth in front of Misha.

Misha's eyes followed the sledgehammer, his panic beginning to reach a crescendo. He knew what the sledgehammer was for. Sweat began to roll down his face, getting into his eyes, burning them and blurring his vision. He desperately wanted to wipe it away. He tried to scream, again and again, but all he could hear were muffled grunts. He tried to kick, but his legs were immobilized.

What am I going to do? he wondered in horror. He could feel his heart thudding in his chest, despite the drug, and at the same time thought that he might close his eyes and pass out at any minute, succumbing to the drug's soporific effects. *I've got to stay awake*, he told himself. *Got to stay awake!*

"Now, because of *you*, I'm not going to be getting that nice tax-free wad of cash," the young man continued. "Now, because of *you*, they may go after your wife or your kid or your whore. But you know what? I don't care. I don't care what *they* want anymore."

"I"—he paused and thumped a hand against his chest—"want *you*." He pointed an accusatory finger at Misha, glaring, then straightened up and smiled at him crazily. He suddenly turned and grabbed one of the heavy patio tables and scraped it across the floor. *Just the thing*, he thought. Jerking Misha's hands by the handcuffs, he slammed them down on the tabletop, holding them there with his free hand. The other held the sledgehammer.

Misha's chest and face felt as if they would explode from the effort to scream, and salty tears began to roll down his cheeks. He was helpless to defend himself, and he knew it.

God help me, he prayed. *God, please help me.*

The young man began swinging the sledgehammer again, rhythmically, back and forth, back and forth, in higher and higher arcs, watching Misha's eyes, enjoying the terror he saw there. Finally, he swung it up to his shoulder, got a good grip, and started to bring it down with all his might.

For a fleeting second Misha imagined he had seen a ghost. *I'm dead,* he thought in a daze. *He's killed me, and I'm already dead.* For nothing else could explain what he fancied he had seen.

Then he felt an explosion of pain, an excruciating white-hot pain such as he had never known could exist. It seemed to blast his hand to smithereens, then consumed his entire being. His head jerked back, and in the instant before he blacked out, his imagination—mercifully, he thought—took over. For he glimpsed Vera, Nicky's Samurai sword in hand, standing over Manny's body, blood everywhere.

Epilogue

⌒⌒

As Vera watched from behind him, Misha gently touched his trembling fingertips to the mezuzah on the door frame. He then leaned over and touched his lips to it reverently. Tears, unbidden, came into her delft blue eyes. She had never seen him do this before, and had always thought it curious that he'd insisted on the cheap mezuzah remaining where he'd put it the day they'd moved into the apartment.

He turned to her. There were tears in his eyes as well, she noticed, but he was smiling, even if ruefully.

Vera reached up and tenderly stroked his tears away and kissed his cheek. She smiled and then turned and unlocked the door. They entered the apartment together, an arm of Misha's slung across her shoulders. In the entrance foyer he abruptly stopped in his tracks and stood still, an alert expression on his face.

"What is it?" Vera asked, looking at him quizzically.

"Where's Nicky?" he replied. "There's no 'Daddy, Mommy. Daddy, Mommy.' " He looked at her, and they both laughed.

"He's over at Sonia and Dmitri's," Vera said. "I thought I told you. He's going to spend the night with them."

"You probably did," Misha said, taking his overcoat off. "And I forgot."

"That's understandable under the circumstances," Vera said, taking his coat, and shrugging out of her own. She hung them in the hall closet, then turned back to Misha. "How about a drink?" she said. "Maybe a brandy? There's a very fancy bottle of something in the kitchen that your new manager sent over. It's supposed to be really special."

"That'd be great," Misha said. "I'll get them."

"No, no," Vera said. "Go sit down. You've exerted yourself enough today." She was already on her way to the kitchen. "I'll get them."

"Okay," Misha said. He walked into the vast double-height living room. A fire flickered in the grate, its flames glinting off the treasures they'd both collected over the years, giving the room a warm, cozy, and homey glow, despite its grand proportions and furnishings.

Misha put another log in the fireplace, then kicked off his shoes and spread out on the sofa in front of the fire. He stared into its dancing flames, pondering the day's events. *How strange its all been*, he thought. *Yet how wondrous.*

Coral Randolph had invited friends of Serena's to her magnificently elegant apartment on the Upper East Side, where she gave a combination memorial service–cocktail party in Serena's memory. When the engraved invitation had come in the mail, Misha had thought that Vera would ignore it or summarily throw it in the garbage.

Well, he mused, *I should have known my wife better than that.* She'd surprised him for the thousandth time.

"We must go," she'd said. "Both of us."

"But, Vera," he'd replied, "don't you think—"

"Misha," Vera had interjected, "it's the least we can do. The two of you had a kind of love for each other after all. And I love you. We owe it to her memory, Misha. We must go. I insist." While Vera didn't relish the idea, she thought it was important that Misha go, with her there to be supportive. He needed to grieve Serena's death properly to help him overcome her tragic loss.

He had acquiesced and was glad now that he had done so. The steely Coral Randolph had been very gracious, warm even, and had wept openly during the short service in her living room. *She's actually human*, Misha thought, *and she really loved Serena.*

Only Jason had spoken, his nicks and scrapes not quite healed, and his brief tribute to his mentor was movingly and lovingly delivered. The service had given Misha at least some sense of closure. The horrors of the days after Manny's attack had only been compounded by Serena's terrible death.

All that beauty! he thought. *All that talent! And the youthful enthusiasm and creative force at work in her. Only to be destroyed by a land mine left over from a war long over.*

He heaved a sigh. *Life's not fair*, he thought. *It's not a fair world.* But as Vera had reminded him, we must try to live as fairly as possible even so, and to remember to be grateful, no matter the circumstances, for the mystery and gift that is life itself.

He smiled to himself. Her advice sounded so much like old Arkady, his long-dead friend in Moscow. It was almost as if Arkady were speaking through Vera, watching over Misha from somewhere beyond the grave.

Thank you, old friend, Misha whispered, his eyes closed prayerfully. *Thank you. For without you, the memory of you and your love, I might have lost everything.*

Misha opened his eyes and looked into the fire again. *I've been so fortunate*, he thought. *To have a companion who loves me so unquestionably, so unconditionally.*

An involuntary shiver ran through him as he remembered that afternoon in Tokyo. Coolly elegant Vera had struck Manny a potentially lethal blow with the sword, although she'd deliberately slammed it down onto his head with the flat side, so as to injure, not kill.

Misha hugged himself, remembering that horrible day. He hadn't known Vera had flown in, that she'd been in his hotel suite sleeping that afternoon. She'd come to save their marriage, she'd told Misha, to fight Serena for him if necessary. She hadn't known, of course, that he'd ended his affair with Serena.

His thoughts turned to Manny. *Poor Manny.* He would never have dreamed that his friend could be so insanely jealous, that he would become unhinged and finally go over the edge. *He'll spend years behind bars*, he thought. *Either in a prison or mental hospital. Who knows?*

With Vera's help, he'd already hired new representation and was negotiating a new recording contract. Under the circumstances, extricating himself from Brighton Beach Records certainly wasn't a problem. He supposed he'd heard the last of them. Sasha had left, simply saying that he and his new girlfriend were going to leave town in search of new adventures. This came as a surprise since Misha, like everyone else, had assumed that Sasha and Manny had been lovers. *Well, it doesn't matter, does it?* he thought. Misha had wished him luck.

Vera quietly came into the living room, carrying two brandy snifters. He looked over at her. *Vera, my avenging angel*, he thought.

She set the crystal snifters down on the coffee table, then eased down onto the couch next to Misha's prone body. "What're you thinking about?" she asked.

"Nothing," Misha said. Then after a moment, he said: "And everything."

Vera tenderly stroked his raven hair, then leaned over and brushed his lips with hers. She sat back up and reached over for their drinks. "It's been quite a day," she said. She handed Misha his drink, and they both sipped quietly.

"It's a shame you couldn't play for the memorial service," Vera said. "It was a wonderful occasion, but your playing would have made it so complete, so perfect, somehow."

Misha looked thoughtful for a moment, staring down at his hand. While the injury had not caused any permanent damage, he'd had two broken bones and considerable tissue damage. It would be weeks before it returned to normal.

He looked up at Vera. "I just don't want to play in front of anybody yet," he said. "I'm just not ready. Can you understand that?"

Vera nodded. "Yes," she said, "but it would've been nice." She looked at him. "Don't you think it's time you started *trying* to play, Misha?"

He was silent for a moment, then nodded. "Yes," he finally admitted. "I guess I've just been . . . afraid."

"There's nothing to be afraid of," Vera said, for she knew that he had lost confidence in himself. "You can start off little by little, taking baby steps, and gradually build up your strength . . . and your courage." She looked at him. "Just a little bit at a time."

Misha smiled. "You're not going to let me get lazy, are you?"

"Nor will I allow you to indulge your fears," Vera said. She took a sip of her brandy and set the glass down on the table. "Why don't you try something now?" she said.

"Now?" Misha said, his eyes widening. "But . . . but Vera, I . . . I—"

"But nothing," she said. She looked at him with a mischievous smile. "Your fingers can move quite nicely, I've noticed."

Misha grinned. "Do you think . . . ?"

"I know," Vera said. "Come on. Get up. Let's go to the piano." She stood and extended a hand to him.

Misha set his drink down and took her hand. He rose slowly to his feet, and together they walked over to the big Steinway grand. He sat down on the stool, adjusting it slightly, and looked at the piano, then up at Vera.

"Where do I begin?" he asked.

She stood at his side, one hand on his shoulder. "Play something for Serena," she said. "A quiet good-bye, Misha."

He looked down at the keyboard, his shoulders slumped. "I don't know, Vera," he mumbled. "I just don't know . . ."

"A nocturne," she said. "Play a nocturne for Serena."

"Serena hated nocturnes," Misha said. "They made her sad."

"It's appropriate," Vera said. "A simple nocturne. She would understand, I'm sure. It's a good way for you to start again. To work your hands."

Misha looked at her doubtfully, then looked back down at the keys again. He sat for a moment, silent, then slowly positioned his hands over the keys. Hesitantly at first, then with more confidence, he began to play.

Chopin filled the vast living room with its sweet sadness, its melancholy strains a fitting good-bye, a reminder of what once was but could be no more. As he played, tears began to fill Misha's eyes. Tears for Serena, tears for himself, for Vera and Nicky and their families.

When he finished, he sat for a moment in the flickering light of the fire, then got to his feet and put his arms around Vera, his head resting on her shoulder, and she cradled him there, stroking his raven hair silently, feeling his grief, his pain, sharing with him this sad good-bye, yet refusing to give up hope for tomorrow, for their family, for their love, and for the joy of life itself.